For Ryan,
My biggest fan.

The Link

By
C.R. Kwiat

ISBN: 0-9762497-9-0

Original text © 2005 Catherine Kwiatkowski
1st edition
Cover © 2005 Catherine Kwiatkowski
Printed by Lightening Source
Publisher: James Ross, Self Publisher

All rights reserved.

Characters and situations in this book are fictional.
Any name similarities to real individuals are strictly coincidental.

No part of this publication may be reproduced in part or in whole, or stored in a
retrieval system, or transmitted in any form or by any means by electronic,
mechanical, photocopying, recording, or otherwise,
without written permission of the publisher.

Part 1: Seven Days of Cyan

Chapter 1
The Collection of 1693 - North Central Europe by the Baltic Sea (Saturday)

The door to an old, wooden dress shop creaked open. A plump, elderly lady with a round face and short gray hair peered outside. Behind her in the gloom of the shop stood Katrine Farmer, a slender woman in her early twenties with dark blue eyes, rosy cheeks, and long, brown hair tied back with a blue ribbon. She peeked anxiously over the woman's head to the dirt street filled with villagers.

"Are you sure they're not out there?" Katrine asked.

"What do they look like, Dear?"

"They have red and black uniforms. Royal guards. They'll be on horses. Maybe they're hiding across the street."

The shopkeeper shook her head and closed the door. "Niemand. Nobody out there fits that description."

Katrine started to rub her hands together as they both retreated into the musty, cold dress shop lit only by a few lanterns on the wall. She looked towards the back room. "And you're sure no one is in the back room?"

The woman walked behind the counter, apparently disturbed. "No one is back there, Dear. I checked twice when you were trying on that dress," she said as she nodded towards the long blue dress her customer now wore. "We're alone."

Katrine shook her head. "I can't shake this feeling that someone's watching me." Katrine took a final look at herself. "Well, I'm in bit of a hurry. I'll just pay for this dress, ma'am, and be on my way."

"Meine name ist Agnes," the shopkeeper said with a smile as she searched for a box behind the counter.

Katrine reached into a jewel-covered handbag and pulled out some gold coins. "Ich heisse Katrine." It felt good to finally say her real name.

Agnes looked up in surprise. "Katrine? Katrine Farmer?" Katrine looked up from the counter, wide-eyed. "I knew you looked familiar the second you walked in here! You look just like your mother! I went to the same church with Mary when you were just a toddler." Agnes smiled warmly at Katrine. "How is Mary?"

Katrine bit her lip, hoping her mother was all right. It had been four years since they had last seen each other. "She's fine," Katrine replied quietly as she placed the coins on the counter.

Agnes stared thoughtfully at the gold coins in front of her. "Word had it that the farms up near Gardenstadt were going through some harsh times about five or six years ago." She nodded toward the counter, then looked up at Katrine with questioning eyes. "Looks as though your farm on Dragon Hill pulled through well." When no explanation came from Katrine, Agnes gave a slight shrug and shifted the coins from the counter into her hand. "Will you be wearing this dress out, or will you be changing back into that lovely dress you left in the dressing room?"

Just thinking about the white gown with gems interwoven throughout the material made Katrine shudder. "I'll be leaving my old dress here. Sell it to someone with a more fitting personality."

Agnes stopped what she was doing and meticulously eyed Katrine, her face conveying confusion. She was about to speak, but was interrupted by a sudden explosion followed by a nearby earth-shattering blast. Katrine quickly fell to the floor and placed her hands on top of her head as the entire shop shook and several dresses fell from the racks. Screams on the street outside penetrated the thick, wooden walls of the shop.

Katrine quickly grabbed her purse and opened the door where she was greeted by a rush of cold, damp air caused by a recent March rain. From the doorway, she watched the townspeople run frantically down the center of the puddle-filled street towards the foothills and neighboring forest at the southernmost outskirts of town. A second blast shook the earth. Katrine watched in horror as a canonball zoomed above the distant trees and crashed into the bakery across the street; a fraction of a second later, she was hit by the shock wave, heat, and splinters of wood. She jumped off the wooden steps of the dress shop and began running down the street.

Katrine was nearly knocked over as she pushed her way through the frantic crowd. Smoke from the burning bakery clouded the street, making it difficult to see and breathe. She tried to ignore the sound of another canonball firing from the bay beyond the trees, but the explosive crash that followed the launch shook her body so violently, she screamed and fell to the dirt. Someone above her tripped over her, knocking her face down into a puddle of muddy water. Suddenly, a hand grabbed her arm and pulled her to her feet.

"Are you injured, Princess Anna?"

It was Paul, her bodyguard. She looked at him with a dazed expression and nodded her head.

"It's not the queen's ship," Paul said as he brushed his long, black hair from his eyes and looked towards the bay. "A couple of fishermen said they saw pirates enter the lagoon. Let's get to the horses."

Katrine quickly wiped the mud off her face with her sleeve and looked behind her to see that the last blast had completely demolished the dress shop. Her face turned ashen.

"Wait, Paul! I need to go back!"

"Your Highness! No!" he yelled as Katrine slipped away from his arm and ran back to the rubble where the dress shop once stood.

Agnes was lying motionless on the street in front of the steps. As Katrine knelt down to see if she was still alive, Agnes began to lift herself. Breathing a sigh of relief, Katrine helped her to her feet and quickly guided her to the side of the street to avoid being trampled by a runaway horse and cart.

"Are you all right?"

"I think I twisted my ankle," her voice trembled. She raised her long dress, looked down at her right black boot, and moved her ankle in circles.

"Let's go, Princess Anna. *NOW!*" Paul said behind her as he impatiently took Katrine's arm and began to pull her away.

"No," she said as she jerked her arm away from his grasp. "I'm helping Agnes out of here." She draped her arm under the shopkeeper's right shoulder to give her support, and then hurried back into the street. "Get to the stables, Paul, before they're leveled and bring us the horses. We'll meet you between here and there."

Paul hesitated. "I can't protect you if I'm..."

"Do what I ask, Guard," Katrine replied angrily.

Paul shook his head, troubled, but turned around without comment and ran down the chaotic street toward the stables.

"Bless you, Katrine, darling..." and with an uncertain air, she mumbled, "Anna."

Katrine didn't want to explain why Paul had called her Princess Anna. She was too preoccupied with the loud explosion that had just sounded from the bay. She looked up into the smoke-filled air and tried to locate the next canonball that was about to hit. A black ball sped overhead and crashed into the rear end of the stables ahead. Panicked, she stood on her toes and tried to see over the scrambling people in front of her. Through the smoke, she caught a glimpse of her horse, along with several others, rearing up on their hind legs and running through the crowd towards the hills. Her eyes searched frantically for Paul in the crowd. He wouldn't have had time to reach the stables, but the debris flying from the impact could have caught him.

A blur of red and yellow in the corner of her eye caught her attention. She quickly turned to see five large men wearing red and yellow jackets over striped short red pants. Each brandished a sword in one hand and a small musket in the other. An equally surprised Agnes gasped as Katrine backed them away from the men towards a wooden wall belonging to a general store. Suddenly they noticed that the streets were filled with men wearing red and yellow jackets. Katrine looked up and down the road dumbfounded, wondering where they had all come from.

"Ungläublich," Agnes murmured. "Are my eyes playing tricks on me, or did these pirates just appear out of thin air?"

Katrine was unsure how to respond. She held her breath and gently guided Agnes against the wall. "They're not interested in us. Let's just wait here until they rob who they want and leave." She looked anxiously toward the bay, hoping that the bombardment with canonballs was over now that the pirates had invaded the land.

"Sir!" one of the nearby pirates yelled toward the bay. "We're going to lose some at the forest boundary if it's not barricaded!"

A transparent blue wall quickly flashed at the far edge of town and disappeared. Katrine swung her head and stared in the direction of the foothills, wondering what the blue flash was.

"Thank you, sir!" the buccaneer said. He yelled down the street at his companions. "Hold them where they stand and wait for the captain!"

Several shots from their muskets fired into the air, causing Katrine to momentarily cower. She looked up the road as the invaders halted the fleeing citizens in their tracks. After several agonizing minutes the people in the streets were lined along the edges as the pirates walked down the middle.

For the first time, Katrine noticed two men walking leisurely up the center of the street from the direction of the bay. Both were blond and clean-shaven, one slightly older than the other. The elder, who appeared to be in his late twenties, had short hair, slicked back on top. He was dressed in a long, white jacket with large gold buttons down the front and on the cuffs of his sleeves. A thick, shiny sword with a handguard made of five finely carved snakes hung at the side of his short, white pants.

His younger companion wore slender black pants and a black button-down shirt. A black bandana held down his sandy blond hair, which had a bit of curl in it and was only slightly longer than his companion's. They bore a striking resemblance to each other, and Katrine was certain they were brothers.

As the two walked up the center of the street and passed the pirates, the pirates each bowed their head and respectfully said 'sir'. Katrine could feel her heart pound as they approached the section of the street directly in front of her. The man in white began to slow until he stopped and placed a hand in front of his mate, causing him to stop.

"Here?" the man in black asked. "That didn't take long." He looked over at Agnes, Katrine, and several others nearby.

"Yes. Here," he replied. He turned in the direction of Katrine and stared. Katrine shook her head in disbelief as the two began to walk toward her. The pirates made a comfortable circle around Agnes, Katrine, and a small man nearby, blocking them from any getaway.

She could feel Agnes grip her arm and squeeze. "What do they want with us?" she whispered.

"Don't worry," Katrine quietly replied as her thoughts drifted towards the worse. "You'll be fine. It's money they want." She *hoped* that was all they wanted, anyway. For the first time, she realized she no longer had her purse. She looked at the puddle in the street where she had fallen and saw it lying in the mud.

The two walked up to the small man first.

"Captain Zor wants to have a look at you," said the man in black.

"And what might he be looking at?" the small man responded as his eyes squinted at the captain's face. He stared defiantly at Zor until a strange look washed over his face. The captain silently walked toward Agnes as Katrine watched the villager bury his face in his hands in apparent shame and fall to the ground.

Katrine could feel Agnes shaking as he stepped in front of Agnes and stood looking at her.

"What do you want?" Katrine asked.

He looked to Katrine. "It's not your turn. Please remain silent."

"Turn for what?"

The captain sighed and glimpsed behind him at his companion. "James?"

The man in black walked over to Katrine. "Let's separate you two for a moment," he said. "Captain Zor just wants to check the color of her eyes."

As James took hold of Katrine's arm, she reluctantly let go of Agnes. She glimpsed at the man sitting in the mud to see if he had been harmed in any way, but he seemed fine; so she turned back to Agnes and the captain and watched silently as their eyes locked. Agnes began to grow visibly upset.

"What are you doing to her?" Katrine asked as she tried to pull away from James.

James tightened his grip on her. "One second more, he'll be done."

"Done with what?"

Agnes' eyes began to fill with tears. She backed away from the captain, dropped to the ground, buried her face in her hands just like the first man had done, and began to cry. The captain now looked at Katrine and began to walk towards her. Katrine's face filled with confusion and fear.

"Who are you?" Katrine demanded.

He smiled. "Who you are is the more interesting question." He stood in front of her and gazed at her with narrow eyes. "Katrine Farmer, peasant, or Princess Anna, royalty?"

Only someone sent by the queen would know both names. "I'm Katrine Farmer, peasant," she answered defiantly. "Tell the queen who hired you that I'm not going back. I'm not marrying him."

He hesitated before a long, drawn-out, "Indeed." He glimpsed at James behind Katrine, and then returned his gaze upon Katrine. "But no queen hired me."

Katrine's eyes scanned the circle of pirates surrounding her. It didn't make sense for the queen to hire pirates when she had guards of her own. She nodded towards the street. "My purse is over there in the puddle. It's all I have with me."

He grinned. "I'm not here for your money." She could hear James laugh behind her.

Katrine took a deep breath and held it for a second before replying, "Are you here to kidnap me?"

He looked mildly surprised. "Perhaps. Would you be worth it?"

"No. The queen's broke. I'm not going to get you any kind of ransom. She'll just find someone to take my place." Katrine felt her anger rise. "She's good at finding replacements for her dead daughter." Her heart nervously fluttered when she realized she had spoken so openly of the forbidden; but at that point, she had nothing to lose.

Zor looked amused. "You're full of stories, aren't you?" He shook his head. "I'm not interested in any ransom, either."

"Then what are you here for? Did you attack this town and kill its citizens with your blasted canonballs just for kicks?" Although the words escaped her mouth, she could hardly believe that they were her own.

Zor's eyes narrowed as he looked at her. "Just for kicks?" He looked at James. "Do people say 'just for kicks' in 1693?"

James shrugged. "I'm not sure."

He returned his attention to Katrine. "I didn't kill anyone. The canons were aimed at vacant dwellings and shops, and they hit their target exactly as I intended." He leaned forward and spoke quietly into her ear. "Hardship builds character, and it looked as though this pathetic village needed a little character-building." He backed up and regarded Katrine with a keen eye. "Perhaps the reason I'm here is to help you."

Katrine looked at him dubiously. "Unless you plan to stop my mother's murder, I seriously doubt it." She hesitated when she saw the expression on his face; he had no idea what she was talking about. She shook her head in disarray. "Am I wrong when I say that you've never even met the Queen of Nezbar? Or even heard of her?"

He stared at her and slowly shook his head. "Show me you're capable of remaining silent for a while. I need to look in your eyes."

Katrine clenched her teeth, reluctant to end up on the ground, emotionally distraught like the other two, so instead she found herself staring at a burning building on the far side of the street. He gently turned Katrine's chin so that she was facing him.

Katrine sighed. "Do what you need to do and then be on your way."

"I require eye contact."

Katrine looked him directly in the eyes. They were dark green with several lighter specks shooting out from the pupil. She waited for her body to begin shaking, she waited for tears to flood her eyes, but she felt no change. The only realization she came to was that he had a very strong, handsome face, and that someone else, somewhere was still watching her. She broke her stare with Zor and peered across the rooftops, looking for her mysterious follower.

Zor peered at James with a bewildered expression. "I can't read her mind."

Katrine snidely remarked, "Is *that* what you're trying to do?"

Zor returned his attention to Katrine and looked her up and down. "You don't have the aura of a witch."

Katrine raised her eyebrows. "A witch?" He made no reply; he simply stared at her as if trying to figure her out. "There are no such things as witches. So, yes. I guess I'm not a witch."

He smiled. "Witches are real. I've known quite a few in my time."

"Really," she responded skeptically. "I once knew a witch, too. But she really wasn't...and they decided they needed to hang her."

"You can't hang a witch," he responded in a matter-of-fact way. "They would simply cut the rope with their brainwave."

Katrine's eyes narrowed. "What makes you the expert on witches?"

"I'm a warlock."

Katrine laughed in disbelief. "A warlock?"

"That's how I knew the names Katrine Farmer and Princess Anna. From Agnes' memories."

Katrine's face grew serious as she peered on the ground at Agnes. Agnes nodded at her with red, wet eyes, making Katrine suddenly feel very unsure of herself. She turned back to Zor, trying to keep her poise.

"Forgive me," she said quietly, "but you haven't proven to me that you can mind read at all. You haven't proven to me that you're a warlock. So I'd very much appreciate it if you would move on to the next person, do whatever it is that you do, and leave me to my own. You've interrupted a rather important journey."

He seemed to consider Katrine's request for a moment, but then turned back to Agnes. "Help Agnes up, James." James let go of Katrine's arm and walked over to a fear-stricken Agnes. After helping her to her feet, Zor took a stance in front of her. His chest lifted with pride as he spoke.

"I am the founder of a society, a utopia. But my utopia is one chef short. I lost him last week when he decided to break curfew. He ran into a couple of guards and got the worst end of it." He glimpsed at Katrine. "From my reading, I find that cooking is your favorite hobby and that you're quite good at it. Your husband is deceased, your overgrown son is a burden, not to mention abusive, and you'd rather not be sewing dresses for the rest of your life. Since your shop is now rubble, I see no reason why you can't join us." Agnes' face filled with protest and she was about to speak when Zor placed his hand on her arm. "Close your eyes." Then she disappeared.

Katrine stumbled backwards until she collided with one of Zor's men. Her throat had disappeared somewhere and her mouth moved wordlessly.

"Now do you believe in warlocks?" he asked turning toward her.

She stared wide-eyed at Zor and finally found her voice. "Where is she?"

"I broke down her body into billions of atoms – excuse me...*pieces* – and flew her through the air. She's now reassembled at her new home with her new family...disoriented and confused, no doubt, but I found it a necessary display to get your attention."

"Bring her back. She didn't want to go."

Zor approached Katrine again. "Look into my eyes, young imposter princess. I wish to have a go at your memories one final time."

"I said bring her back."

"I do not take orders from anyone."

The roof collapsed on the burning building across the street, heightening Katrine's anxiety. She wanted desperately to leave. She angrily found Zor's green eyes and grudgingly waited for him to try to read her mind again, still not believing for a second that he really could. Again he looked bewildered.

"Why can't I read you?"

Katrine did not answer. Her body had become so tense that she felt as though she was going to pull the muscles in her neck. She fidgeted as Zor shook his head and looked at James.

"She's the reason. My instincts tell me we're all here because of this one, so we'll take her now and try to figure her out later."

"What?" Katrine yelled. "I can't go with you! I have to warn my mother..."

"Old family matters do not matter anymore. You have a new family now."

"I DO NOT!" Katrine charged toward a space between the pirates, but they caught her by the arms and swirled her around so that she was held tightly against the front side of one of the men. She kicked hard at his shin and swung her elbow into his soft stomach. He gasped and loosened his grip enough for Katrine to grow limp, fall downward through his arms and land on her knees. She grabbed her long dress, ready to make a second attempt at freedom, but before she could raise herself to her feet and run, she felt the tip of a cold blade nick the side of her neck.

She froze and tried to catch her breath as she followed the blade with her eyes back to Zor. The snakes forming the handguard of Zor's sword hissed and their heads detached to look at Katrine. Katrine gazed nervously at the snakes; then slowly raised her right hand, placed it on the blade of the sword and moved it away from her neck. When she tore her gaze from the metal snakes, she found Zor watching them with equal interest. Moments later the snakes settled down and resumed their original positions.

"I've never seen these snakes get so upset before," Zor said as he looked down at Katrine. "It's certainly a day of firsts."

She wiped her neck and gaped at the blood on the side of her hand. "Yes. It is a day of firsts."

The pirate behind her grabbed her under her shoulders and hoisted her up. She stood tall and put on a bold face as she tried to control the trembling in her body.

Zor lowered the sword to the ground and sighed. He motioned with a wave of his arms toward the foothills. "Look up the street, Katrine."

Katrine looked up the smoke-filled street at the rubble, burning buildings, terrified citizens, and about fifty pirates, all oversized men with weapons drawn.

"Do you seriously believe you can escape a powerful warlock and his little band of guards?"

Katrine felt her eyes begin to water. She turned toward Zor and shook her head. "Why?" she asked earnestly. "Why do you want me? It doesn't make any sense."

"I follow my gut feeling, my instincts, and they're never wrong. You belong in my utopia."

She took a deep breath in order to stop herself from completely losing control of her emotions. "Well, your instincts are wrong this time, and my mother is not going to die because of it."

Zor lifted his arm toward her. "I guess you're going to have to go the same way Agnes went."

Katrine jolted backwards against the pirate holding her. "No." She hesitantly added, "I have a fear of flying."

He smiled. "If you travel by ship with me and my crew, it will take much longer. We're on vacation, so to speak."

Much longer was much better, thought Katrine. More opportunities to escape and reach her mother before the queen's men do. "That's fine. By ship is fine."

Zor nodded. "If you run, you will find yourself being followed by a blue tornado. It will pounce on you and take your legs away. Understand?"

Katrine stared back at him in shock. "What do you mean it will take my legs away?"

"Just that. It will take your legs away." He looked up at one of his pirates and nodded towards the bay. "I'm done here. Let's go."

The pirate called to the others to retreat and there was a second flash of blue at the foothills. Katrine was pushed away from the body of the pirate who held her and directed toward the bay.

"Follow me," a large bald pirate ordered as he turned and walked. Katrine hesitated until she was pushed forward. She reluctantly began to walk toward the small stretch of forest that lay between the town and the bay.

"Let her go!"

Katrine recognized Paul's voice and swirled around in time to see him charging through a small group of Zor's men toward her. She winced as they grabbed him and slugged him in the face. He fell to the dirt and they kicked him several times. Despite the fact that Paul was strong and well-trained as a fighter, he was quickly overwhelmed by Zor's men. Katrine tried to break through a group of pirates to help him, but the bald pirate grabbed her arm and held her firmly in place.

"That would be Paul, I presume," Zor said with mild interest as he waved his group onward with his finger. "Loyal guard 'til the end."

Katrine was pulled in the opposite direction, forced to walk once more toward the bay. She glanced back to see that they had left Paul on the ground, rocking back and forth, clenching his abdomen. She groaned in frustration as she returned her attention to the approaching forest.

Once they arrived at a narrow pathway leading to the bay, her arm was released because it would have been too difficult to walk side-by-side. She had been on the trail only one hour earlier, when she and Paul had first approached the town to give their horses food and water, and she knew that the forest would become quite dense before it thinned near the bay. It would be difficult to follow her if she fled. The pirates were too large to run, and Zor and James seemed too high on the hierarchy to chase after an escaping prisoner. The blue tornado came to mind. Katrine bit her lip. If it were real, it wouldn't be able to weave through the trees. It would have to stay above the tree line, and she could probably lose it in the thicker parts of the forest.

James was right behind her, and behind James was Zor. She wished they were farther back on the trail because it didn't give her that much of a head start before they would try to stop her.

"Tempting forest, isn't it, Katrine?" James asked boisterously. "Bet you're dying to take off."

"She's not going to run," Zor said with quiet confidence.

"Come on, brother. It's obvious she's going to bolt. Any second now."

"She's too attached to her legs to take the risk."

"No. She doesn't believe in your blue tornado. Now if *I* were a warlock, I'd take them away from her right now – *before* she bolts." Katrine glanced at James behind her and scowled. "Whoa! Did you see that?"

"You had that coming, James," Zor said. "When you get your powers and become a warlock…"

"And when will that be? Anytime soon? Has someone had a change of heart?"

"When you get them, I hope you don't take everyone's legs away because you think they're up to something."

Katrine was grateful that Zor's statement ended the conversation. It was obviously meant to discourage her from running, and it was working. But then she felt a bit of hope when she realized that the blue tornado was most likely a bluff; hence, the reason for them to have the conversation in the first place.

As the forest thickened, Katrine took a deep breath. Her heart picked up speed and her body filled with adrenaline; before she could talk herself out of it, she sprinted sideways into the forest.

She couldn't hear anyone following over her own panting as she wove through the trees and jumped over dead, wet logs; but the feeling of being watched still haunted her.

She glanced behind her to see if the feeling had any substance, and terror struck. There was the blue light, swirling in circles to form a funnel-shaped cloud, following her through the trees. She tried to run faster, but the blue light followed with ease. When she tripped over a branch in a small clearing, it stopped and hovered, waiting for her to get up as if it enjoyed the chase too much for it to end so fast. Katrine rolled over and sat up, trying to catch her breath. She pulled herself up slowly as she watched the light hover directly above her, then turned to run again. She took one step; then felt it pounce.

As the blue light picked her up by the legs and started turning her in circles, Katrine screamed and tried to grab onto something, but there was nothing. She could feel her legs bind together, unable to move. Then it dropped her to the wet leaves and sticks below. She tried to scurry to her feet, but something was holding her back. She looked down to see a large fin instead of legs and feet, and she gasped in horror at the sight.

From under her blue dress protruded overlapping bluish-green scales that eventually tapered into a disgusting, thick, green tail fin. She twisted herself around and tried to split the fin apart by moving her legs in separate directions, but there were no legs. It was a single piece that flopped up and down as she tried to squirm out of it.

Katrine heard footsteps approaching. Someone was slowly making their way through the forest toward her. Using her hands, she walked herself over to a tree and leaned her back against it. Stunned, she found herself unable to tear her eyes away from the hideous fin as Zor emerged from the trees, stopped in front of her, and stared at her in silence. Katrine finally managed to pull her eyes away from herself to look up at him.

"What the hell did you do to me?" Katrine cried.

Zor appeared puzzled. "Once again your word usage seems inappropriate for 1693." He sat on a nearby log and picked a blade of grass. "Where'd you hear such an expression?"

"What?" Katrine asked in disbelief. "You want to discuss proper speech for 1693?"

"Yes. Where'd you hear that expression?"

Katrine shook her head. "I have a fin. I don't care *where the hell I've heard it from*...I have a fin!"

Zor placed the blade of grass in his mouth and leaned sideways on the log. "Yes, you do have a fin. And it's truly disappointing. My brother's going to gloat about this for weeks."

Katrine looked back down at the scales, then closed her eyes. She hated him. She wanted to run away so badly, but couldn't. Her fin arched off the ground, then fell again as she tried once more to squirm out of it.

"Please let me out of this thing. I need to get to my mother."

"What about your father?"

Katrine grabbed a fistful of wet dirt and leaf litter and threw it at him with a frustrated cry. "Stay out of my business!" She could hear her heart thumping deep in her ears, uncertain if anger or fear was causing it.

Zor calmly leaned forward, picked up another blade of grass and began to strip the seeds from the stalk. He stared at Katrine with an intense look. "I'm curious how a peasant becomes an imposter princess; and one who can so casually use the word 'hell' in practically every sentence." When Katrine made no attempt to illuminate him, he asked, "Have you really spent the last few years playing princess, or were you really somewhere else? Perhaps taken there by a witch or warlock."

Katrine groaned, looked up at Zor, and angrily replied, "I've been stuck in a blasted castle for the last four years. Where the *hell* would a witch or warlock take me?"

"Someplace a bit more advanced."

She shook her head, completely puzzled. "More advanced? What are you talking about?"

He looked at her in silence for a moment and then threw the blade of grass down. "Just trying to figure you out." He stood up and approached her. "I suppose I have to carry you out of here now."

"Or you can just give me back my legs."

"No. You must learn that there are consequences to your actions."

His words left Katrine weak. Yes, there were consequences to her actions. If she had chosen to stay in the service of the queen – if she had chosen to marry someone five years younger who irritated her beyond belief – her mother would not be in the danger she was in now and she wouldn't be flopping around the forest in a fin, about to be carried off by her warlock captor. Zor leaned over and pulled her up, then hoisted her over his shoulder and carried her back to the trail.

Katrine clenched her eyes shut when James laughed at her. "You know, Zor, you *can* just transport her onto the ship."

"She has a fear of flying," Zor answered as he started down the path. "Besides, it makes you weak when you use your powers for every little chore, and things become so dreadfully boring."

"Well, this is certainly not boring," he said as he patted her fin.

Katrine's face flushed red and she wanted to hide. She could almost feel James gawking at her ugly scales as she flopped up and down with each step Zor took. Zor's shoulder uncomfortably jabbed her in the stomach as he made his way down the trail, but her newly acquired scales seemed to help cushion some of the impact.

She could tell when the path was about to open up onto the sandy banks bordering the sea because she could hear the waves crash against the shoreline rocks and could smell rotting fish guts left behind by the fishermen. Once they arrived at the beach, Zor dropped Katrine onto the sand, allowing her more time to stare at her deformity while he pulled a small rowboat farther onto the shore. As she turned her attention to Zor's crew loading into small boats and rowing towards the main ship, she wanted to cry. Now she had to endure a long trip with Zor, James, and his crew with no chance of being able to run to freedom.

Zor walked over and sat down beside Katrine, but she made no eye contact. Instead, she stared at the waves breaking in the sea. He patted the top of her fin.

"See this?"

"No. I hadn't noticed," Katrine quietly replied.

"This is called a warning. I'm serious about keeping my newly acquired citizens with me, and usually their attempts to escape lead to their own unfortunate demise." Katrine made no response as she continued to stare out to sea, so Zor decided to continue. "I want to have your reassurance that you won't try to escape again. I would hate to see you hurt before I even get to know you."

Katrine turned her head and looked at him somberly. "I broke a pact with a queen, and now she'll be sending her men to kill my parents to teach me a lesson." She turned her head back towards the sea. "I'm not giving you any reassurance. I'll do whatever it takes to get away from you, and if I die trying, then so be it. It's better than living knowing that I didn't even try."

Zor sounded amused. "I was considering giving you back your legs, but I guess that would be foolish, wouldn't it?"

Katrine closed her eyes and buried the side of her face in her hand, wondering why she hadn't lied and told him that she wouldn't run. "I want my legs back."

As Zor stood up, he replied, "I'm sure you do." He turned toward Katrine and held out his hand. "Maybe later when I can watch you closer. Right now, I have a ship to attend."

Katrine groaned and reluctantly gave him her hand. He pulled her up and hoisted her over his shoulder, then walked to a small rowboat in which James was already waiting.

The main ship was a large Spanish galleon with about fifteen canons jutting out from not only the top deck of the starboard side, but also two different levels below. Three large masts held up hundreds of ropes and pulleys, and it reminded Katrine of the large spider webs that she would always find in the old barn at home. Each mast carried two large rolled up sails that flapped loudly in the cold sea breeze. As they rowed to the ship, she stared at the flags at the top of each mast. The middle flag was the Jolly Roger, but the two adjacent flags each had a red letter Z shaped from lightening bolts with a small 'or' on the bottom leg of the Z.

Katrine peered across the water at the setting sun and started to shiver as the oars hit the water and methodically pushed the small rowboat forward across the waves. The lower part of her dress had become soaked not only from sea spray, but also from the splash of the oars and the waves that hit the side of the boat. But the fin part of her body was relatively warm compared to her goose-bump covered arms.

Finally, the small rowboat turned and collided against the side of the main ship, and James secured the rowboat. A rope ladder with wooden steps dropped from above alongside a rope with a loop. Katrine felt utterly humiliated as Zor draped the rope under her arms and they pulled her up the side of the ship. She tried to ignore the snickers of the men as they took hold of her and pulled her over a bronze trim that bordered the edge.

"Tie the brunette to the front mast," Zor ordered the group of pirates as he reached the top of the rope ladder. "Then let's get dinner prepared. I'm getting hungry."

"Ay, Ay, Captain," two of Zor's men responded.

Katrine was carried upstairs to a deck that held the front mast and a large, bronze wheel. The floorboards to the deck creaked with each step they took towards the mast because of a cabin underneath, which Katrine presumed was Zor's because of its large size.

Once at the mast, the pirate dropped her against the pole and began to tie her hands to two metal loops jutting out from the sides of the thick pole. As he tied them, she looked down to the main deck and listened as Zor gave the order to raise the anchor. She watched the crew busy themselves with the anchor and sails, but had to grimace as the ropes around her wrist were tied so tightly that they cut off her circulation.

"They're too tight," Katrine complained as she tried to squeeze her hand. "Can you loosen them just a little?"

"Too tight, eh?" the pirate replied with his arms crossed in front of him. He bent down again and pulled the ropes tighter, causing Katrine to cry out in pain. "There, that's better," he said as he walked away.

"Jerk," Katrine whispered as she watched him descend the stairs. She leaned her head backwards against the pole and contemplated her use of the word 'jerk'. She had never used the word 'jerk', nor knew what it meant exactly, but it seemed the appropriate thing to call him. Just like the word 'hell' had popped into her speech earlier, attracting Zor's attention. "It's just stress," she whispered to herself. "New words are always invented in times of stress."

Katrine watched the commotion on deck as the crew pulled the ropes, lowered the sails, climbed up into their lookout posts, and drank rum to celebrate the success of their trip. They seemed to be having a wonderful time. Katrine, on the other hand, felt like screaming. She had still not been able to shake the strange, eerie feeling of being watched, and her hands were now throbbing with such pain that her eyes were beginning to water.

She closed her eyes and tried to move her hands, wishing desperately that the ropes were looser.

"Just a little looser, that's all I had asked," she angrily muttered. Suddenly, she felt the ropes unravel a bit. She looked behind her to see who had helped her, but there was no one. The knots had just slipped. They were still a bit tight, and she wished the knots would have slipped a little more... then they did.

She looked to the other side of the boat to find Zor, wondering if he was testing her by giving her another opportunity to escape, but he was having a drink with James as they watched the shore disappear on a brilliant red and yellow horizon. No, it wasn't a test. Even Zor knew she wouldn't leave until she got her legs back. Katrine smirked; the big brute simply didn't know how to tie a knot.

She squirmed her hands, trying to get them completely free so that her wrists could recover, but the ropes still weren't loose enough. "Come on," she groaned under her breath. "Get these stupid ropes off." The ropes began to unravel by themselves, but this time she could tell that it wasn't simply knots slipping. There was some force acting on the ropes, untying them. She looked behind her to see that she was still alone as the ropes fell to the deck.

She stared curiously at the ropes for several moments, then turned to face forward again. On the trail, James had made it sound like there was a chance he was going to become a warlock. Maybe the strange powers on which he was waiting traveled through the air, made a mistake and went into her body instead of his, thereby giving *her* the new powers... or something to that affect.

She bit her lip and decided to test her new theory. "I should at least appear to be tied up." She closed her eyes and took a deep breath as she wished the ropes to tie again. When she felt the ropes drape loosely around her wrists and weave through the metal loops, her body flooded with fear. Was she now suddenly a witch? Would she be hanged? Zor said she didn't have the aura of a witch... *What exactly did that mean?* She stared out at the sea, shaking from both anxiety and the chilled breeze. Her mind began to wander, reviewing all the horror stories of women being persecuted for being a witch. Zor said a real witch couldn't be hanged. Could they be drowned? Could they be burned? Or could they breathe in the water and put out fires with a brainwave? What's a brainwave?

The brilliant red sky began to turn into a dreary gray as the sun nearly finished setting. Her muscles were so fatigued from shaking that she forced herself to try to relax and think logically. *Use your powers to escape*, she decided. *Who cares where they came from or what others will think of me, what's important is that I get to mother and warn her.*

She swung her head around to see if the two pirates at the helm had noticed anything unusual about her ropes, but they seemed too busy looking out to sea, discussing mud. Katrine peered across the port bow and wondered whether she should make a jump over the edge to try to escape. Once she swam to land, she would turn her fin back into legs. Katrine stared intensely at her fin and tried to change it into her legs to make sure it was possible, but the fin remained. She groaned with disappointment.

She probably wouldn't have had the courage to dive into the water even if she *did* have the ability to get her legs back. She now had an irrational fear of the water. During the previous summer, she had nearly drowned when she had hit her head on a rock after a dive into a lagoon, and Paul had to drag her out of the water. Drowning had actually been quite peaceful; it was being saved that hurt so much. Choking and suffocating with every breath as she tried to recover was something she never wanted to relive.

Agnes, she remembered. Agnes was magically transported to Zor's utopia. She closed her eyes and wished she could transport home to Dragon Hill. Who cares if she had a fin? She could warn her mother, transport back to the ship, get her legs back, follow Zor to Agnes, and then save Agnes. When she opened her eyes, however, she was still on the ship.

She couldn't get her legs back; she couldn't magically transport from one place to another. But she could do *some* things. Not everything...but some things. Maybe it would be enough to help her escape once they reached land again. The task at hand was to practice using her new powers to see what she was and was not capable of doing.

She looked out on the deck below and watched as some of the crew lit lanterns hung on ropes while others received dinner plates for the evening's meal from a hole that led below deck. The man who had bound her wrists had just acquired his plate of food and was about to sit on a stool to eat. She stared at the stool and whispered 'move.' It slid out from under him as he began to sit, causing him to tumble backwards to the deck and spill his food all over his front side. Katrine took a deep, nervous breath as she watched the crew laugh and tease him. He looked furious. *Serves him right*, thought Katrine.

She looked around for something else to try. A little flag on the edge of the ship was flapping in the breeze. She stared at it and it flapped in the wrong direction. She quickly returned the flag to normal before anyone noticed, then stretched her neck to try to alleviate some of the tension she was feeling.

Katrine noticed James and Zor making their way up the stairs with an extra dinner plate resting in the cradle of Zor's arm. She didn't want to talk to Zor, and she certainly didn't want to eat with him. She leaned her head against the mast and decided to postpone her experiments until they left, in case Zor was somehow able to detect what she was doing. With a quick wish, she tightened the ropes around her wrists a little more, then fidgeted uncomfortably as James sat directly in front of her on a small, wooden ridge separating the upper and lower decks. Zor walked over to the helm instead.

"Steady as she goes," said Zor in a spirited voice.

"Ay, ay, Captain," replied the pirate holding the wheel.

The other man at the helm spoke. "Have I told you that your commanding abilities are far superior to any great sea captain I've ever worked under?" he boasted loudly. "Even Silver, I believe."

"You idiot," the other pirate replied. "Silver is a fictional character. He wasn't even a captain."

"Well, I'll still take it as a complement," said Zor with a small laugh, "since I'm not a real captain either. Carry on."

The two pirates laughed as Zor walked over to James. James was shaking his head.

"Guard Eight is such a brown-noser," James said quietly.

"They're just having fun. It's not often they get out of Cyan to play pirate."

As Zor stepped in front of her, Katrine made no effort to make eye contact with him. She had so many emotions built up inside, she didn't know which one to express.

"Suppose I untie you so you can eat," Zor said. "Do you plan on being problematic?"

"I don't believe I have an appetite," Katrine replied without looking up.

Zor paused, and then dropped the plate of food in front of her before sitting down beside James. Katrine looked at the plate. It had a large helping of fried veal cutlet, green peas, and potatoes with gravy. She was starved and the food smelled wonderful, but she tore her eyes from the dinner plate and focused on the wooden deck in front of her.

"It's going to be cold tonight. It will help to have a little food in your stomach." Zor waved his hand in her direction and Katrine felt the ropes unravel until they completely fell from her wrists. She pulled her aching arms from behind her and rubbed her wrists.

"A thank you might be polite," said James.

Katrine looked up for the first time. James wanted her to *thank* Zor? She took a deep breath and barely managed to stop herself from calling James a word that she had never heard before, nor knew the meaning. Somehow she knew it would feel satisfying to say, however, just as the word 'jerk' had felt.

"Yes, it probably would be polite," she responded coldly. Then she sat silent without any intention of speaking.

"We need to talk a bit about your placement in Cyan," remarked Zor.

"Zor," James cut in, "she hasn't said thank you yet."

"She'll thank me later when she's lived in Cyan for a while."

"Yes, I suppose she will," he said as he gave Katrine a scrutinizing look. "Cyan's going to be your new home. It's filled with only first rate, extremely talented individuals." He paused. "So it will be interesting to see how you fit in."

Zor shot James a look before turning back to Katrine. "Do you have any special talents, such as playing a musical instrument... painting..?" He waved his hand in front of him, asking her for help.

Katrine couldn't mask her confusion. She wasn't sure how to respond to such a strange question.

"Perhaps you're a good cook," James said after Katrine's silence. "Have you cooked any good grilled cheese sandwiches lately?"

"No," Katrine said slowly, her eyes narrowing. "I'm not a cook. But I bet I'm a pretty good swimmer right now."

"What we're trying to find out here is if you have any service or entertainment value," explained Zor. "To find your appropriate house."

"Don't believe for a second I'm going to serve or entertain you." Katrine leaned her head against the mast behind her. "I've already been turned into a mermaid. That should be enough entertainment to last you a lifetime. I'm exempt from any future performances."

James looked at Zor. "She's not cooperating, is she?"

"No. She's not. Perhaps I need to try a different approach." He placed his dinner plate to his side, stood up and grabbed Katrine by the arm. "Let me help you up."

Katrine peered suspiciously up at Zor, then let him pull her up. She felt her fin split down the middle and her legs return. Relief flooded over her as she held onto Zor's arm and regained her balance.

"Now that I've given you something, you can give me something in return – less attitude." He pointed toward the horizon. "While you're up, do you see that little brown speck on the water just south of where the sun set?"

Katrine looked and saw a small boat. "Yes," she cautiously answered.

"That's Paul, following us."

Katrine felt her stomach drop.

"Why do you think he's following us?" he asked inquisitively. "Does he think he can save you?"

Katrine shrugged. "Perhaps."

"Such a fool," he said shaking his head.

Katrine's anger began to rise. "He's not a fool. He's heroic."

"Heroic?" Zor responded with surprise. "Here's a heroic scenario for you. He follows us to find out where we port; then he leaves you at the mercy of your captors to seek help. But from whom, I wonder."

Katrine eyed Zor. "What are you hinting at exactly?"

"Nothing," he said with his eyebrows raised. "But it would take an army to challenge my crew, wouldn't it? Does he know where he can get an army on such short notice?"

Katrine clenched her teeth. "He *helped* me escape the queen. If he goes back to her, she'll hang him for treason. He *won't* be seeking her help."

Zor turned toward Katrine. "You're getting quite worked up over this. Are you in love with him?"

"No," she quickly answered. "But he's a good man. He's always been there for me."

"Keeping a close eye on you."

"No!" She became flustered. "Yes! Because he was assigned to me. That's all! He was hired *after* I arrived at the castle, and he was never told that I was not the princess."

Zor shook his head. "You're so naïve. I bet Paul knows everything about your situation. He was letting you lead him to your home so he could kill your mother himself."

Katrine held back an explosion. "I never told him where we were going." She groaned. "He would never kill my mother."

"Don't fool yourself, Katrine. He's not the nice guy you think he is."

Katrine was beginning to shake with anger. "I didn't see you read his mind in town."

"I don't need to read his mind to know what he's all about. He's playing you. He helped you escape to show you he's on your side; then when he eliminates your real family behind your back, he'll convince you to return to the only other life you have. The queen would prefer to have a voluntary princess as opposed to one who wants to run away."

"I loathe you," Katrine said in a low voice. "You think you know everything about everyone, well perhaps I should give *you* a proper bit of education. Paul is twice the man you can ever hope to be. He's not arrogant like you are, he doesn't play games with people's lives, and he's a *hell* of a lot braver than you are with your boat full of huge, overweight, dim-witted guards surrounding you. You want to know something? Paul has feelings for me, and he's ready to risk his life for me. That's why he helped me escape the queen. He doesn't want to see me married and miserable. You think he's going to turn around when you drop anchor and seek the queen's help? No. He's going to drive his boat right up to the side of this ship and take you on with his oars if he has to. And I doubt you'll have the courage to face him without using your magic."

Katrine swirled around and plopped down by the mast, incensed. She buried her face in the side of her hand so that she didn't have to look at him. Except for the waves crashing into the side of the boat, there was silence, and she half expected her fin to reappear in front of her.

When Zor spoke, his voice was cool. "I shall not let him fall behind tonight. We shall see tomorrow if he wants to challenge me."

Katrine listened as Zor hastened towards the stairs, made his way down the steps, then entered the cabin beneath her. The door slammed, shaking the entire upper deck. Katrine wished that she had seen Zor's face after her speech. It sounded as though she had touched a nerve... which would at least give her a little pleasure.

"I've never heard a prisoner talk back so boldly to Zor before," James commented. "You're either really brave or really stupid." He picked up Zor's tray of food with his and stood up. "Go ahead and eat. I'll be back when you finish to pick up your tray and tie you back to your perch. In the meantime, don't cause any problems." As he made his way to the stairs, he turned to the two pirates at the helm. "Watch her, but don't touch."

"Ay, ay, sir."

Katrine rested her head in her arms. Brave or stupid, she pondered. She raised her head and stared at the lower decks of the pirate ship. Most of Zor's guards were staring back up at her with scowls on their faces. *Stupid* seemed the more appropriate description of her little outburst.

She felt drained. Her body could barely shiver as the night air became increasingly chilled. She weakly reached over to the plate of food left behind and ate what she could before collapsing on the deck from exhaustion. She would experiment more with her new powers tomorrow. There wasn't much she could do in the middle of the sea anyhow.

"I'm going to sleep now," she whispered to the strange presence that had been watching her since the dress shop. "There's nothing more to see, so please just go away."

Chapter 2
1998 - Las Cruces, New Mexico (Saturday)

Alyssa opened her eyes and stared at the white ceiling. It was sterile and colorless, just like the rest of the hospital room. After staring at it for three days in a row, it made her want to scream. The sooner the doctor signed her release form, the better.

She threw off her blankets and walked over to the sink where she splashed water on her face, trying to relieve her dry eyes. Her contact lenses had dried out and she wished she had changed into her glasses before falling asleep. She rarely wore glasses anymore because she not only received numerous complements on her blue-green eyes when the contacts were in, but during soccer practice the ball would sometimes knock her glasses off. Alyssa's nose was much happier when she wore contacts. As she dried her face with the towel, the soft pink glow in her cheeks returned. She wore no makeup, because she didn't need it. Her face was already smooth and blemish free with just enough natural color.

As she finished drying the water around her neck, she stared into the mirror. Next week she would be twenty-one years old, an age that everyone envies. Independent (with her mother and father paying her college room and board, of course), and free to make her own decisions (which usually meant she could pick what she wanted to watch on the dormitory's lobby television on Friday night because everyone else had dates and were out enjoying themselves). It wasn't that she was unattractive, or boring, or dumb – it was exactly the opposite. She was smart and she had high standards, refusing to date just any horny college jock who asked her out. If she accepted a date, he would have to at least *resemble* Mr. Right.

She grabbed a comb and started combing her shoulder-length wavy hair, then pushed her long bangs from in front of her eyes to admire the new section of hair on the right side of her head that she had bleached white. It looked cool. She had made the right decision to dye it. Perhaps it would speed up attracting a potential Mr. Right. It had been two years since she broke up with her last potential... two years without intimate relations and she missed it. Alyssa threw the comb down beside the sink and reluctantly returned to her bed to cover up. The hospital gown revealed too much of her backside and she didn't feel like sharing it with anyone who might want to enter.

A knock on the door ten minutes later was a welcome relief from her boredom. Her two closest friends, David and Samantha, had come to visit. David Lopez, a native from Las Cruces, helped Alyssa through her first semester of college when she was struggling in Algebra, and they've remained friends and study partners ever since. David was a tall Hispanic with spiked hair, a muscular body, high intelligence, and a pleasant down-to-earth perspective on life. He was accepted into Cornell, even had a tuition scholarship, but ended up going to New Mexico State in his hometown due to poor finances. Cornell didn't realize that travel expenses, books, room and board also cost money, much more than David's family could afford. So David ended up living at home, working a part-time job at a convenience store to save enough money to someday move out of his parent's little shack in downtown Las Cruces.

Sami Jazz, on the other hand, had been characterized many times behind her back as a somewhat arrogant, well-to-do airhead. But she wasn't rich like everyone believed. Her dad worked with the Albuquerque police department and her mother was a teacher. She wasn't dumb, either; but being blond and having such a strange last name didn't help curve the airhead jokes. Alyssa had a special fondness for Sami because they had known each other since elementary school and had played on all the same softball and soccer teams growing up. And although Sami was a bit more 'spirited' than most of her other friends, Alyssa didn't like to think of Sami as an airhead.

"We finally made it, Alyssa!" David exclaimed as he trotted through the doorway in front of Sami and dropped a bag onto the floor at the base of Alyssa's bed. "The art convention at UNM started getting slow. So once we decided we had seen it all, we sped all the way from Albuquerque to get here. Sorry you missed it. You would have enjoyed the nude models. I did."

"I'm sure you did," Alyssa replied with a smirk. "Next year you can drag me along."

"Well? Tell us what happened, Alyssa," Sami said with a worried look.

"Craig knows more than I do," replied Alyssa with a rather subdued smile. She had told the story too many times. "He was behind me on his mountain bike. All I remember is reaching the top of the hill and glimpsing backwards to see how far he was behind me. When I turned back around, I saw the fallen power lines and couldn't stop in time. Craig says my bike got tangled and I went flying over the handlebars with a few sparks lighting the way, then slid a good couple of feet on the rocks beside the trail. He also said both the bike and I were flashing on and off like a neon sign, but I believe that's just part of Craig's sick sense of humor."

"May I see the leg?" asked David as he approached her bedside.

Alyssa lifted the blanket off her right leg. "Pretty impressive, eh?" she asked as she turned the side of her leg upward to reveal several deep scratches from sliding across the rocks.

"Ouch! Does it still hurt?" asked Sami.

"It stings a bit, but it's healing fast," Alyssa replied. She covered her leg back up.

"And how's the other part of you?" asked David as he tapped on his head.

"My head's better than ever. In fact, the doctor said there's extra neural activity right about here," she said as she pointed right above her temples on both sides of her head. "Or maybe he said unusual. I don't remember his exact words. But I'll probably be smarter than you now."

"It'll take more than an electric shock to become smarter than me," David replied. "Your best hope would be to acquire a little ESP and become able to read my mind for any answers you might need."

"Ha, ha," Alyssa said sarcastically.

Sami huffed, "I can't believe nobody reported fallen power lines!"

"We were the first to come across them. They probably fell during that storm the previous night."

"I'd sue the power company, Alyssa," suggested Sami. "You shouldn't have to pay for this."

"That's enough, Sami. She's got insurance," said David. "I think she's got enough to stress about without you giving her more." He reached down into the bag he had brought and pulled out a flat ten-by-twelve inch present wrapped in shiny blue paper with a fancy blue and pink bow. "Happy birthday, Alyssa. I even wrapped it in your favorite color."

Alyssa's eyes lit up. "My birthday's not for another week."

"Yes, I know. But if I gave it to you next week, you wouldn't get to look at the babe in January as long."

Alyssa smiled. "You're not very good at keeping secrets."

"I'd seriously worry about this extra brain activity of yours if you couldn't figure out that *this*," David waved it in front of Alyssa's face, "is a calendar." He threw it on top of Alyssa's covers.

Alyssa opened a card attached and laughed. On the card, David had drawn a cartoon figure of a terrified Alyssa riding a broken mountain bike across a power line like a circus tight rope. Below the power line were sharp, dagger-like rocks. "Your cartoons, as always, have most accurately depicted the trials and tribulations of Alyssa Whitman." Alyssa replaced the card in the envelope. "You should try to publish your drawings, David. They're very good."

"Of course they are. I spent four long years drawing and doodling in high school when I should have been doing work."

"Good thing you had something called SAT scores, or I would have never met you."

David sat on the edge of Alyssa's bed. "I made some good connections at the convention. Even met an editor to a children's book publishing house. Maybe I'll give him a call."

"You should." Alyssa tore the wrapping paper off her present. She looked at the calendar and read, "1998: World's Greatest Female Soccer Players. Am I in this?"

"Maybe next year," Sami chuckled. "By the way, coach asked me if you were playing in the tournament this week."

"Just try to keep me away. I'm not going to let a few scratches and scrapes slow me down."

David crumpled up the sack from which he had taken Alyssa's birthday present, stood up, and threw it in the wastebasket. "Are you going to make classes Monday or do you want me to pick up your homework?"

"I can't imagine them keeping me here two more days." She shook her head at the thought. "I really can't wait to get the hell out of here." She sighed. "I'll give you a call tonight to tell you what's up. I think they want to take one more scan of my marvelous brain before I go. Could you do me a favor, David, before you leave?"

"What?"

"Buy me a writing pad and pen from the gift shop. I've been having some very vivid dreams and I want to write it all down before I forget the details. It's great material for my Creative Writing class this semester."

"I will on one condition."

"What could that possibly be, I wonder?" Alyssa said as she rolled her eyes.

"Will you go out with me?"

"Unbelievable," groaned Sami. "When are you going to give up, David?"

Alyssa looked at David and replied, "No, but get me the pad and pen anyway, okay?"

"Fine. Your loss. But I have to send up the pad and pen with a volunteer since we caught the tail end of visiting hours."

Alyssa smiled. "Thanks for stopping by, guys. It gets quite boring here."

They headed for the door when David stopped. "Oh, and a little advice before we leave: give up mountain biking. It doesn't agree with you."

"You sound like my parents. It's only my third major accident."

They waved their hands and disappeared through the doorway. Alyssa sank back into her pillow and closed her eyes. She wanted to dream some more. It was much more interesting than staring at the white walls and watching the nurses write on her chart.

Chapter 3
The Tour (Sunday)

Katrine opened her eyes to find herself lying on the ship's wooden deck by the mast with a small pillow under her head and a fleece blanket covering her. It took a second to realize where she was. The events from the previous day had seemed so far-fetched, she wouldn't have believed them to be true... except there she was, filthy dress, chilled from the morning sea breeze, prisoner of a warlock. She pushed herself up to a sitting position, sore from sleeping on the hard deck, but still grateful James hadn't tied her back to the mast for the night.

The sails and flags above her flapped noisily, drowning out most of the commotion occurring below her on the decks and above her on the ropes and masts. She looked up to a cold, clear sky to see six pirates hanging onto the ropes and nets, rolling up the sails. Six more men were on the middle mast and another six on the mast located at the stern of the ship.

"We'll be dropping anchor soon, Katrine," said a voice behind her. Katrine turned to see Zor with two of his crew standing around the wheel, looking out to sea. "Your boyfriend kept falling behind last night, but I gave him a little push every once in a while to help him keep up. I'm eager to face him in a dual. Perhaps he can lend me one of his oars so we can have a fair fight."

Katrine looked down at the deck, wondering how embarrassed she should feel. She struggled to her feet, then looked over the stern of the ship to see Paul's boat in the distance, being tossed around by the waves like a toy.

"Your destiny awaits you, Katrine," Zor said as he stared across the bow. "Although not yet revealed, there is a reason I took you. I'm sure it will be exciting for both of us to discover why." He gave her a quick smile, then turned and quickly walked towards the lower deck where he shouted orders for his men to weigh anchor.

Katrine turned and realized the ship was nearing a foggy lagoon surrounded by a dense pine forest. White fluffy clouds had fallen out of the sky to become entangled throughout the treetops. She took a deep breath as she stared at the dark forest and remembered the events that had occurred before Zor had interrupted with dinner. She had a new gift of magic, and this time she would have it to help her escape.

Katrine looked for something to practice on. She spotted a pirate sitting on the outer wall of the ship, dangling his legs over the water. *Man overboard*, she thought as she tried to push him off with a wish; but nothing happened. She immediately started to rub her hands together, dreading the implications of a potential loss of power at such an inopportune moment. Maybe her powers didn't work on people, she reasoned. That was why she couldn't get rid of the fish fin or transport home.

To make sure she could still manipulate inanimate objects, she returned her attention to the small flag and wished it to flap in the opposite direction just as she had before. But nothing happened. Trying to mask her panic, she decided that she should probably say the words aloud.

Katrine whispered, "Change directions," but it had no effect on the flag. She shook her head and looked down at the ropes that had bound her at the base of the mast and wished them to wrap around the metal rings, but they didn't move.

Katrine walked to the edge of the ship and stared at the approaching lagoon with a heavy heart and realized that her new powers weren't the only thing missing. She now felt very alone. No longer was there an eerie feeling of being watched. She had told it to leave before she fell asleep – and it did, seemingly taking her ability to perform supernatural acts with it.

Zor walked to the upper level of the ship holding a rope that hung high from the sails above her and began to wrap it around a metal post just over the edge of the ship. As he wrapped the rope, he glanced over at Katrine.

"I'm assuming you learned your lesson yesterday and you know not to run off?"

Katrine held back a groan. "I won't run," she quietly replied. Especially when he was there watching her, she decided.

"Good," Zor said before turning and making his way back down the steps, shouting at Guard Five to take his position at the anchor.

Katrine turned, leaned her back against the ship's bronze edge and watched as Zor helped with tasks that had to be done before they anchored. When she found herself admiring him, she quickly turned away. He was the enemy, the reason she couldn't warn her mother...he was *not* to be admired.

The ship slowed as it entered the lagoon and she could hear the large chain that held the anchor loudly clamor as it was released. The anchor splashed in the water and the rope ladder was thrown over the side of the ship amidst the shouts of the crew.

The man attending the wheel approached Katrine. "Prisoner!" he bellowed as he grabbed her arm, startling her. "Time to walk the plank!"

The man and his companion laughed as she was tossed toward the stairway, causing her to stumble over her dress and lose her balance. She slammed face forward to the deck after a second push from behind.

"Guard Nine!" yelled Zor from the deck below. "Careful with the merchandise! You're not on patrol and excessive force is *not* required."

"Yes, sir," the guard quickly humbled himself. Katrine started to lift herself up when she felt the guard grab her around her waist and stand her up as if she was a rag doll. As she nervously peered behind her, the guard raised his eyebrows and waved his hand down the stairs.

"Proceed to the ladder, Miss," he said in the most pleasant voice he was capable. "This huge, overweight, dim-witted guard offers his most sincere apologies."

Katrine swallowed hard, wondering if she should apologize, but knew it would fall on deaf ears anyway. She turned and quickly made her way down the steps to a rope ladder hanging over the side of the ship.

"Time to go home, boys," Zor announced. He held out his hands and walked around the main deck, touching the guards one by one, making them disappear.

When the guards were gone, James, Zor, and Katrine descended the ladder to a rowboat, then James detached it from the ship and the boat started to swiftly glide across the water toward the shore with no one at the oars. Once they climbed onto the sandy beach of the lagoon, two black stallions appeared from the shadows of the dark forest pulling an open carriage containing two benches which faced each other.

The Link – Seven Days of Cyan

"Now," said Zor as he turned towards the ship, "let's make ourselves a bit more visible." The ship faded into nothing, leaving the open sea in front of them with Paul's small boat in the distance. Between the disappearance of the crew and the disappearance of the ship, Katrine began to feel utterly helpless. He was powerful. Zor smugly crossed his arms in front of him. "Let's see what your boyfriend does."

"He's not my boyfriend," Katrine mumbled as she stared into the sand. "He's my guard." She looked up and watched Paul's boat. For several minutes it remained motionless in the water; then it looked as though it was turning around. Not long afterwards, it was obvious that he was leaving. Katrine hung her head in disappointment.

"Why didn't he come to challenge me? He can plainly see that it's just me and my brother."

Katrine didn't want to respond. She kicked the sand in front of her.

"Nothing to say, Katrine?"

She looked up. "You haven't proven anything yet. You don't know what he plans to do."

"He's going to inform the very queen who threatens to kill your mother of my location. Do you want me to stop him? I can easily capsize his boat."

Katrine raised her head and watched Paul row farther away, unsure what to believe. "If you fear him, by all means, do what you feel the need to do." She turned defiantly towards Zor. "I trust him, though. Don't do anything on my behalf."

James laughed. "I'm getting into the carriage." As he stepped up and took a seat facing the back of the carriage, he remarked, "Too bad Cyan doesn't have a house for gullible females. We'd have a place for you, then, Katrine."

* * *

They rode through the dense pine forest along a small narrow path that seemed to widen as the carriage approached and then completely disappear once the carriage passed. Patches of snow on the forest floor were melting, causing tiny streams of water to trickle across the muddy pathway. The sound of wind rustling through the pine needles and water dripping from branch to branch silenced as they passed.

"The best years of your lives are before you," Zor remarked.

Katrine looked from the forest floor to Zor, angry that he could even suggest he would be improving her life. "My mother is going to die today because of you."

"Oh, wait, Zor!" James jumped in. He pretended to open a book. "You have a beheading at 10, and stabbing at 11...but I don't see any 'killing Katrine's mother' on your agenda. Did I miss it? Perhaps I was doing my nails when you told me and I forgot to write it in."

Zor smiled at James. "Give it a rest." Turning back to Katrine, he motioned towards James with a tilt of his head. "But he does have a point. I don't plan on killing your mother today."

"You know that's not what I meant," Katrine said as she returned her gaze to the forest and shook her head. "A person can still be responsible for a death without actually committing..."

"Then perhaps you should search for the responsible party closer to home," interrupted Zor, "since I had no role in placing your mother in any sort of life-threatening situation."

"But you stopped me from warning her, from saving her."

"From a predicament you placed her in."

Katrine's face flushed red and she quickly looked away when she felt her eyes begin to water.

James broke the silence. "We're approaching Cyan's outer log wall."

The trees cleared and a wall made of vertically placed logs towered forty meters toward the sky. No door was apparent until a section of the wall began to swing open by itself. Katrine's muscles tensed as she peered towards the sky at the top of the wall, and she became certain that once she entered the enormous wooden cage, there would be no way out. She fidgeted to the front of her bench, realizing that she was going to bolt into the forest again. It didn't matter if there was no chance of escape. Her actions were no longer under the control of common sense.

"Stay in your seat, Katrine," Zor warned.

"Maybe you should take her legs away again," James commented.

Katrine's eyes quickly glided from the forest to meet Zor's. "Don't do this to me, please," she pleaded.

"You'll thank me someday."

Katrine grasped the seat to hold herself down as the carriage passed through the gate and the log door swung closed behind them with a loud thud, a sound that seemed to mock Katrine's hope for escape. She stared vehemently at Zor as they entered a landscape that had been completely stripped of vegetation, leaving only a muddy plain behind. About two hundred meters away, in the center of the vast expanse of mud, were trees and buildings. A tall, red, wooden fence was nestled between the windowless, smooth, white walls of the buildings, completely separating the village from the mud.

Katrine quickly grabbed onto the side of the carriage as she felt it lift above the mud and float towards the village. Before the carriage moved too far away from the wall, Katrine peered behind her to see if it was possible to scale the logs behind her. No wires holding the logs together were apparent; there were no ladders... nothing.

"This area is called no-man's land," Zor explained. "No one is allowed to enter this area, except the guards. You met some of them already. They're now back at their house resting up for patrols."

Katrine noticed a narrow concrete pathway that ran one third of the way in from the outer wall perimeter. A large guard walking in the distance patrolled the pathway. She took a deep breath and straightened up, determined to find out everything she could about her new surroundings should the opportunity to escape arise.

As they approached the village, the carriage stopped outside a two-meter tall redwood gate decorated with several carvings of flowers and trees. It had a smooth glossy finish that shined in the rising sun, and Katrine found herself squinting from the sun's reflection, pondering the difficulties she might have if she tried to climb over it.

Zor began to speak. "Past this gate awaits your new home, Cyan, a utopian society consisting of individuals I have collected from several different time periods..."

"Different time periods?" interrupted Katrine.

"Up to the year 2040," added Zor.

Katrine shook her head in disbelief. "And why is 2040 so special?"

"Zor was born," James said. "You can't have two Zors at the same time. Things happen."

"So you expect me to believe you're from the future, along with the rest of Cyan's residents? How stupid do you think I am?"

"Perhaps you shouldn't ask certain questions, Katrine," James said with a smile.

"You will understand everything a little faster if you would restrain yourself from making interruptions," Zor said patiently.

"So time travel is possible in 2040?"

"No, not until about 5120, when a man named Imperius Grumley invents the first time labyrinth."

Katrine's eyes narrowed with confusion. "What's a time labyrinth?"

"A maze made of tall green hedges with hundreds of doors, each leading into a different year. You are coincidentally taken from the same time that I've stationed Cyan, so you will not have the pleasure of experiencing the labyrinth."

"So everyone else in Cyan that you've collected could be returned to their own time without any of their family members ever realizing they were even taken, present company excepted?"

"No. A door that opens into 1356 will be 1357 a year later. Time stands still for no one. One would have to acquire a second labyrinth with a 1356 door to return to the approximate time a citizen was taken. But there is no need to acquire additional labyrinths to return the citizens, since everyone I bring to Cyan wants to stay in Cyan."

"Yes, I'm sure they do," replied Katrine, shaking her head. "Who wouldn't want to be kidnapped and forced to serve a warlock who can mutate your body if you don't cooperate?"

James looked at Zor. "Perhaps you can fuse her mouth shut until the tour's over."

Katrine lost some of the color in her face and looked away, worried that she would find herself mutated a second time.

"Perhaps if I can explain who Cyan's citizens are, you'd understand a little better, Katrine. Each citizen has a natural born gift that had not been properly developed before I removed him or her from his or her detrimental surroundings. They come from families that failed to nurture their genius because of poor finances, unappreciative or uncultured parents and relatives, overburdening domestic responsibilities, or simply, lack of resources. Once they arrive in Cyan, they are assigned to a house with other talented individuals in their field. All the musicians live in one house, the artists live in another, and so on. This atmosphere enables them to quickly reach their full potential, often exceeding even their own expectations. Besides the obvious intrinsic rewards, the people in Cyan also benefit by living a very lavish lifestyle, something they would have never experienced had I not intervened. I am, simply put, their savior."

Katrine bit her tongue to avoid responding and concentrated on watching the decorative wooden gate as it swung open. Trying not to appear too fascinated, she peered past the gate to see the most beautiful village she had ever encountered. The air became warm and had a sweet smell as the carriage floated past the gates and landed on a red brick road bordered by islands of blooming cherry trees and flowers of purple, red, orange, yellow, and blue. A light breeze swept thousands of tiny cherry tree blossoms into the air, giving the appearance of a springtime snowfall in the village.

Behind the trees were square buildings and red slate walkways, filled with people of different skin colors, different hair styles, and exciting new clothing that revealed more of the body than Katrine was used to seeing. If it weren't for the outer wall and guards, Katrine wouldn't have thought they were prisoners. They looked healthy and happy... though their mood seemed to change a bit when they saw the carriage approach.

"Welcome to Cyan, your new home," Zor announced as the wooden carriage wheels noisily rolled over the red bricks below. "After a brief tour of Cyan, I will allow you to eat breakfast in our cafeteria and get acquainted with your new surroundings at a more intimate level."

The first building they rode by was a two-story building with a flat roof made of adobe brick with a brown, stucco finish. Five large windows, three on the second floor and two on the first floor, each had a long, rectangular, flower box suspended directly below. The doorframe and door were made of a dark wood, with the exception of four small glass panes at the top of the door.

"The first building to your right is the hospital, where a couple of very fine doctors work. If someone is injured or sick enough that it will disrupt the routine of Cyan, however, I will sometimes choose to step in and correct the situation."

"The Artist's House is to your left, followed by the Musician's House in the middle. At the end of the street are my Thespians."

Katrine looked through the trees at the houses. Each house was connected to the next, creating a single long wall that ran along the brick road until it ended at the end of the block. It was adobe brick with white stucco. The wooden frames around the doors and windows were painted a different color for each house. The Artist's House had red trim, the Musician's House had green trim, and the Thespian's House had dark blue trim. The roof of the building was flat, but she could tell it was covered with a red tile because of a slight overhang in front. Each house had a small patio made from large, reddish slate rocks that matched the sidewalks.

An uneasy feeling passed over Katrine as she looked at the hospital and the houses. She had never seen adobe walls or stucco. But for some reason they looked familiar to her, and she knew what they were.

Zor continued. "To your right and behind the tree is a job board where daily and weekly postings inform the residents what play I wish to see performed, what music at the weekly concert I wish to hear, and what dinners will be served."

The job board was a large, dark, wooden board on two legs. On it were white pieces of paper tacked to the board with colorful pins.

"Behind the job board is the cafeteria. Most residents choose to eat here rather than at the houses because of the pleasant social atmosphere. I'm sure Agnes is inside at this very moment, laughing and socializing with her new colleagues. The cooks here are a very friendly bunch."

The cafeteria was unique because it was made entirely of dark wood instead of adobe. There were no apparent windows and the front door was made of glass, placed perpendicular to the front wall so that its entrance walkway led directly to the job board. The steep, sloping roof had several chimneys that jutted out from the back side of the cafeteria. They poured out smoke and released an aroma of freshly baked bread. At the apex of the pointed roof was a large, wooden bell tower with a clock.

"Above the cafeteria is the bell tower. The bell sounds five minutes before eight as a warning, and then the curfew bell is at 8:00 p.m. Curfew ends at six in the morning. All citizens must be in their houses during curfew to avoid any guard entanglements."

Curfew raised too many questions. "May I ask a question without getting my mouth fused shut?" Katrine asked with a bit of hesitation.

Zor regarded her in silence before answering, "I suppose."

"If your utopian society is so wonderful, why do you have a curfew? Why do you have guards and a huge wooden wall keeping everyone in?"

"The guards and the wall exist because new residents have not yet realized that Cyan is where they belong. I choose to keep them here against their will until they fully realize what I have done for them."

"So somebody who has fully realized what a service you have done for him or her may be allowed to return home upon request?"

"No one has ever asked. If they did ask, then they haven't fully realized the endowment they have so graciously received and should stay longer until they do."

Katrine shook her head in disbelief as Zor continued with a more agitated tone.

"I require curfew because it gives the guards the opportunity to get out of their house. They had requested ten hours on the grounds of Cyan in a twenty-four hour day, which I felt was a reasonable request. The rest of Cyan's citizens are to be in their homes during curfew, improving their skills in smaller groups. These are my expectations."

"Why can't the guards and the citizens be out at the same time?"

The Link – Seven Days of Cyan

"Too many fights," James answered. "Zor only chooses the best guards, ones that aren't very sympathetic towards Cyan's citizens and have no trouble spilling blood if they need to. We tried letting both the guards and citizens roam the streets together the first year, but there were too many casualties and it created a rather hostile atmosphere."

"It's simple to avoid the guards," added Zor. "Never cross into no-man's land and be in your assigned house by curfew. Two simple rules that everyone is expected to follow." Zor motioned towards the cafeteria. "The cooks' quarters are connected to the back end of the cafeteria, if you want to visit your friend, Agnes, after the tour. Around the far corner of the cafeteria are Cyan's courtyard and the Main House. James and I reside at the Main House."

Once the carriage turned left at the end of the road, Katrine glanced behind her to see the courtyard. Through all the flowers and cherry trees, she could barely make out the Main House enveloping most of the courtyard. She expected it to be a palace or a castle, but instead it was a modest white adobe house that appeared much like the other houses, with the exception that the front wall was composed mostly of large windows with cyan-colored window frames, covered at the top by thick green vines with small purple flowers that draped lazily over the roof. Katrine turned forward in the carriage to find Zor staring at her.

"You will be staying with us," Zor stated, "until an appropriate house can be assigned."

A wave of anxiety swept through Katrine when she realized she would be alone with Zor and James, and she regretted that she hadn't lied about cooking or playing a musical instrument when she had the chance.

"To your right is the auditorium where concerts and plays are performed," Zor continued. "There is also an outdoor stage on the far side." The auditorium was also not adobe. It towered high above the other buildings and was constructed of dark glass, tall white stone columns, and a decorative slanted roof made of marble.

As they approached the next road to the left, she peered down a brick street to see more adobe houses identical to those she had seen on the first street, with each house color-coded a different color.

"The first house, attached to the back of the Thespian House, belongs to the soccer professionals. Not only are these citizens very good at playing a game called soccer, which begins to truly thrive about two hundred years in your future, Katrine, the professionals also begrudgingly serve as soccer coaches and referees for the games I regularly schedule. The fields where soccer is played will soon be in full view to your right after the auditorium and outdoor stage. Each house has a team and is scheduled to play weekly games. Although the people of Cyan may possess extraordinary talent in the field of music, art or drama; during the collection procedure, I also take into consideration athletic ability – thus making the soccer games between houses highly competitive and much more interesting than watching beginners who never improve because of physical limitations," Zor explained. "The cooks are the only house with no team. They are much too busy, some are a bit too hefty, and most haven't an ounce of athletic ability.

"Farther down the street live the gardeners, interior designers, and maids. Although talent is not always required in these areas, I've selected the hardest working, most content workers you'll ever meet. They care about the job they do and never cut corners on quality."

Once the carriage rolled past the auditorium, Katrine looked to her right to see the outdoor amphitheater nestled against the side of the auditorium. A large concrete stage was sunken into the ground, and the lawn surrounding it had rising rows of plush, green, grass benches where an audience could sit. Beside the outdoor amphitheater was a large grassy field, divided into two sections. White lines forming squares were drawn into the grass and centered between two strange white metal structures with nets on opposite ends of each field.

"These are my soccer fields," Zor said. "The first field with benches, called bleachers, is for games and practice; the one farther down is usually just for practice." He looked at Katrine and said, "I imagine you'll make a wonderful soccer player. You're a good runner."

Katrine wasn't sure how to handle the complement, and her face conveyed the confusion of not knowing how to respond, or *whether* to respond. Was he sincere or was he mocking her? Her sprint to escape into the forest was very short-lived. She finally looked out onto the fields, maintaining an expressionless face. A strange, warm feeling passed over her as she stared out at the grass.

The carriage reached the end of the road. In front of them was the tall wooden fence that surrounded the perimeter of the village. One road remained to their left.

Zor turned the carriage to face the final road. "This is the guards' alley. Down this road is the Guards' House, along with a large dirt pit they occasionally use for whatever they wish. As I've already mentioned, the guards patrol no-man's land continuously and the village during curfew. If someone is caught outside their house past curfew, I have given the guards permission to do anything they wish to this individual, because breaking my rules *should* have dire consequences. No one has yet survived a curfew violation, so violations are extremely rare."

James chuckled. "The guards also provide the most interesting soccer games. They certainly keep the doctors on their toes. Their team is undefeated, even against the professionals."

After meeting some of the guards on the ship, Katrine understood why they would be undefeated. Why risk life and limb over a game? James' apparent pleasure regarding the guard games made her shake her head in disgust.

"You know, there *are* rules," she remarked. "Do the refs at least have the courage to issue red cards?"

Immediately Katrine realized what she had said made absolutely no sense. The obscure image inside her head of a man in a black and white striped shirt holding up a red square was not a part of her past.

"How do you know about red cards?" asked James with a puzzled look. Zor also stared at her in silence as he waited for her response. Katrine turned red and immediately buried her face in her hands.

"I don't know," she whispered. "I'm just under a lot of stress."

"Accurate knowledge of the future doesn't simply pop into one's head when one is *under a lot of stress*," James returned.

Katrine angrily looked up. "You're the one who claims to be from the future. Maybe Zor's little memory transfer went in reverse and that's why he couldn't read my mind. You figure it out."

They continued to stare at Katrine in silence as the carriage turned around and headed for the cafeteria. She fidgeted and looked out at the grassy fields as they passed by them a second time. It was the first time she had ever seen fields of this kind, yet there was something very familiar about them... just like the adobe houses... just like the unfamiliar words and expressions she used the day before. Katrine put her head back down in her hands and rubbed her head, dubious that her unexplained 'knowledge of the future' had anything to do with Zor's failed mind probe.

The carriage stopped in front of the cafeteria. "Go and eat breakfast," Zor said. "Afterwards, go to the courtyard where James will meet with you and show you to your room. I have to attend to some business."

Chapter 4
Cyan (Sunday)

When Katrine opened the cafeteria door, the aroma of sausages and freshly baked muffins greeted her. She scanned the crowded room, trying to stay hidden behind a large blue ceramic vase decorated with painted flowers and placed on a small round, wooden table beside the door.

The hustle and bustle of a busy morning breakfast was amplified with the sounds of wooden chairs shifting from under square wooden tables and people traversing across a polished wooden floor. The walls were covered with large oil paintings of colorful scenery – waterfalls and streams, desert canyons, and blue-green forests. Strange round lights, undoubtedly powered by Zor's magic, illuminated the room from above. To the left and back of the cafeteria were two long, wooden service tables filled with trays of breakfast foods: breads, sausages, bacon, steak, eggs cooked in every way possible, berries, melons, crepes, and an assortment of foreign food Katrine had never seen before. There were trays, plates, and glasses at the beginning of each service table that the citizens picked up before they helped themselves to generous portions of the food.

As she stepped out from behind the vase, the cafeteria fell silent. She tried not to look too embarrassed as she reluctantly made her way to the first service table, but she could hear whispers and could feel everyone gaping at her mud-covered dress. She held her breath as she picked up a tray and placed it on the counter.

"Katrine!"

She looked up and instantly felt comforted when she saw Agnes making her way to Katrine from between the service tables.

Although she hardly knew Agnes, Katrine hugged her as if she was a long lost relative.

"Are you all right?" Katrine whispered as they separated.

"Oh, yes, Dear." She looked at the door behind the service tables. "Henry's been an absolute angel."

Katrine looked through the door to see a tall, bald man holding his chef's hat in his hand, watching Agnes.

"He's made me feel right at home." Agnes embraced both of Katrine's hands. "Listen, I've got to get some cakes out of the oven before they overcook. I want to talk later, okay?"

Not sure what to make out of Agnes' behavior, she nodded her head. Agnes leaned over and kissed Katrine on the cheek, and then hurried back through the door to the kitchen.

Dazed, Katrine turned her attention once more towards the food. Everything looked delicious, but she had little appetite.

"Excuse me," a woman behind Katrine spoke. "Are you Katrine Farmer?"

Katrine turned to see a woman about her age with long, wavy blond hair and dark green eyes.

"I'm Ashleigh. Very pleased to meet you," she said as she held out her hand. Katrine halfheartedly shook it. "We'd love for you to join our table after you get your food... if you'd like."

"Thank you," Katrine said quietly. "I appreciate your offer."

As Ashleigh returned to her seat, Katrine's hand started shaking as she spooned strawberries to her plate. She didn't want to sit with anyone. She wanted to be alone; she *needed* to be alone to try to settle her nerves. But instead she was expected to eat and carry on idle conversation with a group of strangers at the same time her mother was possibly being murdered by the queen's guards. She bit her lip and hoped that by meeting some of the other prisoners, she could at least find out if *they* knew how to break out of Cyan.

Katrine finished filling her plate with fruit and a piece of bread, though she knew she couldn't eat any of it, then hesitated before weaving her way through the crowded tables where Ashleigh sat with two other gentlemen. Directly beside Ashleigh sat a young man with reddish hair and faded freckles. Beside him was a slightly older man with very short, black hair and a thin, neatly trimmed mustache. They were in the middle of a conversation when Katrine approached their table.

"So I brought it just to prove it to you. Lucky I had it on when Zor took me," said the redhead to Ashleigh as he stuck his hand out in front of her. On his finger was a large ring with a red stone. The silver band contained several designs, but Katrine wasn't close enough to see them.

"This symbol, right here," he said pointing to it. "Valedictorian." He sat back in his chair with a smug look on his face. "You see, I *am* smart."

"Out of a class of how many?" Ashleigh asked skeptically.

"Thirty, but that's not important."

Ashleigh and the man with the mustache chuckled as Katrine sat down in the fourth chair at the table. Ashleigh turned to Katrine and smiled.

"Katrine, let me introduce you to my friends," said Ashleigh. "This is Robert," she said, placing her hand on the redhead's shoulder. He gave Katrine a nod and smile. "He's an actor from the year 1962, plucked straight out of Canada. And beside him is Jacques. He's from France, 1920. He and I are in the Musician House. He plays the cello and I play the violin. I'm from the United States, 2010."

Katrine's trembling seemed to worsen, but she managed to force a weak smile. The bizarre had just got more bizarre. Katrine looked down at her plate and took a deep breath. Zor had to have tinkered with their minds somehow, making them believe they were from different time periods. She decided that they were not the ones to ask about the possibilities of escape from Cyan.

"I'm just from this time period," she replied, desperately wanting to leave.

"Glad to make your acquaintance, Katrine," answered Robert. "I think you'll find the food here the best you've ever had," he said, nodding at the plates on the table. "Especially the blueberry muffins. You'll have to grab one before you leave."

"So which house are you in?" Ashleigh asked. "Usually Zor places the names and the house of the new arrivals on the job board when he passes by in the carriage. He only has your name."

"I've never seen him leave off the house before," Jacques added.

Katrine's face lost some of its color. "I suppose I'll be staying at the Main House." They all glanced nervously at one another, heightening Katrine's anxiety. "That's bad, isn't it?" she hesitantly added.

"Only because of Zor's girlfriend, Adrian," answered Ashleigh with a nervous grin. "She gets a bit jealous at times...but I'm sure you'll be okay."

"She doesn't have to worry," Katrine replied, shaking her head and stabbing a strawberry with her fork. "I'm not interested."

The Link – Seven Days of Cyan

"Doesn't matter. It's Zor she doesn't trust," explained Jacques. "Witches and warlocks can't read each other's minds, truth rope doesn't work either; so she has no idea whether Zor is being faithful or not. In the past two years, Adrian has pulled three perfectly innocent girls with whom she suspected Zor to be involved out onto the streets past curfew. They were never heard from again, of course." Jacques took a bite of bread. "Zor never even touched these girls. Every girl I have ever known that has been alone with Zor says that he's always acted as a gentleman should. His brother, too." He shook his head. "It's not Zor or James you have to worry about at the Main House, it's Adrian."

Everyone at the table fell silent. Ashleigh's leg began to bounce nervously under the table.

"I don't understand why you're not at one of the houses," Ashleigh finally said.

Katrine stabbed her bread with her fork. "Zor couldn't read my mind. He doesn't know where I belong."

"I don't believe that's ever happened before," said Robert. "Do you know where you belong?"

"Not here," was all Katrine could say. Katrine desperately wanted to change the subject. They were already acting like she was Adrian's fourth victim, and she had more important things to worry about than a jealous girlfriend.

"Come on, guys," Robert said quietly as he leaned back in his chair. "She's just arrived. Let's give her a little time to adjust to her new surroundings before scaring her to death."

Ashleigh's face flushed with guilt. "Sorry, Katrine. I've been here so long that every once in a while I forget how frightening it is when you first arrive. We shouldn't have even brought up Adrian."

"Ashleigh was the *first* citizen, seven years ago," Jacques explained.

Katrine shook her head at Ashleigh. "Don't worry about it. Now if I meet her, I'll know."

Jacques stood up and threw a napkin on his plate. "Well, I hope I'm not being too rude, but I've got to get the outdoor stage ready for the concert." He looked thoughtfully at Katrine. "I may be out of place, but just knowing about Adrian is not going to help you any," he warned. "Adrian is not someone to be shrugged off. She's one of Zor's kind and she's very dangerous, even if she is powerless in this time. Try to get out of the Main House as fast as you can."

"Jacques, that's enough," Robert said.

After Jacques left the cafeteria, Robert sighed. "Sorry about that. Jacques sometimes doesn't know when to let things rest."

Katrine stared down at her plate and found herself still unable to eat. "What did he mean when he said that she's powerless in this time?"

"Warlocks and witches have different power strengths depending on the time period," Robert explained. "Adrian doesn't live in Cyan because she's the equivalent of a human here, and it's probably not safe for her since she can get snuffed out by other warlocks who happen by and don't appreciate her *pleasant* personality. The woman does have her enemies. Zor, on the other hand, set up Cyan in this time because he's very powerful here."

"And probably wants to get away from Adrian for some peace and quiet," added Ashleigh with a smirk. "She can only visit for about an hour, then has to leave for the day."

"Why?"

"We're pretty sure it has something to do with the time labyrinth. You didn't get to go through it, did you?" Robert realized.

Katrine shoved the strawberry around her plate with her fork. "No, but Zor told me a little about it."

"Well, Zor was nearly powerless when he collected me," Robert explained. "He had enough power for his little memory game, though. He approached me, pretended to be an old acquaintance, patted me on my shoulder with a cheerful greeting... and then I just about lost my senses as I witnessed my entire life and more flash before my eyes. After that, we battled it out for almost a good hour as he tried to drag me to his labyrinth door. I can't even begin to explain what a shock it is when you think you're being slammed against the wall of a barn, but you never make contact. Instead, you find yourself falling onto a grassy pathway amidst tall, green hedges, and through a small open archway in front of you, you can see your home." Robert paused with a thoughtful look in his eyes. "Haven't seen home since." Robert sighed, and then took a drink. "Anyway, my point... Zor seemed very worried about getting me through the door before the hour was up. It probably closes automatically if you're a weak or powerless warlock, such is Adrian's case here.

"We've had other warlock visitors from time to time. More powerful, and they ended up staying the entire day. So we're guessing that it's just a magical strength issue with the time labyrinths."

Ashleigh placed her napkin and utensils on her plate, stacked it on top of Jacques', and stood up to leave. "Well, I think I'll go help Jacques set up," she said. "Zor has us play Tchaikovsky's 1812 overture every third week at the outdoor arena in addition to the regularly scheduled concerts. It's one of his favorites. You should come and see the performance, Katrine. You won't be disappointed."

The Link – Seven Days of Cyan

After Ashleigh left, Robert took a drink as Katrine stared at the table. He picked up a napkin and offered it to her.

"Your neck's bleeding a little. Seems I'm not the only one that put up a good fight."

Katrine took the napkin from his hand and placed it against her cut. "I wouldn't call it a good fight," she said, embarrassed.

"Well, I hope you realize there wasn't much you could do to stop him from taking you. Not in this time period, anyway." He threw his utensils on his empty plate. "Since the last thing I wanted to do when I first arrived in Cyan was talk to strangers, my guess is you feel much the same way." Robert smirked, "When I got here, I thought everyone had lost their minds when they claimed they weren't from 1962. Didn't truly believe Zor was a warlock, either. After I recovered from the labyrinth – it makes you a bit disoriented going through – I decked Zor as hard as I could in the nose, which turned out to be about the stupidest thing I've ever done. Turned me into a true believer of warlocks after that... But that's a different story." He leaned over and showed her his ring. "I even have a little of Zor's blood on my ring that I haven't yet washed off, to remind me of that day. Four-year-old blood, that is."

Katrine looked at the ring, but found the 'Class of 1961' inscription more interesting than the small speck of blood stuck in one of the symbols.

"Don't believe I'll ever be hitting a warlock again," he said as he shifted his chair back. "Anyway, I do hope to see you at the concert, Katrine. Music is good therapy for the soul."

Once Katrine was alone, she moved her plate to the middle of the table and lay down her head. She didn't want to believe they were from the future, but Robert was very convincing.

After breakfast, Katrine warily walked to the courtyard. Flowers from the cherry trees covered the brick pathways. To the sides of the pathways were dense patches of brightly colored flowers, just as in the rest of the village. One central red brick path branched into three separate paths, each leading to large, cherry wooden doors belonging to the clean, white, adobe house that encircled half the courtyard.

Katrine sat down on a bench and marveled at the garden's beauty. It reminded her of the Garden of Eden. The garden was so beautiful, you thought you were in heaven; yet you knew the devil was lurking somewhere behind a tree or a bush, ready to tempt you. She gazed up at the trees. No apples, not even cherries. Only cherry blossoms that seemed to fall in a very timely manner, each taking a turn, one after another. It didn't matter that there was no fruit; fruit was not the object of temptation. The temptation was to stay and forget about all the treachery and pain on the other side of the log wall. If it weren't for her mother, she would have considered giving in to the temptation.

"Come on inside. I'll show you your room," said James. Katrine broke her gaze from the trees and looked beside the bench to see James. No longer was James dressed in his black bandit attire. His hair was cut very short on the sides, leaving slightly longer wavy strands on top, and he was dressed very casual in a dark green, cotton shirt and khaki shorts. She had never seen clothes like these in her lifetime, but just like the soccer fields and the houses, they didn't seem that strange.

She stood up and silently followed James through the central wooden door. They entered a large room with brick walls, wooden floors and a wall of windows overlooking no-man's land. A few tall pine trees were placed outside the window to achieve a more scenic view than the vast expanse of mud that lay beyond. To her right was a sitting room consisting of two large brown leather couches surrounding a round, glossy, cherry wooden table; to the left was a dining room consisting of a sturdy, dark, wooden, dining room table with seating for ten. The only barrier separating the dining and sitting rooms was a large, rectangular, brick fireplace with two openings, one leading into the dining room and one leading into the sitting room.

"My room and one other are down that hallway," James said pointing to a hallway on Katrine's right that led from the sitting room to one of the large doors opening into the courtyard. "There's no reason for you to ever go down there. Your room is beside Zor's," he said as he began to walk down the hallway to her left. Katrine followed and looked out the large windows facing the courtyard as James attempted to find the right key for her room from a key chain with ten other keys. Zor's room lay opposite the other large side door leading into the courtyard.

"I don't understand why Zor likes these primitive keys," James muttered to himself as he tried a second key.

"So where is he?"

"Not that it's any of your business, but he's punishing a guard for entering a house last night without permission. We don't need the people terrorized when they're not doing anything wrong. It interferes with progress."

"Progress, huh?" Katrine said resentfully.

"I suggest you keep your sarcasm to yourself until you find out a little more about this village. Zor has done everyone here a great service. They were all victims at one time: victims of mediocrity,

The Link – Seven Days of Cyan

victims of apathy, and victims of psychological abuse." James slid a key into the door's keyhole, unlocked the door, and then opened it to a dark room. "Now they are treated to a lifestyle better than kings. It is a somewhat addicting lifestyle you might find. Given a couple of weeks, you'll realize even *you* won't want to leave it."

James flipped up a small lever to the side of the door and a light came on. Katrine stood baffled outside the door and stared at the light, wondering how James, a mortal like herself, was able to create it without lighting a fire. When she finally managed to pull her gaze from the light, she walked in the room. It was a plain and simple room: no windows, smooth white walls with a few scenic paintings, a small bed with a dark blue blanket, a tall wooden armoire with intricate carvings on the doors, and a small, round wooden table with a matching wooden chair. James walked over to a door on the far side of the room and opened it.

"This is your bathroom. Turn the knobs and water will run out. Red is for hot and blue is for cold. There's also a lever on the toilet; push it down when you're done. Towels, washrags, soap, and other items you might need are in the cabinets. Beside you and right here," he said as he touched right inside the bathroom door, "is a switch that will give you light." He flipped it up and down to show the light turn on and off. "They're powered by the sun, but they still work at night." He pressed a button on the outside of the bathroom door and a low humming sound could be heard. Above the bed, a portion of the ceiling above her bed slid to the side, revealing a window. "You may keep this open so it's not so dark in the morning."

Katrine felt weak and wanted to sit down. Her belief that warlocks didn't exist had to be compromised the day before. Holding sunlight captive to use at night... hidden windows in the ceiling that open with a push of a button... These were not possible, in 1693 anyway. It was too much for her to handle in so short a time.

"If you're going to the concert, I'd wash up and put on some fresh clothes." James looked at Katrine's dress, torn a little from the fin and quite dirty from falling in the mud. "Throw that one away." He opened the armoire. "While you were eating, Zor went to the liberty of supplying you with a new wardrobe. You have casual wear, formal wear, and soccer workout clothes." He picked up a strange pair of black and white shoes with sharp spikes on the bottom. "These are soccer cleats. You'll find them useful when you start playing soccer," he said holding them up to her. "You also have running shoes, high heals, and flats." He closed the armoire door. "The concert starts in about twenty minutes. I suggest going. Staying in your room is only going to turn you into a mental midget, if you aren't one already. After lunch, there's a soccer game you should attend, to start familiarizing yourself with the game." James walked beside Katrine and began to walk through the doorway when he suddenly stopped and turned around.

"So I'm curious, Katrine," he inquired. "Everyone here has been a victim of some type of abuse before Zor collected them and brought them here, but I'm guessing your not here because of your relationship with this queen you keep mentioning. From whom did Zor really save you?"

The question caught Katrine off guard. An image of her father flashed through her mind. She opened her mouth and tried to explain that Zor hadn't saved her from anyone; that he had instead interfered and messed up her life, but the words never surfaced.

James turned and began closing the door. "My brother's instincts are so sharp, he didn't even have to read your mind to know you needed his help," he replied without waiting for a response.

Katrine shook her head in disbelief as the door closed, and then she slowly reached over to the light switch and flipped it down. The room went dark. She flipped it on again and stared at the light until her eyes seemed to burn, then walked over to the bed, sat down, and buried her face in her hands until she felt she was going to break down.

"Pull yourself together, Katrine," she whispered to herself. "Mother needs you to stay strong." She took a deep breath and looked up. "You need to stay strong and keep your wits about you if you're ever going to get out of here," she said before she stood up and walked to the bathroom to clean up.

* * *

The musicians tuned their instruments as the audience gathered and found their grassy seats. Katrine looked anxiously around to see if anyone was staring at her. She had never felt so naked in public before. The dress she chose to wear was the most modest dress she could find in her wardrobe closet, but it still showed almost all her shoulders, and the skirt decorated with pink, purple, and blue scarves completely revealed her ankles and lower legs. After realizing that most of the other ladies were wearing less than she was, she began to relax and search for Robert. She spotted him in the center of the audience, waving his hand at her to get her attention.

As Katrine fumbled past several people who had already taken their seats, she spotted Zor and James behind the last row staring at her. Zor no longer had his hair slicked back with oil, which seemed to change his appearance quite dramatically. Like his brother, his hair was short on the sides and spiked on top with some hair falling just

The Link – Seven Days of Cyan

enough to hide part of his forehead. She quickly turned in Robert's direction, pretending not to see them.

"You look great," Robert said as she sat down beside him. "You're certainly making a few heads turn."

Katrine looked apprehensively at him. "Am I underdressed?"

"No, it's not that at all," he said smiling. "You just look nice."

Katrine blushed, and then quickly lowered her head to try to hide her face. She adjusted her dress once she sat down on the grass and the audience applauded the conductor's entrance onto the stage. It was then that Katrine noticed dark clouds above shift so that the audience was shaded, but the stage was still in bright sunlight. The audience fell silent and the conductor raised his wand.

It was not the first concert Katrine had ever attended, but it certainly had the largest string orchestra and played the most exciting music she had ever heard. Church bells... canons... When it was all over, she sat speechless. Robert had to nudge her to get her attention.

"Good, aren't they?" he asked.

"Yes, very."

She looked up. The dark clouds were now light and fluffy.

"These outdoor concerts always remind me of when my parents used to bring me and my little brother to free concerts they would hold in a field outside our town. We'd usually arrive about an hour before the concert started with our blankets and a half-gallon of ice cream. The challenge was to see if we could polish off all the ice cream before it melted and before too many bugs stuck to it. We always managed to down it all, mostly because my dad could eat half of it without any help. As for the bugs that got stuck in the ice cream... a good bug every now and then never hurt anyone!"

Katrine smiled politely, then watched in silence as the audience began to filter out of their seats, and the orchestra went inside the auditorium to put their instruments away.

Before thinking, she asked, "James told me everyone here has been saved by Zor. Did he save you, too, Robert?"

Robert gave a nervous laugh. "Saved, huh? I suppose he saved me from poverty. After my father passed away, my mom was too poor to provide my way to acting school. Hell, she was too poor to buy a bus ticket to any city that had a stage. Day and night, it was a constant struggle to keep the farm from going bankrupt." He looked thoughtful and a bit sad. "Mother needed my help."

Katrine immediately felt guilty for asking. "Sorry."

"We all have our stories here," Robert said as he stood up and brushed the grass off his pants. "They'll be starting practice at the soccer fields in just a bit, if you'd like to watch; and later on there's a game you might enjoy seeing."

"Sure," Katrine agreed, hoping to find out why she had such strange feelings when she first passed by the soccer fields. As they strolled over to the bleachers, Katrine could make out the top of the outer log wall in the distance.

She bit her lip, and then quietly asked, "Robert, if you thought you could escape from Cyan, would you?"

Robert looked at her with apprehension. "Why are you asking? You aren't thinking about doing something foolish, are you? Katrine, there's no way past the guards and over the wall."

Katrine shrugged her shoulders. "If there was a way, I'd have to try. All I need is one minute with my mother, then I wouldn't care what Zor did to me."

"Look, I understand how you feel. If I had just one minute with my mom and little brother to tell them I'm all right, I know we would all sleep better at night. After that, captivity in Cyan wouldn't be that bad. After all, I love the people here, and I love what I do here." Robert stopped, put his hand on her shoulder, and turned her to face him. "Don't do something that would make Zor angry, Katrine. I've seen him angry before and it's..."

"Don't worry about me busting out of my gilded cage, Robert," she said as she turned away and continued towards the field. "Don't know how, so don't worry. I was just hoping you knew how, that's all."

"No, I don't," he replied as they approached the bleachers and sat down.

Katrine looked out at the field where a group of players were lined up in front of some posts, attempting to kick the ball into a net. She was fairly certain it was called a goal, though she had never heard the term used before in this specific sport. Rarely did the ball go in the net, though. Most of the time it went flying way over the posts.

"Unfortunately, you're here to see the worst team practice – the interior designers. They try to overcompensate for their lack of testosterone by kicking the ball as hard as possible. Drives their coach crazy during games because they're either ball hogs or they just kick the ball to the far end of the field without any specific target in mind. They don't pass to one another and use teamwork. They go through the most coaches, because the soccer professionals just can't stand the job for that long."

Katrine had no idea what testosterone was, but decided to nod her head in interest instead of asking. She stared out onto the field in somewhat of a daze. Everything seemed so surreal, even talking to

Robert. He was like no other individual she had ever met before, but he wasn't exactly from the year 1693... he was kidnapped, just like her, brought to her time against his will by a warlock.

"I never believed in warlocks," she whispered, feeling quite näive.

"Good for you!" Robert said enthusiastically. "There aren't any in your time. Salem witch hunts and all that crap... embarrassing that the human race can go into such a mass hysteria and harm so many innocent individuals."

Katrine turned toward him, confused. "What are you talking about?"

"Zor's a pseudo-warlock, not a true warlock. The first and only true warlock was born a little over three thousand years after I was born. Woester, he's the resident beer brewer, told me the story one night when he brought a keg over to the Thespian's House for a party. He knows everything about everything and talking to him is always illuminating, if you don't mind his..." Robert looked thoughtful, "unusual communication skills."

Katrine didn't care about Woester; it was Zor's story she wanted to hear. "So why is Zor not a true warlock?"

"A true warlock is born with powers. Zor's powers were a gift. Let me see if I remember the entire story. I had a lot to drink that night because we had just won our first soccer game against the musicians. Watch out!" he yelled as he reached out his hand and blocked a ball that was about to hit Katrine. He shook his head in disgust.

"Sorry!" yelled a man with a very feminine voice from across the field.

"Well, you see," Robert explained, "the brain is a very powerful organ, but some of it sits dormant. As humans evolved, we started to use more and more. One day in the year 5100, when most humans used about ninety percent of their brain, an individual named Imperius Grumley was born. He was a genetic mutation." He looked at Katrine realizing she wouldn't know anything about genetics. "He was different... able to use all of his brain. He was capable of moving things by just looking at them, he was able to read people's thoughts and see their memories, able to relocate matter... the first and only true warlock.

"There's several sections in the brain that are capable of emitting brain waves so powerful, they can literally move matter – kind of analogous to how sound waves can move your eardrums. You and I just haven't tapped into these sections yet. Even had the ability to make objects disappear and reappear somewhere else by breaking the objects apart into their individual molecules, then reassembling them somewhere else. He tried to explain the specifics several times to fellow brain researchers, but ended up using so many mathematical symbols and complicated physical formulas that he lost his audience. He eventually gave up trying to explain it to his mental inferiors and resorted to 'Just trust me. It is possible.'

"Imperius married and had two daughters. Found out soon after the death of his wife that he was capable of transferring his powers to other individuals. He would change water into some sort of energy liquid that would stimulate novel neurotransmitters to release between highly specialized nerve cells in the brain. We don't even realize these specialized nerve cells *exist* until about 3350. Once a person drank the energy liquid, the dormant sections of the brain were awakened as the specialized nerve cells started firing, and presto... the person was now a warlock, almost as powerful as Imperius himself.

"The only symptom that Imperius suffered after making the energy liquid was an unexplainable temporary weakening of his power, along with a drain of physical strength, and it took a couple of days for him to regenerate and become full strength again.

"Imperius was generous, empowering most of his family and friends, on a mission to leave his legacy behind. It was soon discovered that the individuals Imperius empowered could also make this strange energy liquid, but were unable to replicate it more than once. Nevertheless, whoever became a witch or warlock was now out of Imperius' control.

"Grumley's older sister, Elise, had a son named Zachariah. He was a very spoiled boy with a mean streak. Before Imperius empowered his sister, he made her promise not to pass on her powers to Zachariah, worried that there would be dire consequences if she did. This, of course, infuriated Zachariah. Zachariah hooked up with one of his friends, Damen Rattimor, another misfit of society from a very dysfunctional family, and convinced Damen to befriend Rebecca, Imperius' oldest daughter. Very pretty redhead. The plan was to persuade Rebecca to empower Damen so that Damen could turn around and empower Zachariah.

"After Damen poured on the charm, Rebecca did befriend Damen. My guess is that it was just out of sympathy. He had a very abusive father who was extremely hard to please... thought his son was weak and cowardly... always insulted and hit him. One day Rebecca gave Damen the energy liquid for protection against his father. Instead of being grateful, Damen turned around and killed Rebecca the day after he drank the energy liquid and then went home to brag to his father about his success. Finally made his father proud, I'm sure.

"Before he even had the opportunity to pass on the energy liquid to Zachariah, Elise broke down and empowered her son." Robert shook his head. "She always gave Zachariah what he wanted in the end. That's why he ended up so spoiled.

"Still weak from creating the energy liquid, Elise tragically died in a fire that very evening. It was no secret that Zachariah was a pyromaniac. He had some ridiculous nickname among his friends, 'fire-hurdler' or 'fire-thrower', something like that. Unfortunately, there was never any solid evidence to prove it was Zach who killed his mother, so he got off." Robert scratched his head. "Who would believe a son would turn on his mother like that?

"Coincidentally, fires began erupting everywhere, killing many of Imperius' friends and family who weren't yet warlocks. (It's near impossible to kill a full strength warlock, so he avoided them during his rampages.) Imperius started to get a bit nervous and tried to empower as many family members and friends as possible before his wild nephew could set them ablaze. Then one tragic day, after Imperius empowered one of his cousins, Zachariah and Damen Rattimor teamed up and killed Imperius Grumley."

Robert nodded his head and had a far away look in his eyes. "I believe Imperius was expecting the attack, because he was prepared for his death." He looked at Katrine. "He had almost given away all his time labyrinths to people he could trust, about seventy total, before Damen and Zachariah stole the rest. They got away with about thirty labyrinths before disappearing into the time line."

Katrine's face conveyed confusion. "Thirty time labyrinths? How do you give away or steal a time labyrinth? I thought they were huge."

"A labyrinth is actually very small. It looks identical to a gold jewelry or music box from the outside, and when you open it up, you can see a tiny green maze, full of tiny wooden doors. Imperius had so many because he was the creator of the time labyrinth; he was the only one who had the smarts *and* the power to make them. It takes a warlock or a witch to get in, because you have to shrink down and transport to the entrance of the maze. Once you are standing in front of the maze, the top of the labyrinth will close... and voila, you become full size again. When you exit a door into a different time, you're not small; you're just the right size. Kind of boggles the imagination."

Robert reached over and blocked another ball. "Each labyrinth even has its own personality: some labyrinths are temperamental, some are easy going, and some are eccentric. You see, Imperius had the ability to communicate with disembodied spirits. Asked them to inhabit the labyrinths to keep the hedges and grass in good condition, kind of like a grounds keeper, and they were asked to give any unauthorized intruders a hard time."

Katrine shook her head, trying her best to comprehend everything Robert was explaining. "So how did Zor get his labyrinth?"

"No one thought Damen Rattimor would ever choose to empower someone else. He seemed to hate everyone, except Zachariah. But many years later, he had a daughter that completely stole his heart, named Adrian." Lifting his eyebrows, he said, "You heard about her over breakfast. Rattimor empowered her and gave her his most valuable labyrinth – the one he stole from Rebecca after he killed her. When Adrian fell in love with Zor, she empowered him before her father even knew she was having a love affair. She *had* to tell her father after turning Zor into a warlock because she was in a weakened state and needed protection from any of Grumley's pseudo-warlocks who might happen by. Zor wasn't able to protect her because it takes a day or two to fully establish the new neural connections.

"All hell broke loose, excuse the expression, when Rattimor found out what she had done. After she recovered and was at maximum power, she was still quite peeved at her father's reaction – I guess she felt like he was treating her like a child – so she stole a labyrinth from her father and gave it to Zor. Needless to say, Rattimor practically disowned Adrian when he discovered who had his missing labyrinth. Threw her out of the house and refused to speak to her." Robert caught a third soccer ball flying at him and threw it back to one of the players skipping across the field. "Can't tell you much more than that. Woester was either too drunk or he didn't know any more." He looked out on the field. "It amazes me how a team can be this bad."

Katrine shook her head. "My luck. Seventy to a hundred warlocks bouncing through all of time, and I have the privilege of being kidnapped by one."

"Yes, the probability of encountering a pseudo-warlock is quite rare, I have to admit," Robert said as he dodged another ball. "About the same probability as the interior designers winning a game."

Katrine looked out at the field and watched them practice passing. "Something is very familiar about this game. It's strange."

"I'll tell you what I can about the game if you like. Maybe you'll figure out why it's familiar to you."

"I'd appreciate that."

Robert proceeded to tell her the object of the game, the rules, strategies – everything he could think of before lunchtime was upon them. Katrine didn't understand why she already knew most of what Robert told her, and she probably could have told Robert that he didn't need to continue his lesson, but he had a very pleasant demeanor and for the first time in a long while, she felt completely comfortable sitting with a man and talking. When they finally got up to meet Ashleigh and Jacques at the Musician House for lunch, the stress of being trapped and unable to warn her mother quickly returned.

They arrived at the front of the Musician's House to find that Ashleigh and Jacques were already on their way out the door, apparently in the middle of an argument by the look on their faces.

"I still believe he should be transferred to the Gardener's House," Jacques said with a snarl as he closed the front door behind him.

"He's just angry that Josh fired the first canon too late," Ashleigh explained to Katrine. "Interrupted his timing a bit."

"Don't pretend it didn't throw you off," retorted Jacques.

"I'm not listening to the canons, Jacques. I'm watching the conductor. We're finished talking about it, okay?"

Jacques and Ashleigh continued to snap at each other throughout lunch about the performance. When they weren't paying attention, Robert leaned over and whispered in Katrine's ear, "They argue like this after every concert."

* * *

The queen's guards had probably reached Dragon Hill by now. Katrine closed the *2014 Rules and Regulations* book to the game of soccer and laid it on the bench beside her food tray. She appeared calm and collect from the outside as she watched the cherry flowers fall from the courtyard trees, but she felt like screaming on the inside. She had been anxious the entire day; she even tried kicking the soccer ball on the sidelines before the soccer game to try to take her mind off things, but to no avail.

It was during dinner that she decided to eat alone in the courtyard. James and Zor were in the cafeteria eating at a small table in the corner, and it was difficult to restrain herself from throwing the cafeteria's large blue vase at their table. Eating alone had its drawbacks, however. Too much time to think. Her body ached and her mind was exhausted. Katrine stood up and made her way inside the Main House to her bedroom. Once she closed the door behind her, she searched for a lock, but there was none. She threw herself down on the bed and closed her eyes.

Chapter 5
Escape (Sunday night)

The sound of the courtyard door closing in front of Zor's room several hours later woke Katrine. She opened her eyes and lay still on the bed as she listened to footsteps approach her bedroom door, then pause. She could feel her face go white when he knocked on her door a couple of times before opening it. Zor flipped on the light and stared at her, then his eyes drifted above and beside her.

"Get up," he ordered as he walked into her room. Katrine timidly lifted herself from the bed and stood up. He took her arm and gently backed her against the wall. Laying his hand on her left shoulder, he lifted her chin up with the other hand so that they were eye to eye. Katrine realized he was trying to probe her mind, or whatever it was he did, and started to squirm. He pushed her harder against the wall and gave her a look of warning.

"Stay still and make eye contact."

Katrine swallowed nervously and didn't move. She looked him in the eyes, but again felt nothing. Finally, Zor lowered his arm, and then turned to walk out of the room.

"Curfew started about a half hour ago. I'll be locking your door at night until I can trust you won't try to run. It's for your own safety," he said without looking at her.

He closed the door and Katrine could hear him lock it from the other side. She stood there in silence, contemplating what had just happened. He still hadn't been able to read her mind, and she soon realized a possible explanation: the strange feeling that there was someone else with her, watching her, had returned. Her heart began to pound as she realized her magical powers may have returned as well.

Katrine looked at the bathroom door. "Shut," she whispered. It closed all by itself. She took a deep breath, determined to attempt her escape before her powers had a chance to abandon her again.

Katrine quickly placed her ear to the bedroom door and strained to listen as Zor and James talked in the hallway.

"Still no reading?" asked James.

"No."

"And she's really not a witch?"

"The aura around her is different than a witch. It must have been so weak during the collection that I didn't even notice it, even when I was looking for it. But now it's grown stronger." There was a pause. "She's not a witch, James."

"Are you suggesting what I think you're suggesting?" James asked in a hopeful voice.

"Yes. But I want to run a few questions by Adrian first. Her father has had considerable experience with this."

"Adrian is not going to be real happy about her staying in the Main House."

"She'll be reasonable once I explain things. Don't worry," Zor replied. "I'll be back in the morning sometime. Goodnight."

"Goodnight... and good luck."

Katrine listened as James and Zor walked back to their rooms and shut their doors. She waited for several minutes, listening through the door, before she decided it was safe to make her exit.

She closed her eyes and once more wished she was at Dragon Hill, hoping that her magic would work better than when she tried to transport off the ship. Now she had some kind of aura, according to Zor. She opened her eyes to find herself still in her room.

"I guess we're doing it the hard way," Katrine whispered as she ran over to her armoire and quickly changed into the soccer clothes Zor had left for her. She sat down on the bed and slid on her cleats, figuring that the spikes on the bottom would help her get across the mud in no-man's land a little faster.

"Okay," she said as she finished tying her shoes, "a little backup protection." She peered down to her lap and wished for a sword she had left behind at the castle. To her relief, it appeared across her lap.

For the first time, Katrine was grateful she was forced to mimic the real Princess Anna, someone who had a secret passion for fencing. Her sword was not as decorative as Zor's, but it had some sentimental value. It was a simple silver blade with a gold-plated hilt wrapped in leather. Paul had given it to her after she had won her first dual with him, though she was convinced he had let her win. Katrine raised her left hand and made another wish. On her hand appeared a long, white glove covered with thick chain mail.

She stood up and hung her sword and glove on a belt that she quickly wished to appear around her waist. Walking as quietly as the cleats would allow her, she made her way to the back bedroom wall and laid her hands on it. Her body felt an adrenaline rush as a large hole appeared, and she quickly climbed through into no-man's land.

The mud seemed to grab hold of Katrine's shoes as she turned to the hole in the wall and replaced the missing section. Now, should anyone enter her room, she figured they would look for her on the grounds of Cyan before no-man's land. Dim light from the dining and sitting rooms illuminated the pine trees that hugged the building, then gradually disappeared as it traveled across the mud, leaving the outer log wall completely masked in the dark. As she stepped forward to begin her journey, she noticed a lantern in the distance, swaying from side to side as the guard holding it walked in her direction. Quickly, she peeked through the large window of the Main House to make sure the rooms were vacant, then hid from the guard behind one of the pine trees.

The guard's slow pace began to frustrate Katrine as her legs stiffened from squatting below the low branches of the pine tree. Frequently glancing through the windows, she decided she had to speed up her escape before Zor or James happened to pass by. She stared at the guard and tried to make him disappear, then tried to influence him to walk faster. Everything she wished for had no effect on the slow, steady pace of the guard. Finally she made a wish that he would fall asleep... standing up if possible, rigid. That way his lantern would stay lit and any other guard that should appear wouldn't suspect anything. She watched as the guard's silhouette stopped in his path and drooped his head to the side.

"Something actually worked," she grumbled. She waited a minute to make sure he was truly asleep, then started walking across the mud to the outer wall. With every step, her shoes grew heavier, nearly slipping off her feet as the ground suctioned around them. She was less than a quarter of the way to the wall and she could already feel her legs start to fatigue.

"This is ridiculous," Katrine whispered in disgust. She bit her lip, and then raised her arms to her side. "Fly." She remained firmly planted to the mud. With a sigh, she grabbed her sword and peeled the mud from her shoes.

"Well, then. How about a nice dry pathway?" She could see the shiny mud before her darken as it dried into a smooth, flat walkway leading into the dark. "Now why didn't I think of that sooner?" She put her sword back in her belt and began to run as fast and as quiet as she could towards the outer wall.

Almost to the wall...

Rrring...

Katrine looked in the guard's direction to see where the ringing had come from.

Rrring...

It was just in her head.

Hello?

She looked around to see who spoke. It was a young woman's voice, but Katrine was alone. *Really* alone. Her heart beat wildly as she realized the presence had disappeared. She reached the wall at the end of no-man's land and laid her hands on it.

"Don't fail me now," she pleaded. She wished for a hole, just as she had in her bedroom, but nothing happened. "A hole, please, a hole. That's all I ask," she urgently whispered. Still nothing. Katrine stared bewildered at the intact logs before her, pounded them in frustration with her fists, then sat down with her back against the wall and closed her eyes.

"This can't be happening," she whispered. She opened her eyes and looked across the mud at the windows of the Main House. She had sealed up the hole she had made in her bedroom, leaving the front doors to the Main House her only way back to safety. She stared at the tallest tree in front of the windows, hoping it was close enough to the building for her to jump onto the roof.

Katrine noticed the guard's lantern begin to sway. He had woken and was looking behind him to see if any other guards noticed him sleeping. He then continued to walk straight towards the dry pathway Katrine had made. Katrine took a long, deep, quiet sigh, and decided she would be seen if she passed in front of the guard. She had to go behind him before he ran into her dry dirt pathway.

Pushing herself up very slowly, she left the dry dirt for the mud that ran alongside the outer wall. With every step, the mud squashed to the sides of her shoes. As the guard came closer, she tried walking slower to deaden the sound, but it just made the sound last longer. Finally, she stopped and stooped down to make her image smaller. The guard walked slowly along the concrete pathway until he passed her, then stopped a short distance later when he reached the dry dirt Katrine had made. Katrine didn't move; all she could hear was her breathing. If the guard looked behind him against the wall, she was sure he would be able to spot her in the dim light given off by his lantern.

Confusion spread across Katrine's face as the guard suddenly extinguished his lantern, leaving them both in the dark. Only the faint light radiating from the Main House could be seen in the distance. The guard had already passed between her and the windows, so not even his silhouette was apparent. She listened closely, but there was only silence. She waited a few minutes before she slowly stood up to restore circulation into her legs. A few more minutes passed, but still the only sound she could hear was her own breathing. The guard was still there, somewhere, waiting for her to move.

They stood in a standoff for what seemed an eternity until Katrine noticed the next guard's lantern appear in the distance. If she waited any longer, she would have to contend two guards.

She took a step. The mud sloshed loudly as her foot broke free and came down again. She paused nervously, but the guard made no sound. She took another step. He still did nothing. She continued slowly towards Cyan, step by step, until she neared the concrete pathway. Her sweaty palms grabbed the glove and the sword from her belt. She quickly pulled the glove onto her left hand and squeezed the hilt of her sword. The guard would be able to attack her quickly once she hit the concrete path, but she had still not heard any movement from his direction.

Katrine reached the concrete and stood ready, then slowly walked backwards on the concrete to increase the distance between herself and the guard... then she heard him move. The pounding of her heart at that moment blocked out all other sounds as she took to the mud and ran as fast as she could towards Cyan, repeatedly stumbling along the way and barely able to keep her shoes on her feet. Her run felt no faster than a fast walk on dry earth and she soon fatigued and stopped to try to catch her breath. She held her breath so that she could listen for the guard, but the pounding of her heart in her ears was still too loud. Exhausted, she began to walk.

As Katrine neared the trees, she could hear the guard's footsteps in the mud between her bedroom wall and the beginning of the dry dirt pathway she had made. She looked across the muddy field and could finally make out a silhouette of a very large man about the same distance from the Main House wearing long, strange eyeglasses that projected outward from his eyes. She quickly wiped the sweat off her hand and sword handle with her shirt in order to get a better grip. She was tired. The guard was huge. No one had ever survived a curfew violation, she remembered Zor say.

Katrine finally made it to the trees outside the windows of the Main House. Her plan to avoid the guard altogether before climbing the tree and jumping onto the roof had to be abandoned when he stepped in front of the tree and gave Katrine a wide, nearly toothless grin. He was a large, robust man with a short, black beard and a single eyebrow extending over both his eyes. The few teeth he had were checkered gold. The strange glasses he had worn were now hanging at his side, swinging with each movement he made into a small gun with a very wide muzzle attached to his hip. Despite having the gun, he seemed to savor the moment as he slowly drew a sword from a sheath attached to his back.

"Appears somebody escaped from their cage. You're the new girl, aren't you?" he said with a gleam in his eyes.

Katrine, exhausted from fighting the mud, kept her distance as she scraped the heavy mud off the bottom of her shoes with a dead pine tree branch she had found on the ground. She said nothing to the guard as she tried to recall everything Paul had taught her, but the only lesson she could call to mind was the lesson on 'avoidance'. The guard before her was twice the size of Paul, and she knew she wasn't going to win if they got into a fight.

"I was watching you the entire way. Night vision goggles," he said with a smile as he lifted the strange eyeglasses at his side. "I know how exhausted you must be, so just tell me when you're ready. It's not often that a curfew violator has a weapon. It makes things much more interesting than just shooting you." He coughed up a chunk of mucus and spit it off to his side. "Just tell me when you're ready, Missy."

Katrine moved sideways while still facing the guard in order to get a little closer to the tree she wished to climb. She held her sword up, but already her palm was so sweaty she had a hard time getting a good grip. She looked at the guard's face as he smiled at her. He was probably very stupid, she hoped. Sound sincere.

"Where I come from..." Her voice was too shaky, so she tried to steady it better. "....before a dual we touch our swords together for a moment as a promise of fair play." She would have considered rolling her eyes had she not been about to die. The guard took a step nearer. "I'll consider it a promise that you won't use that gun at your side when you find yourself losing."

"Seems a reasonable last request," he said with a laugh.

Katrine swallowed the lump in her throat as he extended his sword to touch Katrine's. She quickly lunged after his sword and grabbed it with her gloved hand. Trying not to look the guard in the face, she stabbed him in his abdomen as hard as she could, then let go of both swords. Flinging herself through the branches of the tree to the trunk, she quickly threw off the glove and started climbing through the dense tangle of branches while the guard keeled over below and began yelling words that Katrine had never heard before.

Her clothing became snagged with every step up she took; and she felt her arms, legs, and face scrape against the jagged branches as she squeezed between them. Glancing below, she could see that the guard had already removed her sword and was approaching the tree. The tree began to shake as the guard started climbing below.

Katrine was almost to the top of the tree when she felt the guard's hand clasp around her foot and pull her downward. She let out a small cry as she grasped the branches nearest her and began to dangle from the tree. With her free foot, she stomped on his hand as hard as she could while he pulled her downward. The muscles in her arms felt as though they were ripping.

Wearing her soccer cleats finally paid off and Katrine was glad she had taken the time to get most of the mud off. She scraped and stabbed his hand until she finally felt his grip fail, then quickly twisted her foot free and scurried farther up. Once she was above the level of the roof, she pushed off from the thin tree trunk and fell on the roof's pebbly surface, tearing the skin from her lower arms and setting her legs on fire.

Katrine quickly got to her feet and ran to the other side of the Main House. As she bent down to grab hold of the vines that crept down the front side, she felt a bite on her left arm. She yelled out in pain and grasped her new wound, then looked back in shock to see the guard in the tree with his gun aimed at her. He had shot her, but she had not heard the gunshot.

Before the guard could shoot again, Katrine jumped over the ledge and grabbed the vines to help break her fall. Her ankles and knees jarred painfully as she landed, then she stumbled as fast as she could to the main entrance of the house. The door opened; something finally had gone right.

A tremendous relief swept over Katrine as she struggled through the door and closed it behind her. She limped to her bedroom and tried to open the door, but it was locked, so she slumped down and sat on the floor, too exhausted and in too much pain to move. After taking a deep breath, she looked up in front of her at the window overlooking the courtyard. All at once, her heart leapt into her throat. The guard stood outside the window, staring in at her. She stared back in terror, wondering if he would enter the house. Finally, he smiled at her, smeared his bloody hand across the windowpane, turned around and left.

Katrine placed her right hand over her gunshot wound and held it tight to try to stop the bleeding. The bullet had luckily just grazed her. She closed her eyes and leaned her head against the wall behind her, trying to catch her breath, hardly aware that James had come out of his room and was now standing over her. When she realized his presence, she looked up at him to see him staring with an expressionless face at the blood on the window.

Without a word, James unlocked her bedroom door and stood waiting for Katrine to enter. Katrine slowly lifted herself up using the wall for what help it could give, and then limped into her room. She sat on the bed and watched as James walked around her room, looking for anything unusual. She expected him to ask questions, but there was only an uncomfortable silence.

Finally, James walked to the bedroom door and placed the key in the door, ready to lock her in again.

"Need I say anything about staying in your room for the rest of the night?"

"No, I will," Katrine quietly replied.

He shut and locked the door. Katrine collapsed on the bed, unable to move.

* * *

Alyssa Whitman hung up the phone in her dormitory room and checked the time on her wristwatch. "Crap," she said to herself. "How'd it get so late?"

She grabbed a cola from the refrigerator, walked over to her desk, and sat down in front of a stack of loose-leaf papers with several pages of shorthand scribble. A look of concentration washed over her face as she tried to figure out what to write next. After several minutes of tapping her pen on the paper, she shoved her notes to the side and opened the writing tablet David had bought her. She had already written about twenty pages. She skipped past several blank pages from where she had last left off and began to transcribe her shorthand notes onto the tablet.

"I can hardly keep up with you, Katrine," Alyssa whispered before taking a drink of cola.

Chapter 6
Dragon Hill (Monday)

A loud knock on the door woke Katrine with a start. James opened the door.

"You're going with me to breakfast. You've got twenty minutes to get ready." He threw a roll of gauze on the bed beside her. "Here's something the doc gave me to wrap your arm. I don't need you bleeding all over the breakfast table." He slammed the door behind him as he left.

Katrine struggled to get up. She was stiff, sore, and the gunshot wound on her arm ached and burned. She walked to the bathroom to clean up as best she could, but many of the scratches that had clotted began to bleed again as she ran the washcloth over them. She held her breath as she rinsed the wound on her arm, and then firmly wrapped it with the gauze James had given her. From the armoire, she picked out a pair of jeans, though she felt very uncomfortable wearing pants meant for men, and a long sleeved shirt, hoping to hide the scratches she acquired from climbing the tree and falling on the pebble roof. She found herself unable to do much about two deep scratches on the left side of her neck and a scrape across her right cheek.

James escorted her to the cafeteria where they sat in silence and ate. Behind James, Katrine could see Ashleigh, Jacques, and Robert at a nearby table. Ashleigh, who seemed particularly stressed at the sight of Katrine's scratches, whispered with wide-open eyes to Jacques between glances. Robert quietly leaned back in his chair with a thoughtful, disappointed expression on his face. Katrine wondered why she felt the need to explain to Robert, someone she had met only yesterday, that she hadn't tried something foolish. She would have made it out if the guard hadn't been so slow. After all, her less-than-reliable powers would have still been working when she reached the wall if the guard would have walked a little faster.

The silence soon became unbearable.

"Is Zor at Adrian's?" Katrine asked as she slid her fork through her eggs.

"Already know about Adrian, do you?" James asked before taking a bite of toast. "Zor's been back for quite a while. He's at the hospital talking to Guard Eleven."

"Aren't you going to ask me anything about last night?"

"No need to. I already know what I need to know."

"And what is that?" she asked looking up from her eggs.

"All in good time, Katrine," he replied as he sipped his coffee. She was sincerely hoping for a better answer, for it seemed he already knew more about what was happening to her than she did.

They finished eating and walked to the courtyard together. Zor was already standing on the brick pathway, waiting beside a large cherry tree. He motioned for Katrine to sit on the bench in front of him. As she sat, Zor reached behind him to a fork in the tree where he pulled out her sword and glove, then threw them at her feet. Katrine took a deep breath and stared at the blood on her sword. She had never stabbed anyone before.

"Where did you get these?"

Katrine looked down at the brick pathway and stared, uncertain if she should answer.

"Did they just appear in your lap with a wish?"

Katrine looked up, surprised. "Something like that," she answered cautiously.

"Did you have a strange feeling someone else was present at the time?"

Katrine eyes narrowed and her mouth dropped slightly open.

"I'll take that as a yes."

James walked a few steps closer to Zor. "You think she's linked, Zor?"

"Yes, but it's not yet fully formed. It's still a little difficult to tell when she's connected. Once it becomes stronger, it'll be very obvious."

James cracked a big smile. "You're instincts sure zoomed in on her fast. Impressive."

Katrine found herself growing angry. "What do you mean 'is she linked'? Connected to what? What's not fully formed? I deserve..."

"I'm sorry, Katrine," Zor said with disappointment in his face. "I shouldn't have taken you."

"I know you shouldn't have…"

"It's not your fault, Zor," James interrupted. "Your instincts guided you to someone special who was in trouble. You didn't know."

"So now take me home," Katrine said looking between the two of them. "You made a mistake, so now take me back."

Zor and James looked at each other in silence, and Katrine knew there was something wrong.

Zor peered thoughtfully at Katrine. "It's not that simple."

"Sure it is," she answered.

Zor's stare began to unnerve her. "Cyan's a secret society," he simply stated.

"You pose a threat to Cyan, Katrine," James explained. "If you have the capability of escaping with your new powers and spreading the word about where we are and what we do, it would severely disrupt Cyan's functioning. Then there's the possibility you may become righteous and try to destroy what we've built here by liberating the citizens. There are simply too many potential problems your existence can create now that we've brought you here. It's truly unfortunate, but we're going to have to get rid of you." Katrine sat in shock, wondering what he meant exactly. James looked over at his brother. "How are we going to do it? The guards? Or shall we just do it ourselves, right here, right now?"

Katrine lost the color in her face and slowly rose to her feet, eyeing the brothers anxiously. She wasn't sure how she was going to get away from them – they stood on both sides of her, trapping her against the bench – but she wasn't going to just sit there and let them kill her.

"The details of her demise can wait for now, James," Zor said as he stared at Katrine. "I want to know a little more about our guest before we decide to do anything rash. You're alone right now, aren't you, Katrine?"

Katrine immediately realized why he was asking. "No, Zor," she warned.

Zor started walking towards her. "Get ready for a wild ride, Katrine."

As Zor reached his hand toward her, Katrine sprang in the opposite direction and tried to dodge past James, but James grabbed her by her injured arm. With a painful cry, she kicked and struggled as hard as she could to get away, but he managed to push her down to her knees and pin both her arms tightly behind her back. She yelled in frustration and tried to squirm her arms free as Zor walked up to her.

"You have no right!"

The Link – Seven Days of Cyan

James hoisted her to her feet so that she was face to face with Zor.

"My past belongs to me, no one else. If you're going to kill me, then do it. But you have no right to delve into my personal life before you get rid of me." He placed his hand on the side of her neck, and she felt her neck lock into position so that she couldn't look away. Helplessly, her eyes met his. "Zor, please don't," she whispered, pleading.

Then it happened: her entire life flashed through her mind at unbelievable speed. Her body started to feel weak as she had to relive so many things she tried so hard to forget... three years of physical abuse by her drunken father; and the day her mother went into town and two strangers dragged her away, kicking and screaming, while her father turned the other direction. Katrine could still vividly remember the sound of gold coins jingling in his pocket as he walked back to their farmhouse. The memories continued to show her four years at the castle, but oddly returned to the humiliating day she was sold. An image of her father's callous face filled her head.

When it was over, Zor took his hand off of her and backed away in silence. Katrine was unable to look at him as James released her arms; but the lengthy, unexpected silence made her slowly look up. Zor appeared thoughtful as he stared at her.

"I'll transport you to Dragon Hill," he finally said.

"What?" James yelled in surprise. Katrine tried to wipe the puzzled look from her face, but couldn't.

"On two conditions, Katrine," Zor continued. "First, you must come to me immediately when you feel your powers have returned. Second, you must never try to escape Cyan again."

James' face grew red. "Zor, we agreed that if this should ever happen we were going to eliminate..."

"We'll sever the link from the other side, then she'll be no more powerful than any of our other citizens, and no longer a threat." Zor looked back at Katrine. "Well?"

Katrine stood silent for a moment. "You're not going to kill me?" she asked quietly.

"No. Unless you fail to meet my two conditions."

Katrine imagined a lifetime of captivity in Cyan. Even if it *was* the most interesting place she had ever been, the idea didn't thrill her. It had been so long since she was able to walk free and make her own decisions. It was the price she would have to pay, however, to know she did what she could for her mother, even if it might be too late. There was always the possibility that the guards were delayed, or that her mother had been away when the guards arrived. There might still be a chance to save her.

"Fine. You have my word. When can we go?"

"Now."

"What do you think you are doing?" James angrily protested. "You *never* get involved in the family matters of our citizens!" Zor looked as though he was about to explain, but James interceded even louder. "If you risk the life we have here, Zor, I'll never forgive you."

"Remember your place, James," Zor said calmly.

"And what's Adrian going to make of this?" he quickly responded. "She can take your powers away if you give her enough reason."

"Adrian has no reason."

"Yet." James gave his brother a disapproving look, then turned and stormed into the Main House.

Zor walked up to Katrine and took hold of her arm. "Close your eyes, otherwise you'll get an unpleasant surprise."

Katrine closed her eyes as her heart began to race with anticipation. She became dizzy and felt as though she was being lifted from the ground and spun around. Finally, the sensation subsided.

"We're here."

Katrine opened her eyes and found herself in shock as she stared at her old farmhouse. It was in ruins, but not from a recent attack. It was wrecked from years of neglect. There were holes in the roof, the front door was falling off, and the weeds were so overgrown that they had burst through the cracks in the floorboards on the front porch. She turned to the fields and the animal enclosures. No crops had been planted; no animals were present. The only sound was the wind blowing through the tall weeds and trees on Dragon Hill.

She walked slowly towards the house, stunned. The floorboards creaked as she walked up the steps and into the house. Most of the furniture was still there; spider webs connected one piece to the next. She started feeling faint as she inhaled the fine dust that had managed to escape contact with puddles from a recent rain.

She made her way into the bedroom where the entire family had slept. Kneeling down beside her small bed on the floor against the wall, she slipped her hands under the mattress until she felt a small slit in the material. She slipped her fingers through the material and pulled out a necklace. It was a locket with a simple gold chain. Her two grandmothers had pitched in together to buy it for her on her sixth birthday, but she kept it hidden from her father when he started squandering the family's valuables and plunging into debt.

Katrine opened the locket and took a deep breath. It was empty. A small purple stone that she and her mother had found when they were walking together along the beach was no longer there. Only her mother knew where Katrine kept it; only her mother could have taken it. It was a worthless stone to anybody else, but to her it was priceless – a keepsake reminding her of the first time her mother had brought her to the sea when her father was far away on a trip. Nothing particularly interesting happened. They were just together, and it was a fond memory.

She stuffed the necklace into her shoe, determined to keep it hidden from Zor in case he wouldn't let her keep it – since she now had a new family.

Katrine walked out the back door. There was one more place she had to look before Zor brought her back to Cyan. She gazed up the hillside and felt as though a dagger had pierced her heart. There were two new headstones in the family cemetery, struggling to peak out of the tall weeds. She couldn't bring herself to walk to them, so she just stared until Zor walked up beside her.

"I'm not bringing you back here, Katrine. You have to go see who they are, or you will never know."

"I already know who they are," she whispered. She looked over at Zor with a glimmer of hope in her eyes. "Can you bring me back in time to save her?"

Zor looked down at the grass, apparently disturbed by her question; then he sighed and looked at Katrine. "You can't save her. Two Katrines can't exist in a single time period because you have only one soul. If I brought you back to a time when you are alive, your soul would split between your body now and your body from the past. You would become so self-absorbed and so unmotivated, you wouldn't even remember why you had traveled back in time." He looked up towards the hill. "You should check to make sure they're your parents before we leave. Like I said before, I'm not bringing you back."

Katrine clenched her arms tightly around herself and slowly started walking as Zor followed alongside her. She didn't want him there. What if she started to cry? They were obviously her mother and father's graves.

They ascended the hillside and stopped in front of the stones. Katrine read the names of her parents: Mary Farmer, Frank Farmer. Just as she suspected from the moment she saw her dilapidated old home, the date on the stones read 1689, four years ago. The two men who had taken her to the queen must have decided to tie up loose ends before they left for the castle. The secret was safer that way. Someone from Gardenstadt, the nearest town that they frequented, must have found their bodies and buried them.

"Katherine and Irene," read Zor as he looked at the headstones behind her parents'.

"They were my grandmothers. My name comes from their names... but you already knew that, didn't you?" she asked quietly. "You now know more about me than my own parents did."

She stared thoughtfully at her parents' headstones. No longer was she worried about crying in front of Zor; she was far from it. Instead she felt anger. It was all her father's fault. He had destroyed their family with his greed, all for a few gold coins and one less mouth to feed, and now her mother was dead because of him.

She quickly turned and headed for a small shed beside the house. Once at the shed door, she picked up a nearby shovel and started pelting the locks with it, but they wouldn't budge. She looked up at Zor, who was still at the cemetery staring intently down at her parents' graves.

"Zor!" she yelled up the hillside. He looked down at her. "Would you be so kind and open this door for me?"

He waved his hand and she could hear the shed door in front of her open. She flung the door to the side and stepped into the dark, damp shed. Her father's still used for making bourbon, as well as other choice drinks, loomed before her in the darkness, like a silent killer. She and her mother had wanted to smash it ever since it was made, but they were always afraid of the consequences. She lifted the shovel high in the air and swung it down with all her might, smashing it to bits and pieces. With each swing, she pictured her father. It was the closest she would ever get to revenge for all the times she and her mother had been hit.

Zor appeared in the doorway of the shed, blocking most of the light that was entering. Katrine dropped the shovel to her side and looked at the broken glass and coils that lay on the ground before her. Now she felt like crying, but she would wait until she was alone.

"I'm ready to go now, Zor."

Chapter 7
Creative Writing (Monday)

Alyssa closed the calculus book and put her head down on the desk. "Let's call it quits for a while, David. I can't concentrate anymore."

David closed his book and leaned back in the chair. "You'll do fine on the quiz tomorrow." David rubbed his eyes. "You're dorm room has terrible lighting. Either let's do this at the library next time or get rid of the stupid aluminum foil on your windows."

Alyssa didn't like studying at the library. Her dorm room was her domain, her kingdom. She had it all to herself since her roommate bailed at the beginning of the fall semester due to homesickness, and luckily, they hadn't assigned a replacement.

Along the west side of the wall were two large desks. The desk closest to the door that was primarily used for studying was cluttered with books and papers, pens and crumpled up paper balls. Some of the paper balls had fallen onto the tile floor to mix with a few dirty socks. The second desk closest to the bathroom had turned into a place to stash her extra clothes, a small refrigerator, an illegal stove, and dishes. Above each of the desks were a couple of large shelves filled with books, soccer team pictures, and several photographs of her parents. She was an only child. Her father was an electrical engineer and her mother was a teacher who worked at the same high school as Sami's mother.

Alyssa's bed, a twin bed with a small bookshelf attached lengthwise, was shoved against the east wall behind the main door and just below one of two aluminum foil covered windows. The spare bed was perpendicular to hers, leaving a comfortable space at the foot of her bed. Unfortunately, the spare bed jutted a little ways into the doorway of the sink room, which bothered Alyssa a little, but it was better than having both beds side by side along the entire east wall, which made her room look too long and narrow. On the right of the sink room was a door that led into a bathroom that she shared with two other girls next door. On the left was a large closet with a sliding door. Alyssa filled the entire closet herself and was unsure how she would ever make room for a roommate should one get assigned.

Alyssa glimpsed at the aluminum foil covered windows. "It gets too hot in the afternoon without the foil," Alyssa said as she slid her chair backwards and stood up.

"Alyssa, it's January."

Alyssa walked over to her small refrigerator, pulled out a yogurt, and plopped down on the bed behind David. "Then I like the privacy. Want some?" she asked holding the yogurt out.

"No, thanks. I'd rather have a hamburger."

"Can't eat at the library, David. I'll just buy another lamp for you, okay?"

David started clearing his books and stuffing them into his backpack when he noticed the writing tablet he had bought her. "Started on your story?"

"Yeah. Read it and tell me what you think so far."

David read the story in silence as Alyssa finished her yogurt and got dressed for soccer practice.

"Well, what do you think?" she asked as she looked in the mirror and pulled her hair back into a ponytail.

"Don't get me wrong... what you have is fine..."

"But?"

"Well, for starters, what are all the blank pages in between...?"

"Oh, I'll fill those in once I get time," she said, waving her hand nonchalantly before she continued putting up her hair. "How was what I have so far?"

David appeared confused as he flipped through the tablet. "Well, as you've probably already guessed from the blank pages... there are some very large chunks of the story missing." He grabbed the blank pages between two fingers and held them up. "What happens between the time she falls asleep on the pirate ship and the time she wakes up in this strange prison room?"

"I'm not sure yet."

"Not sure yet? How can you not know what happens? You write the second part of the story like you know what has happened."

Alyssa picked up a water bottle and began to fill it with water. "Like I said, I'm not sure what happens yet." She screwed the lid on and turned towards David. "So, aside from the fact there's a large chunk missing, how do you like it?"

David appeared flustered. "It's hard to critique with that 'chunk' missing. Where did Paul disappear? Did he sink? Where did the ship and the pirates go? Why is the room she woke up in so nice if it's supposed to be a prison? It is a prison, right? How did she make that hole in the wall? How did she conjure up the sword and glove? Did she end up using them for anything? She's running along a dirt pathway to the outer wall of what? What is all the mud about? What's on the other side of the wall?"

"David, give me a break. I'm not finished yet. I realize I haven't explained everything... I just haven't had time to write it down. Besides, some of your questions I can't yet answer."

"You can't answer? Do you at least know how she got these strange powers?"

"Not yet! I've been busy studying for this stupid calculus quiz!" She grabbed her soccer bag. "That's the last time I ask you to read my story," she said in disgust. She picked up her soccer shoes and angrily stuffed them into the bag.

"Don't get so defensive. I was just trying to understand."

Alyssa stopped and sighed. "Sorry, David. The truth is maybe there's something wrong with me. When I start thinking about the story, it's like I have little control over what's happening. I'm just watching it, and if I stop thinking about it, the story goes on without me, and I find it difficult to find out what has happened in my absence. It's the extreme of the proverb 'a novel writes itself'." She stuffed her water into the bag and zipped it up. "I'll tell you what, though, when I'm thinking about Katrine, the images in my head are really vivid... almost like being there myself."

David stared across the desk at the wall and tapped his fingers nervously, "Let me get this straight. You're telling me you have little control over the story you're writing?"

"Yeah." She threw the bag over her shoulder. "Katrine has a mind of her own and makes her own decisions, chooses her own arguments, uses her own words...sometimes. I don't make the decisions for her; I'm just a reporter trying to get it all down on paper – except, of course, when it comes to the magic. Then it seems I have some influence. I decided it was okay for her to have the sword and glove, and to make the hole in the wall, but I thought just magically transporting to Dragon Hill was too boring and didn't let her do it. Where's the challenge?"

Alyssa noticed that David looked worried... overly worried. She must have sounded simply crazy. She shook her head. She *did* sound simply crazy, even to herself, and she wished she hadn't told David so much.

"When's your next doctor's appointment?"

Alyssa smiled. "David, I'm pulling your leg. You're so gullible. I just haven't had much time to work on it because of the calculus quiz. The answers to all your questions are right here," she said as she pointed to her head. "They're just my little secrets for the time being. I'll give you the story a little later when it's more complete."

David shook his head and smiled. "Don't worry me like that."

Alyssa bent over and kissed David on the forehead. "You're such a sweetheart."

"Boyfriend sweetheart?"

"Brother sweetheart."

Chapter 8
The Link (Monday)

Katrine ran down Cyan's soccer field and passed the ball to Ashleigh, then Ashleigh kicked the ball through the goal posts. The whistle blew and the musician's coach yelled for everyone to take a water break. They walked towards the sidelines to get a water bottle.

"Haven't you had enough, Katrine?" Ashleigh asked. "You've been out here four hours since lunch. You'll be sorry in the morning if you don't stop now. Besides, you're already better than most of us out here."

"It's helping me get my mind off things." Unlike the first two hours of soccer practice, she no longer felt the need to crouch in the corner of her bathroom, bury her head in her arms, and cry over something she couldn't change. She had done that plenty before lunch.

"Are you ever going to tell me what happened?" Ashleigh asked, nodding toward Katrine's legs.

Katrine picked up the water bottle and took a drink. She had put on her soccer shirt and shorts to practice and the scratches from the pine tree were obvious. She didn't care anymore about appearances. In fact, she didn't care about much of anything after seeing her parents' graves earlier that morning.

"I broke curfew and had a fight with a tree and a pebbled roof."

"What! Are you crazy?" Everyone nearby turned in their direction. Ashleigh looked around nervously, and then lowered her voice. "What were you thinking? How did you expect to get past the guards and the outer wall?"

"I just thought I had a way," Katrine casually explained.

"What about that?" she asked as she pointed to where Katrine had bandaged her gunshot wound. "A tree?"

"It's nothing." Katrine noticed that the rest of the team was staring at them, whispering. "I'll explain what I can later. Now is not the time," she said in hopes of ending the conversation.

"Is Zor angry?"

"He doesn't seem real angry."

"Maybe he's impressed that someone actually survived a curfew violation." Ashleigh took a drink and looked across the field, then sighed. "He may not be angry with you, Katrine, but he's angry with the musicians."

"Why's that?"

"We play the guards on Friday. Perhaps we botched that last concert more than I thought we had. I *knew* he was going to set us up with the guards. He always gives me this strange look the day before he announces that we play them... a look of concern." Ashleigh shook her head. "But he still sets it up."

Katrine glanced behind her at the guards' alley. "Has anyone ever refused to play them?"

"And risk punishment? Zor's punishments aren't like two days in solitary confinement. They last a lifetime." Ashleigh took a final drink and wiped her mouth with a towel. "We basically don't play them anyhow. If you try to get the ball, you get the living crap kicked out of you. Last time I had a bruise on my shin that didn't heal for weeks. We all just try to stay out of the way as they dribble the ball towards our poor goalie. The goalie seems to end up on the ground whether or not he's trying to block the ball. He could be clear at the other end of the field and they'll still take him out. We draw straws before the game to determine who our eight goalies will be. Four for each half. That way one person doesn't have to bear it all."

The coach signaled for the team to return to the field. They began jogging toward the center of the field to practice heading the ball when Katrine felt the presence return. She stopped, uncertain what to do.

"What's wrong?" yelled Ashleigh once she realized Katrine had stopped.

Katrine hesitated for a moment, and then decided she had better keep her promise. "I think I'm going to call it a day. I'm getting a headache from all the heading I've done today."

Ashleigh nodded in approval and raised her hand to wave goodbye.

* * *

Zor and James were reading in the sitting room when Katrine walked in the Main House. She stopped suddenly in front of the door;

the uncertainty of what Zor was going to do momentarily left her paralyzed.

"It's back, isn't it?" Zor asked as he looked up from a magazine. Katrine nodded. "Take a seat at the end of the table," he said as he got up from the couch, tossed the magazine down and approached the dining room table. Katrine sat down and Zor pulled up a chair so that he was directly in front of her.

"This is going to be simple, Katrine. All you have to do is let me inside your mind. Stare into my eyes and wish my spirit in your body."

"What?" Katrine asked as she quickly rose from her chair. Zor placed his hands around her waist and gently pushed her back down.

"You made a promise, Katrine. Nobody is going to get hurt from this, and it will only take a few minutes."

Katrine looked out the window and stared at the pine tree she had struggled to climb the previous night as she tried to gather enough courage to face Zor. Her gaze was interrupted when James sat down at the other end of the long table to watch.

"Now, Katrine," Zor said. She turned to face him. "Stare into my eyes and relax."

Katrine sighed, and then looked into Zor's eyes. It was the fourth time she had to look into them so closely, so intently, and each time she did, they seemed to mesmerize her even more. His lighter green rays seemed to shoot out of his pupil like an exploding star into a dark green night.

"I can't do this without your help, Katrine. Concentrate on merging our souls; bring me in," he whispered. She took a deep, nervous breath before she wished Zor's spirit in her body. The images in front of her eyes blurred and she could barely make out Zor's features. When her vision went completely dark, she wasn't sure if she had closed her eyes or not. She could hear Zor talking inside her head.

"There is somebody watching you. You must travel to the other side to see who it is. Do you see that light?"

In all the darkness, a single point of light floated in the background. "Yes," Katrine replied in her mind.

"Go toward it and go through."

The light grew in size until it overcame her, leaving her temporarily blinded.

"You're eyes are closed, Katrine. Open them."

She opened them and a picture slowly formed before her eyes. It was a tablet with writing on it. She could see a woman's hand beside it, tapping a large pen on the table.

"A story about us, Katrine," she heard Zor say enthusiastically. "How wonderful. Katrine, when we talk like this, she believes it's her own thoughts... the characters in her book have just possessed her mind. Tell her to take a break, and make sure she closes the tablet."

The woman sighed and dropped the pen. *You're right. A break* **would** *be nice right about now.* The woman closed the tablet. Written on the cover was 'Alyssa Whitman, Spring 1998, Creative Writing'.

"That came a little easier than I expected," remarked Zor. "Tell her to splash some water on her face, but not to stop thinking of us. The water will refresh her so she can focus on her manuscript better."

Katrine did as she was told. Alyssa got up from the chair and went to her sink. Katrine's vision went dark as she listened to the water splashing, then the light returned. Alyssa was looking in the mirror as she wiped her cheeks and neck with a small, white towel. She was an athletic woman about the same age as Katrine. She was dressed in a yellow tank top, and her wavy brown, hair was tied back in a ponytail. A couple of strands of hair, some white, had fallen out and were now stuck to the sides of her face from the water.

"Another beautiful brunette," remarked Zor. "Your soul has good taste."

Before Katrine could make sense of Zor's comment, a knock on Alyssa's door sent Katrine whirling. Katrine grabbed onto her wooden chair with a tight grip as she sped out of Alyssa's room, back into darkness, and back into the light of the dining room.

It took a moment for Katrine to realize she was staring into Zor's green eyes once more. Unexplainably, neither moved. Instead of looking away, she continued to stare, as did he. Beyond his entrancing eyes dwelled the soul of the only man who knew all her secrets, and she felt a strange bond to him.

As Zor's hot breath hit her chin and traveled down her shirt, she began to feel aroused. She quickly looked away when she realized what was happening, but could still see out of the corner of her eye that a grin had spread across Zor's face. She held back a groan, angry that she had not come to her senses sooner.

"You are excused. You may want to wash up a bit before dinner." He stood up and shoved his chair under the table. "I watched you practice today. What did I say about you having a special talent for soccer?"

Katrine stood up confused and started slowly walking towards her room, then turned. "Aren't you going to explain to me who she is?"

The Link – Seven Days of Cyan

James spoke to Zor, "It would probably be best not to tell her."

Zor looked as though he was considering her request as he took a seat beside James at the table.

"I have a right to know," Katrine said a little more forcefully.

"So you do," Zor said.

"Zor," warned James, "you could risk her warning..."

"She won't believe, James," he replied. He looked at Katrine. "Simply put, she's your future soul in a different body. Many people decide to return after they die, like you did after this lifetime. Occasionally it happens that a part of the brain is able to make contact with past lives, such as Alyssa contacting you, but it is usually interpreted as just a daydream. That's all we'll ever be to Alyssa, even if we talk about her like we're doing now. We're a daydream... a story for a creative writing class."

"How does that explain my powers?"

"Just like a daydream, she can manipulate what happens, although most people with her ability would prefer to just watch. She will sometimes do what you wish her to do. Sometimes, however, she may deny your request for whatever reason, perhaps to make her story more interesting. If she is not thinking of you, you have no powers because she's not there to hear your wishes. It's really a strange phenomenon, and I can't explain where the powers originate. The power of a link is quite a bit different than that of a witch or warlock."

"A link?"

Zor leaned back in his chair. "You are what we call a 'link' because her mind is now linked to yours. You probably even picked up some of her memories, which would explain the red card comment you made during the tour."

"It also explains the twentieth century clichés you've picked up," James added.

Katrine felt overwhelmed. Finally a few things made sense: the familiar adobe houses, soccer, and the words she used, but had never heard before – they were from Alyssa's memories; the reason she lost her powers when she woke on the ship – Alyssa wasn't thinking about her; the voice she thought she heard running across the mud – it was Alyssa's; the inability to disappear and reappear somewhere else – Alyssa didn't allow it. She turned and started to walk back to her room in a daze, then stopped when she remembered what Zor had said in the courtyard.

"This morning you said you were going to take care of it from the other side. What are you going to do to her?"

Zor paused. "I'm going to sever the link."

"How?"

"I'll do whatever is necessary, Katrine. Go wash up."

Katrine felt faint. Because of her, Zor now knew Alyssa's name and what she looked like. "Are you going to kill her?"

"Wash up, Katrine," Zor said a second time, this time impatiently.

Katrine hesitantly turned and went into her bedroom. Leaving her door slightly ajar, she sat down by the opening and listened.

"Alyssa Whitman."

"Where is she?"

"New Mexico State University. She had NMSU soccer team pictures up on a shelf in her dormitory. 1998."

"Soccer player, huh? I hope you can keep your head on straight with this one." James paused. "You do have that door in your labyrinth, don't you?"

"Yes, I got Woester from it four years ago. I'm powerless through that door."

"So you'll have less time to take her out. An hour should still be sufficient. Do you know what day?"

"Calendar on the wall shows they're in their last week of January, on a Monday. My labyrinth has never given me a hard time when I've asked it to open on specific days."

"When are you going?"

"Tomorrow."

* * *

Ashleigh, Jacques, and Robert appeared dumbstruck after Katrine had finished telling them over dinner about her curfew violation and Alyssa.

"So do you have any ideas how to stop him from going after her?" Katrine wearily asked.

"Is Alyssa with you right now?" asked Robert, shifting his chair eagerly up to the table.

"Yes."

"May I see? Can you move something?"

Katrine could see that they all were interested. She looked around the room to make sure Zor and James weren't present, and then focused her attention back to the table. The saltshaker rose into the air, flew over to Robert's plate, and started shaking salt on his French fries. Robert leaned back against his chair as if afraid, yet a huge smile spread across his face.

"That's too cool," Robert said.

The shaker suddenly dropped onto his plate.

"And now she's gone. Not very reliable," Katrine explained.

"Hey, Katrine," Ashleigh spoke up, "Maybe you can help us out with our soccer game against the guards!"

"It depends on whether Alyssa's there. After all, she might be *dead* by then," Katrine answered resentfully. Ashleigh's face flushed red with guilt as Katrine sighed. "If she's around, I'll see what I can do. It's up to her, I believe."

Jacques leaned back against his chair. "You know the one you might want to talk to about your problem is Woester," he said. "I don't think we can help you much."

"The beer brewer?"

"He knows the most about those two," replied Jacques. "When the brothers get a little tipsy, they do a lot of talking. Woester is usually there pouring the drinks for them."

"He's an odd fellow to talk to, however," remarked Ashleigh. "He only talks in rhyme."

"It's his punishment for spilling the beans about Zor's name one day," added Robert. "Woester let a group of people know that Zor wasn't his real name. He got the name from a comic book he used to read as a kid." He paused thoughtfully. "Woester hates poetry. It was a wicked punishment for him. Can't stand to hear himself talk."

"Don't ever make fun of Zor's name, Katrine," warned Ashleigh. "Poor Earl Morrow did... made fun of it when he didn't know Zor was listening. Zor said Earl had put his foot in his mouth, and now he has toes in his mouth instead of teeth. Earl has to sip his food through a straw now. Not to mention he's really gross to look at."

Robert stood up and wiped his mouth with a napkin. "Woester will be at the play tonight. He goes to all of them except the ones with a little rhyme thrown in. Have Ashleigh point him out to you, Katrine. I've got to go and get ready. We're having the play on the outdoor stage, so I've got to help set up the backdrop before I put on my makeup."

"Did you notice we're doing a musical next week, Robert?" asked Ashleigh. "Both Jacques and I have been selected to play."

"Great! I'll be sure I'm not one of the singers. Too much pressure with you guys critiquing."

Ashleigh pointed across the table at Jacques. "It's not me you have to worry about. It's him."

Jacques just shrugged and smiled. "I expect only the best from you, Robert."

In the early evening before the play started, Ashleigh pointed out Woester. He was an elderly gentleman with a receding hairline and gray hair. His tall, thin stature seemed to shake as he took his seat in the grass. She wanted to introduce herself to him, but the lights on the stage turned on and music from a set of speakers to her side began to blast. As she turned her head towards the stage, James and Zor passed in front of her and took their seats. It was hard to concentrate on the play. For the next two hours, she stared at Zor, the man who would murder the woman who possessed her future soul.

The play ended just before curfew, so everyone cleared their seats quickly and hurried back to their houses. Zor and James walked ahead of Katrine towards the Main House. When she saw that they had entered the center door, she quickly entered through the door in front of Zor's bedroom to avoid them. She shut her bedroom door behind her and lay in bed waiting for them to lock her in, but they never did.

That night Katrine had a dream. She was floating in circles with hundreds of wooden doors inside a green tornado. Suddenly, everything went black and she could hear voices. They were echoes she could barely hear.

"Is her soul split?"

"No."

"Good. I'll put the cabinet in the room across the hall."

The green tornado returned, the doors returned, then she fell into her bed. Katrine woke up and stared into the darkness of her room, trying to remember her dream. She had already forgotten the words that were spoken. All she could remember was that her dream was green.

Chapter 9
Job Announcement (Tuesday)

Morning came with a blast and a loud crack. Katrine rose from her bed and opened her door to look outside.

"Your boyfriend's back," said Zor with a smile as he passed by her on his way to the dining room.

Katrine approached the courtyard window and looked out to see a canonball and several arrows hovering in the air. Another blast vibrated the window in front of her. She watched as a canonball crashed into an invisible ceiling above Cyan. It bounced a couple of times, and then rolled to a stop not too far from the first ball. She shook her head and went back into her room. Paul had gone back to the queen for help and had somehow managed to convince her that he wasn't guilty of treason. Zor was right that he would go back to the queen; but he had also been wrong about Paul, she realized. Paul wasn't following her to kill her parents on the queen's orders. The queen had them killed four years ago.

The noise continued all morning. Most of the residents found the show very amusing because Cyan had never been under siege. As Katrine walked to the cafeteria, she saw that the Thespian House had set up several chairs on the front porch of the house. They sat and made bets on where the canonballs would stop rolling once they impacted the ceiling.

"Katrine!" yelled Ashleigh. Katrine looked away from the Thespian House towards the job board where Ashleigh and a dozen other female residents had gathered. "There might be a way out of here for you," she said with a smile. "No fights with guards or trees; and Zor wouldn't have to worry about you somehow destroying Cyan, because you won't *remember* Cyan."

Katrine looked between the heads of several excited women. A large paper tacked to the wood read:

Job Announcement:
Wanted: Princess Anna of Nezbar
In order to satisfy a treaty signed six years ago, the arranged wedding
between Princess Anna of Nezbar and Prince Phillip of Papau
must commence immediately.
Any female individual interested in becoming the princess
must apply in person in the cafeteria at 3:00 p.m.
If selected, you must undergo a permanent change in appearance
and memory loss of Cyan and any previous life.

Katrine turned around and began to head towards the cafeteria. "I'm not interested."

"Are you sure?" asked Ashleigh. "It may be worth a try."

"I don't believe I'd like the people." The only reason she'd go back, Katrine thought, would be to seek revenge against her mother's killers, whoever they were. "I hope *you're* not considering it, Ashleigh."

"No. I already have someone dear to my heart," she said with an airy smile.

Katrine gave Ashleigh a suspicious look, but then flinched as the shadow of a canonball swept over them. It slammed into another ball above them, and then ricocheted off four others.

"Yes! That's five!" Robert yelled from the thespian's front porch. "Pay up, boys." There were moans as several colorful plastic coins were flung at him. "I'm all set for this week's poker game! Thank you, gentlemen."

After Robert picked up the plastic coins, he stood up and noticed Katrine and Ashleigh walking to the cafeteria. His eyes lit up as he pocketed the coins and ran across the street.

"So, how'd you like the play?" asked Robert as he opened the cafeteria door for them.

"You made a splendid Horatio," remarked Ashleigh.

Katrine smiled as he waited to hear from her. "Yes, you were very good." In truth, she had no idea how well he had performed. She was staring at Zor throughout the entire play.

"They almost had me play Hamlet, but I told them that would be a bit too much with La Bohéme coming up."

"You look too Canadian to play Hamlet," said Ashleigh.

"That's what makeup and hair dye are for," he explained. "I didn't exactly look like a Canadian Horatio, did I?"

There was a pause. "I guess not," Ashleigh decided. "Good."

They entered the crowded cafeteria and were welcomed by the aroma of sausages, breads, and pastries. The sounds of dishes and silverware being stacked and distributed at the beginning of the bar mixed with the sounds of chairs shifting across the wooden floor and laughter from a small group of artists in the corner.

"I'm going to save a table for us. Pick up a drink for me, would you?" said Ashleigh before making her way to an empty table. Katrine and Robert waited in line for their turn to pick up a tray.

Robert leaned forward and quietly asked Katrine, "So are you Princess Anna?"

Slightly flustered, Katrine turned to face Robert. "Uh, no, I'm not."

"It was a second identity of yours, wasn't it?" he said with a sly smile.

"You're very quick, Robert," Zor answered. He and James had just stepped in behind Robert and were waiting in line. Katrine swirled around so that her back was towards them.

"That's not very polite, Katrine. Where are your manners?" James loudly clamored.

Katrine still didn't turn to face them.

"The cafeteria appears to be quite crowded this morning," James continued. "Perhaps we can join you for breakfast."

Katrine couldn't stand the thought... not on this day when Zor was going to kill Alyssa.

"I've lost my appetite," Katrine said as she turned to head towards the door. James stepped in front of her and stopped her.

"Where do you think you're going? You're being extremely rude."

"Let her go," Zor said calmly.

James looked angrily at Zor, and then stepped aside. She walked to the door, then turned to face Zor.

"I'm no threat to Cyan. I'm going to keep my promise and stay," Katrine explained. "Killing Alyssa is *wrong*."

Zor said nothing as he looked at her. Katrine hesitated for a moment, and then turned and walked out the door.

Chapter 10
Quarter Final (Tuesday)

It was a corner kick. Alyssa knew Sami would nail it. Corner kicks were her strong point. Sami kicked the ball up; it curved in the air right towards her. Alyssa jumped up as high as she could and headed the ball towards the goal. It skimmed the goal post and glided effortlessly into the net as the goalie from the University of Texas dove for it. The team went ecstatic. It was perhaps the best goal Alyssa had ever made. They were now up one goal before half time. As the half time whistle blew, a few of the players ran over to Sami and Alyssa and slapped them on their backs with words of praise.

The players hustled off the field towards their respective benches and grabbed their water bottles. Alyssa's eyes scanned the crowd. It was larger than usual because they were playing one of their biggest rivals; there were about fifty spectators, instead of the usual twenty. Women's soccer hardly ever drew a large crowd in Las Cruces.

"That was quite a goal you made," said a man's voice. "You're very talented."

She turned to see a man in his late twenties with short, blond hair approach. He was dressed in a heavy, dark blue pullover and khaki shorts. Alyssa tried not to stare too long at his muscular legs, for it was the legs that Alyssa found most attractive in a man.

"Thank you. It was a lucky shot," she replied with a smile. She looked again towards the stands. The stranger wasn't leaving, and it became obvious to her that he wanted to stay and talk with her some more. She looked again at him. He was oddly familiar. "Have we met? Are you in my biology class?"

"No."

Alyssa looked at him curiously. "Oh. I just thought you looked familiar."

"Perhaps I'm the man of your daydreams."

His comment caught her off guard and she laughed with amusement. "Don't you mean *man of my dreams*?"

"No."

"No?'

"You have no control over your dreams. You do over your daydreams. I'd rather be someone you consciously think about."

Alyssa smirked. "Well, you have some very interesting pick-up lines. Get many girls with them?"

The man smiled and replied, "You're the first I've ever been interested in trying them on. Is it working?"

"I don't believe it is. Sorry." Alyssa noticed the team gathering to talk about the second half. "Well, I've got to go."

"Good luck in the second half," he said with a gleam in his eyes. He turned and strolled casually towards the stands as Alyssa joined the team.

Sami nudged her while the coach was talking and asked, "Who was that?"

"Just a fan."

"I'd try to get to know that one if I were you. Nice legs, eh?"

Alyssa smiled and told Sami to be quiet so she could listen to the coach. Throughout the first part of the second half, Alyssa found herself sneaking peaks at the stands to try to find him. When UTEP scored and tied the game, however, she forgot about him. The game stayed tied until there were five minutes of play left. Sami passed the ball to Alyssa, who had a clear path to the goal. UTEP's goalie dove after Alyssa's shot and barely managed to knock it away. Another teammate ran forward and kicked it in before the goalie could pick herself off the ground. After the final whistle blew and the teams slapped hands (only a few had spit on them), the team celebrated until the stands were almost empty and the other team had gone home. New Mexico State would get to play tomorrow in the semi-finals.

As Alyssa packed her shoes in her bag, she looked up at the nearly vacant stands. Her fan was nowhere to be found. Perhaps he would show up at tomorrow's game, she hoped.

Chapter 11
Paul and Punishment (Tuesday)

Robert was right about the interior designers. Katrine was tired of running out into the street to retrieve the ball and tired of their bragging to see who could kick the ball the farthest. Near the end, she believed that it was a conspiracy by the interior designers to frustrate the coach and try to make him quit. They went through six coaches last year; they were already on number five for this year with four more months left to go.

Today everyone, including herself, was becoming irritable as the bombardment of the village continued. As she picked the ball up, she noticed Zor emerging from the courtyard and heading towards the cafeteria for the Princess Anna interviews. She kicked the ball back to the field and anxiously headed to the cafeteria.

Katrine opened the cafeteria's door enough to peek inside. Ten women were standing in a single row in front of Zor and James as if in an army inspection. A smile crept across Katrine's face when she saw that James was fuming. Alyssa was probably still alive.

Zor slowly walked in front of the women, viewing them one by one, until he stopped in front of a smaller blond-headed woman wearing a yellow dress.

"You've got the job, Tiffany. One less trumpet would benefit the orchestra," he said to her. Katrine couldn't tell if she was happy that she had got the job, or if she felt insulted about his trumpet remark. She seemed a little of both. "Everyone else is dismissed."

Katrine turned to leave, but Zor quickly yelled for her. "Katrine, I'd like you to join us."

Katrine gave a nervous sigh and turned to go back inside.

"I'd like to get this messy business behind us as soon as possible. So much fuss over two regions so insignificant that they don't even make most history books. Your arm please," he said as he pointed to Katrine's arm.

Katrine looked down at her arm in confusion.

"Give it to me," Zor clarified.

Katrine walked closer and lifted her arm towards him.

"I just need a few cells for its DNA."

"D and A?" Katrine asked.

Zor picked some dry, flaking skin off from beside one of her scratches and pushed it deep into a small muffin sitting on a table behind him. The muffin briefly glowed a faint blue before Zor placed it in the woman's hand.

"Tiffany, it was a pleasure having you in Cyan. Now take a bite."

Tiffany timidly raised the muffin to her mouth and took a bite. A strange look spread across her face, then she closed her eyes and fell to the floor. Katrine watched as Tiffany's hair grew longer and darker; her face distorted longer, then shorter, until it looked like Katrine's; then her body shook as it grew taller and changed in proportion. Katrine didn't watch her body change, however, because her eyes were transfixed on Tiffany's new face. It was identical to her own right down to a freckle on her right cheek, minus the scratches. It was like looking in the mirror. A cold chill ran up Katrine's back and she shuddered.

Once the transformation was complete, the new Princess Anna lay on the floor, unconscious. Her yellow dress disappeared, and a long, white dress took its place.

"Is she all right?" Katrine asked.

"She'll wake up outside of Cyan on the way to her wedding. Won't remember a thing. They'll like her like that. Won't have to worry about her running away again."

Katrine looked up at Zor. "Is Alyssa all right?"

Zor looked at Katrine, and then knelt down to pick up Tiffany.

"Of course she's all right, Katrine!" yelled James from behind the food counter. He grabbed a bottle of beer and flipped off the lid, then took a gulp. "He visited her during a soccer game. Can't kill a soccer player during a game, you know!"

"It was not the time or the place, James," Zor returned, irritated.

"Katrine, leave us. I want to have a word with my big brother," James bellowed.

"I don't have time now," said Zor as he flung Tiffany over his shoulder and carried her through the door. Not wanting to stay in the cafeteria alone with James, Katrine followed. Parked outside on the main road was a carriage with only a driver's bench, drawn by the same two black stallions that had pulled the carriage during her tour. Zor slid Tiffany's changed body into the back and climbed up onto the driver's seat.

As the horses started trotting towards the village gates, the loud crack of a canonball hitting another overhead startled her. Zor pointed to the sky and turned the arrows and the canonballs into cherry flowers that began to fall from Cyan's ceiling, one at a time and in no particular rush. Katrine could hear a groan of disappointment from the Thespian House's front porch. She crossed the street to find Robert.

* * *

"Can't tell you how lucky it is that she's a soccer player. He may never go through with it now," said Robert as they watched the flowers fall. Ten minutes had passed since Zor had left with the carriage. Katrine and Robert were the only two left on the thespian's porch. "She's probably why you're so good at the game."

Katrine could hear the outer log wall open and shut. Zor would be returning soon.

Katrine sighed, "He's coming back. I'd rather not be here when he arrives, Robert."

"Would you like to go inside the auditorium and watch Ashleigh and Jacques practice for the next concert? It's quite entertaining. They've got a real mean conductor."

"Sure," she said as they rose from their chairs and made their way toward the auditorium. The village gates could be heard opening and closing at the end of the street. Katrine turned around to look, then froze when she noticed someone else in the wagon with Zor.

"What's wrong, Katrine?"

"You go on ahead," she said, barely paying Robert any notice. Robert watched with Katrine as the carriage neared. Katrine started to feel faint when she realized that Zor had not merely delivered a princess to the queen's army, he had traded her for Paul. Paul was bound and gagged in the back of the carriage. His long black hair covered most of his face as he hung his head toward the carriage floor.

"Who is he?" Robert asked Katrine, but Katrine didn't answer. Zor drove the wagon past her and stopped at the entrance of the courtyard. She walked toward the wagon as Zor pulled his prisoner down.

"Why'd you take him?" Katrine asked, trying to control the anger in her voice. Paul looked up at Katrine in shock.

"Surprise!" Zor said to Paul before turning to Katrine. "He needs to be taught a lesson for this attack." He pushed Paul down onto the courtyard's brick pathway. Katrine rushed over and helped him up.

"But not until you receive *your* education, Katrine. Take him into the dining room and sit him in a chair."

Puzzled, Katrine helped Paul into the Main House where James was sitting on the couch reading. James closed his book, stood up, and walked to his room without a word as Katrine led Paul to a dining room chair. She sat down beside him as Zor untied Paul's ropes.

"Struggle and I'll turn your brain into mush with a lightening bolt, just like I did to that soldier outside the wall who tried to attack me," he warned Paul.

Grabbing Paul's wrist, Zor placed it against the chair's armrest and murmured a few words under his breath. A thick black rope with no beginning or end held his wrist to the chair. Zor placed his hands around Paul's neck and again mumbled some words. A thinner blue rope appeared around his neck.

"On your wrist is black rope," Zor explained. "If you even think of escaping, it tightens. It tightens even faster if you squirm your hands and try to escape. Around your neck is truth rope. It tightens when it's not satisfied with the conversation. If you are withholding any important information, or if you downright lie, it will tighten. It loosens when you decide to come clean with the truth. I suggest not lying to the point where you can't talk your way out of it."

Katrine was at a loss. It was Katrine who had never told Paul the truth, not the other way around. She should have been the one with the truth rope around her neck.

"You are to start the conversation, Katrine, by telling him your true identity. I'll be out in the courtyard and will assume your conversation is over when you leave. Don't take the gag off of him until I'm out of earshot. I've had enough of your personal guard in the short time I've been with him and don't care to listen to him further."

As soon as Zor left, Katrine leaned over and untied the gag.

"What was that all about?" asked Katrine.

"Nothing. I swear I just saw you handed over to the queen's army outside."

"It was an impostor. Zor made her."

"What an *amazing* likeness." Paul scanned the room. "Look around and try to find something to cut through this rope." A strange look spread across his face.

"What?"

"The rope tightened."

"I suggest you stop planning an escape. There's no way out."

"Kick hard on the chair and maybe it will break. Okay! Okay! I'm staying!"

Katrine could see his wrist being squeezed against the armrest by the black rope, causing his hand to turn slightly red. He sighed and sat back in his chair, waiting for Katrine to say something.

"You're supposed to start," Paul finally said.

"I know. I'm just having trouble."

"I'll save you the pain. I know you're not the princess. You're a peasant girl taken off a farm."

Katrine felt her heart leap into her throat. "You knew all this time? How did you find out?"

"The queen told me."

Katrine could see the blue rope tighten around his neck. A worried look spread across Paul's face.

"How did you find out, Paul?" Katrine asked again, a little more leery.

Paul hesitated and the rope tightened more. "I knew all along," he finally said. "I was the one who first spotted you in a market and informed the royal family of your remarkable resemblance to the princess. She had already fallen ill at that time." The rope loosened only a little.

Katrine couldn't believe what she was hearing. She stared in disbelief at the tight blue rope around his neck.

"It seems you have something more to tell me." Katrine was beginning to fume, uncertain whether or not she wanted to hear more.

"You don't want to know."

"What else did you do, Paul?" she asked more forcefully.

He hesitated. "I was the one who met with your father and convinced him to sell you. I got a bargain. He was easy after I got a few whiskeys down him."

Katrine quickly stood up from her chair and walked to the other side of the table. She couldn't stand to be so close to him, and she shuddered to think of all the times she was grateful he was there at her side.

"Were you responsible for killing my parents, too?" she asked, trying to control the shaking in her voice.

Paul's eyes narrowed. "They're dead? *We* didn't kill them."

Katrine expected the rope to tighten, but it didn't.

"They were killed right after I was taken away."

"How could you know that? We didn't even make it back to Dragon Hill."

"Zor brought me," she informed him. Katrine leaned against the wall and fought back the tears. He seemed so cold to her now. Not even a sympathetic word about her parents.

The Link – Seven Days of Cyan

"I trusted you all these years," she said in disbelief. After a pause, the truth rope around his neck tightened a little.

"That was my job... to earn your trust," he decided to say.

"To what end?"

"To ensure that the secret did not get out."

"Suppose I had told someone."

"They would be dead soon after." The rope loosened to its original state.

Katrine stood speechless, and then shook her head. "I even thought you had fallen in love with me. Was that all a show?"

Paul looked uncomfortable. The blue rope started to tighten.

"Partly. I do still care for you, Katrine."

"Really," Katrine said skeptically. "But most of it was an act."

"It was important for me to get as close to you as possible in case I needed to do... well... some persuasion." The rope didn't change.

"Persuade me to do what?"

"To return to the castle should you escape."

Katrine began to tremble. "But you helped me escape!"

"My job wasn't to prevent you from escaping."

"What was your job then?"

"To follow you if you fled, ensure your safety, and persuade you to return on your own accord. That way we would trust the secret would remain safe even after the marriage."

Katrine shook her head. Zor had been right about Paul from day one. She stared at Paul's neck and noticed that the blue rope tightened again.

"You're not telling me everything," Katrine said half-heartedly.

"I'm not going to tell you everything. It's irrelevant now and you don't need to know."

Katrine stood in silence. Paul was probably right, but she decided to ask anyway. She wanted to see the truth rope squeeze his neck.

"What are you keeping from me?"

Paul looked Katrine straight in the eyes and said, "I am *not* going to tell you."

The blue rope tightened a little more, but Paul did not waver. Katrine became furious. She kicked the chair in front of her as hard as she could, causing the entire table to shift from the chair's impact.

"Zor said you were following me home to kill my parents! Was he right?" she yelled.

Paul didn't look at Katrine. He made no attempt to speak, and the truth rope tightened even more. With a frustrated groan, she stormed out of the dining room into the courtyard, passing Zor without any notice.

* * *

Katrine sat in the auditorium and stared at the empty stage. It was made of shiny wood and had an orchestra pit in front. There were four large sections of black, velvet chairs and one balcony booth on the side wall where she presumed Zor and James would sit to watch. The booth was decorated in crimson velvet fringe and drapes. Crimson banners decorated the dark walls and six huge glass chandeliers hung throughout the room, but they had been dimmed ever since orchestra practice had ended.

Katrine had been there for hours, just staring at the empty stage. She felt a fool for trusting Paul so much. She had actually *enjoyed* his company.

Ashleigh approached from the back of the dark auditorium and sat down in the chair beside Katrine.

"Robert asked me to check on you. He said it probably involved a man and it would be best if I came to talk to you."

Katrine continued to stare at the stage as she spoke. "Zor showed me that someone I trusted was ... well, very untrustworthy. Why would he bother doing that?" She took a deep breath. "I don't know the good guy from the bad guy anymore. I don't know who to trust."

Ashleigh was silent for a moment. "Perhaps Zor revealed what he did because he's becoming a bit taken with you. I mean... why is he going after Alyssa instead of you? You didn't see him yesterday after you left the cafeteria before breakfast. He sat with us, but he had this solemn look on his face and didn't say a word. He usually chats with us about the latest concert or play. Made us feel a little uncomfortable."

"I really didn't want to hear that, Ashleigh," Katrine remarked gloomily. "If you're right, I hope he doesn't expect me to ever return such feelings, because I won't. I could never be with someone who has destroyed so many lives."

Alyssa looked surprised. "I don't think he's destroyed my life, Katrine."

"Everyone in Cyan has been stripped of his or her family and friends to be brought here to entertain him. There's no higher purpose. He's not doing it for *you* so that *you* can reach your full potential, or whatever his lame justification is. Cyan is nothing more than a village of slaves trying to please their master."

The Link – Seven Days of Cyan

Ashleigh stood up. Katrine could tell Ashleigh was upset with her and she regretted that she had said anything.

"Curfew is in an hour," Ashleigh politely stated. "You should get something to eat. We've already eaten."

Ashleigh walked up the aisle and left the auditorium. Katrine put her head down in her hand and imagined toes in her mouth instead of teeth.

* * *

The five-minute warning bell sounded as Katrine entered the Main House. Paul was still in the chair with the black rope squeezing his wrist, truth rope tight around his neck, and the gag back in his mouth. Zor and James were on the other side of the table playing poker.

"Good news, Katrine," said James with a smile as she walked toward her room. "We've decided to let him go."

Katrine paused, wishing there was truth rope around James' neck. She looked at Paul and felt nothing. She had somehow managed to bury her hatred and anger after three hours of staring at the empty stage.

"Goodbye, then," she said to Paul before walking into her room and closing the door behind her.

The curfew bell rang as Katrine lay on the bed and stared out her ceiling window. She listened to James and Zor play cards in the lobby until James yelled 'royal flush!' and Zor groaned with disappointment. Soon after, she could hear their chairs move across the wooden floor and could hear Zor talk to Paul. She slid out of bed and eavesdropped against the door. Strangely, she didn't have to strain as hard as she did the first night to hear their voices through the door.

"The carriage is waiting for you on the street we came in," said Zor. "Just help yourself in, and it will take you to the outer wall gates."

Katrine shook her head, realizing they were sending Paul out to the guards. Nobody deserved to be fed to the guards; not even Paul. It wasn't Paul who had killed her parents. She sighed and closed her eyes. The last thing she felt like doing was to put her neck on the line to try to save Paul. But he had saved her life once by pulling her from the water before she drowned. She felt obligated to return the favor.

"Alyssa," she whispered, "I need you now!"

Alyssa had been showing up quite a bit since Katrine had visited her in her dorm room, but she never stayed long and Katrine never tried contacting her, never asked her to do anything for her... but now Katrine needed her.

The lobby door opened and shut.

Alyssa!

Paul's in trouble? Rescuing the weasel sounds like a bit of fun. A lot more interesting than sitting and staring at an empty stage.

Katrine's heart began to beat faster when she realized she had made contact. She could sense that her connection with Alyssa was growing stronger, for Alyssa already knew what was happening. Oddly enough, Katrine could also sense what was happening with Alyssa: she was lying on her dormitory bed, reading a book about a boy named Harry.

Katrine quickly put her ear to the door again. James and Zor had started a new game of poker. She decided she would have to try to save Paul with them in the dining room, or she'd be too late. She slowly turned the doorknob and opened the door, making no sound with Alyssa's help. She quietly sneaked down the hall until she was in front of Zor's room and opened the door to the courtyard. Again the sounds from the door and from the courtyard were silenced until she closed the door behind her.

She heard a heavy thud and a moan followed by several laughs that echoed around Katrine. Katrine quickly crouched behind a tree to see what was happening. On the main pathway, four guards had already found Paul and had him surrounded. Paul was on the ground trying to get back on his feet when a guard pushed him back down with his boot.

Katrine wished that Paul was outside the outer log wall, but nothing happened.

Come on, Alyssa, Katrine thought. *Just this once. Transport him out of here!*

Again nothing happened. Katrine watched in horror as a guard drew his sword and sliced it across Paul's left arm. Paul grabbed the cut with an agonizing yell. As the guard's sword rose in the air again, Katrine quickly turned it into a long stemmed rose - thorns not included.

The confusion in the guard's face when he saw the flower was quickly replaced with a startled expression as he flew through the air and landed with a hard thump several feet back from where he had stood. The other three guards also took flight as Katrine ran to Paul and pulled his arm.

"Come quickly!" she said as she led him back to the courtyard door in front of Zor's bedroom. The guards were getting back on their feet when Katrine whispered 'sleep'. The guards fell back down to the ground and began to snore. Once more, Alyssa muffled the sounds as Katrine led Paul into her room and shut the door.

"How did you do that to those men?" asked Paul with a bewildered look. Katrine paced quickly back and forth as she rubbed her hands tightly together.

"You are getting me into so much trouble, Paul. I can't believe I'm doing this, especially after you ruined so much of my already pathetic life." She stopped and pointed angrily at Paul as he held his hand over his cut arm. "And don't you *dare* drip blood onto my floor!"

She marched over to her armoire and grabbed a long scarf, then threw it at Paul. "Wrap your arm while I figure out how to get us out of this mess." She stared at her back bedroom wall and sighed. "It would have worked before had Alyssa not left for a phone call. It'll work now."

Katrine placed her hands on the wall and a hole appeared. She made the dry dirt pathway clear to the outer log wall, and then wished a hole through the log wall.

"Now go, Paul. Run like crazy in that direction," she said as she pointed out to the dry dirt pathway.

Paul approached the hole and looked out.

"How did you do that?"

"I *don't* have time to explain. You've got to get out of here."

Paul looked out of the hole, and then turned back to Katrine. "Aren't you coming with me?"

"No. Hurry up and go," she urged. "There's a way out at the end of the dry dirt."

Paul quickly leaned over and kissed Katrine on the forehead. She fought back the urge to punch him as he pulled away.

"Thank you." He crawled through the hole in her bedroom wall and began to run.

Katrine watched as he ran out of sight. It was too dark to see all the way across no-man's land, so she impatiently waited until she thought he had enough time to climb through the outer log wall's hole she had wished on the far side. She was about to seal up the holes and turn the path back into mud when she saw Paul running back toward her room.

"I am in such big trouble," she said to herself as she watched him approach.

"There's no way out on the other side, Katrine," huffed Paul as he tried to catch his breath.

"There's got to be!" she frantically replied. Alyssa had not yet left her.

"There's not."

Katrine looked past Paul across the mud, unable to see anything.

"Maybe I'm too far away. Maybe I have to see what I'm doing." She hesitated, trying to figure out what to do. "You'd better be telling the truth," she said as she started climbing through the hole. Zor had taken the truth rope off his neck and she had no way of knowing.

They both ran as fast as they could across no-man's land. Katrine noticed a guard with a lantern in the distance, and then quickly made him fall asleep before he got any closer. Finally, she was at the wall with Paul behind her. She felt around, but there was no hole.

"Alyssa, you've got to do this for me!" she whispered. "I don't have much time!"

She continued to feel for the hole in the darkness. The logs beneath her hand finally disappeared and her hand fell forward onto something that seemed to bite her. She jerked her hand back. Across the circular hole she had just made shined a bright blue light. She reached forward again and touched it, and once more it gave her hand a shock.

"What is that?" Paul asked behind her.

"It's obviously something Zor put up," Katrine angrily answered. She stared intently at the blue light and wished it was gone with all her might, but it remained.

"Maybe we should go back," Paul said.

"Shut up, Paul! Going back is not an option! What am I going to do with you? Hide you under my bed?"

Katrine continued to stare at the blue light. She could tell Alyssa was trying to help, but it wasn't disappearing. Finally, the blue light began to dim, but Katrine was getting a terrible headache from the process.

Suddenly a bright light and an earth-shattering crack threw Katrine backwards to the ground. She tried to catch her breath as another bright flash fell from the sky. The ground shocked her body, and Katrine lost her breath a second time. She struggled to look up. Gazing down at her was Zor, James, and about ten guards. She had never seen Zor so angry. Her head felt heavy from the lack of oxygen, and when she finally began to breathe a little easier, the air was different and didn't allow her to recover quickly. She tried to sit up.

"I wasn't going to leave, Zor," she managed to say.

Zor held out his palm towards Katrine, and she felt her face turn white as his palm began to glow. A bolt of lightening shot out of his hand and hit her in the shoulder. Katrine yelled out in pain as it threw her back into the mud. She clamped her hand over her burning shoulder.

"That is for interfering. It is my mark to remind you that you now belong to me and you will respect my authority. Remove it and I'll put it back the exact same way."

Katrine looked under her hand. In the dim light of the guards' lanterns, she could see under her torn, burnt shirt a large letter 'Z' with a tiny cursive 'or' written on the bottom line of the Z. She had been somebody's property for the past four years and would not let it happen again.

"I do *not* belong to you, Zor," she dared to say. "I never will."

Three lightening bolts accompanied with deafening thunder fell from above to each side of her body. Katrine screamed and put her arms over her head. She could feel the electricity shoot up and down her body, leaving her paralyzed and breathless once more.

"Bring her back to her room," Zor ordered two guards. The guards grabbed her under her arms, hoisted her up, and dragged her towards the village. Katrine tried to stop her body from shaking, but her nerves would never settle. She looked to see what fate had befallen Paul, but he was nowhere to be seen.

The guards dragged her through the hole in her bedroom wall and tossed her onto the bed. Zor walked through the wall, grabbed her hand and bound it to the headboard with black rope.

"I wasn't going to leave, Zor," she said again, still unable to stop her body from shaking.

"I believe you. If I didn't, those last three lightning bolts would have been full power and aimed straight at your head." He looked at the back wall and sealed up the hole. "You still are to be punished for breaking curfew... twice now. I'll be back when Alyssa's gone."

The room was cleared and Zor slammed the door behind him. Katrine closed her eyes, trembling. She could feel tears begin to fall down her cheeks.

Pull yourself together.

Let's see how well you *hold yourself together after nearly getting struck by lightening*, Katrine angrily thought in response.

Yes, I know. But you can't let Zor see you this way. You're supposed to be tough.

Katrine was about to reply when she realized Alyssa had just responded directly to Katrine's thoughts.

Alyssa? Do you realize I'm talking to you?

Of course I do.

Katrine's breathing quickened.

Now listen. When he comes back, don't show him how you feel. Straight face, walk tall. Nobody's going to want to read about a sissy.

Read? Alyssa, you've got to listen. I'm real. Zor's real. He's already shown up to one of your soccer games. You've got to be careful. He plans to kill you.

Boy, I hope writing this time travel stuff doesn't trip me up. I want an A. Well, good luck with this punishment business. Remember, don't let him see you scared.

Katrine shook her head in disbelief, and Alyssa disappeared.

* * *

Straight face...walk tall... Katrine walked beside Zor down the road that would eventually turn into the guards' alley. James was behind them following along with a few other guards who wanted to watch. It was the second time that Zor had made her feel like a spectacle. The fish tail was still more humiliating... for the moment.

They had said nothing to each other since Zor came into her bedroom and released the black rope, and the uncomfortable silence reminded her of when her father was angry with her and was trying to decide what he was going to do with her.

Zor finally broke the silence. "You put me in a difficult position, Katrine." Katrine made no response and they walked a bit farther in silence. "As founder and leader of Cyan, I have no choice but to enforce the rules that I have set. You were lucky when you violated curfew the first time. In fact, you're the first to ever survive a curfew violation. I foolishly thought you had learned your lesson and wouldn't repeat such a mistake, but you proved me wrong tonight."

"Half of Cyan knows about your first little escapade," interceded James. "If they get news of this one, the people are going to get the wrong idea about the guards. Any blood spilled because of a foolish citizen who thinks they can escape will be on your hands." The guards walking beside James grunted in agreement.

Zor continued to speak. "Now I am forced to resort to more drastic measures to make you understand that the rules I set in Cyan are to be followed, no matter who you are. Whatever happens to you tonight, I do it out of necessity."

Katrine's face grew pale when he said 'whatever happens to you tonight'. Didn't he know what was going to happen? Her thoughts repeated faster: *straight face, walk tall, straight face, walk tall...*

"I will never understand why you tried to save him," Zor said. "I even revealed to you who he truly was."

"Is he dead?" Katrine asked quietly.

"His lifespan is shortened quite a bit, that's for sure," James smirked.

"Indeed," remarked Zor.

Katrine looked out at the soccer fields as they began to near the guards' alley. Some of the guards were practicing.

"What did you do to him?"

"Turned him into a dung beetle and put him in a septic tank under the Main House. It was amazing how his entire brain fit so easily into a dung beetle's head. I preserved his thought processes because I wanted him to know that for the rest of his days... he would be feasting on my shit." James and the guards gave a little chuckle behind her.

"Good thing you saved him from the guards, Katrine," James said. "The dung beetle punishment is so much more interesting."

Katrine turned to James. "He didn't deserve to get killed by the guards," she said, trying to justify her actions.

"I read Paul's memories, Katrine," Zor responded. "Like I predicted, he was following you back to Dragon Hill to kill your parents. He would have made it look like an accident so you wouldn't have suspected any royal involvement, then he would have convinced you to go back to your other life, since there would be nothing left for you at Dragon Hill."

Katrine stopped walking, not wanting to believe him. Zor stopped and turned towards her.

"I bet he was surprised when you told him your parents were dead. Someone did his job for him."

Katrine's heart sank as she remembered the conversation. Paul *was* surprised when she told him her parents had been murdered.

"Well, if the royal family had nothing to do with their deaths, then who did?" Zor turned around and continued to walk, so Katrine ran in front of him and stopped him. "Please, do you know?"

Zor looked thoughtfully at Katrine, then looked up at the night sky and shook his head before returning his attention back to her. "I'm not sure why I'm telling you this, because it's counter-productive to your stay in Cyan. But I do love a good mystery." He sighed. "You haven't lost both your parents. One of the graves was empty, Katrine."

Katrine stood dumbstruck, and then a faint smile spread across her face. Her mother was alive. It had to be her mother. The rock from her locket was gone. She would have taken it with her before she left the farm. The headstones... her father wouldn't have bothered with such nice headstones. He would have made wooden crosses so that he could return to his bottle of bourbon faster.

"Now why'd you do that?" asked James. "You cheered her up before punishment."

Katrine's smile quickly faded.

"Let's go," Zor said as he took hold of Katrine's arm and turned her in the direction of the guard's alley. They walked to the front entrance of the Guard House and Zor knocked on the door.

"Send him out," Zor said to the guard who answered.

The worried look on Katrine's face was quickly replaced with one of extreme anxiety as Zor led her to the pit. Lanterns on all sides above the pit lit up, illuminating a dirt hole as big and as deep as a small house. A rope ladder in front of them was the only way down. Many of the guards started to gather around the outer edge of the pit.

"Please don't make me go down there," Katrine gravely requested. The hole terrified her, and the guards gathering to watch didn't make her feel any braver.

"I'm not going to make you do anything, Katrine," Zor answered. "But your only weapon against Guard Eleven," he said as her sword appeared in his hands, "is down there." He threw the sword down into the pit. "Guard Eleven has requested a rematch. I've granted him his request."

At that moment Katrine heard a familiar laugh. She whirled around to see Guard Eleven approaching her from behind, swinging his sword at his side. Katrine shot an angry look at Zor, then jumped onto the ladder where she quickly made her way to the pit's floor to retrieve her only defense.

She picked up her sword and swirled around to see Guard Eleven jump from the middle of the ladder to the dirt below. He smiled at her, revealing the large gaps between his checkered teeth.

"I can't tell you how much I've looked forward to this," he said, eyes gleaming as he raised his sword and approached her. Katrine took a deep breath and squeezed the handle of her sword.

The guard raised his sword and swung it at her. She blocked it easily, but almost lost hold of her sword. She hastily put both hands on the handle and raised it to block his next swing. Again, the sword nearly jolted from her grasp as the two swords clashed. With his every swing, she found herself stepping back and struggling to keep hold of her weapon. With every block she made, she barely had time to recover before she had to make another. He was too strong and Katrine's hands and arms were tiring fast. She could see in his face that he was just playing with her.

Then it came. He swung at her with such force that Katrine's sword flew out of her hands and tumbled across the dirt floor. The bones in Katrine's hands and lower arms vibrated with such pain from the blow, she cried out and clenched her arms tightly against her body. She could hear cheers from above echoing throughout the pit. The guard placed the tip of his blade under her chin and raised her head to face him.

"You'd be a worthy opponent if you were a man. I think you've got the skill, but you certainly don't have the strength," he said as he removed his sword from her chin and poked her upper arm.

He pushed her over backwards with his boot, then walked to pick up Katrine's sword. Katrine watched with relief as he stabbed both weapons deep into the dirt wall. She gathered a handful of dirt and scurried to her feet as he turned around and approached her. When he was close enough, she threw the dirt in his eyes and ran past him toward the other side of the pit. He had not expected the attack and was wiping the dirt from his eyes with a growl. She could hear the crowd above boo her.

Katrine had hoped to find the ladder extended for a possible getaway, or at least a delay of the inevitable, but someone had brought it to the surface. She frantically looked around for something to defend herself, but could find nothing as Guard Eleven started to charge after her. In the shadows of the tall walls, she finally spotted a rock. She dove for it and threw it at the guard's face as hard as she could, again surprising him as it hit him in the nose. He roared in anger as she tried to run past him, but fell to the floor when he kicked his leg out and tripped her. She had almost regained her stance when she felt the guard's hand grab her ankle. She twisted her foot until her shoe fell off in his hand, then scampered to her feet and ran for the swords buried in the wall.

Katrine had just managed to wrap her hands around the hilt of her own sword when she felt the guard's arms grab her around her waist. She yanked desperately at the sword as he pulled her away. The sword finally slid out and was in her hand, but the guard whirled her around and threw her down to the ground so hard that she lost her grip. Her sword fell in the dirt, just out of reach.

The guard immediately straddled his legs over her and sat on her back. She struggled to breathe as his enormous weight smashed her to the ground. Katrine closed her eyes and lay still as she listened to the crowd above cheer again for their colleague. She shuddered when he grabbed her hair and leaned over so that his vile-smelling breath hit the side of her face.

"Now the fun begins, Princess."

He pulled her to her feet with her hair and hit her in the stomach, knocking the wind out of her. His elbow knocked her hard on the side of her face and sent her whirling to the ground. She tried to crawl away without having recovered her breath, but a kick to her abdomen caused her to fall back in the dirt. She gasped for breath and began to choke on the dirt she inhaled. Another kick to her body caused her to roll over so that she looked towards the night sky. The lanterns were blurring and the guards above were just shadows. She could tell they were shouting and yelling at her, but she couldn't hear them.

She felt her head jolt to the side and begin to pound. Her vision became narrower. She closed her eyes. She could see the farm. She could see her mother. Her mother's had to be the empty grave. It just had to be...

Chapter 12
Semifinals (Wednesday)

Alyssa limped off the field, furious. There were only ten minutes in the game left and she wouldn't be able to play the final minutes. The only consolation was that a red card was given to the woman who kicked her. She threw herself down on the bench and crossed her arms. The trainer came over and questioned her about her ankle, moved it one direction, then the other, then gave her a bag of ice to hold on it. When he left, Alyssa slammed the ice down on the bench beside her and looked out to watch the game.

Sami slid over to sit beside her. "Good game, Alyssa. Guess who showed up again," she said as a huge grin spread across her face.

"I don't know. Who?" Alyssa angrily asked as she stared out at the field.

"Look behind you in the stands!" she cried out, barely able to stay sitting.

Annoyed, Alyssa looked at Sami, and then glanced behind her at the stands to see that her fan from the previous day had returned. She had completely forgotten about him since leaving the fields the previous day. He saw her look back at him, gave her a smile, and lifted a couple of fingers to say hello. Alyssa politely smiled and turned back toward the game.

"You should ask him out," suggested Sami.

"Sami, I'm trying to watch the game."

"We're up by two and they're playing terrible. Now get your mind on more important things."

"Sami, I'm not going to ask a stranger out. He's probably some stalker or psycho-killer."

"You don't ask strangers out; you don't ask friends out. You're going to end up forty and alone if you don't get with it *now*."

"I'll ask someone out when I'm interested in him."

"Oh, come on! You can't tell me you're not interested in him. He looks intelligent, he's good looking, and he likes soccer. What more could you ask for?"

Alyssa sighed and looked at Sami. She was a hopeless romantic.

"Yes, he's got my attention, but he'll probably say no. I bet he already has a girlfriend and..."

"Wrong! Would someone who has a girlfriend ask me if you had a boyfriend?" Sami asked with an enormous grin.

"Sami, please. I'm trying to watch the game."

It was not the response Sami wanted to hear. "Fine. Forget I even mentioned him, but I'm beginning to think you have lesbian tendencies." She stood up and trotted to the other side of the bench.

"I am *not* a lesbian!" Alyssa yelled over to Sami. The rest of the team on the bench started to laugh as Alyssa groaned in frustration and buried her head in her hands.

The final whistle blew. They would get to play University of New Mexico in the finals. As Alyssa threw her shoes into her bag, Sami walked by.

"He's leaving. You may never see him again, Rainbow Child."

"Okay! I'll say hello!" Alyssa yelled. Sami just smiled and kept walking.

Alyssa picked up her bag and started toward the gate. She could see her fan lingering around the exit, viewing a tournament board that hung on the fence. She felt ridiculous searching for a pick-up line herself.

"So, does the man of my daydreams have a real name?" He turned around and smiled, then held out his hand.

"John Albrecht."

She took his hand and shook it. "Alyssa Whitman. Listen, if you weren't busy tomorrow, I was wondering if you would like to meet at the union for a coke or something."

"That sounds great. What time?"

"How about three? I'll meet you at the Crossroads Snack Bar."

"Okay, I'll be there," he said with a nod. "I really enjoy watching you play. You're by far the best player on the team."

"Thanks," Alyssa said, trying to stop herself from blushing. "Are you coming to watch the finals on Friday?"

He appeared disappointed. "No, I've got classes. I wish you luck, though."

The Link – Seven Days of Cyan

"I'll see you tomorrow at three, then." She gave a little wave and hurried nervously to her car. She wasn't used to asking men out, but it had gone well.

Alyssa walked to her car and began to unlock the door. She looked back to find John, but he was nowhere to be seen.

Chapter 13
Adrian (Wednesday)

Katrine lay motionless on a soft, warm bed and tried to open her eyes, but only the right would open. All she could see was a smooth, white wall a meter to her right and a white ceiling with pictures of waterfalls and mountains. She stared and wondered where she was when footsteps began to echo through the room, growing louder with each step. An elderly man with a smooth, shiny scalp and thin wire spectacles leaned over Katrine and smiled.

"Glad to see you're awake."

"Where am I?" Katrine whispered.

"At the hospital. I'm Doc Norman," he said as he walked over to the counter and picked up a tube. "And you are the one who put Guard Eleven in here a couple of days ago. Simply amazing." He walked over to Katrine's burning shoulder. "Can't say I've seen a burn like this one before," he said as he removed a bandage, rubbed ointment on Zor's mark, then taped a new bandage over it.

Katrine turned her head to look at him. "There's a sharp pain when I breathe."

"Just a small fracture in your left rib. You've given me a lot of business lately: a stab wound, a fractured rib and a broken nose within sixty hours."

"My nose doesn't hurt."

"Guard Eleven's does," he said with a smile. "Good shot."

Katrine gave a weak smile, satisfied that she had done at least a *little* damage to her opponent.

"I've noticed a lot of interesting things since your arrival, in fact." He returned the ointment to the counter. "Did you know Zor spent nearly the entire night in here just sitting, staring at you?" Katrine's smile vanished as the doctor returned to adjust her pillow.

"He's *never* stayed with a patient before. It seems you're giving him a lot to think about." He looked at her and sighed. "Can't do much for your bruises at the moment, but I believe I'll have something for you a little later."

"Thanks."

"Get some rest. If you need me, just press this button," he said as he placed a remote with a button in her right hand.

After placing his hand on Katrine's shoulder and giving her a small pat, the doctor left the room. Katrine closed her eyes and rested until she heard more footsteps enter the room about fifteen minutes later.

"Is that her?" a woman angrily asked.

"Yes, Adrian," answered Zor.

Trying to appear asleep, Katrine kept her eyes closed and remained motionless.

"I want her out of the Main House, Zor."

"She's still linked. I need to keep a close eye on her."

Katrine listened as Adrian approached and stood directly over her. "What's going on?" she asked. "You've visited her other side twice now and you haven't killed her."

"I haven't had the opportunity. I only have an hour and both times I arrived during a public activity. I'm not going to do it in front of a crowd. I'll do it when I get her alone."

"That's ridiculous!" she yelled as she turned towards Zor. "Just kill her and disappear through the doorway."

"It's a valuable door, Adrian. I've gotten several people from it. I don't need my picture posted on the FBI list at every post office should I choose to return to Alyssa's time period for a collection."

Adrian turned back to Katrine. "Then get rid of this one. No one will miss her."

"She's valuable to Cyan."

"Don't give me that! She's just a worthless peasant girl!"

"She'll be going to the Thespian House. Not only is she a very strong soccer player, but she's also an exceptionally good actress. She's already earned the respect of the other thespians from rehearsals for the next play."

"I'm looking forward to the next play then. What's this?"

Katrine felt Adrian begin to tug at her shoulder bandage. Zor rushed over and held it down.

"The guard stabbed her. You should leave it covered so it doesn't get infected. I need her to heal as fast as possible so she can play in the next soccer game. The thespians only have one good forward."

Katrine could tell from Adrian's breathing that she didn't believe him.

"Adrian, I think your hour is almost over. I'll walk you back to your labyrinth. Give me about fifteen minutes to change and I'll meet you at your place. We'll go to lunch and spend the afternoon together."

"You seem to be trying to get rid of me. Is there something more going on here than I'm aware?"

"Adrian, now is not the time or place to discuss..."

"I want to stay. Just bring me back with your labyrinth."

Zor hesitated. "I don't think that's wise. You know if the door closes and you're on the wrong side, your labyrinth is released from your ownership. If any witch or warlock happens by..."

"You know my labyrinth's special. No one's going to find it, so don't try to lecture me on how I should act, Zor. I'm the one that got you in this business, remember, and at great personal risk. I could have been murdered in my state of weakness after I changed you."

"Murdered?" Zor raised his voice in disbelief. "Your father was there protecting you the entire time... which is more than I can say you'll do for me."

"When you come to your senses and realize my brother is a worthier recipient than James, then I'll protect you from Daddy's wrath. If you turn Rehnny into a warlock, I bet Daddy would even warm up to you a bit."

"Look, we'll talk this afternoon. We've already said too much in present company."

"I don't care what she hears, Zor," Adrian said as she walked to the right side of Katrine's bed and leaned over until Katrine thought she could feel Adrian's breath on her face. A loud metallic clang sounded above Katrine's head on the metal bedpost, causing Katrine to startle and open her eye. Adrian, a skeleton of a woman with sunken, pale eyes; thin lips; and very long, flat, shiny, black hair, was glaring at her from only a foot's length away. "She won't be here much longer, I believe."

"Leave her alone, Adrian. It's not your place to decide who lives and dies in Cyan."

Adrian looked up at Zor, then back down at Katrine with a mischievous smile. "He defends you. I don't believe he's ever stood up to me like that before."

"Adrian, your door is about to close. You best be going."

Adrian stood up and walked to Zor. "Yes, I best be going. I no longer believe I can trust you to bring me home."

"Don't be ridiculous. I've lost three girls because of your unfounded jealousies. I just don't want to lose four."

Adrian gave a huff, and then walked quickly out of the room. Zor groaned and silently followed behind.

Adrian's cackling voice and cold stare still weighed heavily on Katrine's mind when the doctor reentered the room.

"It's been about a half hour since they left, wouldn't you say?" Doctor Norman approached Katrine's bedside and held out a muffin. "Zor gave me instructions early this morning to give this to you after Adrian's visit. Charming lady, isn't she?"

"Yes. Simply charming," Katrine feebly replied.

"Well, don't worry. She can only visit once a day, so you have the rest of the day off!" he exclaimed happily. "Now eat this. I'm curious what's going to happen."

Katrine looked dubiously at the muffin, wondering if there was somebody else's D and A in it. Becoming somebody else didn't seem like such a bad idea at the moment, however. The doctor put the muffin to her mouth and she took a bite. Instantly, she began to feel warm inside. The pain throughout her body started to melt away, her left eye opened painlessly, the burn on her shoulder cooled, and the gunshot wound on her arm no longer ached. She felt completely rejuvenated.

The doctor stared at her wide-eyed and grinning. "I've got to order about a dozen of those muffins before the guards' game." He grabbed a mirror from a drawer and gave it to Katrine. "Not only are the bruises gone, but also the scratches."

Katrine sat up and looked in the mirror. There was not even a trace of the cut Zor had given her on her neck during her collection. She quickly looked over at her shoulder and tore the bandage off, but became disappointed to find that Zor's name was still there.

"I see he left his lovemark," remarked the doctor.

"It's not a lovemark." Katrine tried to stick the bandage back on, but it wouldn't stick because of ointment on the tape. "May I have a different shirt before I go? One that will cover up this desperate attempt for ownership?"

The doctor gave a warm smile. "Of course. I'll retrieve one right away. Zor told me that you need to see your friend, Robert, about a play once you leave. Apparently you need to start memorizing lines."

Katrine took a deep breath as she pictured herself up on a stage, in front of about four hundred people, acting like she was someone else. But then... she spent the past four years acting like someone else.

C.R. Kwiat

* * *

Robert's face appeared strained before he burst out laughing. "A dung beetle?"

Katrine imitated Zor's voice. "I wanted him to know that for the rest of his days, he'd be feasting on my shit."

"He said shit?" Robert asked. "I've never heard a bad word out of that man's mouth the entire time I've been here."

Katrine smiled back at Robert. She hadn't told him anything about her attempt to free Paul and what happened afterwards, and a simple 'Zor decided to be nice' comment when Robert asked her about her healed scratches worked nicely.

Katrine leaned back on the couch. She was in the thespians' main living area. Each wall was lined with a plush beige couch, leaving a large space in the center of the room for the thespians' nightly improvisations. Surprisingly, the room had a warm feeling to it, due in part to the dim lighting from lanterns spaced along the wall between hung photographs of several famous actors and actresses.

Katrine lifted a script from her lap and flipped through it. "I only started learning to read three years ago, but I think I can handle this. I'm a better reader than I should be, if that makes sense. Ever since I've become linked with Alyssa, I sometimes know things I've never learned in this lifetime. That photograph, for example," she said as she pointed across the room. "The Great Stone Face, Buster Keaton. Alyssa watched a movie with him in it during a history class in high school."

"Amazing... Knowing things you've never learned."

"Every time we connect, I get a little smarter. Can't say it hasn't changed me. I don't feel like I'm from 1693 anymore."

"You don't exactly act like you're from 1693 either."

"No?"

"Nope. I remember my grandmother... overly conservative and very uptight. You come even before her day. So, does Alyssa pop in often?"

"Yes. Most of the time I think she gets bored and goes back to her own life, especially if I don't ask her to do anything."

"Bored?"

"Well, sometimes she visits when I'm eating, sleeping, staring at a stage... not very exciting material for her book." Katrine started to shift forward on the couch, ready to stand up. "I've got to go talk to Ashleigh."

"That might be a good idea. She's a bit put off by being called a slave."

A guilty look spread across Katrine's face. "I really blew it."

The Link – Seven Days of Cyan

"Katrine, you'll find that Cyan means different things to different people. Your situation is understandably bad, but it's not that way for everybody here. Have you seen Agnes lately?"

"No, not since we arrived."

"She is the most cheerful woman that's ever hit Cyan. Turns out her son was a real hardship. Twenty four years old and still demanding that she do his cooking and cleaning. It stressed her out every day she had to take care of him. He was thankless, rude, abusive... a real loser. She told us this morning she probably wouldn't go back if she could. And Ashleigh – both of her parents died when she was an infant. She ended up hopping from foster home to foster home before Zor brought her here. He saved her from death on a hospital bed after childbirth. She was bleeding uncontrollably and they couldn't do a blessed thing to save her. She was just a teenager. Now she couldn't be happier being forced to live in the same house with Jacques. (Don't tell her I told you.)

"As for myself, I miss my family like hell; but I realize that I can't presently change my situation, so I just need to make the most of it. Does it really matter if I play a role in a play for a hundred Canadians or for Zor? Both will result in food on the table and a roof over my head. Face it, the people here are first class, and I truly love what I'm doing. You can't say that much for the millions of people working jobs they hate to make barely enough income to feed themselves, let alone their families."

Katrine stood up and slowly walked toward the door with Robert. Robert opened the door and leaned against it as Katrine began to leave. Before she stepped out into the sunshine, however, she found herself stopped in the doorway, needing to tell Robert one more thing.

"I met Adrian today."

Robert looked worried. "How did it go?"

"I don't think we're very fond of each other."

"Well, be careful. Don't get caught alone with her. If she tries anything, she'll probably try to throw you out to the guards after curfew like the others."

Katrine gave him a weak smile, then walked out shaking her head. She had enough of the guards to last a lifetime.

Chapter 14
The Date before Finals (Thursday)

"I can't believe I'm thirty minutes late! He probably took off," Alyssa said looking at her watch as she and Sami approached the entrance to the Crossroads Snack Bar.

"Just tell him the truth: practice went over. I want the entire scoop afterwards. I'll be sitting on one of the couches in the corner doing history. Come see me."

They entered the snack bar and stopped at the door, searching for John. Alyssa spotted him at a round table with two drinks sitting in front of him. She gave a small groan when she noticed the look of disappointment on his face, then hurried over to the table as Sami departed to the corner of the room.

"I am *so* sorry, John. You must think I'm the rudest woman who's ever asked you for a drink."

A smile of relief swept across his face. He quickly stood up and pulled out a chair for Alyssa. "I was worried you weren't going to show."

"Practice went overtime. The finals are tomorrow morning and coach is stressed, so we ended up super-analyzing a video of yesterday's game. Anyway, thanks for buying the drinks."

John sat down. "Got you a regular cola. Is that okay?"

"Yes, fine." Alyssa took a drink and sat back in her chair. The awkward silence that Alyssa always hated on 'dates' took control for the first few seconds.

"So, you're a student here, right?" she asked.

"Yes. I'm a second year psychology major. And you?"

"English. Also second year." Another awkward pause. Alyssa took a second drink to try to look relaxed. She noticed how calm John

The Link – Seven Days of Cyan

looked, even during the uncomfortable pauses. She tried desperately of think of something to say. "I knew a psychology major once."

"Yeah?"

"Really screwed up in the head."

"Most psychology majors are," he laughed. "That's why they're in psychology."

"And why are *you* in psychology?"

"To study the psychology majors."

Alyssa laughed. "Do you ever get to visit mental hospitals?"

"No, just book work. I've got to get my education before I meet the truly disturbed. Wouldn't want to jump to any false diagnoses."

"What's there to diagnose? For most of them it was because their parents were screw-ups, so now they're screw-ups... they're overly angry, they feel inferior, and they can't stop taking it out on others."

John leaned back in his chair and smiled. "Is that what you believe?"

Alyssa quickly sipped her drink to give her time to think of her answer. She had just made a statement that probably made her look ignorant and she needed a good response.

"Well," she said as she wiped her mouth with a napkin, "I believe that if a person isn't loved or taught discipline when growing up, they won't know how to show love or discipline when they're grown." She slowly nodded, believing she didn't sound *too* far-fetched and uneducated. "They become social misfits, and then the problems just worsen. They're miserable and they often take it out on society."

"But so many people show tremendous resiliency when they grow up in a dysfunctional environment. I believe most of the time they become better people, not worse."

"If better means they can tolerate more, then I suppose you're right."

"No. I mean better as in becoming a beneficial member of society."

"I'm not sure I hear about those cases often. It'd be refreshing to hear one," Alyssa said with her eyebrows raised.

John looked thoughtful. "I'm not sure I can think of one at the moment."

Alyssa smiled. "You've just proven me right then."

"Fine," John said as he took a drink and shifted his chair closer to the table. "Here's one for you. Read it in a book. Two young boys, ages nine and five, lose their mother to cancer. She refused to get medical help because their family was too poor to pay for treatment.

She told her boys that God would save her if it were meant to be. God didn't save her, to the boys' surprise, and she died, leaving them with a drunk father who never wanted to have anything to do with them, and he always let them know it."

Alyssa thought she detected a hint of anger in his voice.

"Coincidentally, the nine-year-old was very talented for his age when it came to the game of soccer. But when the mother died, he was no longer allowed to play. He and his brother would have to report to their room every day immediately after school. Everything they loved was taken away from them. If the older brother dared to stay after school to kick the soccer ball with the school team, his father would beat him for his tardiness. The boy's frustration grew as he watched his peers excel and succeed through the years, while he did nothing but report to his room to do homework and read comic books.

"When the oldest brother was fifteen, the last thing he loved was taken away from him: his brother. There was an argument and the oldest boy dared to stand up for himself... ended up hitting his father, which landed him rather quickly in military school.

"After a year of blindly following orders, he ran away from school and met a woman. They fell in love and she changed his life. The woman had... resources."

"Resources?"

John took a drink as he searched for the right words. "Influence. Powerful friends. With her help, he began a program that helped others in similar situations as his own."

"Children with Drunk Fathers Anonymous?"

"No, it was more than that. He helped gifted and talented individuals whose creativity or ability to improve oneself was being stifled by family members or friends."

Alyssa's eyes narrowed. "How did he do that?"

"He did whatever was necessary to help these individuals reach their potential."

Alyssa smirked, "You're answering like a politician, John. Can you be more specific about what he did?"

"Removal from the environment that hindered their progress."

Alyssa gave a small laugh. "This sounds like the theme to a book I'm writing. Hope I didn't read what you read and am merely regurgitating old ideas." Alyssa nodded thoughtfully. "So what happens to the younger brother?"

"His older brother helped him. Removed him from his dysfunctional environment."

Alyssa leaned back in her chair. "Something just doesn't sit right with your story, but I can't quite pinpoint it. The program he started... It's like CPS run amuck, screwed up at a whole different level. Taking children away from their families so they can play soccer better." She sipped her drink as she stared at him, entranced by his dark green eyes. "This woman who helped him... I bet he didn't really love her."

"No?"

"No. She was merely the means to an end. She was used."

John sat silent and thoughtful, and then replied, "Just because she helped him get out of his situation doesn't mean he didn't love her for other reasons as well."

"Well, you tell me. How long does their relationship last?"

"The book didn't say."

"I bet another girl comes along, one that royally screws up his life. Makes him lose everything. True love is messy, you know. Not all neat and convenient, like you're describing."

John smiled. "And how much do you know about true love?"

Alyssa looked down at the table with a guilty smile. "I've just read my share of romance novels."

"Is that appropriate reading material for an English major?"

Alyssa laughed. "Got to read it all."

"So let's talk about *your* interests. What kind of classes are you taking?"

"Lots of English classes, of course. I guess my favorite right now is Creative Writing. Like I said before, I've been working on a manuscript. Hope to get it published someday."

"What's it about?"

"Witch-warlock stuff. I really don't want to say more until I can get the whole story down on paper. At first, I had a lot of trouble making it flow. I was writing the stories in chunks, and I wasn't exactly sure what belonged in between the 'chunks' until recently, but now it's all tying together quite nicely. When it's finished, I'll let you see it."

John looked very interested. "So now it flows?"

"Yes. What helped is that I got to know my main character better. I talk to her in my head and I pretend she talks back."

Alyssa noticed John's mood suddenly change. "You have a dialogue with her?"

"Don't commit me to a loony bin, John. I'm sure a lot of authors talk to that little voice in their head when they're writing."

John forced a smile. "Of course." He looked at his watch. "I'm sorry, Alyssa, I've got to run."

"Oh?"

"I promised a friend I would pick him up. His car broke down today and I'm his only ride."

"Oh, of course," Alyssa replied with a nervous smile as they both stood up.

"Do me a favor, Alyssa."

"What?"

"Don't talk to that voice in your head. It's probably not healthy, from a psychological standpoint."

John gave Alyssa a quick kiss on the forehead and rushed out the door, leaving Alyssa with a feeling of dread. She walked over to Sami's couch and plopped down beside her with a disparaged look on her face.

"Oh, no. What happened?" asked Sami as she looked up from her history book.

"He thinks I'm crazy."

Chapter 15
The Blue Box (Thursday)

Katrine stepped out of the shower and wrapped herself in a towel. Her body tingled as the water dripped downward across her skin onto the floor. She felt renewed, refreshed... completely invigorated. She had no cuts, sores, scrapes, or bruises; Alyssa was still alive after Zor's third visit; and she had just finished a very good soccer session. Now she was looking forward to a pleasant dinner with her friends. She took a deep breath and her heart gave an unexpected flutter when her thoughts drifted toward seeing Robert.

She opened the bathroom door and stepped into her room to see Zor in front of her open bedroom door, wearing a tuxedo, staring at her. She froze when she noticed him and could only stare back in silence, nervously wondering what he was going to do. Something deep inside Katrine stirred as he watched her stand and drip water onto the floor, and she was uncertain if she would turn him away if he tried something. She hated herself for what she felt as he stared at her; she was weak and despicable, and she hoped it was because of the crush Alyssa had on the man. It was affecting her common sense. Or maybe she was under some sort of spell, completely unable to control her own emotions. It had to be a spell. The last time she saw him, he was throwing her sword down into the guard's pit.

"We're going to dinner and the opera tonight," Zor finally said. "I have a dress picked out for you already." He motioned toward the bed.

Katrine looked on the bed to see a long, slender, sparkling blue dress. The bodice had spaghetti straps. Any spell she might have been under was broken in an instant.

"I'm not wearing it."

"Yes, you are."

"Then put a jacket with it. I'm not parading your ridiculous name tag around for everyone to see." Katrine knew she was making him angry, but she was no longer afraid of him. Nothing he could do would be worse than the guard's pit, and her interpretation of the doctor's comments was that Zor was guilt-ridden for allowing the rematch.

"I'm not changing the dress, Katrine. You will wear what I tell you to wear."

"Then I'm not going to dinner."

"Then you'll wear that towel for the rest of your stay!"

Zor pointed to the armoire. Its doors slammed shut and Katrine could hear a clicking sound as it locked. Katrine stared defiantly at him as she heard the main door to the house open and close. James walked up behind Zor.

"Is there a problem?" James asked curiously when he noticed the standoff.

"No," Zor replied. "Katrine was just showing me what she was going to wear to tonight's performance."

James looked down at the dress. "Is she going with you?"

"Yes. Meet me in the cafeteria in ten minutes, Katrine."

As Zor closed the door, James raised his voice, "May I have a word with you, big brother?"

Although Katrine felt like screaming and throwing something, her curiosity outweighed her anger. She hurried over to the door and placed her ear against the wood.

"A date? Do you know what will happen if Adrian finds out?"

"First of all, Adrian doesn't need to find out. Secondly, it's not a date. It's more of a fact-finding mission."

"How so?"

"Alyssa told me today that they can communicate with each other. A dialogue."

There was silence. "Has a link ever been known to do that?"

"They're never alive long enough to grow such a strong connection."

"If she becomes too powerful, Adrian may be the least of our worries. You need to..."

"I don't need to be told what to do, James. Everything is under control."

There was a pause. "Sure it is." James started walking towards his room. "I guess I'll go ahead and eat, since I now know I'm dining alone tonight."

"Meet me in the opera box after the show. I may need your help."

The Link – Seven Days of Cyan

Katrine could hear James mumbling as he walked down his hall and slammed his bedroom door. She turned to her bed and stared at the dress.

"Alyssa," she whispered. "I need your help."

* * *

Katrine walked in the cafeteria door. Everyone inside wore tuxedos and long evening gowns for the opera afterwards. Katrine carefully adjusted the corsage of orchids attached between the strap and bodice so that it completely covered Zor's name.

Zor sat at an empty table near the back of the cafeteria. As she walked to the table, she passed by Ashleigh, Robert and Jacques. Robert looked at her with a gleam in his eyes and was about to stand up and pull a chair out for her when Katrine motioned for him to stay seated. He looked confused as she walked by him.

"Can't," Katrine whispered to him. She walked up to Zor's table and stood.

"Nice corsage, Katrine."

"I'm leaving if you take it off."

Zor sighed and waved his hand at her chair. It slid out from under the table and pointed in her direction.

"Always a gentleman," Katrine remarked as she sat down.

"I'll put the extra effort into chivalry when you put a little extra effort into civility."

"After that little rematch you set up, I'm not sure I want to put any effort into civility."

Katrine leaned back in her chair, crossed her arms, and gazed at the painting on the wall behind Zor until a waiter came to their table and placed a silver tray in front of them.

"Roast duck with sautéed vegetables," the waiter said as he poured wine. After the waiter left, Zor raised his wineglass in the air.

"A toast to the quiet life."

Katrine sneered at his toast, then raised her own glass. "Which is certainly not to be found here."

"You have no idea what it's like for a warlock outside of Cyan, but here it's just fine food, good weather, nice scenery, great entertainment... the quiet life."

Katrine took a sip of wine and considered drinking enough to get drunk. She swirled her glass and watched the wine sway from side to side.

"Woester can make a splendid wine," Zor remarked. "He puts it together and I age it in just ten minutes. I hide it in one year and pick it up in another. Only rarely does someone discover it before I pick it up."

Katrine put the glass down and sighed. "What's the point of all this? Do you think that just because you and I share something in common that I feel some sort of connection with you? It'll take more than a couple of abusive drunk fathers to get me interested."

Zor leaned back in his chair with worry in his face. "What I told Alyssa was just a story out of a book."

"No, it wasn't," she curtly remarked.

Again Zor hesitated, seemingly uncomfortable. "What else can you and Alyssa do?"

"What do you mean?"

"You talk to each other. What else is different from when you first noticed you were linked?"

"Nothing."

"All I have to do is look into your eyes."

Katrine looked at him apprehensively, and then dropped her gaze to the tabletop, uncertain how much to tell him.

"I want to know how this corsage can so conveniently pop up when you need it. *Convenient* is the key word in the question, if you hadn't noticed."

"It seems you already know of what we're capable."

"I want to hear it from you."

She looked up at him. "I can contact her. There, now you've heard it."

There was a pause. "What else?"

She let out a bothered sigh. "Aside from the fact that I can read college level material; recognize every slang and cuss word in the late twentieth century; do integrals and derivatives (whatever *they're* for); explain the structure of DNA and proteins... absolutely nothing. Oh, and I could probably drive a stick-shift, given the opportunity."

Zor looked at her, seemingly fascinated. "You think you can drive a stick-shift?"

"I know just about *everything* she knows. And in the instant we connect, I can tell you everything she's been doing since we last were linked. The same goes for her."

"Do you feel the same feelings? Like the same things?"

"We certainly have different taste in men."

Zor smiled. "She can't stop thinking about me, can she? Leaving so abruptly today actually had its benefits."

Katrine was furious, but did her best to sit still in her chair and keep her voice low. "Can't wait to get her alone, can you?"

Zor didn't answer. He surveyed the food and started cutting the duck. Katrine tried to calm herself down as Zor fixed the plates.

Alyssa was running out of time and acting hostile towards him was not going to help her any.

"What can I do to convince you not to go through with it?" she asked quietly. He looked up at her with a mouth full of duck and chewed, with no intention of answering. "I've told you already I'm no threat to you or Cyan," she continued. "I'm not going to try to escape. I won't try to destroy your utopia."

Zor swallowed. "That's very kind of you." He took another bite.

Katrine sat back in her chair and watched him eat. He seemed extremely pleased. She grabbed her wineglass and downed what she had left, and then slammed the wineglass down on the table. Zor looked up from his plate, grabbed the wine bottle, filled her glass again, then looked back down at his plate and returned to eating his food like a hungry coyote at a garbage can.

Katrine picked up her wineglass and stared as the wine swirled around the sides. *Why the hell not?* She downed her second glass... then a third... then a fourth... then she lost count. The room wouldn't sit still, so Katrine had to put her head down on the table in front of her to steady herself.

"Your hair is getting in your food. You should eat some of it. It'll help you sober up enough so I won't have to carry you to the auditorium."

"Just give me another magic muffin to sober up."

Zor quietly chuckled. "I'm not sure I have time to make one. They're actually quite complex."

Katrine looked up at him. "Well at least you had the good sense to make one for me after you landed me in the hospital." Katrine's heart fluttered nervously. The alcohol was making her say stupid things. She bit her lip, wondering if Zor was getting angry with her for her candor; but instead, he looked thoughtful. He stared into Katrine's eyes as he sipped his wine.

Katrine put her head down again on the table, believing it would be in her best interest to change the subject. "So how come you don't play soccer anymore?" she asked with her head still down. He was silent. She looked up at him and tried to steady her head.

"If my mother had lived, I would have kept playing and excelling. By the time I had the opportunity to play again, the gift was gone. I won't play if I'm not the best, so I guess I'll never play again."

Katrine put her head down on the table again. "You were just out of practice. If you truly were talented, then it would have come back quickly." She paused. Before she could stop herself, she boldly said, "You're what I call a quitter." He was quiet, so she looked up again to see if he was about to zap her with a lightening bolt. Instead, he was staring at the table with a solemn expression. "Why don't you just hocus pocus yourself and become the player you've always dreamed of becoming?"

"It wouldn't mean anything."

Katrine put her head back down on the table a fourth time. Throwing caution to the wind, she mumbled, "A quitter with integrity." Despite the silence on the other end of the table, she decided she was finished lifting her head; it was making her too dizzy.

"I suppose that's what Alyssa would think as well," Zor said with a distant voice.

"Yes. I suppose," Katrine said as she began to drool on the table. She quickly slurped it back in her mouth once she realized what was happening.

* * *

Tears rolled down Katrine's cheeks as she watched Rudolpho hold Mimi's dying body and cry out with such sorrow, it sent shivers up her spine. "Mimi! Mimi!" he cried. The anguish in his voice was amplified as it echoed throughout the auditorium.

Katrine felt something on her knee and looked down to see that Zor had placed a white handkerchief in her lap. She quickly turned away as she snapped back to reality. She did not want him to see her cry, so she concentrated intently at the crimson satin fringe surrounding their booth, trying to indiscreetly wipe her eyes dry with the back of her hand and ignore the sad song of the orchestra.

When the opera ended, the audience sat speechless, and then gave the singers a standing ovation. As the chandeliers descended from the ceiling and turned on, the audience and performers filed out of the auditorium. Soon only the stagehands were left cleaning the theater. As the five-minute warning bell sounded, the stage manager clapped loudly and told everyone to go home. They would finish cleaning tomorrow.

Katrine began to squirm in her chair as the door to the opera booth opened and James walked in.

"It was certainly refreshing sitting with the little people," James complained. "The gardener next to me kept asking me to translate." James walked to the front of the booth and leaned against the edge. "So now that we're all here, what are we doing?"

Zor stood up and faced Katrine. "Contact Alyssa."

"She can do that?" James asked with surprise.

They both stared at her in anticipation, making Katrine fidget and feel trapped. She closed her eyes, and then opened them with a look of trepidation.

"What's wrong?" asked Zor.

"You have to wait about five minutes."

"Why?"

"She wants to see if the captain can save the Enterprise."

Zor plopped down in his seat and sighed.

"Which captain?" asked James with a smile. "I liked the bald one the best."

Katrine ignored him and the three sat in silence until Alyssa was contacted again.

"She's here now," Katrine said, breaking the silence.

"Tell her to turn off the TV," Zor said as he stood back up. "She's got another chapter to write, titled 'The Blue Box'.

The lights of the auditorium dimmed and Katrine noticed a large blue box composed entirely of light appear on the stage. It appeared to be the same blue light that had stopped her from getting Paul out of Cyan.

"The game is simple, Katrine," said Zor. "Make the box disappear. When and if you can, I'll give you another more difficult box to vanish. Notice the size of the box. It's large enough for a redheaded thespian to fit inside and suffocate." Katrine looked at him with a sick feeling in her stomach. "Yes, I've seen the way you two look at each other. If I think you're not trying your hardest, James will fetch him and our boring game will get a lot more interesting. Then I'll know for certain that you're trying your hardest. Understand?"

"Yes," Katrine weakly replied.

"Then go ahead," Zor said as he turned and looked out to the stage. The box was already gone. "A bit too simple, I guess," Zor said with a baffled look on his face.

Another box appeared whose blue light shined brighter than the first. Katrine looked at it, and it disappeared. When the fifth box disappeared as fast as the first, a worried look spread across both Zor's and James' face.

Zor turned to his brother. "I'm going down to the stage to lessen the distance between myself and the box. You run the show from up here." James gave Zor a nod.

Zor appeared on the stage below. Katrine stared at Zor and tried to make him disappear, but it didn't work. She watched intently as Zor raised his hand, reached forward and created another blue box.

"Okay, try that one," said James.

Katrine looked at it. She considered squinting her eyes in deep concentration and then just making the box fade, but the fear of Robert being placed inside was too great. She made the box disappear as quickly as the first. James cussed.

Zor paced and scratched his head, then mumbled something to himself. A small black book appeared in his hands.

"Imperius Grumley's *Book of Unmemorizable Spells*," James said in awe. He turned to Katrine and proudly stated, "My brother is the only warlock besides Imperius himself who knows how to summon that book. Very strong stuff inside. Spirit magic."

Zor flipped through the pages slowly as he walked. Finally, he stopped, looked center stage and mumbled words again. The box appeared. Katrine stared at the box and wished it gone, but it remained. She concentrated harder and it started to fade. Finally, it disappeared completely.

"Seems Imperius' spirit world is getting a surprise!" Zor yelled up to James. James shook his head in disbelief and cussed once more.

Zor continued to flip through the pages of the black book while Katrine took a deep breath and sat back in her chair, uncomfortable with what was happening. Again there was mumbling down on the stage, but Katrine stared at the chandelier instead of the stage.

"Katrine," said James. "The box is waiting."

"Alyssa's gone," she lied.

"Shall I get Zor up here to verify that?"

Katrine leaned her head sideways in her hand and shook her head. "No, I'll get her back," Katrine said in a defeated voice. She leaned forward in her chair and stared at the new box, trying to make it disappear, but it remained. She concentrated harder to at least try to make it fade, but still nothing happened.

"Shall I fetch Robert?" James asked Katrine.

Panic struck. "I'm trying my hardest! I swear!" She looked down at the box again and begged Alyssa to make it disappear, but it only faded a little, and then came back full strength.

"You're putting on a show for us, Katrine. I'm getting Robert," James said as he headed for the door. Katrine jumped out of her chair and flew between James and the door.

"I'm trying the best I can! You've got to understand that," she angrily protested.

Zor appeared in the booth. "We'll give her one more chance, James. Then you may fetch the redhead."

Katrine walked away from the door to the front of the booth, eyeing James mistrustingly the entire way. She peered down at the box again and wished it would disappear with all her might, but again it just grew dimmer for a second or two before returning to its original state.

The Link – Seven Days of Cyan

"I'm glad to see there's a limit to your powers. I was getting worried," Zor said as he made his way out of the booth. "Let's get back to the house."

"You don't want me to get Robert?" James asked.

"No, she was trying her hardest."

"Are you sure?"

"Were you trying your hardest, Katrine?"

"Yes," Katrine replied as earnestly as she could.

"See," said Zor to James with raised eyebrows as he walked out of the booth. Katrine closed her eyes and took a deep breath. She felt dizzy, uncertain whether it was caused from the stress or the alcohol still in her system. She stumbled to a chair, sat down, and closed her eyes.

She had almost dropped to sleep when she heard James ask, 'Why do *I* have to carry her?'

Chapter 16
Guards vs. Musicians (Friday)

"Whoa!"

Robert jumped up from his chair as water ran off the breakfast table into his lap. It was the second glass of water Ashleigh had spilled that morning.

"I'm so sorry, Robert!" Ashleigh yelled as she grabbed her napkin and tried to stop the rest of the water from rolling off the table. Katrine raised her head from her hand to watch the commotion. She had a splitting headache from drinking too much the night before.

"Ashleigh, you've got to settle down," said Jacques as he gave Robert his dry napkin. "All you got last time was a bruise. That's all you ever get. I was the one that couldn't slide my bow across the strings for a week."

"Can't you talk to her, Katrine, and make sure she's going to be there?" asked Ashleigh in frustration. "I'm going to have a nervous breakdown!"

"The game is during her economics class... on a Friday. Believe me, she'll be at the game." Katrine took a drink of her coffee and shook her head. "I don't know how much I can get away with if Zor and James are there."

"We need to keep them away somehow," said Robert excitedly as he sat back down in his chair. "Any ideas?" He looked around the table as they all sat in silence, thinking.

"What can we possibly do that he can't fix in an instant with the wave of his hand?" Jacques asked, disheartened. "Besides, we don't need to risk punishment."

"What if you make Zor and James fall asleep!?" Ashleigh suggested. "You did it to the guards. They may never suspect!"

The Link – Seven Days of Cyan

"Katrine will get in trouble," stated Jacques. "Let's just play the guards like we always do."

Ashleigh sat back in her chair with anxiety written all over her face.

"I agree with Jacques," Robert added. "Sorry, Ashleigh."

Katrine took another drink of coffee. She was finally waking up and her head was starting to clear. She stared down at her coffee, and then had an idea.

* * *

Katrine walked down the brick pathway leading from the Main House with a smile on her face. She saw Robert waiting for her at the edge of the courtyard, pacing nervously. When he saw Katrine, he stopped and smiled.

"The luncheon worked?" he asked. Katrine nodded in response. "I don't believe it!"

"They stayed up late last night playing chess," Katrine explained. "I got up for a drink of water around two thirty and they were still up playing."

"We'll have to send Agnes some flowers for the herbal tea and pasta. She really knows her stuff. Did they suspect anything?"

"Playing your spacey music after lunch had them a bit curious, but I think they reasoned I was being extra nice to save Alyssa. I hid the space heater in my room, cranked it up full blast, and cracked my bedroom door. It probably helped a little. I don't know how much time we have, though, so let's hurry."

As they began to walk towards the soccer fields, Robert took a deep breath and said with sigh, "This is what gives life true meaning."

Katrine looked at him, feeling quite perplexed by his statement. "A guard game?"

"It's the classic good versus evil fight. Take for example, musicians versus artists. Hip hooray for the winner, but it's truly not that exciting. Now, winning a guard game is another story! It's what makes life exciting... conquering evil."

Katrine smiled and gave a little laugh. As they approached the fields, Katrine was mildly surprised that only a small crowd had gathered to watch. Robert explained that nobody liked to attend the guard games because the true spirit of the game was never honored.

On the far side of the bleachers, Katrine saw the guard team sitting on a bench. They were dressed in red and black uniforms with a devil on the back and front left shoulder of their shirt where the number was displayed. On the bench in front of Katrine sat the musicians. They had light blue uniforms with their numbers displayed over a large picture of a violin on the backside and a harp on the front shoulder. Each team stood up and walked out onto the field for a coin toss as Katrine and Robert made their way up the bleachers behind the musician's bench.

"Check out the monster they have for a goalie," remarked Robert, pointing toward the far goal.

Katrine looked over and couldn't stop the grin that slowly spread across her face. It was Guard Eleven... number eleven on the team. He still wore a bandage over his broken nose.

Robert and Katrine sat down as the referee walked onto the field between the two teams with the ball. Katrine summoned Alyssa, and Alyssa arrived in an instant. Alyssa's professor had been discussing the stock market trends in the early 1920's with the most monotone voice he could muster, and it usually sent Alyssa whirling helplessly into daydream mode.

"She's here," Katrine whispered to Robert.

Jacques and Ashleigh had been nervously glancing back and forth between the referee and the stands ever since the referee walked onto the field. Robert smiled and gave them a thumbs-up signal.

To everyone's surprise, once the ball rolled into motion, Jacques charged after Guard Thirteen to fight for possession of the ball. Guard Thirteen suddenly froze, unable to move his feet, completely glued to the ground. Jacques kicked the ball away, maneuvered around him, and dribbled towards the goal as the other musicians stared in disbelief. Each time a guard neared Jacques, the guard froze into position.

After Jacques kicked the ball at the goal, the ball picked up incredible speed in midair and crashed squarely into the goalie, Guard Eleven. Guard Eleven was thrown off his feet and thrust against the net by the ball, then lay on the ground with a stunned expression plastered on his face. The guard team, now able to move again, rushed over to him.

"Are you okay?" they all asked. Guard Eleven placed his hand over his stomach, struggled to his feet, and angrily wiped the grass from his uniform as the few people in the stands went ecstatic.

"What kind of playing was that?" he yelled at his team. "Are you all a bunch of sissies?"

Robert turned to Katrine and remarked, "That was kind of boring. You need to get a bit more creative."

"Like what?"

Robert thought for a moment. "How about severe stomach cramps?"

"That doesn't sound much better, but we'll give it a try for one play since I don't have any better ideas."

A guard dribbled towards the goal. As he was about to pass Ashleigh, he stopped and keeled over, clenching his abdomen. The ball rolled to Ashleigh's feet. She looked at the ball nervously before she passed it to another musician. Another guard nearby fell to the ground in pain. As the musicians passed the ball up the field, the guards fell one by one. Finally, Jacques acquired the ball again and shot. The ball picked up speed in mid-air and plowed down Guard Eleven just as before. Score: 2-0. Guard Eleven remained rolling back and forth on the ground in pain, trying to catch his breath. Only one team member went over to him to help him up, but he got punched.

"You're right," remarked Robert with disappointment in his voice. "That was just as boring as the first goal." He rested his chin in his hand, deep in thought. "Oh, you'll like this one. It's crude," Robert said with a smile. "Put a strong laxative in their water."

Katrine laughed. "Show no mercy in the fight against evil, eh?" She tapped her feet against the bleachers as she thought about the possibilities... as she thought about the guards jeering and laughing at her from the periphery of the pit. "But the guards are in desperate need of being humiliated, aren't they? I'll do it, but I'll save that play for a little later, out of respect for the musicians."

The crowd was growing at a phenomenal rate. Katrine looked down the road toward the courtyard, but there was still no sign of the brothers.

"Extreme tunnel vision, Robert." The spectators burst out laughing at the guards' jerking head movements, their eyes darting around the field like chickens trying to find the ball. They ran into each other and fell down; they kicked at the ball and completely missed it; they tripped over their own feet. It looked like an episode of the Stooges.

The musicians' forward kicked the ball toward the goal, but it flew too high. Katrine quickly changed its direction and speed, causing it to pounce directly down on Guard Eleven's head and ricochet back up into the top of the goal's net. Score: 3-0. The guards called a time-out when Guard Eleven stayed sitting on the ground holding his neck and head. This time, no one tried to help him up.

The musicians quickly gathered, and Katrine could tell that Jacques and Ashleigh had informed the team what was happening because their team kept peering up at her from their huddle. A beast-like roar sounded across the field and everyone turned to see Guard Eleven back on his feet, staring at Katrine.

"I think he knows about you, Katrine," Robert whispered in her ear. "You might want to lighten up on the goalie a bit."

"He'll get over it," replied Katrine, determined to throw her punches while she could. Katrine watched the rest of the guards take a drink of water. One guard broke free from the huddle and headed down the road towards the Main House. Laxatives take a little time, Katrine thought as she turned her attention back to the rest of the guards. As they drank, she quickly changed their water into a tasteless, clear solution of full-strength laxative.

Time out was over. As the guards headed back onto the field, Katrine watched the guard that was walking toward the Main House. With a wish, his shoestrings untied, then wrapped tightly around his ankles so that the guard fell to the ground. He tried to kick his feet apart, but they were bound too tightly. Katrine turned back to the field. "It's your turn, Robert. What do we do?"

"Have a guard score on his own team."

"Good one."

Guard Fourteen had possession of the ball. The ball started rolling around his feet. He tried to maintain control of the ball as he turned in circles several times. Disoriented and confused, he set out toward Guard Eleven. The team tried to stop him, but each slipped and fell to the ground before they got too close. Guard Eleven moved to the far corner of the field in anticipation of the next soccer ball bullet. Guard Fourteen shot towards the goal, but Katrine quickly changed its direction. It traveled with amazing speed to the corner of the field where it pelted Guard Eleven in the knees so hard you could hear them crack, then ricocheted back towards the goal where it made a hard ninety-degree turn into the net. The guards jumped to their feet, ran over to Guard Fourteen, and proceeded to beat him up.

"Only broke two or three laws of physics with that one," remarked Robert as he watched the fight.

Guard Eleven couldn't get back up, and no one would help him. There was a long delay as Doc Norman and one other doctor attempted to drag him off the field. He fought them furiously, too proud to accept any help. Guard Two reluctantly became the new goalie.

Katrine looked down the road towards the Main House. Zor, James, and the guard, who was now barefoot, were walking in front of the auditorium towards the field.

"Stay here, Robert," she said as she stood up and stepped down from the bleachers. Katrine walked to the opposite side of the large crowd that had gathered so that Zor couldn't see her.

The ball was in motion. Before Katrine had the opportunity to do anything, she realized there was a change in the guards' performance. The guards started moving slower, and they all appeared

The Link – Seven Days of Cyan

quite panicked. Some stopped and squirmed. Some stood straight up with their butt cheeks clenched as tight as their muscles would allow. Katrine looked to the sidelines where the doctors were treating Guard Eleven's knees. He was looking at her with a scowl on his face, and Katrine frowned when she realized he had not drunk the water along with the rest of his team. She winked at him, and his uniform turned bright pink with a white-lace trim. Barbie dolls replaced the devils on his uniform, and a large pink bow appeared on the top of his head. The doctors jumped back in surprise and stared at the guard. As Guard Eleven caught sight of his new uniform, he looked as though he was going to explode. He fell painfully to his knees and tried to crawl toward Katrine. She looked at him amusingly, and then noticed that behind him at the end of the bench was a large box full of spare uniforms and equipment for the guards' team. With a wish, the contents of the box began to glow pink as everything inside was changed to Barbie-doll attire.

She turned her attention back to the field. No one but the guards, Robert and Katrine knew what was happening to the guard team. Katrine couldn't help but to smile and give a little chuckle as Jacques easily swerved through the guards and scored the fifth goal. The new goalie made no attempt to stop it; the look of concentration on his face was not directed towards the soccer game at hand. She could hear Robert above in the stands burst out laughing over the cheers of the audience.

Katrine felt a hand grasp her arm, and she turned to see Zor's disapproving face. James was behind him with a similar expression.

She smiled timidly. "You've missed a good game so far."

"Come with me," Zor said pulling her arm. "You are officially thrown out of the game."

"Aren't you going to start the game over, Zor?" asked James.

Zor paused and looked out at the field.

"No. It's about time the guards had a little challenge. They've been getting lazy on the field."

Zor led Katrine in front of the bleachers toward the Main House. As they walked, a musician near the sideline saw them and caught Ashleigh's attention. Katrine gave Ashleigh a faint smile and a little wave goodbye as a look of worry spread across Ashleigh's face. Immediately, she raised her hands and called a time-out.

Zor sat Katrine down on the bench in the courtyard and bound her wrist to the bench's armrest with black rope. He had spoken the black rope incantation so quietly that Katrine couldn't hear it despite her efforts.

"I'll leave you out here until the game is over. It's a bit stuffy inside." He turned to leave, then stopped. "By the way, that was wonderful tea you gave us. Did Agnes give it to you?"

"I told her it was for me. Sleepless nights, you know."

Zor nodded his head and leisurely strolled away. "Beautiful day for a game."

Once alone, Katrine leaned back on the bench and watched the cherry blossoms fall. It was curious how the trees never ran out of blossoms to drop; there was always another blossom waiting for its turn to fall. She could hear a cheer come from the fields and she smiled. The musicians weren't going to stop playing.

Katrine was drifting off to sleep when she heard soft footsteps approach. She opened her eyes to see Woester strolling down the brick pathway in leather shoes, brown pants with a matching vest and beanie hat. He tipped his hat to her as he approached.

"Woester?" Katrine asked with a smile.

He nodded his head and replied:

> *"So Zor and James mentioned*
> *a link now lived in Cyan.*
> *It appears you are her?*
> *I offer my hand."*

Woester held out his hand and Katrine shook it.

"I've been wanting to talk to you for some time now. Would you mind?"

> *"To share a bench*
> *with a pretty dame-*
> *I'd be foolish to refuse,*
> *I'd be truly lame."*

Katrine chuckled. As Woester sat, he took special notice of the black rope binding her to her spot.

> *"I see that you are bound with Zor's black rope.*
> *You are not in a lot of bad trouble, I hope."*

"No more than usual, I believe." She paused, wondering why he was strolling the courtyard instead of watching the game. "Zor's not here if you need to see him. He's at the game."

The Link – Seven Days of Cyan

"It's during the games
I come here to be alone.
This garden, you see,
reminds me of home."

Woester leaned back against the bench and took a deep breath of fresh air.

"I had some of your wine last night. Literally knocked me off my feet. Very good," remarked Katrine. Woester smiled. Katrine sighed nervously. "You don't mind if I ask you a few questions, do you? I hear you're the resident expert about a great many things."

Woester shook his head and replied:

"Don't mind at all.
I'm at your beck and call."

"I overheard James and Zor yesterday. They mentioned something about links never being alive for very long. Do you know anything about links? Do you know what they might have been talking about?"

A look of concern spread across Woester's face.

"Well, I've heard that a link is a treasure
of which all can take pleasure.

But of the twelve links known through history,
none of them have survived.
They've been killed by witches and warlocks
who refused to keep them alive.

What risk they present to the powerful?
I'm not exactly sure what they fear.
But I do know a link's power is equally strong
no matter the day or the year.

It seems it is lucky Zor found you first,
for you still look very much alive.
In this magical village he's protected you
ever since you have arrived."

Katrine stared at the ground in front of her, in shock. Had Zor saved her from other warlocks and witches? Was he trying to destroy her link with Alyssa so that she'd *always* be safe from them? She may be safe from most of the witches and warlocks while in Cyan, but not safe from a crazy witch named Adrian. She shuddered as she thought of Adrian's pale skin and sunken eyes above her when she was in the hospital. Adrian was angry... angry that Katrine was in the Main House, angry that Zor wouldn't empower Adrian's brother.

A question rose in her mind as she remembered the conversation between Zor and Adrian. "Zor has the power to turn James into a warlock, doesn't he?"

"Insightful you seem, correct you are,
but James is still not a warlock thus far."

"Why hasn't he done it yet? Is he afraid of Adrian, even though he's more powerful than she is in this time period?"

Zor is not yet able to share
the gift of power with his brother.
Adrian wants the gift elsewhere,
so she won't protect her lover.

And protection he needs
from those who have power.
Many enemies he has,
Many relationships sour.

Katrine smirked, "I imagine he does have his share of enemies: Adrian's father for dating his daughter, and Grumley's supporters, for much the same reason – dating the daughter of the man who killed Imperius Grumley. Seems to me it would be in Zor's best interest to dump the witch."

"Grumley's supporters?
The name Grumley I've not heard.
Perhaps you might share a story?
My ear you have lured."

Katrine looked at him confused. "Robert told me that *you* were the one who told him about the Grumleys... at a party after the actors defeated the musicians."

A name like Grumley
would be hard to forget.
Although I am old,
I'm not senile, yet.

Katrine sat silent, wondering if Robert had made up the story or if he just remembered something wrong. A loud cheer and then a gunshot echoing from the fields suddenly interrupted her thoughts. Several streaks of blue light streaked across the invisible ceiling of Cyan. She could hear screaming and shouting in the distance. She leaned over to try to see what was happening down the road, but too many trees blocked the way.

"Trouble's a brew.
I must bid you adieu."

"Thanks for the conversation, Woester. I look forward to your next wine."

After Woester departed, Katrine listened to the fighting sounds down the road. For the first time, she looked at the black rope and wished it wasn't there. It tightened around her wrist, so she quickly looked away and thought no more of it. She would have to wait until Zor came to release her.

As the sounds finally began to die down, she saw Zor and James heading towards the courtyard. James was furious and stomped past her with a scowl on his face. Zor, on the other hand, couldn't appear more delighted.

"I haven't been to a good old fashioned soccer riot since my last visit to England!" he said to Katrine before leaning over the black rope and releasing her.

"I heard a gunshot," Katrine said as she rubbed her wrist.

"One of the guards got carried away and tried to shoot the referee. I swerved the bullet upward in the nick of time. He didn't deserve to get shot. He's a good ref."

"Did you cancel the game?"

"It'll count. Musicians 7-1. A clarinet player scored just before the guards called a team bathroom break. They were running a bit too slow." Zor smiled. "Some of them wanted to change clothes, but their spare uniforms had mysteriously turned pink."

"*Wow.* I wonder how that happened."

"Indeed. The referee disqualified them because they didn't have matching uniforms. A tuba player shot the last goal, instigating the riot." Zor looked at the Main House. "I think I'll avoid James for now. Give him time to cool off. There's ice cream in the cafeteria to celebrate the guard's first defeat, if you're interested."

Zor leisurely walked to the cafeteria as Katrine hurried towards the fields. No guards were left on the grounds, for they had all retreated to their house. Katrine found Jacques and Robert on each side of Ashleigh, supporting her as she hopped off the field. Ashleigh had one foot lifted off the ground, yet she was beaming.

"Is your ankle broken?" Katrine asked with a worried look on her face as she approached.

"It might be," she replied. A huge grin spread across her face. "I kicked the guard pretty hard." Katrine smiled back in disbelief.

"How about you?" asked Robert. "Is Zor angry with you?"

"No. He actually seems quite thrilled over the whole scene."

"Good," Robert replied. "Would you mind picking up some ice cream and bringing it over to the hospital? Since that's where everyone in Cyan is meeting anyhow, we decided to have the party there. Oh, and they're postponing dress rehearsal tomorrow *three hours* so we can all sleep in, just in case the house party lasts a little too long, as it usually does. Performance is still at six."

Katrine stood at the edge of the field stunned as she watched her friends hobble away to the hospital. She had completely forgotten about the play.

Chapter 17
The Final (Friday night)

The five-minute warning bell sounded. Katrine walked along the brick pathway towards the Main House with the screenplay in her hand when she heard yelling. Through the window she could see James and Zor arguing in the sitting room, so she decided to go in the door opposite Zor's bedroom. The yelling stopped as soon as she opened the door and stepped inside. She quickly and quietly slipped into her bedroom and closed the door behind her, then sat down against her door like she had so many times before to listen. It didn't take long for them to start arguing again.

"You have to do it tonight, Zor. When Adrian comes tomorrow to watch that play and Katrine is still in this house without a bruise on her body, she'll take everything we have away. She'll take your powers away," James warned.

"She's not going to do anything," Zor reassured James. "We've been together too long for her to make a move like that."

"You're a fool. You saw how she acted with those past three girls. There wasn't even any reason to believe you were unfaithful. Why don't you think she'll go even more ballistic when it *is* the real thing?"

"I keep telling you that there's nothing like that going on."

"I'm not stupid!" James yelled. "You bring her to Dragon Hill to save her mother, you make sure she finds out the truth about Paul... eliminating the competition, are you? And what about that punishment? You punished the guard more than you did Katrine! Triple patrols for the next month? What's that all about?"

"He went overboard. It was supposed to be a fencing rematch... nothing more. When he knocked the sword out of her hand, that should have been the end. Everything that happened after that was unauthorized. He put me in a difficult position."

"A difficult position? She tried to escape Cyan after she made a promise! She tried to rescue that slime ball! I'm *glad* Adrian was spying on you from the guards' house. Katrine would have received no consequences whatsoever for her actions if she hadn't..."

"Are you finished?"

"No! Don't like talking about the fight? Okay, let's talk about the dinner... the opera... What's with that dress? You let her practically drug us... you let her get away with humiliating the guards! Didn't you notice during the riot that even the interior designers were standing up to the guards? You're asking for a complete breakdown of the system!"

"Katrine is not a threat to Cyan," Zor retaliated. "In fact it's her only home..."

"Now *there's* an interesting topic as well! Why haven't you moved her to the Thespian House since she's *no longer a threat to Cyan?*"

"I'm not quite sure she really belongs in the Thespian House."

"You told Adrian she was going to the Thespian House."

"Well, I'm not sure I want her there anymore."

There was a pause. "Now who's acting like the jealous one?"

"Don't even suggest I'm behaving like Adrian," Zor angrily responded.

"You told Adrian she was going to the Thespian House. What's she going to think if you change it? Can you make her any more suspicious than she already is?"

"I'm tired of this conversation."

"You'll tire of a lot more than this conversation when you lose your powers and Cyan..."

"That's enough, James! I didn't go to Alyssa's final today because I'm going to get her alone tonight and finish her! And Katrine will be out of the house before Adrian arrives tomorrow! There! Does that make you happy?"

Katrine could hear Zor stomp past her bedroom and slam his bedroom door.

"Don't weasel out, Brother!" James yelled after him. As he walked out the front door, she could hear him mumble something about visiting Woester.

Alyssa, Katrine thought, *Don't let John get you alone. He's going to kill you.* She repeated her thought over and over until she was certain Alyssa had heard her.

The Link – Seven Days of Cyan

Quiet! I'm in the middle of a quiz. I'm trying to concentrate!

* * *

It was eight o'clock Friday evening when Sami and Alyssa walked along the university's sidewalk toward the dormitories with their backpacks.

"Have a good weekend in Albuquerque. Drop by my folks'. I think they picked up something for your birthday," Sami said with a smile.

"Sure you don't want to go up with me?"

"No. I've got too much homework. Besides, I don't trust that wreck you call a car. I'm waiting for the day it can't make it back up Nogal canyon and we're stuck waving our thumbs in the air."

"Be careful in the parking lot, Sami. Want me to walk you to the car?"

"No. I have a couple of bottles of pepper spray in my bag."

"A *couple* of bottles?"

"Dad sent them. One was for my backpack, one for my purse…"

"…but you don't carry a purse," Alyssa said with a nod.

Sami waved goodbye to Alyssa and took off towards the parking lot behind the English building. "Call me when you get home so I know you made it!"

Alyssa continued to walk up the sidewalk toward her dorm room. She was tired and hadn't had a good day. Not only had they come in second place in the tournament, but she also had a strange, guilty feeling all day when she thought about John. His sudden departure from the snack bar was an obvious signal that he wanted to bail from any sort of relationship with her. After all, she had dialogues with the main character in her book. She had a voice in her head. Why would a psychologist want to get involved with someone losing her mind?

As she passed the union, her heart fluttered. John was sitting under a light on a bench just outside the union entrance, reading a book. She wondered if he wanted to see her, or if she should just keep walking. As she looked at him, he glanced up and saw her. To her relief, he smiled and waved her over.

"How did the team do this morning?" he asked as she approached.

"We lost 1-2. All our shots were missing." There was an awkward pause which Alyssa always noticed. "About yesterday…"

"I'm really sorry I had to run off like that. I would have liked to stay a lot longer."

Alyssa felt a tremendous relief. Maybe she hadn't blown it after all. He stood up and brushed dirt off his jeans.

"May I carry your books for you? They look heavy."

Alyssa smiled. Nobody but David had ever offered to carry her books for her. She gave her backpack to him and they walked slowly together past the union towards the dormitories.

"They're showing a movie in about fifteen minutes at the union. Would you like to go?" John asked.

Alyssa felt a nervous excitement. She would have never considered going had it been anyone else. She was tired and she was planning to get up early the next morning to start her trip.

"Sure," she said as nonchalant as she could. "Just give me a second to freshen up in my room and I'll be ready."

Dodging a group of students trying to play football in the dark, they walked together across a small outdoor amphitheater and several sidewalks until they approached her door. She took out her keys and unlocked the door.

"Wait here," she said as she took her books from John. "I'll be out in just a second."

Alyssa went into her room and closed the door behind her. She felt like jumping and screaming with joy, but refrained because she knew he would hear. She quickly threw her backpack onto the bed and rushed over to the sink to splash water on her face. As she was drying off with a towel, she heard the main door behind her swing open. She spun around to see John shut and lock the door behind him.

"I thought I asked you to wait outside," she said with a quiver in her voice.

Without a word, he slowly walked toward her.

Chapter 18
Round One (Friday night)

Katrine sat at the dining room table and stared at the script. She was hoping her concentration would improve in the dining room, but she still found it nearly impossible to memorize what few lines were given her. As she turned the page, she realized once more that she had no idea what she had just read, so she flipped it back to start over. Her mind kept wandering to Zor's room. There had been no sound from within for a good half hour. He had to be with Alyssa. She lay her head down and closed her eyes.

"What are *you* still doing here?" a woman's voice hissed. Katrine raised her head to see Adrian across the table, staring at her with hate-filled eyes. She was dressed in a black robe that camouflaged the black hair that fell below her shoulders. "Your eye seems to have healed rather quickly. Where's Zor?" she angrily questioned.

"He might be in his room."

"I'm not a fool! He's not there! Where did he go?"

Adrian's glare felt so threatening, Katrine found herself unable to speak.

"He's with her, isn't he? He's with your counterpart!"

"I don't know."

Adrian looked out the windows toward the courtyard with her hands on her hips and took a deep breath. With a growl, she turned, picked up one of the dining room chairs, and threw it across the table at Katrine. Katrine quickly leapt out of her chair to dodge it.

"All this nonsense is ending tonight!" she yelled before turning and stomping out the door. Katrine walked over to the window and looked out, not sure what to expect. Robert's warning to avoid being alone with Adrian repeated over and over in her head.

143

Finally, she saw what she had been most dreading: from the darkness of the courtyard, Adrian appeared, followed by what must have been the entire guard soccer team, some still in uniform, out for revenge.

Katrine quickly ran into her room and closed the door behind her. Since there was no lock, she sat with her back against the door and tried to slow her frantic breathing.

"Alyssa," she said aloud. "I need your help now!" There was no answer. "This is an emergency... a matter of life and death here..." Still no answer. "Please, Alyssa," she whispered as she heard the main door open.

"Katrine!" Adrian called. "Seems the team would like to have a word with you."

Katrine pressed her back against the door to keep it shut as Adrian tried to push it open.

"I'll be back," Adrian said through the door. "Seems the guards brought a few things to help me out."

As Katrine listened to Adrian return to the guards, the adrenaline flowing through her body made her feel lightheaded. She looked around her room to try to find some kind of weapon... *anything*...

Katrine let out a startled cry as something came crashing into the door above her head. She looked up to see a section of wood pushed forward. Another crash into the door. She could see the tip of an ax peek through the splintering wood above her shoulder. Katrine swirled around and planted her feet against the door.

"Come on, Alyssa!" Katrine cried in a panic. "Where are you?"

With the third ax swing, the ax completely broke through her thin door and lodged into the wood. As Adrian struggled to release it, Katrine scurried across the floor into her bathroom where she quickly slammed the door and held it closed with her feet. She was out of doors to hide behind.

The ax started its assault on the new door. It was a thicker door and it took Adrian a second or two to release the ax from the wood. Katrine could hear Adrian pause to catch her breath.

"You're just delaying the inevitable, Katrine."

Katrine knew Adrian was right, but only if Katrine didn't start fighting back. She held her breath and quietly stood up, then placed her hand on the door handle, waiting for Adrian to resume the attack on the door. As soon as the ax struck the door, Katrine swung the door open, pushed Adrian backwards with a strong kick, and grabbed the ax still lodged in the door. As Katrine pulled at it, Adrian recovered and jumped onto Katrine's back, wrapping her arms tightly around her throat.

Both fell backwards between the bed and the wall as the ax finally dislodged. With barely enough room to maneuver, Katrine raised the ax over her head and tried to beat off Adrian, but Adrian quickly unwrapped one of her arms from Katrine's throat and grabbed hold of the handle. She felt it slip from her grip as Adrian pulled it further behind her head. She pushed her legs against the side of the bed to help her turn and soon wriggled her way out of Adrian's neck hold. Quickly, she struggled to her feet as Adrian gained full control of the ax. Adrian swung with all her might at Katrine's leg, but missed as Katrine jumped onto the bed, scrambled across the room, and ran out the door.

The guards were outside lined up against the windows, like spectators at an out-of-control hockey game. Katrine ran to the opposite end of the dining room table as Adrian came out of the bedroom with the ax, smiling.

"What does Zor find so special about you, anyway?" Adrian asked as she walked around the table. Katrine countered Adrian's movements, always keeping the table between them, ready to dodge a flying ax.

"There's nothing going on, Adrian," Katrine answered earnestly as she tried to catch her breath and recover from Adrian's neck hold.

"If that were true, you would have been dead soon after he discovered you were a link."

Katrine was at the table's end closest to the door when she heard the door rattle. As she glanced behind her to make sure the guards weren't entering, she heard the ax cut through the air. She tried to duck in time, but the ax handle hit her on the head, causing her to falter. Before she could fully recover, she felt Adrian jump on her back and push her down to the floor. Adrian grabbed Katrine's hair and started to drag her to the main door where the guards awaited.

Katrine tried to get back to her feet, but Adrian kept stomping on her shoulders with her thick, heavy boots. The cool air from the door as Adrian swung it open signaled to Katrine that she was running out of time. With all her might, Katrine lunged at the open door and pulled it shut as hard as she could, smashing Adrian in the doorway. Adrian screamed angrily as Katrine sprawled her body behind the door and began to push the door shut. Finally, Adrian released her grip on Katrine's hair, allowing Katrine to scramble to the sitting room and pick up the ax from the floor. She leaped over the couches, turned, and held the ax up with two hands, ready to defend herself.

Adrian's nose was bleeding. She wiped the blood with the back of her hand, and then opened the door as wide as it could open.

"You have my permission to come in and get her," Adrian said in a low, controlled voice, but the guards didn't move. "Come in and drag her out to the courtyard! Zor will never find out!"

"Sorry, ma'am. We have orders," replied Guard Fourteen.

Adrian screamed in frustration. "Are you all cowards? I'm the one who made Zor what he is today! I override any orders he gave you!" Still the guards did not move. "Give me this," she said as she grabbed Guard Fourteen's knife from his side. "Get me some more knives. I'll finish her myself."

Katrine ducked behind the fireplace as the first knife flew through the air and smacked the glass window behind her. She peeked around the corner and watched the guards hand her more knives to throw.

"Adrian, can't we talk about this in a more civilized manner?" Katrine called out.

Adrian threw a knife, barely missing Katrine's ear as she ducked back behind the fireplace. Katrine could hear her walking past the dining room table and quickly moved to keep the fireplace between them. Another knife went flying past. She barely dodged a fourth knife that flew through the opening of the fireplace. Before long, they had circled the entire fireplace and were back where they started, with Adrian near the front door.

"Adrian!" Zor's angry voice sounded in the room. Katrine immediately gave a sigh of relief and leaned her back against the fireplace. "What do you think you're doing? Are you insane?"

"I'm just doing what you seem incapable of doing."

Katrine decided to peek around the corner, but another knife went whizzing by her head. She ducked back and closed her eyes.

"Stop it, Adrian. The link is severed and Katrine is moving out tonight." Katrine sank to the floor in disbelief. "Come into my room to settle down."

"You expect me to believe that you killed Alyssa?" Adrian asked.

"Yes, I finally got her alone. That's all I was waiting for. You know I would never betray you."

There was a pause. "Bring me home, Zor," Adrian said calmly. Another pause.

"Wouldn't you rather visit Woester and have a drink? He just finished perfecting his Oktoberfest."

"I would like to go home... *now*," responded Adrian a little more forcefully.

"Of course. We'll take my labyrinth."

"No, we'll take mine."

"Fine, we'll take yours."

Katrine could detect a note of worry in Zor's voice, but she didn't care. They deserved whatever they did to each other. They walked into Zor's room and were gone. Katrine stared out the window in front of her at no-man's land and tried to contact Alyssa, but there was no reply.

Chapter 19
Round Two (Saturday)

"What happened here?" James asked.

Katrine woke, opened her eyes and looked up at James. She was still sitting against the fireplace with the ax across her lap. It took a moment to realize where she was as she stared out at no-man's land at the rising sun.

"I asked what happened here," James repeated with growing agitation.

"Just a visit from our friendly neighborhood witch," Katrine weakly replied.

"Where's Zor?"

"With Adrian."

James was silent, and then he lost control. He gave a frustrated yell as he kicked the chairs and table several times. When he stopped, he was out of breath. Katrine dared not say a word.

"Contact Alyssa," he ordered. "We're going after my brother."

Katrine's anger began to rise. "She's dead. Zor killed her."

"I seriously doubt that. Contact her."

"I've already tried."

"Try again!" he yelled as he kicked the ax from her lap.

Katrine irately looked up at him. "Fine!" She clenched her eyes shut and called out to Alyssa.

Good morning! It's such a wonderful day for a road trip!

Katrine's heart began to pound when she heard Alyssa's voice in her mind. *I thought you were dead! Why didn't you answer me last night?*

Although she asked Alyssa for an explanation, she already knew what had happened.

Very busy... with the most spontaneous, most passionate lovemaking I've had my entire life! I didn't feel like talking to that little imaginary voice in my head at the moment. Unfortunately, we had to stop when his pager went off. His brother got in a small car accident and John had to rush off to the hospital. Bummer. But he gave me his phone number!

Katrine opened her eyes in shock.

"What?" James asked.

"They..." Katrine sat speechless for a moment. "They..." She looked up at James, held out her hands, and locked her fingers together.

James shook his head. "Let's hope Adrian doesn't find out. She's angry enough about you still being here." He grabbed Katrine's arm and lifted her from the floor. "Zor's certainly giving her all the reason she needs to suck the power from his body."

"She can do that?"

"She gave it to him. She's the only one who can take it back. When did they leave?"

"Last night."

"Then she's had time to do it already. Come with me, and make sure Alyssa stays with us in case we encounter Adrian."

Katrine stopped and jerked her arm from James' grip. "I've had enough Adrian for a long while! Zor can take care of himself."

James grabbed her arm tightly and pulled her up to his angry face. "If Zor is powerless, who's going to stop Adrian from going after Alyssa, then you? Zor is the only one who *can* and *will* defend you. Do you understand? *I* am not a warlock. I am a helpless, insignificant little mortal like yourself. You need to stop Adrian before she strips you of your help and your power."

Katrine looked at James and squirmed. He had such a tight grip on her arm that it throbbed. She nodded.

"Is there anything that might distract Alyssa and prevent her presence?"

"No. She's driving on a highway."

"Good. Let's not waste anymore time."

They approached Zor's room. James took out his set of keys, unlocked the door, and they entered.

Zor's room had large windows on three of his bedroom walls, each with light tan drapes pulled off to the side. Katrine walked towards the window immediately to her right as she walked in the door. Her room was on the other side of the wall, yet in the window she could see the ocean and a brilliant sunset on the horizon. The window that should have shown no-man's land showed a rich, luscious pine forest with a waterfall in the background and yellow flowers in a foreground meadow. To the left of the door where there should have been the hallway and the courtyard, she saw red rock canyon lands through the window. She watched as an eagle swept down from the top of a rock and landed on the top of a saguaro cactus.

"It's called Revolutionary TV, from 2037," explained James as he walked over to Zor's redwood bureau drawers. On the only wall that had no window, Katrine noticed a display case on the wall with Zor's sword. She felt strange as she looked at it. It was almost as if the snakes that formed the handguard were looking at her. Pushed against the wall under the display case was a large bed covered with a dark green comforter. It had a wooden frame that matched the bureau drawers and a large armoire that towered beside the bed.

"Where is that compass?" James mumbled as he sifted through Zor's bureau drawers.

Katrine looked over at James, noticed a small, round, gold box on the dresser top beside him, and walked over to it. The top had several intricate designs surrounding a cherry tree, all in gold inlay. She tried to pick it up, but it wouldn't budge from the dresser top.

"The only one who can move a labyrinth is its owner," James said as he opened the bottom drawer. "Aha, there you are." He pulled out a gold compass and squeezed it in his hand. "Okay, I need you to get us to the entrance." He lifted up the top of the gold box. Inside Katrine could see a tiny green labyrinth. James pointed at one of the corridors.

"Adrian's door is somewhere around here, but the only place we can enter the labyrinth is here." James pointed to the only gap on the outside perimeter of the maze. Everything was so small that Katrine could barely make out the gap. "Here's where I need you. Get us in. Shrink us down and place us in front of the entrance." Katrine gave James a dubious look. "Do it, Katrine. All you have to do is wish it," James said impatiently. "You're wasting time."

Katrine looked down at the entrance point and visualized herself with James in front of the gap. Suddenly, they were together in front of a gigantic bushy hedge. She cowered as the top to the gold box closed above her. All was dark until blue sky appeared above her. James quickly grabbed her hand and looked down at his compass.

"To Adrian's door," he told it. The arrow pointed down a hedgerow. They weaved through the bushy hedges, turning left, then right, then right again. Wooden doors were along each hedge, spaced

The Link – Seven Days of Cyan

several meters apart from each other. Each door had several dates and names burned into the wood. Katrine started to feel dizzy and began to stumble more and more with each turn. Her grip on James' hand tightened to prevent her from falling.

"Stop, James. I feel as though I'm going to pass out."

"Here, take this and follow the arrow."

He handed her the compass. When she took hold of it, she regained all her senses and her head cleared instantly.

"Intruders get lost and sometimes pass out in the labyrinth without a compass," he explained. "When someone has a compass in the hedgerows, it usually means they have permission to be there."

Katrine sighed, looked down at the compass, and then led James. By the time the compass pointed directly at Adrian's door, James was about to fall down. Katrine reluctantly handed him the compass. As James recovered from his dizziness, Katrine read the years and names burned into the wood of Adrian's door. The years were sequential, ending in 1923. She glanced at the door beside Adrian's and something immediately caught her eye: '1962 Robert Tebaeu' was the third year down. The last year listed on Robert's door was 1966.

"Only the last date listed is accurate?" she asked as James knelt in front of Adrian's door. Perhaps she could risk an unapproved visit to Robert's family, should the opportunity arise. If not to escape, she might at least be able to tell Robert's mother that Robert was in good health and happy.

James turned to Katrine. "Yes, now shut up and get over here." Katrine moved closer to James. "You have to place your hand on the door and tell it to open at Adrian's palace in a vacant room upstairs. Tell it not to close until we return. Otherwise, it'll close after an hour."

Katrine shook her head, realizing how awkward she would feel talking to a door. "Can't you do it?"

James looked impatient. "It won't stay open longer than an hour if I open it, but it will listen to you. You're the one with the power."

Katrine groaned, then knelt down and placed her hand on the door. "Open inside Adrian's palace, upstairs in a vacant room. Stay open until we come back through." Her hand fell forward as the door completely disappeared, revealing a quaint sitting room through the doorway. She looked back at James and he nodded in approval.

They silently crept through the doorway into a room with shiny, wooden floors and dark furniture; around a large fireplace in the wall were several large, brown, paisley chairs. Katrine looked behind her to see that the inside of the labyrinth had turned invisible. All she could see was a rectangular distortion where she had stepped through the door, appearing much like when heat from a desert rises and distorts everything in the distance.

Katrine followed closely behind James as they crept into a long, stone hallway decorated with golden trim. Arches adorned with golden, horned angels were spaced throughout the hallway, separating each door that James and Katrine peered into as they quietly made their way down the hall. Finally James found Zor in Adrian's library. He grabbed Katrine's hand and led her inside.

It was a large room with dark, wooden bookcases completely covering the right adjacent wall and the opposite wall from the door. A large reading table with a red shaded lamp on each end was placed in the same corner where the bookshelves met. Two soft, red-cloth chairs with dark, wooden frames surrounded the table. A large letter writing desk was centered against the left adjacent wall from the door. Zor was bound to its wooden chair on the far side of the desk with a rope made of blue light. There was no sign of Adrian. When Zor saw James and Katrine walk in, his face became apprehensive.

"Why did you bring her here?"

"Because she's going to help you," replied James. "Are we too late?"

"Yes, she already extracted my powers... filled the vase and then dumped it all into a sink. Washed it away forever." He took a deep breath. "She's planning on visiting Alyssa this morning. If Adrian finds out what happened between us last night, Alyssa's not going to be the only one dead."

"Where is Adrian now?"

"She's in the kitchen eating breakfast. She'll be back any minute." He looked at Katrine. "You can get me out of this. You possess stronger magic than some of Imperius' spirits. This is much weaker. Get me out of this, then I'll show you how we can save Alyssa."

Katrine walked towards Zor and stopped. She looked at him and felt herself unable to move. Part of her felt angry, part of her felt violated, and part of her felt embarrassed. He had gone to bed with Alyssa... her future soul. She felt as though she should have had *some* sort of input in what happened. Alyssa had no idea who she was dealing with. How dare she act so reckless.

Zor didn't have to make eye contact with her to know what she was thinking.

"I wasn't using her," Zor explained quietly. "I really do care for her."

"You have feelings for her after just three short visits?" Katrine asked, never breaking eye contact with him.

"Yes, I do." Zor sighed. "Maybe it was love at first sight. Maybe... as I got to know you, I started wanting Alyssa more and more. Alyssa's *you*, Katrine, with the same spirit, but without the anger..." Zor looked earnestly at Katrine and spoke in a defeated voice. "I wasn't taking advantage of her. I just wanted to be with her."

Katrine shook her head and tried to speak, but no words came out.

"Both you and Alyssa are in trouble," Zor explained. "Get me out of this so I can help you."

"How convenient that you showed," cackled Adrian. Katrine quickly turned to see Adrian standing in the doorway, still in her black robe. "Saves me a trip to Cyan and makes things a bit easier for me," she sneered as she slowly circled Katrine like a vulture.

Katrine felt tremendous pressure followed by a sharp pain in the center of her right lower arm. She cried out as the bones snapped in half. Katrine grabbed her arm with her opposite hand and quickly repaired it with a wish. As she did, she felt her feet lift off the ground. She flew backwards through the air and slammed against the wall beside the door, knocking the wind out of her.

"Stop, Adrian!" Zor yelled.

James backed into the corner of the room, uncertain what to do. Katrine looked up, trying to catch her breath.

"This is going to be fun," laughed Adrian.

Katrine could feel her upper leg start to strain and bend. She grabbed her leg and stopped it from snapping. Again Katrine felt herself flying across the room. She placed her hands in front of her and barely managed to stop herself from hitting her head on the top of a bookcase. She slammed into the shelf, fell to the ground and groaned, then felt herself take flight a third time. Her back slammed against the wall beside the door and she slumped to the floor. As she tried to recover, she felt a pain in the back of her neck as Adrian tried to snap it. Katrine became furious.

"Stop it!" Katrine yelled as she waved her hand at Adrian. Adrian flew across the room and hit the bookshelf on the opposite wall. As she was suspended against the shelves, Katrine simultaneously snapped all of Adrian's leg bones, arm bones, and ribs. A loud crack sounded throughout the room as Adrian shrieked and fell to the floor. She wriggled in pain on the ground, and then fell silent. James and Zor appeared shocked; Katrine wondered if she had killed her.

"That was not supposed to happen," sneered Adrian as she looked up at Zor. Then she glared at Katrine and disappeared.

Zor anxiously peered over at the letter desk. "She's going after Alyssa." Katrine looked on the desk to see a golden box whose top was closing. "James, use my labyrinth and go after her. Do what you can to stop her until I can get there, and play it smart. She's very powerful in 1998."

James ran out of the room.

"I'm going, too," Katrine said as she struggled to her feet and turned towards the doorway.

"You can't, Katrine," Zor quickly said.

Katrine stopped and angrily turned towards Zor. "And why not?"

"Only one soul in a single time period can exist. Your soul would be split between yourself and Alyssa. Whether or not you still have powers, they'd be worthless. You won't even care what Adrian does to you with a split soul. I already explained this to you at Dragon Hill, Katrine."

Katrine stood silent for a moment. "How do I know you're not just making this up?"

"My mother would be alive today if souls didn't split. I tried to go back in time to cure my mother's cancer, but was unable to move once I stepped through the doorway. Adrian had to pull me back into the labyrinth."

"I am *not* Alyssa. She's a different person."

"You share her soul. Why do you think I avoid collections for Cyan in years after 2040, the year I was born? There's the risk of stepping into a time period where I've been reincarnated." He sighed. "Adrian's powerful in ninety-eight, so we have to act before Adrian finds Alyssa and distracts her. You *have* to release me before she disconnects."

She looked at the glowing ropes, still uncertain whether she wanted to release him. Something Adrian said needed to be explained. "What did Adrian mean when she said *that was not supposed to happen*?"

"I just never told Adrian how strong you had become. Please, before it's too late."

Katrine looked at Zor's desperate face and decided she had little choice but to believe him. She stared at the glowing ropes and they disappeared.

"Quickly," he said as he jumped up, grabbed Katrine's arm and led her to a small, dark room across the hall. Zor flipped on a switch inside the door and candles all along the walls began to burn.

There was a cabinet with a golden top in the center of the room. The rest of the room was bare. He swung a cabinet door on the opposite side of Katrine open, grabbed something, and quickly closed it. He placed a large golden vase on the counter top before Katrine.

"It's a solid gold transfer vase. You can use it to equip me with enough power to save Alyssa from Adrian."

Katrine couldn't believe what he was asking. "I'm going to give you powers?" She started to feel angry. "How do I know Adrian took your powers away in the first place?"

"Warlocks and witches have a different brain structure than a mortal, and it creates an aura around their body. If you look for it, you'll be able to see it with Alyssa's help. Alyssa can tell if it's gone. She can tell if I'm mortal."

Katrine looked dubiously at him, then her eyes drifted to the air around his body. The air was normal; there was no aura. She didn't know how, but she could sense that he was no longer a warlock. He felt different.

"You can give me power, Katrine, without depleting your own, and I can use it in 1998. Even if I still had Adrian's power, it wouldn't have helped me in Alyssa's time. I was powerless. I still would have needed your help." He backed away from the table. "I swear I'll help her if you do this."

Katrine folded her arms tightly in front of her. Woester had told her that the power from a link worked in any time period. She would be making Zor more powerful not only in 1998, but all the other years he was previously powerless. How many more people would be collected because of her?

"You may choose to take the gift back when I return, if that makes the decision easier for you."

It did. She stepped closer to the vase. "I'm only doing this so Alyssa has someone to help her."

Zor looked both relieved and excited. "That's why I'm doing it as well," he answered.

"What do I do?"

He moved up to the table with Katrine. "Place both your hands on the vase," he instructed. "First, fill it with the purest water you can imagine."

Katrine closed her eyes. She could see the water molecules colliding with each other. She peered into the vase and saw the water.

"Now imagine the water turning into pure power. It'll glow. Try to make it glow as bright as possible." Katrine looked up at him suspiciously. "Adrian is very powerful in Alyssa's time," he explained. "It would all be pointless if I'm weaker than her."

Katrine shook her head, unable to believe what she was about to do. She closed her eyes and visualized pure power... as strong a power could be. She could tell that the vase was lighting up. She opened her eyes to see it glowing bright yellow. The light was so intense that she could no longer see Zor on the other side. When she could do no more, she took her hands off the vase. Zor walked around the counter to her side, apparently awestruck.

"I didn't know yellow was possible," he whispered as he stared at the glowing vase.

Katrine started to feel lightheaded and weak. Her knees gave out and she started to fall, but Zor caught her. He helped her sit on the floor against the wall in the corner of the room.

"I imagine you'll feel very tired for a couple of hours, just like warlocks and witches do after they fill a vase. You're welcome to fall asleep while you try to recover. Most links do." He stood up and walked to the vase. "Is Alyssa gone?"

"No."

"We don't need her anymore. You may want to convince her to leave. Daydreaming when someone's trying to kill you isn't a good idea." He walked around the cabinet and stared at the vase with greedy eyes.

"Is she gone yet?" he asked impatiently.

Katrine was having a hard time concentrating. "I think so." Her body felt like it was sinking into the ground as a tremendous weight seemed to push her from above. "Is this where I die?" she whispered.

"This is where other links have been murdered, but not you. I'm not going to hurt you."

Katrine could barely keep her eyes open. She heard the cabinet door open and she forced herself to look up. Zor had taken out another gold vase that glowed with a bright blue light. She tried to speak, but was too weak. She could only watch.

"For a moment, I was seriously worried Adrian wasn't going to leave this behind. It took a little sweet talk and convincing," Zor said with a smile. "How sorry she'll be when she finds out her mistake."

Zor poured the glowing blue water from the second vase into the vase Katrine had just filled. The glowing light turned a bright greenish yellow. He drank it quickly. His body glowed, then returned to normal.

"Go to sleep, Katrine. I'll be back after I take care of a bit of nasty business."

Chapter 20
Road trip (Saturday)

The highway seemed pretty empty for a Saturday. Alyssa flipped through the channels of the radio. There were no good stations, so she turned it off again. She had forgotten her cassettes, which made the long, boring ride almost tortuous.

Her mind started drifting to the night before, when she was with John. What could have been a very ugly situation had turned into the most amazing, wonderful experience she had ever had. She laughed aloud and shook her head when she recalled him kneeling on the floor with his hands tied behind his back, asking her to let him stay and make it the most memorable night they've ever had. Alyssa started humming the birthday song. This birthday couldn't get any better.

Something moved in the rear view mirror. She looked in the mirror, but there were no cars behind her, so she reasoned that it was probably a turkey vulture swooping across the road. She kept humming.

"Can you please stop that incessant humming!" a very unfriendly voice behind her complained. Alyssa jumped and the car swerved. As soon as she regained control of her car, she quickly looked in the backseat. There was a woman with black hair, dressed in a black robe.

"How the hell did you get in my car?" Alyssa yelled as she started to pull the car over to the shoulder.

"No, we're not stopping here." The car's steering wheel turned so that the car returned to the driving lane. Alyssa pressed hard on the brake pedal, but nothing happened. She was still speeding along at seventy miles per hour. She turned back around to look at the woman.

"I'm Adrian. Very pleased to meet you," the woman said with a smile. She was sitting back comfortably with her arms folded.

"I don't care who you are, how did you get in my car?" Alyssa repeated as she looked back and forth between the road and Adrian, pretending she still had control over the car.

"Listen to me carefully," Adrian said as she unfolded her arms and leaned forward so that she was face to face with Alyssa. "I... am... Adrian." She leaned back and folded her arms in front of her again. "You don't have to pretend to drive. I've got full control of the car at the moment."

Alyssa turned away and stared at the road in shock. She tightened the grip on her steering wheel and tried to change lanes, but it wouldn't budge.

"This is not happening," Alyssa whispered.

"So, I'm curious," Adrian said. "Zor... oh, excuse me, *John*... told me a little about what happened last night. I'd like to hear your side of the story."

Alyssa said nothing. She stepped on the gas, but it didn't speed up the car. She stepped on the brake, but again there was no response.

"What happened last night, Alyssa? I want to know or I'll plunge you right into the side of a mountain."

Alyssa took her hands completely off the steering wheel and watched the car glide smoothly along its course. She turned to Adrian and stared.

"You're a figment of my imagination," Alyssa said quietly to herself as she stared at Adrian.

"No," corrected Adrian. "You made a real connection to a past life... to a pitiful creature named Katrine." She leaned forward again so that she was in Alyssa's face. "And unless you answer my question about last night, I'm going to end your life much faster than I planned. What did you two do?"

Alyssa wondered if she was still in bed asleep and hadn't even started her trip. Her daydreaming had become so much more vivid and realistic since the accident, why not her dreams, too? Whether she was awake or asleep, Adrian seemed real enough at the moment and wasn't going away, so she decided to play along until she could figure out what was really happening.

"We went to watch a movie."

"That's what he said. You're both lying. He can hide it, but you can't," she said as she started to place her hand on Alyssa's chin. Alyssa quickly knocked it away.

"Don't you *dare* touch me," Alyssa warned.

Adrian looked surprised at first, then sat back again and laughed. She looked out the window with a thoughtful look. "Did he stay until the end of the movie?"

"Yes."

"Must have been a very short movie. I suppose it doesn't much matter anyway. John and I have only one more matter to attend to, then we'll travel our separate ways, I suppose." She paused before she spoke. "But I hate a man who cheats. He needs to be taught a lesson."

Alyssa noticed something moving behind her and turned further around to see a strange distortion on the driver's side rear door.

"That's my getaway when you go plummeting off a mountain. I hope to make your death as painful as possible... to thank you for the bone-shattering experience you gave me just a little while ago," Adrian explained. "Well, I'm pretty sure I've waited back here long enough... an entire thirty minutes before you broke your little connection with Katrine. Unbearable boredom, I'll tell you, especially in this God-forsaken desert." She placed her arms on the back of the front seat and looked out the front windshield. "Well, let's see what's available."

Alyssa had given up trying to drive and now inconspicuously rested her hand on top of her seatbelt buckle. As Adrian looked out at the passing mountains, Alyssa slowly released her seatbelt and held it in place.

"There's a nice steep decline coming up here a bit," Adrian said as she noticed the sign by the side of the road. Alyssa looked ahead and swallowed a lump in her throat. It was Nogal canyon. She looked at the floor on the passenger's side to try to find something to hit Adrian with, but there was only trash from a fast food restaurant. The car began to speed up and shake as the car peeked over the edge of Nogal canyon.

"This is even better than I had hoped for," Adrian said when she saw the canyon. "Good thing you have your seatbelt on. You're going to need it."

The car started shaking more violently as it accelerated past eighty-five miles an hour on the downhill.

"Goodbye, Alyssa," Adrian said. "It was nice *not* knowing you."

Adrian started to move towards the distortion as the car cut right and headed off the highway. Alyssa jumped from her seat, turned, and latched onto Adrian's robe before she could pass through.

The Link – Seven Days of Cyan

"If I'm going down, you're going down with me, Witch!" Alyssa yelled.

The car began to toss violently as Alyssa managed to pull herself over the seat using Adrian's robe.

"Get off of me!" shrieked Adrian as she tried to squirm out of her grip.

The car started to roll and Adrian fell on top of her as they smashed into the ceiling of the car. A blue light appeared around Adrian's body, causing Alyssa's skin to sting and bones to vibrate. The car turned upright and Alyssa fell on top of Adrian again. Her body was on fire everywhere the blue light touched her. The pain was too real to be a dream. Alyssa tried to kick herself away from Adrian's glowing body as the car started on its second flip. The door at her feet flew open as the roof began to cave in. Alyssa tried to push on the seat toward the open door to get out of the car before Adrian landed on her again. She slammed once more into the ceiling of the car, then Adrian's glowing body landed on top of her. Paralyzed by the pain, Alyssa couldn't move, even to scream. Finally, the car righted itself again and Adrian began to fall away. As Alyssa fell, she pushed herself closer to the door. The car began rocking between the right and left tires, and she was finally able to push herself out the door.

Alyssa tumbled onto the shrub-filled slope of Nogal canyon and let out a sigh of relief as she watched the car continue down the slope and crash into a small pile of boulders at the bottom. She stared at the car as she tried to catch her breath, hoping Adrian would just disappear through her labyrinth door, but she didn't. The blue light faded, and she could see someone moving inside the wrecked car.

Alyssa stood up and winced in pain. Her left knee felt as though it had completely shattered. She returned her gaze down the slope to see Adrian now standing beside the car, looking up at her.

"This would be a good time to wake up," Alyssa said to herself as she turned and tried to limp up to the highway. Suddenly something knocked her backwards. She tumbled down the slope over rocks and shrubs. Every time she managed to grab hold of a bush to stop her fall, she was pushed even harder, causing her to lose her grip. Finally, she hit the wide canyon floor and lay motionless on her stomach with her face buried partially in the dirt.

"That's got to hurt!" yelled Adrian.

It did. Alyssa strained to lift her shoulders and saw Adrian casually walking towards her only a short distance up the desert canyon floor. Alyssa looked down at the dirt below her and took a deep breath. With a groan, she lifted herself from the ground and struggled to stand up, hardly able to believe what was happening. When she finally lifted herself, Adrian was nearly on top of her.

"Don't trip!" Adrian yelled as Alyssa turned to limp away. A big rock suddenly stopped Alyssa's hop and sent her flying face forward into a huge, densely padded prickly pear cactus she could have sworn wasn't there a second ago.

Tears came to Alyssa's eyes as she tried to move. The thousands of spines in her body seemed to dig even deeper when she tried to lift herself out. She began to concentrate on her breathing, although passing out probably would have felt better than staying conscious.

"Okay," Alyssa whispered to herself. "This is just like bicycle accident number one. You can get out of this."

She could hear Adrian approach and stop beside her.

"Guess you didn't see the cactus. I tried to warn you," Adrian said calmly.

"Adrian!" yelled a man's voice from behind Alyssa. "You were told to wait."

Alyssa could feel two hands grab her around her waist and pull her out of the cactus. It was hard to keep her breathing quiet as he moved her, and she whimpered in pain with each breath. The man dragged her across the dirt and sat her against a boulder. She looked up to see a blond man, about the same age as herself, who bore a strong resemblance to John. Adrian was standing behind him with her arms angrily crossed. The man looked up and saw the car in the distance.

"You weren't supposed to do anything until Zor showed. What if he failed to get it?"

"Hogwash, James. He had plenty of time. She stopped her daydreaming and started fiddling with the radio," snarled Adrian.

"We have to be sure, Adrian!"

Adrian gave an angry puff. "This is nonsense. Look, I'll just read her mind and find out." Adrian started walking towards Alyssa, but James blocked her path.

"We're following the plan, Adrian," James said adamantly. "We wait until Zor shows."

Adrian glared at James. "I *don't* have a lot of time, James. I didn't tell my labyrinth door to stay open because I didn't want to risk this slut hearing me and breaking the connection. My stupid labyrinth opens her damn doors too fast. She does it on purpose just to piss me off." Adrian kicked a rock. "This entire plan is ridiculous. He could have forced the power out of that simpleton Katrine the day he found out about her."

The Link – Seven Days of Cyan

"You know Zor is not that kind of person," James responded.

"It would do him some good to take a few lessons from the others... like my father," she argued. She kicked some dirt and started to pace. "Did you see what that peasant wench did to me at my house?"

"Perhaps she was a little peeved about all your ax-chopping, knife-throwing, bone-breaking, wall-slamming escapades. What were they all about? You weren't just trying to scare her, were you? You were really trying to kill her! How is Zor supposed to get the power from her if she's dead?"

"I guess I lost my head," Adrian said nonchalantly.

"You could have blown everything. One week of staging arguments with my brother for nothing."

"You both did well. I'm sure that deep down Katrine believes that Zor cares enough to protect this wench from his raving lunatic girlfriend. I'm sure both of you will get nominated for best actor," Adrian answered sarcastically. "The problem is I believe Zor's act is not just an act anymore. What's even *more* pathetic is that I can't even figure out which wench he wants! I think he wants *both* of them!"

James smiled. "What man *wouldn't* want two women?" he joked. Adrian immediately gave James an evil glare that made his smile quickly disappear. "Adrian," he sighed. "You're being ridiculous. He loves you. Rants and raves every night about how wonderful you are."

James turned away from Adrian and knelt down in front of Alyssa. He started to brush the dirt from Alyssa's face, but she jerked her head away, unable to stand him touching her. She glared back angrily as he let out a sigh.

"Alyssa, I would have shown earlier but the labyrinth wouldn't open inside your moving car. I need a password for tricks like that." He rubbed his forehead and then shook his head. "This is just one very bad dream."

"This is just one very *good* dream, James," Adrian corrected. "He really does love me? Rants and raves and all those things you just said?"

"Yes, Adrian," James said wearily. "I get sick of listening to him go on."

Adrian clapped her hands together and held them in front of her. "Wonderful!" Her eyes narrowed mischievously at Alyssa. "Isn't it ironic, Alyssa, that by empowering Zor to save the other side of the link from the jealous girlfriend, you've instead signed your very own death certificate? We simply don't need you any longer now that we have the vase filled."

"That's enough, Adrian," James said.

"There. Zor's here. Now I can finish her off, like he promised I could," remarked Adrian. James stood up and looked up the canyon bed. Alyssa could hear footsteps approaching her from behind.

"How did it go?" James asked.

"Good. She was generous," the voice replied. Alyssa closed her eyes, wanting to cry as she recognized John's voice.

"It's about time! Where's the vase?" Adrian asked. "You were supposed to bring it."

"Well, there seems to be a change in plans, Adrian," replied the voice. "Not only did I drink the entire contents, but I also mixed the contents of the transfer vases before I drank."

"You did *what*?" Adrian yelled hysterically.

"I mixed them. So unless you and Katrine work together to take the power back, which I don't see happening any time soon, you no longer have that control over me. No more putting up with your jealous rages, your insane rantings, and your nasty temper. I owe you nothing and you can't do anything to me. I'm probably fifty times more powerful than you now."

Alyssa heard the footsteps approach her side. She opened her eyes and looked beside her, but all she could see were footprints in the dirt. No one was there... only the voice.

"I made you!"

"That's another thing I won't miss: that ridiculous 'I made you who you are' comment every time I turn around." The voice paused. "You won't be getting any of Katrine's power, Adrian. It's integrated with the warlock's power, which can only be shared once. I choose to share it with my brother, no one else."

Adrian screamed such a terrible scream that shivers ran down Alyssa's aching spine. Adrian quickly threw her palm towards the voice and lightening shot out. It disappeared into thin air just before a faint, greenish-yellow light appeared beside Alyssa. Alyssa watched as the light began to swirl much like a whirlwind in a dusty desert. It rose into the air and floated towards Adrian. Adrian stepped backwards in horror at the sight and shot several lightening bolts into it, but they just disappeared. Adrian closed her eyes as a dome of yellowish light flashed over the canyon. When she opened her eyes, she appeared shocked that she was still in the canyon and the swirling light was nearly upon her. With a quick shriek, she turned and fled towards a dirt road that ran under the highway's bridge. The light slowly followed, hovering slightly behind its prey, and then it attacked.

The light circled around the screaming Adrian, picked her up in the air and tossed her in circles. She grew smaller and smaller. A pink, wrinkled skin slowly replaced the black robes with each turn in the yellowish cloud. Her arms and legs shrank until they were short, stubby, and pink; her ears shrank to be tiny little pink holes; a snout grew, and two very long incisors sprouted from the top of her mouth. Finally, it was over. The animal dropped to the ground and the light disappeared.

James walked over to the small animal sniffing around in the dirt.

"I see you haven't lost your sense of humor with your newly acquired powers. Was that yellow I saw?"

"Amazing, isn't it?" said the voice. "Letting their connection grow stronger had its risks, but it certainly paid off. I can finally transfer my powers over to you without becoming vulnerable. Did your little ears hear that, Adrian?" the voice raised. "I don't need you to protect me while I recover. I'll be strong enough even *after* the transfer."

James gave a huge grin and nudged the animal gently with his foot. "What the hell is she, anyway?"

"Naked mole rat," replied the voice. "A very powerful naked mole rat. Before she regains her senses and figures out what's going on, it's probably best you take her through my labyrinth to 1980, where she's powerless. Drop her somewhere in Africa. Maybe she'll get lucky and find a mate."

James bent down and scooped Adrian up. "So, you'll pick up Adrian's labyrinth for me?"

"Yes. I'll take care of it. Its door probably closed when she changed. Labyrinths don't consider animals suitable owners."

"If it didn't close, it'll close soon," James commented. "She didn't give it instructions."

Alyssa quickly closed her eyes and woke Katrine, then told her to try grabbing Adrian's labyrinth before she left.

"Well, Alyssa," said James as he walked up to her. "It was a pleasure meeting you. I'm sure you'll feel better soon." James passed beside her and disappeared.

It was quiet. Alyssa glanced at the desert floor and noticed that the set of footprints had turned towards her. She became extremely nervous despite how weak and nauseous she felt from the spines lodged throughout her body. She struggled to look up to where she thought his head might be.

"John?" she whispered.

"Have a happy birthday, Alyssa," the voice whispered.

The footsteps walked towards her until they stopped directly in front of her. She jolted with surprise when she felt a hand touch her forehead. It gently brushed down her face and closed her eyes. Suddenly, all the pain disappeared from her body, leaving a tingling sensation behind.

She took a deep breath and opened her eyes to find herself in her car, parked on the shoulder of the highway leading up the other side of Nogal canyon. Her emergency blinkers were flashing on and off, and the 'HOT' light was lit up. Alyssa stared blankly at the dashboard for what seemed an eternity. She didn't trust herself to look up. She was going crazy.

A tapping on the window made Alyssa jump. She looked up to see a short, middle-aged Hispanic man outside her window.

"Are you okay?" he asked through the window. Alyssa glanced in the rear-view mirror to see a potato chip delivery truck parked behind her. She shook her head in confusion as she tried to answer the man.

"I guess," she said quietly, more to herself than to the man outside.

"Looks like you've overheated. Pop the hood and I'll have a look."

Alyssa looked up at him, bewildered.

"Pop the hood," he repeated.

Alyssa nodded her head slowly and surveyed the dashboard, trying to concentrate on where the release for the hood was located. Finally, she found it and popped the hood open. As the man looked at her engine, Alyssa slowly got out of her car and looked down at the canyon floor. The boulders her car had crashed into were there, but the large prickly pear cactus she had fallen into was not. She stared down at the canyon trying to discern if it had really happened.

"Looks like you have a leak in your radiator hose," the man explained. "I'll dry it up and wrap it with duct tape. It should hold 'til you get to the next town. I can top you off with some water," he said as he passed behind her, heading towards his van.

Alyssa rubbed her face upward with her hands, then pulled her hair on the way down as she looked out. There were no footprints below, no marks in the dirt that she could see, no sign that anything at all had happened.

The man had returned to the car and the sound of duct tape being torn off its roll echoed through the canyon.

The Link – Seven Days of Cyan

"Can you start her up? I'll add some water directly to the radiator," the man said as he peeked around the hood.

Alyssa turned to the man. "What?"

"Can you start her up, and I'll add some water to the radiator?"

Alyssa shook herself out of her daze. "Of course."

She got in the car and started it. She wouldn't tell her parents... or anyone. The man slammed the hood down. She'd make another doctor's appointment. Her head still wasn't quite right after the bicycle accident. The man gave a smile and wave. She returned the smile and wave, and said thank you.

Just get home, she thought. If it had really happened, someone would have stopped and tried to help her. She looked to see if any cars were coming. Maybe for the rest of the trip she should try to think up a different story with different characters. The addiction she had developed to her present story was turning unhealthy.

Alyssa quickly glanced into the backseat to make sure no one was there, and then pulled back onto the highway.

Chapter 21
Free (Saturday)

Katrine gazed across a wheat field towards a small farm town. The Canadian air was cold as it whipped down her tie-die T-shirt and up her bell-bottom jeans. Alyssa had dressed her in what she thought was appropriate for 1966, but had made the mistake of giving her a short-sleeved shirt instead of a long one. She rubbed her hands up and down her arms to try to warm up, but stopped when her right hand touched the scar that Zor had put on her shoulder the night she tried to get Paul out of Cyan. Alyssa wouldn't let Katrine take it off. She said that every main character needed some sort of physical distinction to separate them from the rest of the characters. Katrine was back to being a character in a fictional story. Only for a fleeting moment when Alyssa had wakened her at Adrian's and told her to grab the labyrinth did Alyssa believe Katrine was real.

Out of the corner of her eye, she finally saw what she had been waiting for: Zor stepping through his labyrinth door she had left open. He stood a short distance from her and examined his surroundings, and then started to walk towards Katrine until he saw her take a step back.

"I was on the way to Adrian's when I noticed this door open. You need the compass I have to get back to Cyan," Zor explained.

"You got what you wanted from me, Zor," Katrine said quietly. "You no longer need me."

"I know that you're angry with me, but it would be foolish for you not to return to Cyan. The others can't detect your presence there. Out here you're exposed... vulnerable. They'll take you, force you to fill a transfer vase, then kill you so that you can't share your powers with anyone else."

Katrine scoffed, "A link is a treasure from which all can take pleasure... unless you're dead."

"Been talking to Woester, I see." He sighed. "He was partially correct. You can't give everyone your power. Only those who are primed to accept it. Only witches and warlocks. A regular human doesn't have the brain structure to hold onto a link's power."

Katrine plucked some of the wheat in front of her. It was time to 'put all her cards on the table' as she heard Robert once say.

"Do you know where you are?" she asked.

Zor looked over the fields at the town. "I believe we're outside Robert's town in Canada."

"This is the field that they used to mow down every year to have a concert. Robert used to go with his parents and his younger brother. I suppose you know a thing or two about the close bond that brothers can share."

"I suppose I do know. I would do anything for my brother."

Katrine looked across the field and watched the breeze bend the tips of the tall yellow grass. "Yes, you've certainly shown as much." Katrine threw the blade of grass down. "What you do to families, no matter how well you justify your actions, repulses me, Zor. You were poor once. If you were forced to choose, would you have chosen to stay with your brother and be poor, or would you have chosen to never see your brother again so that you can be free to *play soccer?*"

"Who's to say that Robert would choose the same way I would?" Zor questioned. "You can't apply such hypothetical situations..."

"If your mother was still alive..."

"Don't talk about my mother, Katrine."

"If your mother was still alive," Katrine asked louder, "and you disappeared without a trace, can you imagine the pain she'd go through, always wondering if you were dead or alive? And what about your brother? Wouldn't your disappearance be traumatic to him? Can you even conceive the pain you cause when you tear families apart?"

"Time heals all wounds."

"Your mother is gone, Zor. Do you no longer miss her? How many years has it been?"

Zor folded his arms in front of him and sighed. "Loss makes a person strong."

Katrine shook her head and replied with disappointment, "But if the loss doesn't *need* to happen? Zor, you at least know your mother is dead. The families of Cyan's citizens have to cope with not knowing what's become of their loved ones."

Zor seemed to become impatient. "Katrine, I am *not* going to release Cyan's citizens no matter how much you bring up my past. Yes, everyone in Cyan has a mother, and perhaps most mothers miss their children when they disappear. But Katrine, most of the citizens in Cyan have parents like my father. And do you know what? I have no idea whether my father is dead or alive, nor do I care. *These* are the types of families I've split up."

Katrine shook her head. "Not all of them. Robert, for example."

"Robert's a special case."

"I'm sure Cyan is full of *special cases*."

"No, it's not. Come back to Cyan so that you can learn their stories."

Katrine took a deep breath. "I'm not going back with you. I suppose it would be very easy to get me through that door once Alyssa arrives in Albuquerque and stops thinking about me, but I'm hoping you have the good sense to just leave me here. There's no place for me in Cyan and if you force me to return, I'll make your life miserable. I'll destroy your utopia... somehow."

Zor sighed. "You won't try to destroy the only place you are truly safe and could call home. You may not belong to the Thespian House, the Musician House, or the Artist House... but you do belong at the Main House, Katrine. Like it or not, we have a future together."

Katrine glared at him. "Yes, there's no doubt in my mind we have a future together. For now, though, I'd like to be free. I haven't been free for a very long time."

Zor looked across the field at the town. After a long pause, he nodded his head.

"I suppose Robert's family would like to hear how well he's doing. I'll tell him you visited." Zor began to walk towards the labyrinth door. "If you get into any trouble, contact Alyssa. I plan on spending a lot more time with her now that the 1998 door will take me a bit more seriously. I'll come to help you."

Katrine shook her head in disappointment, realizing she could do nothing to keep him from seeing Alyssa. Zor was about to step through the door when Katrine remembered.

"Zor?"

"What?"

"The empty grave."

The Link – Seven Days of Cyan

It felt awkward to ask him, especially after she had just finished threatening to destroy Cyan, but she had to know. Katrine held her breath nervously as she waited for his response.

"It was your mother's."

A tremendous weight seemed to be lifted from Katrine's shoulders.

"Did she kill my father?" She felt almost ashamed after she asked the question. Her mother was not a murderer.

"I don't know. My powers don't work that way. When you settle down a little and realize how much you need Cyan, how much you need me, you are welcome to return. Then I'll help you find your mother. I'll leave the door open for you." He reached into his pocket and pulled out a compass. "It will bring you back to Cyan, nowhere else. I'm giving my labyrinth orders not to let you open the other doors." He threw it to Katrine and she caught it. He gave Katrine one final look. "You won't be able to stay away, Katrine." He stepped through the door and was gone, but the distortion remained.

Katrine started walking towards Robert's village. She slid her hands in her jean pockets to try to warm them and felt a cold metal box in her left pocket. She pulled out Adrian's labyrinth and a compass she had found in the top letter desk drawer. They now belonged to her.

Zor was right. She couldn't stay away. She had too much unfinished business in her own time.

171

Part 2: Master Rattimor

Chapter 22
Picking up the Pieces

Katrine dropped the shovel in the wet grass of Dragon Hill, sat down to rest beside her father's grave, and hugged her arms around herself. The gray sweatshirt she wore was not enough to keep her warm since she had stopped working, and the sweat on her body was turning frigid. She had just finished reburying her father's remains and was exhausted. Using an old glass that she found on the kitchen floor inside the farmhouse, she rinsed her mouth out with water. Although she spit the water out, the sulfur and dirt taste in the farm's well water was still better than the taste of vomit in her mouth.

Katrine looked below at her old, decrepit home and felt peaceful. The enormous task of finding all her father's shattered remains was finally completed. It had taken about two hours to scour Dragon Hill's slope to find the smaller pieces of bone fragments; about three hours to collect the bones below that had landed in the old chicken yard, backyard, and on the roof of the farmhouse and shed; then one more hour to collect what dirt she could find to cover the bones and fill the empty holes she had found in front of her parents' headstones. Even if Alyssa had stayed with her, Katrine wouldn't have asked her to help with the cleanup. It was something Katrine had to do out of respect for the man who had raised her. What began as a short trip home to read the maker off the headstones to her parents' graves turned out to be a long and arduous morning that ended with her finally making peace with her past and forgiving her father. With each of the larger pieces of bone she picked up, she tried to recall a different memory from her past. It gave her a chance to remember that before her father started drinking, he was a loving, hardworking, generous man. The turning point in his life came only after a couple years of crop failure and after losing much of the livestock to disease. A man who can't provide for his family will first turn on his family, the individuals who most love him... perhaps out of embarrassment, perhaps out of resentment. Whatever the reason he changed, Katrine decided to no longer judge him based on the last three years she had lived with him, but rather the first fourteen years when she was growing up.

As Katrine peered across the farmyard to the distant hills, she once again tried to understand why someone would assault her father's grave in such a heinous manner. It had to be a warlock, because a regular human wasn't capable of blasting a decayed corpse out of the ground. She felt sick to her stomach once more as she thought of the scene she happened upon once she exited the labyrinth. Zor wouldn't commit such a crime. James... maybe. Perhaps he was angry with her for taking Adrian's labyrinth; but it still seemed unlikely James, if he *was* a warlock by now, would vandalize her father's grave in response.

As Katrine tried to reason why Adrian might have done it before Zor turned her into a naked mole rat, the sound of a horse galloping towards her from the other side of Dragon Hill startled her. She stood up to see a tan horse ridden by a man with a large, straw cowboy hat appear on the summit above her. She turned and walked anxiously down the hill towards the farmhouse where her labyrinth door awaited just inside the back door.

Katrine could hear the horse begin to gallop down the hill through the trees toward her, pausing momentarily at the family cemetery. Katrine broke into a run and was almost to the shed next to the house when the horse came upon her and skidded to a halt directly in her path. She stopped and looked up at a middle-aged man who could have starred in a colorized television western that Alyssa's father had watched during her visit to Albuquerque... with the exception of two pierced ears. He had on a black and white polka-dotted sheepskin vest with a pink, button-down shirt underneath, jeans covered with leather chaps, and old, black boots. A large rope tied into a lasso was attached over the edge of his saddle with a hook. Earrings below each ear dangled clear down to his shoulders. It would have been a comical sight had Katrine not known why he was there.

"I'm looking for a woman named Katrine Farmer. I'm an old friend of Frank's, her father," he said with a smile that unnerved her.

"She's in the house. I'll go get her," Katrine replied, trying to mask her apprehension. She began to walk in front of the horse, but he moved it in front of her. She tried to walk behind the horse, but the cowboy backed the horse up, again blocking her from the house. Katrine stopped, sighed, and looked up at the man. "Can you make it sit, too?"

The man chuckled. "No one's in the house. You're Katrine."

"What do you want?" she asked, annoyed with his antics.

"Frank wanted me to drop by every once in a while after he died to make sure you're all right." He looked at the house. "You haven't been home."

"I've been on Sabbatical. I'm fine. Now would you mind moving your horse? I'm getting cold and I'd like to go inside." She tried to move in front of his horse, but he moved it in front of her once more.

"That's an interesting outfit you have on... for 1693," he remarked about her jeans and gray sweatshirt.

Katrine looked him in the eyes, tired of the game they were playing. "Interesting earrings *you* have on," she responded. They stared at each other with the most serious faces, waiting to see what would happen next.

"You give off a very human aura when your other half isn't with you, Katrine," he finally said. "Hard to believe there's such a high price on your head. Bringing you in just seems a little too easy," he said as he grabbed the rope from beside the saddle. "Nevertheless, I aim to collect that prize."

Katrine backed up slowly, in shock. "What do you mean there's a price on my head?"

"What I mean is that someone wants you so badly, he made it worthwhile for me to grab you and give you away instead of keeping you all to myself."

Katrine swallowed and tried to maintain her composure. "What prize could possibly be better than a transfer vase full of a link's power?"

"Fifty percent of the transfer vase contents along with a space labyrinth, a labyrinth that opens up into any alien nation on any planet in this galaxy. And you look like the aliens so they can't detect you. Word has it that the warlock named Grumley created just one before he was killed, and it's soon going to be mine, mine, mine," he said as he adjusted the lasso.

Katrine took a step backwards, turned around and started sprinting towards the cemetery as she tried to call out to Alyssa, begging her for help. She could hear the horse gallop up from behind, and soon after, a rope flew over her head and draped tightly around her, binding her arms to the side of her body.

"Always wanted to do that... lasso me a girl," he chuckled as he pulled her closer to the horse. Katrine attempted to keep calling Alyssa, but couldn't concentrate.

"Listen, cowboy!" she said angrily as she tried to lift the rope back over her head. "You don't know who you're dealing with."

He looked thoughtful for a moment, then hopped down from the saddle.

"Considering the man who has put a price on your head, you may be right. I was hoping to *drag* you to my labyrinth door, but I suppose it would be a lot wiser to transport you out of here and get you to the master as quick as I possibly can," he said, then added, "since I don't know *who I'm dealing with*." He pulled her closer and she resisted with all her might.

"I don't know any *master*! There's been a mistake!" Katrine yelled as the man reached out to grab hold of her arm. Suddenly a blinding green light from the top of the farmhouse flew and hit his head, causing him to release the rope and drop Katrine to the grass. When the light disappeared, the man above her had an absent, glazed-over appearance on his face. Out of the corner of Katrine's eye, she saw the familiar funnel-shaped cloud that had once turned her legs into a fin; but this time it was light green, not blue. Katrine shifted back on the ground as best as she could as the funnel-shaped cloud encircled the cowboy, picked him up, and turned him in the air. He shrank in size, grew brown fur, black eyes, and long whiskers. When the funnel cloud disappeared, a small field mouse dropped to the ground and scurried away, squealing madly. Katrine looked over to the roof of the farmhouse where she saw Zor calmly sitting on the edge, then closed her eyes and fell back to the ground with a sigh of relief.

Katrine lay on the ground and listened to Zor's footsteps as he approached. When he stopped above her, she opened her eyes and looked up at him.

"Thank you."

Zor waved his arm and the rope around her disappeared, releasing her arms. "It would make my life much easier if you'd just come back to live in Cyan. You're lucky I noticed the strange look on Alyssa's face when you called her." Zor leaned over and held out his hand for Katrine to take. She did and he lifted her to her feet. "Alyssa's a busy woman, you know. She can't go into a daydream state every time you're in need of help. She's got soccer, class, a new boyfriend..." He turned and started taking the stirrups off the horse. "I've got to get back to my date. She thinks I went to the men's room." He lifted the saddle and blanket off the horse and threw it to the ground.

"If you would tell me how to get the labyrinth door to follow me, I wouldn't need Alyssa's help," she told him, remembering that Adrian had made the labyrinth door stay in her moving car.

Zor turned towards Katrine, irritated. "Every labyrinth has passwords that will allow you to do different things, such as order the doors to move with you... or open the door twice in one day. I don't know any of your passwords." He slapped the horse on the thigh and watched the horse take off running, then grumbled, "Don't even know mine because dear 'ol daddy Rattimor never told Adrian." He turned back to Katrine after the horse disappeared over the hilltop. "You know, James has been rather difficult to live with since you stole the labyrinth I promised him. You'd better find your mother quickly, because I do intend on taking it away *soon*. Stay closer to the door, next time. You might not get so lucky with the next warlock." Zor gave her the same worried look a father would give a daughter, then disappeared.

Katrine bit her lip and wondered if she should have told him that her father's grave had just been blasted into hundreds of pieces and that there was a price on her head, put out by someone who had a space labyrinth. She sighed and decided that it was best he didn't know yet. He would just force her to abandon the search for her mother and bring her back to Cyan. He would read about everything in Alyssa's book, anyhow.

As Katrine started to walk towards the back door of the farmhouse to return to Robert's Canadian farmhouse in 1966, she remembered the original purpose of her visit: to find out who cut the headstones. Perhaps whoever cut and carved them would remember who ordered and paid for them. She quickly made her way back to the family cemetery and peered at the back of the headstones. Her face flushed white as chalk. Above the makers, Smith & Coal, was a note engraved in the stone: *I shall hunt your mother down and shatter her bones like your father's should my daughter not be returned.* Signed *Master Rattimor.*

Chapter 23
Elation

Alyssa and Sami sat side by side on the bench, waiting for their turn to play in their weekly practice soccer scrimmage. Alyssa couldn't stop her legs from bouncing up and down and couldn't stop smiling.

Sami leaned over, still looking out at the field. "What's got into you? Stop smiling."

Alyssa turned to Sami. "I did it."

"Did what?"

"*It.*"

Sami turned to Alyssa in disbelief. "With who?"

"That blond-haired god that you pressured me into seeing."

Sami shook her head in disbelief. "Jesus, Alyssa. I just thought you would go out for dinner or something, not jump into bed with him the first chance you had."

"I know," Alyssa replied, trying not to burst out in sheer joy. "It's not like me, is it?"

"I should say not." Sami looked back onto the field. "Well, how was it?"

"Unbelievable. I never thought it was possible to feel so good." Alyssa shook her head. "He was simply amazing. I've never met anyone like him. He's so... *intense!*" She swiveled on the bench so that she faced Sami. "And it's not just his lovemaking. Everything about him is intense. Even when he's quiet, he's got this intense look on his face," she said as she raised her hand in front of her face and imitated John. "It's so attractive. You know how women fall for men in uniforms," she tried to explain. "Well, it's like that. And he's *smart*. I had lunch with him just a couple of hours ago. He knew everything about everything... music, opera, art, theater, sports, zoology. I couldn't stump him on anything. I think he's even smarter than David." She looked down to the grass, shook her head, and smiled. "I am hopelessly infatuated with him." Alyssa took a deep breath and exhaled slowly. "I can't get him out of my mind."

Sami laughed. "Boy, you do have it bad." The ball came rolling up to the bench. Sami quickly picked up the ball and threw it back onto the field. "So, how'd you two get together for the nasty deed? You know... in case there's something I can use should I get a boyfriend someday."

Alyssa smirked. "It's too embarrassing to tell."

Sami looked suspiciously at Alyssa. "This I've got to hear."

For a moment, Alyssa's face became strained as if trying to hold back the most wonderful secret. It didn't take long for her to give in.

"Okay. You win. So last Friday, I'm walking to my room and I see him. He asks me to the movie they're showing in the union, I say yes, and then he walks me to my dorm room. Of course, on the side of caution, I tell him to wait outside. I go inside to fix my hair or whatever, and he walks in my dorm room and locks the door behind him."

"Oh, my God. Weren't you scared out of your mind?"

"To say the least. I grab my hair dryer, ready to pelt him over the head with it. He walks quietly to the middle of the room and scans my spare desk, the one with all my clothes on it, and he picks up a bandana. I think he's going to strangle me or something, so I warn him to leave or I was going to scream at the top of my lungs. He tells me to calm down, that he wasn't about to hurt me. I had my hair dryer gripped so tight, I probably cracked the plastic. Now, get this... he ties the bandana into a circle, places his hands through it behind his back and twirls one of his hands around a couple of times so that his hands become bound, then he kneels down on the floor in front of me."

"You've got to be kidding," Sami said, a smile slowly spreading across her face.

"Then he says something like... 'Before you knock me senseless for invading your room, please hear me out. From the very first moment I set eyes on you, I have been unable to get you out of my mind. I want to become much more to you than just one of your fans, because since I've met you, Alyssa, you've come to occupy my every thought, every dream. With everything I do, your image interferes, and I find myself wishing I was at your side. You may ask me to leave, and I will. But I hope you let me stay to make this the most memorable, most passionate night of your entire life. Do what you want with me, but just realize that if you knock me out with that hair dryer, you're still going to have to drag me out the door to get rid of me, and I weigh nearly two hundred pounds.'"

The Link – Master Rattimor

"Whoa. What'd you do?"

"Cracked up. I mean, it was such an outrageous scene." Alyssa nodded. "I thought it was a man's legs that turned me on, but his chest... Mmm. He was built."

"Did you let him untie his hands?"

"Eventually," Alyssa said with a mischievous smile. "Can't make love without hands."

Sami turned back towards the field. "Well, I guess I'm happy for you."

"Guess?"

"It just makes me a little nervous. Seems he knew exactly what to do to get you in bed. You've got to be careful around men who are used to getting exactly what they want."

Alyssa nudged Sami on the shoulder. "Don't rain on my parade, Sami. He would have left had I asked, but I didn't. I *wanted* him to stay." She sighed with a glazed-over look. "I certainly don't regret it."

"I hope you didn't tell David. It'll break his heart."

Alyssa shook her head. "No. He doesn't need to know."

"Well, if you and...?" She waved her hand, asking Alyssa for help.

"John."

"If you and John actually develop a long lasting relationship, David's going to have to find out."

"About *going out* with John, not the sex."

"They go hand in hand! Poor David."

"Sami, David and I are just good friends."

"I *know* that. It's just he's so sensitive. He's not going to take the news lightly."

"I wish he would get out more and try to meet someone."

Several girls yelled from the field, "Alyssa! Sami!" They looked out at the field to see everyone staring at them. "Pay attention and get out here! We're losing!"

Chapter 24
Gardenstadt

Katrine looked across the dirt street of Gardenstadt, a somewhat sleazy town near Dragon Hill, knowing that she was about to do something very stupid: journey too far from the labyrinth door. She shivered in the cold air as people walked the street in front of her and looked at her curiously because her hair and long dress were soaked on a day when there wasn't a cloud in the sky. But she could do little about appearances at the moment since Alyssa was too busy rushing off to class.

Katrine contacted Alyssa at 6:30 in the morning, knowing that was the time she would be tossing and turning, hitting the snooze button on her alarm clock repeatedly, moaning to herself that she didn't want to get up. In her restless state, Alyssa didn't mind helping Katrine dress in some appropriate clothing and help her enter the labyrinth. But when Katrine found out that it hadn't stopped raining inside the labyrinth since the previous day and asked Alyssa for an umbrella, it was too late. Alyssa was already stumbling towards the shower, unable and unwilling to concentrate on anything. So Katrine walked in the rain to the 1693 door, knowing full well it was her own fault she was becoming soaked.

After Katrine's visit to Dragon Hill the previous day, Katrine had upset her labyrinth, which apparently had a female soul because of the pleasant voice that sounded from the doors. The conversation started when she asked the door out of desperation to open at Smith & Coal's workshop. The town where Smith & Coal was located wasn't too far away from Dragon Hill, but Alyssa still refused to give her any help when it came to transporting.

"Sorry, dear," replied the door. "Rules are rules, and all labyrinths are bound to them. Opening once a day is all that is allowed, unless you know the password, of course. Try tomorrow at sunrise. I'd be happy to do it for you then."

"But I need to find my mother before Adrian's father does. He's threatened to kill her," Katrine tried to explain.

"You can't be talking about Damen Rattimor. He was such a nice, young fellow. I seriously doubt he's going to kill your mother. I loved having him visit when he was dating my first owner, Rebecca Grumley. Now *she* was a remarkable woman, not like that Adrian... but I haven't heard from Rebecca for years. Have *you* seen her lately? Adrian thought she had taken a vacation to Australia and decided to stay."

Katrine sat down on the grassy lawn in front of the talking door, wondering if she told the labyrinth the truth, it would somehow be grateful and would open the door at Smith & Coal's as a favor.

"I heard from a friend that Rebecca was killed by Damen Rattimor after she empowered him."

The labyrinth fell silent, then Katrine noticed dark clouds appear above her and it started to rain.

"Would you please open the door just one more time today?" Katrine begged.

"I'm much too sad to do *anything* at the moment. Please, just come back tomorrow."

So the rain that had started yesterday had not yet stopped when Katrine entered the labyrinth that morning. She waited two hours in the rain to make sure Smith & Coal would be open, since she didn't want to be stuck dawdling outside their shop too long like easy prey waiting for Rattimor's bounty hunters. Then in her haste to get out of the rain, she wasn't specific enough when she told the door where to open. Consequently, it opened in the back room of Smith & Coal's workshop. Luckily, no one saw her walk out of the labyrinth door, and she managed to successfully sneak into the front business room undetected by Mr. Coal, who was busy cutting a new headstone for a recently deceased elder.

The fifty-year-old, gray-headed businessman with a strong Irish accent proved surprisingly helpful. He remembered everything about her parents' headstones because he had a dream about them the previous night, which seemed much more than just coincidence. Nevertheless, Katrine found out that Ms. Patty Horton, the madam at the brothel across the street, had ordered, paid for, and picked up the headstones.

Katrine's mother was the only woman from her church who would talk to Ms. Horton, and it didn't surprise Katrine that her mother would turn to her for help over the other gossiping churchwomen. Katrine couldn't stand the women who went to her church, but she would always go on Sundays because it was expected of her, and the last thing she wanted to do was to disappoint her mother.

Now Katrine peered across the street at the brothel in her wet dress, knowing that she'd be much safer if she waited until tomorrow to talk to Madam Horton because she would be able to move her labyrinth door right outside the brothel's door. But waiting another day was out of the question if she was to find her mother before Master Rattimor. She looked around to see if there were any obvious signs of a warlock or witch watching her. No one appeared to be dressed inappropriately, and as for people watching her... well, just about everyone was watching her. She was the only one in a drenched dress on that cold, sunny day. She recognized some of the faces from visits to the town four years ago, but most were foreign or forgotten faces.

Katrine took a deep breath, hurried across the street, and knocked on the door. Madam Horton, a large lady with curly, long black hair tied up in red satin ribbons, answered the door. She was dressed in a long, low cut, shiny, satin, red dress with a slit clear up to her very large thigh.

"Katrine!" she exclaimed excitedly. She quickly grabbed Katrine's arm and pulled her inside, then looked out at the street nervously before closing the door and locking it. Watching Madam Horton as she peeked out a window, Katrine had to rub her eyes. For a moment, Katrine believed to see the entire front wall glow green before returning to normal, but no one else seemed to notice. Hesitating, she turned around to find herself in a room full of flowers and several scantily clad girls lounging lazily on large flower print couches. A strong smell of spice in the room almost choked her, and the air was warm and humid. In the back of the room was a winding staircase that led to a balcony with several bedroom doors.

"Girls," Madam Horton said in a most serious manner as she nodded her head towards the stairs. They groaned, stood up, and slowly made their way up the stairs and into their rooms. Madam Horton looked at Katrine's wet dress and made her way to a front closet to pull out a pink dress. "I've seen stranger things than a girl in a wet dress on a sunny day, so I'm not even going to ask." She handed the dress to Katrine and turned away from her so she could dress with some privacy. Katrine looked at the dry dress, modest by brothel standards, and decided a change in appearance was not a bad idea. She started to undress as Madam Horton rubbed her hands together.

"I've been thinking about you," the madam said anxiously. "Do you know about your parents?"

"My father's dead," Katrine replied with a bit of remorse. "I'm looking for my mother. Mr. Coal told me that you were the one who ordered the headstones."

The Link – Master Rattimor

"Your mother came to me the day after your father died. He killed himself, Katrine. Put a bullet through his head when he realized what he had done to you." Katrine stopped dressing, shocked. Madam Horton turned her head around to look at Katrine and said, "He loved you, you know. Came here once after drinking too much and bored one of my girls to death talking about you and your mother." Katrine lifted the dress over her shoulders and sat down on the couch, still stunned. "First and only visit, Precious, so don't worry."

It wasn't the brothel visit that disturbed Katrine. It was the fact that her father had killed himself over what he had done to her. She put her head down in her hand, wishing her father was still alive so that she could tell him how much she loved him and that she forgave him.

"Last night there was this strange black cloud that covered the moon," the madam said excitedly. Katrine looked up, remembering that Mr. Coal had also mentioned the black cloud, but thought it was part of his dream. "I believe it was some type of omen," she continued, "for it came upon me like death and tried to splinter my head into a million pieces, sucking out the memories I had of your mother when she first came to ask for help four years ago. Then it left in a blink of an eye when I finished recalling her first departure to find you. Then this morning, I can't tell you how many strangers, most certainly Nezbar guards in disguise, have been knocking on my door, asking your whereabouts. And now here you are! What is going on, Precious? Why are you back? Did your mother ever find you?"

Katrine opened her eyes wide. "Do you know where she is?"

"She went to get a job as a maid at the castle."

"What?" Katrine asked in disbelief. "I never saw her!"

"Dear, dear. Not in Nezbar. Yes, she tried Nezbar first, but someone recognized her. She came running back to me soon after, in fear of her life! We decided that adding a stone beside your father's wouldn't be such a bad idea." She paused in mid-thought and looked as if she had just realized something. "How did you know your mother was still alive?"

"Please, Ms. Horton, it's a long story," Katrine said quickly. "Where's my mother now?"

Madam Horton began to shake with both fear and excitement, her breasts nearly escaping their satin prison. She rushed over to the couch, sat down beside Katrine, and took Katrine's hand tightly into her own. "She had talked to a worker in the fields and found out about the wedding, so she decided to go to Papau, my precious, to seek employment, not Nezbar. Haven't heard from her since."

"Papau?" Katrine asked faintly. She had escaped with Paul on the very day she arrived at the castle. Her mother hadn't found her in time.

A loud crash was heard against the door, startling both Katrine and Ms. Horton. "Quick, dear," the madam said with a wild look in her eye as she jumped up from the couch and pulled Katrine up. Madam Horton ran to the closet and grabbed a long red wig, then quickly led Katrine towards the back of the room to a door behind the staircase.

"Through the kitchen, out the back door. God's speed and good luck. Find your mother and make sure she's well," she said as she placed the red wig on top of Katrine's head and tucked in her hair. Madam Horton stopped for a moment with worry in her eyes, then kissed Katrine on the forehead. "Be careful."

"Thank you," Katrine said with a nervous glance towards the front wall, then she slipped into the kitchen and out onto the street as a second crash into the brothel's front door shook the entire building.

Katrine took a deep breath and began to walk down the street towards the corner, attempting to look calm and in no particular hurry. As she walked, she tried not to stare too long at the people who were holding small black cards, reading them as they walked around, inspecting the others who walked the street.

Alyssa, she thought, *I'm going to need you to get back to the door. Please.*

Can't right now. I'm in the middle of calculus.

But I really have a bad feeling about this, Katrine responded as she watched a large man reading a black card pass her, then pause with a strange look on his face. Katrine started to walk a little faster. *Can you at least spare a little time?*

Look, the instructor goes down the row and has us take turns answering the homework problems. I've got five people in front of me before I go. That's how much time you have, so hurry.

But you've got to leave until I call you. I think they can detect you when you're around.

You know, you are really making this difficult!

Katrine started walking faster, rounding one corner, then the next, passing six more men and one woman, each holding a black card, until Smith & Coal's workshop finally came back into view. A small group of people had gathered in front of the brothel's front door, so Katrine turned her head in the opposite direction as she began to cross the street. Near the entrance of Smith & Coal's, she noticed a young man, about eighteen with brown hair, watching her with a gleam in his eye. She slowed a little and tried to walk a little more casual, but he stepped in front of the doorway and held up a black card.

The Link – Master Rattimor

"Long brown hair," he read loud enough for several nearby people to hear. Her wig flew off the top of her head and landed behind her. Katrine stopped and stared at him as he continued reading, "Blue eyes, approximately one point seven meters high. Will probably visit both Smith & Coal's and the brothel in the small town of Gardenstadt, or be found at the servants' quarters at the Nezbar castle." He looked up from the card and smiled. "I can spot a brothel wig a kilometer away."

Katrine's eyes darted from the young man to the people who began gathering around her, then back to the man in the doorway while she frantically called out for Alyssa to return. The young man in front of her was also aware of the crowd gathering around Katrine.

"I found her first, everyone! Fair is fair," he announced boastfully to the crowd.

A strange sound like a gas torch being lit behind Katrine changed the young man's expression quickly. Katrine turned her head around just in time to see a bald man in his fifties, wearing a black suit, hurl a ball of fire past her, hitting the young man in the midsection and hurling him through the side wall of Smith & Coal's where he exploded and set the shop on fire. Many of the people walking the streets screamed and ran into the nearest building, leaving Katrine surrounded by about twelve onlookers who were pocketing their black cards with hungry looks upon their faces.

Paralyzed only a moment at the sight of body parts flying out the side wall of the shop, Katrine began to run for the door of Smith & Coal's, but was stopped when the bald man appeared in front of her, blocking the entrance. He had beady, dark eyes set too close to a long, crooked nose. She swallowed nervously and backed away from him.

"It's not who found you first," he said with a smile. "It's who's the most powerful." He reached down to the ground and picked up a severed foot. "This boy was weak and cocky. Not a good year for him, I guess." He threw the foot to his side.

I'm here! You should have heard it. The idiot class clown just made the funniest wisecrack.

"I see your other side has now joined you," the bald man in the black suit remarked. "Don't try anything, you'll only get hurt. I'm not just an ordinary warlock, you see. I've already acquired the powers from a link, with a little help from my dear friend, Master Rattimor himself."

Boy, this guy's full of himself. Hold a fist above your head. I'll show him a thing or two.

Katrine quickly made a fist and held it above her head. She could feel it tingling and looked up to see her fist glow yellow. Before she realized what was happening, several streams of yellow light shot out in all directions, each directed at the warlocks and witches that encircled

185

her on the street, with two shooting straight into the bald man in front of her. Everyone surrounding her collapsed where they stood. Katrine looked at the fallen bodies with wide eyes.

"Wow," Katrine whispered.

It's my turn next. Gotta go. Get out of there fast, Katrine. Looks like I could only stun the more powerful ones.

Katrine hurried to Smith & Coal's shop, which was now ablaze, and reached down to the doorknob when her body was lifted up in the air and thrown backwards to the street. She landed on her back with a hard thud. The bald man stood up with a fireball in his hand and approached Katrine.

"Alyssa!" Katrine yelled as she tried to scurry to her feet, but ended up tripping on the long, pink dress she wore. "Help?"

"Too bad my good friend wants you alive. You're going to be begging me to let you die after I get through with you," he said angrily as he raised the fireball above his head.

Katrine turned her face toward the dirt and covered it with her arms, shaking and about to scream, when she heard the ball of fire drop to her side. She peered up to see a green ray of light originating behind her and striking the bald man in the head. He fell to the ground, motionless, and the ray of light disappeared. Katrine looked at the brothel's rooftop to see Zor standing, staring silently at the fallen bodies on the street.

Katrine quickly scrambled to her feet and ran back to Smith & Coal's door. As she reached for the doorknob, she realized that her hand, along with her entire body, had an eerie green glow surrounding it. Opening the door, she was momentarily knocked backwards by the heat from the fire that had already devoured the walls and wooden workbenches of the shop. Katrine gathered her dress tight around her waist, held her breath and rushed inside.

As Katrine hurried through the workshop, her face felt as though it were shriveling up from the heat, and her eyes watered so much that it became difficult to see clearly. Just as she was about to enter the back room where her labyrinth door awaited, she heard a moan. She stopped and looked down to see Mr. Coal laying face down on the floor beside his workbench. On his back rested a bloody hand. Katrine looked out the hole in the front wall where she thought she saw movements and knew at once she wouldn't be able to drag Mr. Coal out the front door.

Katrine leaned over, still holding her dress to her waist, and dared to take a breath. As she inhaled the smoke and began to cough, she knocked the hand off Mr. Coal's back and shook him.

"Come on, Mr. Coal," she said urgently before a cough. "You're too heavy. You have to wake up!"

The Link – Master Rattimor

A rafter fell near the front door, startling Katrine. She looked over the flames of the workbench to see that no one had yet followed her inside. Katrine let go of her dress, turned Mr. Coal on his back, grabbed him under his arms, and pulled the heavy man using all her strength through the back room's doorway. Lightheaded and dizzy, it took her a moment to realize that the edge of her dress had dragged too close to the wall and was now on fire. She gave a panicked cry at the sight, but her attention was soon shifted away from her dress when she noticed two or three silhouettes appear in the front door behind the flames.

The fire in front of the approaching warlocks disappeared, then a light flashed and flew towards her, only to ricochet off the green light that surrounded her body. With a final lurch, Katrine fell through the labyrinth doorway into the grass and rain, and the green light around her body disappeared. She grabbed Mr. Coal's pants and pulled his legs quickly through.

"Close!" she yelled to the door, and the door closed just as a dark figure stepped in front of it. She coughed again, staring at the doorway, half expecting the warlock on the other side to open it, but it remained closed.

She sank back against the hedge behind her and watched the rain put out the flames on the edge of her dress. The rain felt wonderful after the heat from the fire, and the smell of wet grass was a welcome relief from the smoke. Mr. Coal started to stir.

"I hope you're ready to believe in the impossible, Mr. Coal," she said quietly, "because I can't bring you back for a couple of days."

Tomorrow at sunrise she would be visiting her old fiancé's castle in Papau. A small smile crept across her face when she realized the black card read that she might be found at Nezbar's castle. Master Rattimor was looking for her mother in the wrong place. For the first time, Katrine felt a bit of hope, for she believed she finally had a chance to get to her mother before Rattimor.

Chapter 25
New Love

Alyssa walked out of her calculus class and rubbed her tired eyes. When she looked up, she saw John leaned against the hallway wall in khaki shorts and a dark green pullover, waiting for her with a smile on his face. She felt butterflies in her stomach as she smiled and walked over to him.

"What are you doing here?" she asked suspiciously. "I thought you had class on the other side of campus."

"Skipped out early to catch you. Would you like to go for coffee or a muffin at the union?"

"Definitely coffee. I need to wake up. Got caught daydreaming and answered the wrong problem in front of everyone."

"Well, then?" he said as he took her backpack, slung it across his shoulder, then offered his hand to her. She gave him a warm smile as she placed her hand in his, then they walked out of the building into the fresh morning air.

She loved the feeling she had when she was in a new relationship: she was jittery, excited, and she wanted everyone to look at her and her gorgeous new boyfriend. Envy me, she thought as she passed the students walking in the opposite direction. The beginning of a relationship was the best part.

She looked up at John's face to see if there was any indication he wanted to let go of her hand because of the sweat accumulating on her palm and noticed that he had a distant look.

"Something wrong?" Alyssa asked quietly.

He looked over at her and seemed to snap out of his daze. "Oh, nothing. Family matters. Nothing to worry about."

"Is your brother okay?"

John looked at her with a puzzled face. "Why wouldn't he be okay?"

"The car accident."

"Oh, yes, that. He recovered fine."

The Link – Master Rattimor

When they entered the snack bar at the union, Alyssa groaned when she saw how long the line was just to get a cup of coffee. But when John told Alyssa to save a table, he arrived at the table with the coffees a mere minute later. She was about to ask him how he got the drinks so fast, but John began to speak.

"I read your story," he said as he sat down and slid Alyssa's coffee across the table.

"I just gave it to you yesterday!"

"I guess I couldn't put it down."

Alyssa let out a small sigh of relief. "So it wasn't too bad? I was worried you would get angry that I used the story about the two young boys you told me about last week… and I used your pick-up line at Nicole's soccer game… and a few other things, if you hadn't noticed."

"No, it all seemed to fit well into the story. But I wanted to talk to you a little about the ending," John said as he took a sip of coffee.

"What about it?" Alyssa asked nervously.

"It's too open-ended. You end with Zor warning Katrine about warlocks coming after her, she has no idea where her mother is, and isn't she even going to *try* to free Cyan? It seems you're only half way finished with the book. You *are* going to continue writing the story, aren't you?"

"I suppose I could continue," she said hesitantly, "but quite honestly, the story is interfering with my concentration. It's always on my mind, and I wanted to start getting away from it. I've written one hundred seventy some odd pages in about a week, only by staying up 'til one or two every morning. I'm tired, I'm starting to drag on the soccer field, and I'm beginning to fall behind with my homework. I kind of need a break from it. After all, I have more classes than just Creative Writing."

John sat back in his chair with a thoughtful look on his face. "You're not going to be able to get it out of your mind until the story is truly finished. I bet you already have some good ideas about Katrine's struggle to ward off the other warlocks."

Katrine took a drink of coffee and looked over at the food court where the students were waiting in line, irritated at John for wanting her to continue writing the story. Didn't he listen to all her excuses *not* to continue it? Did she have to tell him that if she continued writing it, she was worried she'd completely lose her grip on reality just as she had on her trip up to Albuquerque?

"Well?" probed John. "Any ideas?"

She looked back at him and stared. If eyes had the power of persuasion, his certainly did. She let out a sigh and decided to tell him, since it was best at the beginning of a relationship to share common interests... and he was obviously very interested.

"Well, I do have a few ideas," she said, tapping her fingers on the table. "Let's see... Using Adrian's labyrinth, Katrine travels back to Dragon Hill where she runs into a warlock, but Zor saves her. The next day she faces twelve or so warlocks at once. Nicole saves Katrine by allowing her to shoot some sort of energy ray from her fist in all directions, rendering the warlocks surrounding her unconscious. Something like 'Raiders' when they open the sandbox." She felt stupid talking about energy rays, but John moved his chair in closer, looking extremely interested.

"Now, why would there be twelve warlocks after her at once? That seems like an unusually high number of warlocks to encounter at one place in one time period."

Alyssa gave a small smile, surprised he caught on that it was an unusual circumstance. "Adrian's father, Master Rattimor, offers a prize for Katrine's capture because for some reason he thinks she had something to do with Adrian's disappearance."

It almost seemed John's face lost some of its color, then he sat back in his chair with the most serious, thoughtful look Alyssa had ever seen. He stared at the table in silence, so Alyssa decided to continue in hopes he would share what he was thinking.

"I haven't yet figured out, however, how he finds out Adrian is missing, seeing that she and her father hadn't been on speaking terms since Adrian started dating Zor... according to what Robert told Katrine in Chapter Four."

John looked up at Alyssa with a glossy look. "Rehnquist."

"What?"

John shook his head and his glossy look disappeared. "Sorry. Create a brother named Rehnquist Rattimor. He can go squealing to Daddy like a pathetic, sniveling, brainless, low-class rodent once he finds out his beloved sister is missing." John appeared to be growing angrier with each word. "Adrian took care of him because he was quite incapable of..." He stopped himself from finishing the sentence, then exhaled slowly. "Rehnquist is a good name for a low life character, don't you agree?"

Alyssa smiled nervously, uncomfortable with John's sudden change in behavior. "Yes," she answered quietly.

"I suppose it stands to reason that Adrian's father would assume Katrine is responsible for his daughter's disappearance." He tapped his fingers on the tabletop beside his coffee cup with a look of concentration. "Make Rehnquist so much of a dimwit that he's unable to see that Adrian and Zor's relationship had been falling apart for the past couple of years. He knows about the link, but is sworn to secrecy by Adrian. Once Adrian turns up missing, only a week after a link shows up..." John shook his head. "So, does Katrine ever intend on telling Zor?" he asked with an agitated voice.

"No. She's worried he'll halt the search for her mother."

"Well, that seems like the logical action to take."

"Adrian's father is after Katrine's mother. He wrote on the back of her father's headstone a message that he was going to blast her mother into a million pieces if Adrian wasn't returned. Katrine would like to find her mother before Master Rattimor does... understandably so." Alyssa shook her head in disbelief. "You should have seen how he splintered her father's remains. Pieces of bone and dried flesh were all over the farm and Dragon Hill. Pretty gruesome."

John appeared surprised and Alyssa realized that she had just talked about her story as if it had really happened. She quickly took a drink of coffee, waiting for John to comment on her grasp on reality.

"It's still foolish for Katrine not to tell Zor. He can protect her, and maybe even help her find her mother."

Alyssa let out a sigh of relief, happy he hadn't noticed her mistake.

"Chapter One, John. Zor says that her old family matters do not matter anymore. She has a new family. Chapter Six – James states that Zor doesn't get involved in the citizen's family matters." John appeared disturbed at her response for some reason, so Alyssa decided she needed to change the subject. She gave a little laugh. "I can't believe you read the entire manuscript since lunch yesterday; which, by the way, was absolutely wonderful."

To her dismay, bringing up lunch had no effect on his mood. He looked down at his watch. "I have to run. I need to show up early for my next class to talk to the instructor." He downed the rest of his coffee and wiped his mouth. He was about to stand up when he stopped himself.

"May I mention something else about the manuscript?" he asked. Alyssa nodded her head reluctantly, anticipating the worst. "Katrine's feelings towards Zor are very ambiguous," John began. "One minute she's telling her friend, Ashleigh, she could never be with him, then a few chapters later you write that Katrine probably would *not* have stopped Zor from making an advance on her when she had just stepped out of the shower. So which is it?"

Alyssa sat back in her chair, surprised a man would care about the more intimate side of the story. "Well," she said slowly as she tried to figure it out for herself, "I think it's more of a lust thing. He's an attractive man with status and power, which almost any woman could fall for, but she'll never allow herself to get close to him emotionally because she doesn't respect what he does and she'll never be able to completely trust him. He doesn't care for her anyway."

John looked confused. "Why do you say that?"

"I thought you read the book, John. Everything he does and say is just to get her to trust him enough so that she fills the vase for him. It was all an act."

"But not only does Zor give her back her freedom at the end of the story, you said Zor lets her keep the labyrinth to find her mother, a gesture that would seemingly illustrate that he *does* care," John answered. "Maybe some of it was an act in the beginning..."

"It was *all* an act, John. And maybe Zor let her keep Adrian's labyrinth because he likes to see Katrine fight. Every time she's gone back to her own time, she has an encounter with Rattimor's warlocks, and Zor's been there every time to watch her contend. Perhaps it's a turn-on for him, or perhaps it's just part of his next scheme that will end with Katrine filling a transfer vase for James. That's why he kept her alive. He still wants to use her. Rattimor and Zor are probably best friends, for all we... I mean... for all *Katrine* knows." Alyssa sighed and looked away. Why wasn't he leaving to talk to his professor? The longer she talked the more mistakes she made. What if she ended up spilling the beans about how she had no control over that little voice in her head that seemed to constantly interrupt her thoughts with menial requests? *I need in the labyrinth...I need some different clothes...I need some money...*

"Anyway," Alyssa said, trying to wrap up the conversation, "Zor will get his just rewards when Nicole dumps him. He seems to have a real interest in her. You know...in the last chapter, he mentions that he still wants to see her."

"You think she's going to dump him?"

"Yes. After she finds out his true identity. Everything he's told her, just like with Katrine, has been a lie. Can't have a relationship with someone you don't trust."

John sat quiet for a moment. "Does that mean you trust me?" he asked with a curious look.

"You seem pretty trustworthy," she said with a smile, "but then I've only known you for a little over a week." Her face grew serious and she raised her eyebrows. "I'm watching you," she teased.

She could tell John was forcing a smile, and she felt like kicking herself.

"Would you mind if I stopped by your place tonight?" he asked as he threw his napkin in his empty coffee cup.

The Link – Master Rattimor

"I have a friend helping me study until about seven. After seven is best," she replied.

"Great," he said as he stood up, leaned over and gave Alyssa a gentle kiss on her lips. "I look forward to it."

She watched as he walked away, threw his cup in the trash, and left the union. She stared at the table in silence for nearly ten minutes with a very unsettled feeling, reviewing the conversation in her head and trying to figure out why John had reacted so strangely to some of the things she had said. Finally, she threw her napkin in her cup and left the union for her next class.

Chapter 26
Separation

Katrine watched in silence from the kitchen table as Mr. Coal replaced a broken hinge on a door leading to the backyard. Robert's mother, Brandi Tebeau, was humming a tune as she washed the dishes. The large woman with long, thick, reddish-brown hair seemed a lot cheerier since Mr. Coal showed up that day, especially since in the few short hours since his arrival, he had already fixed a broken water spigot, a busted window frame in the living room, and a clogged pipe above the stove.

Katrine told Mrs. Tebeau that Mr. Coal was her uncle from Ireland, visiting for a couple of days. Mrs. Tebeau still had no idea who Katrine was, or that she was from a different time. In fact, Katrine hadn't told Robert's mother anything. How does a person say 'I'm from the past. Your son is fine. He was captured by a warlock and is now in theater'?

Mrs. Tebeau had given up the search for Robert only recently and had placed his room for rent to make a little extra money. So with Alyssa's help, Katrine paid her with American cash and moved in. She was the first to occupy Robert's room since his disappearance, and she could tell that it bothered Mrs. Tebeau.

Robert's younger brother was now in high school and involved heavily in after-school sports. Katrine didn't see much of him, which was fine since he always became extremely flirtatious with Katrine when his mother wasn't looking. Katrine was in no mood.

As for Mr. Coal, she wasn't sure he had a true grasp of what had happened to him. He adjusted so effortlessly to the fact that he was now almost three hundred years in the future, Katrine was certain he thought he was still unconscious from the fire and in some sort of dreaming frenzy. Just like Mrs. Tebeau, he was also in a spirited mood as he fixed up the homestead. He had even volunteered to assist with the crops that year. The idea of leaving Mr. Coal in 1966 made Katrine a little uncomfortable. What were the implications of taking someone out of their own time period and placing them in another?

Katrine put her head down on the table and closed her eyes. The warm kitchen and the smell of apple pie baking in the oven were not too unlike Cyan's cafeteria. She actually missed Cyan, guards excepted... and she missed Robert, too. How desperately she wanted to tell his mother that he was all right.

"That's my son, Robert," Mrs. Tebeau said. Katrine looked up from the table to see that Mr. Coal had finished fixing the hinge and was now staring at a picture on the kitchen wall. "He disappeared on us four years ago," she said quietly before turning back to the dishes, no longer humming.

"Run off?" asked Mr. Coal sympathetically.

"I don't know. That's the worst part... not knowing. He could be dead and buried; he could be living it up in the city, tired of the poor country life." She scrubbed frantically at a pot, her eyes never looking up. Her voice started shaking. "Not knowing is the worst part. It's a mother's nightmare." She sniffed.

Katrine put her head back down to the table and listened as Mr. Coal walked over to Mrs. Tebeau to try comforting her, but he made things worse instead. Katrine listened to Robert's mother completely break down and cry until Katrine found herself fighting back her own tears. Not knowing *was* the worst part. Her own mother had probably experienced the same grief. Katrine certainly had. And now, not knowing how close Rattimor was to obtaining her mother was eating her up inside. All she could do was sit and wait until the labyrinth door to 1693 decided to open again. Sitting and waiting. It was just as agonizing, if not more, as it had been the previous day.

Katrine looked up to see Mr. Coal holding Mrs. Tebeau in his arms and decided that she could no longer just sit there. Perhaps she could try a few potential passwords and open the labyrinth door earlier; perhaps she could sweet talk the labyrinth into breaking a few rules. Katrine wiped her eyes, stood up and started to walk out the kitchen door to the backyard. Just beyond the backyard's tree line was a fallow field in which she took her labyrinth to disappear. She dared not leave it in Robert's house when she was gone in case somebody "less than normal" should happen by in her absence. Katrine was about to close the kitchen door behind her when she found herself stopped in her tracks, unable to leave without saying *something* to Mrs. Tebeau.

"Mrs. Tebeau," Katrine said quietly before turning to face her. Her stomach fluttered nervously as she quickly tried to recall the dozens of lies she had conjured up since her arrival to tell Mrs. Tebeau about Robert's well being. She looked into Mrs. Tebeau's tear-filled eyes. None of the lies were good enough. "Robert's alive and happy, but he misses you terribly. I promise I'll try my hardest to get him back for you."

Mrs. Tebeau stood speechless, and Katrine knew she had made a mistake. Now she would be expected to explain herself. Mrs. Tebeau opened her mouth and struggled to ask, "How...?"

Katrine backed away from the door. "Just trust me, Mrs. Tebeau," she said as earnestly as she could, then she turned around and broke into a run for the field as the door slammed behind her. As she neared the field, she could hear Mrs. Tebeau rushing out of the house, calling after Katrine.

"Alyssa, I need you again," she said aloud as she ran through the trees bordering the backyard.

What now?

Katrine hesitated. Alyssa seemed especially irritated about being summoned. "I'm going to need in the labyrinth, with queen attire... perhaps a white dress similar to the one I gave Agnes in the dress shop before it was demolished." Katrine stopped behind a pine tree and looked around to see Robert's mother running toward her from across the backyard. "I also need a photograph of myself with Robert... smiling and on a stage."

You can't be serious.

"I'm not sticking around to tell Robert's mother why I know he's all right. If she sees a picture, at least she'll believe he's alive and well. If you don't do this for me, I just made matters much worse for her."

Fine. Is this what you had in mind?

A photo of Robert and Katrine appeared in her hands. They were dressed up as Romeo and Juliet, smiling and holding hands on a stage with a castle backdrop.

"Perfect."

Unbelievable. I can't believe I'm doing this.

Katrine dropped the picture to the ground in the middle of a pathway Mrs. Tebeau was sure to take, then ran along the tree line to duck behind another tree. Grabbing the labyrinth from her pocket and placing it on the ground, she covered it with dead pine needles and leaf litter before lifting up the top. She wished herself in, and soon after found herself standing at the entrance of the vast green labyrinth. After the top lowered and the darkness turned into sky, Katrine once more found herself in the rain wearing the gaudy white dress she thought she would never see again.

The Link – Master Rattimor

"An umbrella, too... before you leave." A large red umbrella appeared in her hand. "Thanks, Alyssa. I won't need you for a little while, so you can take off." Katrine pulled out her compass, raised her umbrella, and started to walk into the first hedgerow.

We need to talk, Katrine. I'm ending the story. I'm not going to come to your aid anymore.

Katrine stopped in her path, uncertain how to respond.

Things are just getting too weird, especially after last weekend. If I don't put the story on the shelf, I'm going to completely lose my grip on reality. You feel so real to me, it's scary... so no more. The next time you call, I'm ignoring you. It's the only way to make you go away.

"Please don't do this to me, Alyssa. I promise I won't need you much longer. You have no idea what's at stake here!"

Any last requests before we say goodbye?

Katrine dropped her umbrella and slumped down to the grass, unable to believe she was about to be abandoned... by her very own soul. She looked dismally down the hedgerow and stared.

Well?

"I guess a small sack of food would be nice," Katrine said quietly. "I'll probably be living inside the labyrinth for a while." A sack of food appeared at Katrine's feet.

Anything else?

Katrine threw her head back and sighed as she stared at the dark clouds. Rain was falling on her face, but patches of sunlight were finally starting to appear.

"An accurate pencil drawing of my mother, since you're so good at pictures."

A colored pencil drawing appeared in her hands. Katrine quickly shielded it from the rain with her hand and looked at it. A tall, slender woman with blue eyes and straight, shoulder-length brown hair with a touch of gray creeping in was standing on the front porch of the farmhouse. Her face strongly resembled Katrine's, with the exception of the wrinkles around her eyes. The smile on her face was pleasant, relaxed, and a bit crooked. When Katrine looked at the photograph and saw her mother's face for the first time in four years, she wanted to cry.

Bye now! Good luck.

"Goodbye, Alyssa. Good luck to you, too," Katrine answered somberly. Alyssa disconnected, and Katrine had never felt more alone.

Chapter 27
Viruses

Alyssa yawned as she turned the page and studied the figure from her biology book. It was a diagram of a virus: protein capsule with DNA inside. It looked like a space ship with some sort of drill coming out of the bottom. David sat close beside her at the table in her dorm room.

"So it requires your cell's machinery to reproduce," David explained, "Your ribosomes... your nucleotides... Since they can't reproduce by themselves, they aren't considered living." He looked at Alyssa staring blankly at the book. "What's wrong?"

Alyssa looked up at David. "Sorry, I just need a small break." She shifted her chair away from the desk. "Do you want a cola?"

"Sure."

Alyssa stood up and walked to her small dorm refrigerator where she pulled out two colas and popped them open. She handed one to David, then threw herself down on the bed behind him. David stared at her.

"You look nice tonight," David said before he took a drink.

"You're not too hard to impress. All it takes is beat up running shoes, jean shorts, and a long-sleeved, maroon T-shirt. Whoever you end up with will be lucky," she replied with a smile.

David shook his head and rolled his eyes, then pulled out a book from his open backpack on the floor and started to flip through the pages.

"What's that?"

"Criminal psychology. My cousin gave it to me for Christmas. It's pretty fascinating. Take a look," he said as he closed the book and handed it over to Alyssa.

Alyssa opened it to the table of contents. "Glad I don't have a cousin like yours."

"You don't have any cousins."

"Good thing. Cuts down on weird Christmas gifts like this. I mean, really... Chapter 4: Mass murders, Chapter 5: Hostage situations, Chapter 6: Arsonists... Merry Christmas," she said in disbelief as she closed the book and handed it back to David.

"So my cousin's found a creative way to get rid of his old textbooks. What's the big deal? Besides, it might just save me a few bucks if I take the class next semester." David threw the book on the desk and leaned back in the chair. "What's that?" he asked as he stared down at Alyssa's wire wastebasket. "That's your *Seven Days of Cyan*, isn't it?"

Alyssa took a drink, then replied, "Yeah. I decided to trash it. It was no good."

"What are you talking about?" He reached down and pulled it out. The entire tablet had been filled with black, blue, and red ink, along with numerous scribbles and scratch-outs. "The second time you let me read it, I thought it was really good. I didn't discourage you, did I?"

"No," Alyssa said, shaking her head. "I just decided I didn't like it. I want to start over... perhaps some story about a girl who meets a boy... in the army... she likes him but he's gay..." Alyssa rolled her eyes and stared at the aluminum foil that covered her window. "I don't know. Writer's block."

"No, no, no!" David exclaimed, shaking his head. "Look," he said as he reached down into his backpack, "I even made you a cartoon drawing of Zor." He pulled out a paper and handed it to Alyssa. Alyssa looked at it with an expressionless face. Zor was drawn in his pirate garments with a mermaid over his shoulder and a pirate ship in the background. She handed it back.

"It's very good. I give you permission to make a comic book with the story." David gave Alyssa a look of disappointment and was about to argue with her more when he was interrupted with a knock at the door. Alyssa looked at her watch.

"Crap, I didn't realize it was getting so late," she said as she jumped up from the bed to answer the door. She opened the door to see John in jeans and a dark green, button-down, cotton shirt.

"Come in, John," Alyssa beamed as she opened the door wide enough so that he had enough room to walk in and around David's chair. David stood up with an uncomfortable look on his face that Alyssa noticed immediately.

"David, this is John. John, David," she said as pleasantly as she could. They shook hands, both with fake smiles on their faces.

"Old friend of Alyssa's?" David asked John.

"No, new boyfriend," John stated bluntly. Alyssa closed her eyes and wished desperately that she had watched the time more closely.

"David," she said in the sweetest voice she could muster, "I met John last week at the soccer tournament and since then we've gone out a couple of times."

David nodded his head, "Oh... that's great, Alyssa." There was an uncomfortable silence as Alyssa smiled nervously between David and John.

"Drink, John? All I have is cola."

John looked at Alyssa. "No, thank you," he said with a smile, then he looked back at David and the smile disappeared. The uncomfortable silence returned, so Alyssa clapped her hands together. "Well! We were just wrapping things up here. Right, David?"

"Actually, we should look over the RNA viruses a bit better," he replied without taking his eyes off John. Alyssa rolled her eyes and plopped down on her bed, uncertain what to do.

"You don't look so good," said John to David as he sat down on the bed beside Alyssa. David's face turned red and a strange expression spread across his face. He sat in the chair for a moment, glancing back and forth between Alyssa and John, then sprang up, ran for the bathroom, and slammed the door behind him. Alyssa jumped up from the bed and ran to the bathroom door as sounds of David throwing up into the toilet filled the small room. When the sounds subsided, Alyssa gave a quiet knock.

"Are you okay, David?"

"Yes, fine," replied David as he flushed the toilet and opened the door. "May I use your sink to rinse out my mouth?"

Alyssa backed up against the closet door, for the smell on his breath repulsed her. "Maybe you should go home and crawl into bed."

"Don't worry about me. Probably just a little food poisoning." He turned on the water, gurgled water in his mouth and spit into the sink. Wiping his mouth with a small hand towel, he walked hunched-over back to his chair. "I feel much better now."

Alyssa looked over at John and shrugged her shoulders when David wasn't looking. John looked back at David.

"Are you sure you're okay?" John asked as David's face turned bright red a second time.

"Excuse me," David said as he jumped up from his chair again and ran to the bathroom. As he slammed the door shut behind him, Alyssa shook her head and sat down on the bed closest to the bathroom.

"Maybe he's got a virus," John said with a smile as the sounds of David throwing up a second time filled the room. Alyssa couldn't help but to laugh.

When David came out of the bathroom to once more rinse his mouth, Alyssa stood up and went over to him.

"David, you need to go home," she said bluntly.

David looked nervously at John, then turned his back to him. "I'm not leaving you alone with him," he whispered to Alyssa, practically knocking her down with his foul breath. "You don't know him well enough."

Alyssa appeared as irritated as she possibly could. "I'm not a little girl, David. I've been alone with him before," she whispered back angrily. Alyssa wasn't sure why they were whispering. The room was so small, it was obvious John could hear everything. "Now go home."

"No!" he whispered back equally angry before gasping in pain and grabbing his abdomen.

"Yes," Alyssa said calmly in a normal voice. "You're not dying on my floor. Now rinse out your mouth while I get your things together." She walked over and picked up David's backpack from the floor, then hoisted it onto the chair. "Go to the hospital and get your stomach pumped or something." She grabbed his books and started packing them away as David rinsed out his mouth. When he finished, he walked over to Alyssa

"I don't like this, Alyssa," he said, suspiciously eyeing John.

"Well, I don't like you puking all over my room." She placed his backpack in his hands and opened the door. "I'll see you tomorrow in class, but only if you're feeling better, okay? Thanks for the help."

"I'm calling you tonight."

Alyssa shook her head, annoyed. "Whatever."

After David hesitantly left into the chilly night, Alyssa closed the door behind him. "Sorry about that. He can be just a little overprotective."

John smiled and stood up from the bed. "I thought he would never leave," he said as he put his arms around her and gave her a slow, gentle kiss on the lips.

"Wow," she whispered after he finished. She shuddered and smiled. "I picked something up for you at the bookstore," she said excitedly as she pushed him away and turned to rummage through her desktop drawer.

"What's this?" asked John. Alyssa looked behind her to see John holding David's drawing of Zor.

"That's Zor. David drew it. Good, isn't it? I told him he should write comic books based on the character." She noticed John's face become flushed. "Is it too warm in here? I can turn down the heat a bit if you like," she said as she reached towards the back of the drawer and grabbed a small sack.

"No," John said as he sat down, still staring at the drawing. "I'm fine."

Alyssa sprang up with the sack and pulled out a wooden pen. "It's a good one. I hope you like it," she said as she handed it to him. She bounced down beside him on the bed with a smile.

John clicked the pen and scribbled a little beside David's drawing. "It's nice." He clicked the pen closed, attached it to the drawing, and laid it on the floor. "How can I ever show my gratitude?" he said as his hand touched her leg and slid upward. Alyssa smiled and raised her eyebrows.

John gently pushed her backwards until she lay flat on the bed, his hand caressing the side of her body. He leaned over and kissed her gently on the forehead, then took his hand and stroked the side of her face. Alyssa closed her eyes in a dreamy state as she felt him kiss her temples, then the side of her neck. She felt herself falling deeper into her blankets and she started to panic inside when she felt herself become *too* relaxed. She tried to open her eyes, but couldn't. She was tired and couldn't move. Barely conscious, she hoped John would forgive her for falling asleep. When she heard him whisper in her ears, "Sweet dreams," she knew it would be all right.

Chapter 28
The Castle in Papau

Every possible password Katrine tried the previous day had not worked and the door to 1693 stayed closed, but the skies inside the labyrinth had finally started to clear, which gave Katrine a chance to eat dinner without having to hold up her umbrella the entire time. Even when it did rain, the labyrinth, which Katrine found out was named Rose, spared Katrine and left her a dry space in front of the door.

Katrine didn't get much sleep. Every half hour or so she would try to open the door, but Rose kept telling her 'You have to wait for sunrise, Deary, unless you know the password, of course'. Finally the sun rose and Katrine opened the door just outside the servants' quarters inside the courtyard belonging to the castle in Papau.

The castle was situated against the sea on the edge of a rocky cliff. It was one of the larger castles of its time, consisting of eight large stone towers and several smaller turrets, all connected with large, indoor, stone passageways. The courtyard inside the main wall was filled with grass, trees, rocks, benches, and a small pond – suitable enough for a royal evening stroll. The servants' quarters and kitchens were separated from the main towers, but an indoor corridor between the servants' quarters and one of the smaller towers provided easy access for the servants.

Katrine started shaking in nervous anticipation as she entered the servants' quarters, but few of the servants noticed since they bowed down to the floor the instant they noticed Katrine. Katrine took a deep breath as she quickly scanned the long, narrow room filled with little more than beds and washbasins. Her mother was nowhere to be seen. She stood up as straight and proud as she could.

"Rise and carry on with your duties," she instructed. The servants hesitated for a moment, then slowly rose from the ground.

Instead of continuing their activities, however, they backed up against the wall beside their beds and stood at attention.

Katrine walked slowly down the row of beds and stopped in front of a teenage maid. As Katrine approached her, she could tell the girl was trembling.

"Have you seen this woman?" Katrine asked as she held out the picture of her mother.

The girl looked confused, then she gave a small curtsey. "Yes, two days ago was the last I saw of her, Your Royal Highness."

Katrine's heart started beating wildly. "Do you know where she is now?"

"You sent her to the dungeons, Your Royal Highness."

Katrine became pale. "Why would I do that?"

The girl looked increasingly puzzled and started shaking even more. "She went crazy, Your Royal Highness."

Katrine tried to mask her panic. "What do you mean? How did she go crazy?"

The girl's eyes narrowed and she shook her head. "Don't you remember?"

"Lillian!" shouted a deep voice from farther down the row. Katrine looked over to see the head servant, a tall, gray-headed man. "You will not question Your Royal Highness! Answer the question."

"I beg your forgiveness, Your Royal Highness," Lillian said in a wavering voice. "She claimed she was your mother and dared to touch you without permission, even started shaking you, so you sent her down below."

Katrine clenched her fists in anger, wanting desperately to strangle Tiffany, Cyan's ex-trumpet player who had taken her place as Princess Anna.

"Thank you for your assistance," Katrine said as nobly as she could.

Katrine was about to turn and leave when she heard a scream. The room grew darker as a black film began to cover the windows. Through the cracks of each window squeezed a black cloud that broke into smaller pieces once it found itself inside. Each piece of black mist was shaped like an upside-down teardrop about twenty centimeters high, possessing a single, dark purple eye in the center. They zoomed through the room, flying up, down, and around each servant like tiny ghosts. The head servant gave a painful cry. Katrine looked over at him and backed up in horror as she watched one of the black ghosts exit his left ear, then give an ear-piercing shrill. Katrine was about to charge out of the room towards the dungeons when two ghosts flew in front of her and stopped her. They inspected her from top to bottom with their large eyes until a third black ghost flew beside them and spoke in a high shrill that almost hurt her ears.

"Too young. She was brought to the dungeons." They zoomed off through the hall towards the entrance of the main castle.

Katrine tore off her shoes and broke into a run amidst the flying black ghosts. As the hallway leading from the servants' quarters reached a main corridor in the castle, the black ghosts split up. Katrine turned right and ran as fast as her large dress would allow her towards the dungeons she had been shown during her first visit to her fiancé's castle. She raced downstairs and turned from one stone corridor to the next, losing more and more of the flying ghosts with each turn. She passed servants running and guards drawing their weapons to strike down the strange invaders, but their swords swung clear through them with no effect. Still several black apparitions were ahead of her as she neared the dungeons. She quickly stopped at one of the guards swiping his sword through the air.

"Give me the keys to the dungeon!"

The guard seemed surprised to see Katrine running through the hallways. "You must stay with me, Your Highness. It's too dangerous for you to be here alone."

"Give me the keys *now*, or I'll have your head cut off!"

With confusion in his eyes, the guard reached down to his belt and unhooked his keys. Katrine grabbed them and ran as fast as she could to the end of the corridor and down steps to a gate leading into the dungeon. A strong smell of urine hit her nose as she pulled at the gate to see if it was already open, but it was locked. Katrine fumbled with the keys, trying several frantically, as the sounds of screaming prisoners met her ears. She looked through the bars to see the black ghosts zoom back and forth through the dungeon, some of them entering and exiting the heads of the prisoners, causing them to cry out with such pain, Katrine was having a hard time controlling her shaking hands to hold the keys. When she finally found the right key, she flung the gate open and jumped down a small set of stairs to a wet, straw-covered floor. Most of the black clouds were now flying out a small barred window near the stone ceiling. She ran around the dark room, frantically looking at the shackled prisoners along the walls, but her mother was nowhere to be seen.

She turned to an old, skinny, whimpering man chained to the wall, and held out the picture of her mother. "Have you seen this woman?" she yelled.

The man clamored and stuttered nervously. "It entered my head! It told me the Eyes of Rattimor are looking for Mary Farmer, then it entered my head and recalled my memories. It was looking for Mary!"

"Well, where is she then?" Katrine yelled angrily.

"She was right there a minute ago," he said as he nodded towards an empty set of shackles on the opposite wall. "She just disappeared! Poor, poor Mary. She was such a kind woman. They must have taken her."

A guard that Katrine had not noticed behind her stepped forward and hit the man in the face with a baton. "Crazy old man! Who's Rattimor? Where'd the prisoner go?"

Katrine placed her hand on the baton and lowered it in dismay, then walked over to the empty set of shackles that the old man had indicated and felt like fainting. How could someone have forced her mother to stay in such an awful place? If her mother had been at the servants' quarters, Katrine could have saved her. She glanced out the barred window to see the Eyes of Rattimor form a single black cloud and drift away in the sky.

She closed her eyes and took a deep breath, then turned quickly and looked at the guard. "Follow me!" she said angrily as she lifted her dress and charged out of the dungeon. "Rattimor is a witch who can take on the appearance of others. The black ghosts were just a distraction. Rattimor's got the prisoner and she's probably still in the castle. Find her and we'll find our missing prisoner."

Katrine stormed down the cold, stone hallways, unable to think of anything but revenge. She didn't care if there was a warlock or a witch possibly waiting to bring her to Rattimor, for she welcomed the thought of being brought to him now... to set things straight about Adrian's whereabouts. As she neared the corner, she recognized a voice approaching – her own voice. She turned around to the guard following her.

"Give me your sword!" she ordered, taking it from him without waiting for a response. She turned the corner and stared face to face with her own – white wig, elaborate gold and white dress, caked on makeup... the new Princess Anna. Katrine made a fist and hit Tiffany in the face as hard as she could, sending her spiraling down to the floor, then took the sword and put it against Tiffany's neck. With blood flowing from her nose, Tiffany looked up at Katrine in shock, not only unable to believe that someone had the nerve to hit her, but also unable to believe *who* had just hit her. The handmaiden accompanying Tiffany gave a scream and backed up against the wall; the guard seemed uncertain what to do.

"You don't understand how bad I want to hurt you," Katrine said in such a threatening voice, she even surprised herself. She looked at Tiffany's fear-stricken eyes and paused, then threw the sword against the wall with a cry of frustration. Taking a deep breath to try to calm herself, she spoke harshly to the guard behind her. "Guard, take this witch to the dungeon and put her where Mary had been shackled. I'll return shortly with our escapee." She turned and began to storm away, realizing for the first time that she had traveled too far away from the servants' quarters and her labyrinth. The last thing she wanted was to become delayed at the castle when she could be seeking help from Zor or searching for Master Rattimor's residence.

"Stop that woman!" she could hear Tiffany yell. Katrine turned to see Tiffany struggle up to a sitting position and point to the guard. "Your name is Gregory, your sister is my handmaiden! Her birthday was last week and I gave her half a day off! Now stop that imposter and find out who she is!"

"Yes, Your Highness!" the guard answered as he turned and began to chase Katrine.

A wave of panic engulfed Katrine as she broke into a run down the stone corridor. The echoes of Tiffany calling out for the other guards to assist and the sound of Gregory's heavy boots pounding the stone floor as he pursued Katrine caused such a noisy commotion that Katrine nearly ran into a guard responding to the cries as she turned a corner.

"Guard!" Katrine yelled as she grabbed his sleeve and pulled on it, attempting to appear more frightened than she already was. "You've got to help me. The guard named Gregory has gone crazy and is trying to attack me! He's already attacked one of my handmaidens! Do you hear her screams?"

The guard pulled his sword as Gregory turned the corner. Their swords clashed, sending a metallic clang in all directions down the empty stone hallway.

"Stand down, Gregory," the second guard warned as Katrine took off running again. She turned the last corner towards the servants' entrance and could hear Gregory in the background frantically trying to explain that Katrine was an imposter.

Charging through the servants' quarters and out to her labyrinth door took no time at all. Before she knew it, she was in the tranquil row of hedges inside her labyrinth, yelling for the door to close. She sat down in the grass to catch her breath and grasped her throbbing hand, but hitting Tiffany was worth the risk of getting caught. It was the high point of her day.

The rain had stopped and the sun was breaking through bright and fluffy clouds. She would have found the labyrinth enjoyable and peaceful had she been there with her mother, but now Rattimor had her.

Chapter 29
Master Rattimor

As soon as the sun rose the next morning, Katrine put her hand on the labyrinth door. "Robert's room in Cyan, but only if Robert's there," she whispered. It opened up into a dark room in which the only sound was Robert's breathing. "Don't close until I tell you. Okay, Rose? I might be coming and going today."

"It's an unusual request. We're supposed to have a command each time you enter and exit... but I'll do it for my favorite link! I really enjoyed shopping with you yesterday, by the way. The 1932 door sure had some nice outfits, but I still think Robert will like you in that outfit the best," Rose said, regarding Katrine's khaki pants with pockets along the sides, hiking boots, and a blue, button-down, long-sleeve cotton shirt she had stolen from a camping store.

"Shhh..." Katrine raised her finger to her lips.

"Sorry, dear," Rose said a little quieter. "I just have never had anyone spend so much quality time with me. Not even Rebecca, bless her sweet heart. I'll try to bloom some flowers for you on these boring green hedges while you're gone."

Katrine smiled, then quietly crept out of the labyrinth into Robert's room and made her way over to where she could hear him sleeping. She reached her hand forward until she felt him, then gave him a little nudge.

"Robert?" she whispered.

Robert stirred. "Who's that?" he sleepily asked.

"It's Katrine."

"Katrine!" Robert whispered as he sat up in bed. "What are you doing here?" He reached beside the bed to his bed stand and turned on a lamp. He was in a beige T-shirt and his red hair lay on his head in every direction, but he looked very nice to Katrine.

The Link – Master Rattimor

"I thought your mother might enjoy seeing you, even if it's only for a little while. I can't promise Zor won't end up dragging you back once he finds out."

Robert looked at the labyrinth door, which appeared as a section of the back wall swaying back and forth. "Katrine, we're in the Main House. They were expecting you to try this, so they brought me here," he said with a worried look on his face.

Katrine glimpsed around the room for the first time. It was similar to her old room, but arranged differently with the bathroom on the opposite wall. It was the room beside James'. "Then I guess you better get going," she replied with a smile.

Robert threw off the covers, smiling and shaking his head in disbelief, then quickly slipped on his soccer shorts that were thrown on the floor beside his bed. Katrine led him to the labyrinth door and pulled him inside. His face beamed when he recognized the labyrinth's hedges and doors. Katrine held out his hand and placed the compass in it.

"Just tell it to go to the entrance of the labyrinth. Once you step out of the labyrinth, it'll first go dark, then you should find yourself behind a tree near your backyard. You don't need any power to get out. You better hurry."

Robert looked confused. "Are you staying?"

She stared at him, wishing she could go with him, but it had already been nearly twenty-four hours since her mother had been taken, and she didn't want to be stuck in 1966 waiting for Zor to come to her.

"I have to talk to Zor." She swallowed unable to believe what she was going to say. "I need his help to find my mother. Go, Robert, before it's too late." She put her hand over his hand holding the compass. "Bring him to the entrance."

Before she could let go, Robert grabbed her, pulled her close, and passionately kissed her. When he pulled away, Katrine was trembling and could barely keep her balance.

With a smile on his face, he said, "I can't *tell* you how much I've been wanting to do that."

Katrine stood speechless, unable to move, as Robert turned, looked down at the compass, and began to hurry away.

"Robert," she said weakly before he turned the first corner. He stopped and looked at her. "That was nice," was all she could say in her daze. They smiled at each other, then Robert disappeared around the corner.

Still staring at the corner where Robert had disappeared, Katrine began to head out the labyrinth door when she collided into James, still dressed in long pajamas and a bathrobe. He grabbed her wrist and displayed the most unpleasant scowl on his face.

"It's too early for this, Katrine. Couldn't you have waited until after breakfast?" He looked down the pathway and yelled, "Robert, come back or she's going to spend some quality time with the guards!"

Katrine shook her head with disappointment. "Let him go home, James. Just for a day."

He grabbed her chin and made her face him. "No. Zor is the only one who decides who will leave and who will stay," he angrily replied. Robert appeared around the corner, also discouraged. "Go back to the Thespian House, Robert. Curfew just ended, so the guards won't be out to give you any problems. I'll deal with you later."

Katrine looked down to the ground, unable to face Robert as he approached them.

"It's okay, Katrine," Robert told her as he passed.

James held out his free hand and stopped Robert. "The compass." Katrine lifted her gaze enough to see Robert place the compass in James' hand and exit the labyrinth. James looked around. "Nice labyrinth. Soon to be mine. Tell the door to close when we exit."

"No," Katrine replied quietly.

James took a deep breath. "Fine," he said as he clasped his hand over Katrine's mouth and walked her through the door. "If you're not going to tell it to close, then you're not going to tell it to stay open either." As soon as they were in Robert's room, a metal pole leading from the floor to the ceiling appeared. James shoved Katrine's wrist against the pole and murmured words under his breath, causing a black rope to appear around her wrist and the pole. "We'll wait an hour and let the door close on its own." He pulled up a wooden chair, sat down, crossed his legs and arms, and stared smugly at Katrine.

Katrine rested her forehead against the pole and closed her eyes, knowing that Rose would never close the door until she was instructed. She was stuck there for a while. "I need to talk to Zor."

"He's not here. He's been very busy lately."

Katrine looked out the bedroom door that Robert had left open to see the sun begin to light up the courtyard. "Busy doing what?"

"Preparing for Rattimor's imminent attack: changing Cyan's air... bringing in new prisoners. One prisoner looks strikingly similar to you, but about twenty-five years older. She arrived early yesterday morning and is in the Gardener's House." Katrine watched as James opened his hand and a small, shiny, purple pebble appeared. Her eyes instantly welled up with tears as the enormous stress that had been building up inside her for the past several days released itself.

"You have my mother?" she asked, trying not to break down completely.

"Yes."

The Link – Master Rattimor

Katrine closed her eyes and leaned her head against the pole once more, trying to maintain her composure in front of James. "Thank God," she whispered.

"Zor told me to tell you, should you be foolish enough to show your face here, that he's going to hold onto the pebble and locket," he said as the locket she had left in her room appeared in his hand, "until all is resolved with Rattimor. Do you understand?"

"Fine, fine," she agreed. "I don't care. As long as my mother's safe." He put the pebble in the locket, then it disappeared completely. "May I see her?" she asked eagerly.

"Once you close the door."

Katrine was about to agree, but something was stopping her: a lack of trust. Zor could have conjured up a duplicate stone since he knew what it looked like from his mind reading. If her mother wasn't there, losing the labyrinth would halt her search.

"I'll close it after you let me see my mother. I promise," Katrine tried to bargain.

"Then I guess we're waiting, because I'm not letting you go until the door is closed."

Katrine gave a frustrated yell and tried to pull her arm away from the pole. The rope tightened, nearly cutting off all circulation in her hand. The sight delighted James, and he stood up to get a closer look.

"Isn't this stuff great? It took a lot of practice to get it right. My first was a failure because Zor somehow transported out of it. The second one, he couldn't transport, but he was able to relocate the chair I had him bound to. This one looks good, though." He looked up at Katrine with a smile. "And I'm the only one who can take it off, so try not to cross me too much. You see," he said as his eyes lit up even more, "each rope has a password. I choose the password when I put it on, and it's needed in order to take it off. I'm the only one who knows it. Even if Alyssa managed to wake up and connect with you, she wouldn't be able to take it off." Katrine looked confused as he sat down with another smug look on his face. "I love being a warlock."

"What do you mean if she managed to wake up?"

"Haven't you been wondering why you haven't been able to contact her for a while?"

"I haven't *tried* contacting her," Katrine replied, irritated.

"Zor put her to sleep and she won't wake up until he lifts his little spell," James said with a smile. "We wouldn't want you running around, filling transfer vases left and right for Rattimor in case he got hold of you and put a butter knife to your throat. You're so gullible and easy to manipulate."

Katrine turned her head away from James. She wanted to make a snide remark, but she knew there was a bit of truth to what James said.

"I hope you realize," James continued, "Daddy Rattimor's already got the best of two other links. If he gulps down one more transfer vase, he'll be so powerful, he'll be able to read the mind of a warlock. Then we'll all be sorry. If he reads my mind, you'll find yourself saying 'welcome back' to your little friend Adrian.

"But there are worse things that can happen than Adrian's return," he continued, shaking his head and sitting back down. "The only warlocks to ever fall victim to another have been those weakened after a power transfer or those who had the unfortunate luck of being caught in a time period where they had little or no power. A third vase downed by dear 'ol Daddy Rattimor would probably make him powerful enough to kill a full strength warlock. He'd be damn near unstoppable."

Katrine sighed, then looked at her red hand, wondering how long she would be able to bear the pain before giving in to James and closing the door.

"Why did Zor have to go after Alyssa? Why didn't he just put me to sleep?" she asked, trying to get her mind off her throbbing, red hand.

"Zor plans to, but it's not enough to just put you to sleep. If Alyssa connected with you while you were sleeping, Master Rattimor wouldn't have too hard of a time finding you. You now give off an obvious aura of power since you and Alyssa have grown such a strong connection. Putting Alyssa asleep makes it more difficult for Rattimor. Then he'd have to find you *and* Alyssa to get what he wants. Zor's waiting for you now in 1966, ready to sing you a little lullaby, but he's having a bit of trouble locating the labyrinth to find you."

"The all-powerful Zor can make mental midgets out of warlocks, but he can't even find my labyrinth?"

"*My* labyrinth, and a very valuable labyrinth at that. When it belonged to Rebecca Grumley, her father, Imperius, put a spell on it so that its life force was masked and undetectable by other warlocks. Witches and warlocks have no trouble finding living objects; non-living objects are a different story. Very hard to detect."

"Show me my mother and I'll tell you where I've hidden it, in addition to closing the door."

"I was hoping to save that piece of information for my first mind reading, but I wanted to wait for Zor just in case I screw it up. They can sometimes be painful if certain precautions aren't taken." He smiled. "And I don't necessarily want to hurt you, I'm just interested in finding out what my brother finds so fascinating about you."

The Link – Master Rattimor

Katrine stared at him. "Didn't he already share with you all my 'deep, dark secrets'?"

James sighed. "No, he hasn't told me much of anything. Has some strange ethics code and won't share with me anything that might be considered private and personal if it's not necessary. He believes the mind probe should be used only to determine worthiness to participate in Cyan, nothing more." He paused and looked at Katrine's bright red hand. "Aren't you going to ask me to loosen the rope?"

Katrine looked again at her hand. "No," Katrine replied quietly. "You'll probably just tighten it more." James gave a chuckle and looked very amused.

Katrine stood and waited in silence for five more minutes as the throbbing in her hand increased; she knew she wasn't going to be able to take the pain much longer. "If you're not going to let me see my mother, can you at least offer more proof that she's here?" she finally asked.

James looked thoughtful. "You've become a bit more mistrusting than you used to be. There might be hope for you yet." James stood up and his bathrobe changed into jeans and a long-sleeved gray T-shirt. He walked over to the bedroom door and stared out at the courtyard. "Zor said he snapped her up from the dungeons of urine in the nick of time. Does that mean anything to you?" He turned to see Katrine smile with relief.

"Yes, it means a lot. I'll close the door."

James shook his head approvingly.

"Just promise me, James, you'll take good care of the labyrinth. She's sensitive."

As Katrine looked at James and waited for his response, she saw a black cloud descend upon the courtyard behind him. Instant terror flushed across her face, and James turned to look out the window in response. Unable to take her eyes off the cloud as it started to break apart and scatter in all directions, Katrine hardly noticed as James ran to her, grabbed onto the black rope, and said the password. The black rope disappeared and James yanked her into the labyrinth.

"Go to 1966 and tell Zor that Rattimor is in Cyan!" James yelled as he shoved the compass into her hand.

"James, don't let him get my mother!"

"He doesn't know your mother is here, you idiot. He's after me and Zor." He exited the labyrinth and turned around. "Close the door, Katrine... *now*," he warned. But Katrine couldn't bring herself to tell Rose to close the door. She watched as the Eyes of Rattimor swooped into the room and surrounded James. James looked nervously back at the open labyrinth door and said nothing as a purple mist seemed to envelope James. Two of the black ghosts swirled around his wrists and pulled him

213

out the door. The ghosts disappeared from the Main House, and Katrine could hear nothing except her own breathing. She strained to look out into the courtyard and could see the black cloud disappear behind the cherry trees, on its way to the rest of Cyan.

Uncertain what to do, Katrine grabbed hold of her hair with both hands, pulled, and groaned in frustration. If she went to find Zor, he would put her to sleep. If she stayed in Cyan, she could at least make sure that if her mother was recognized and captured, Katrine would be there to explain to Rattimor what happened to Adrian. James was not about to tell Rattimor what happened to Adrian and wouldn't care if he hurt Katrine's mother. *Someone* had to be there for her mother.

Katrine quietly stepped out of the labyrinth and hid the compass between the mattresses of the bed before she peeked out of the doorway. The Eyes of Rattimor were nowhere to be seen. She ducked below the windows and crept out the main door into the courtyard. Still no black ghosts were apparent, but she could hear screaming and shouting down the main streets of Cyan. As she slowly edged through the flowers and trees of the courtyard to its outer perimeter, her eyes grew larger as she watched hundreds of black ghosts dragging the citizens out of their homes in their pajamas and leading them by their wrists down the street towards the soccer fields. She crouched down as best she could into the flowers and vines and watched as a purple haze enveloped each individual as they were pulled forward.

Katrine waited silently until it seemed all the people and ghosts were at the soccer fields, then slowly crept over to the auditorium where she hugged her back against the wall to stay out of view. She peeked into the front entrance of the auditorium, but all was dark inside. She leaned over and quickly walked past the glass doors of the auditorium, then made her way to the corner of the building and peered across the outdoor stadium to the soccer fields where a new platform above the bleachers was erected. Three men were on the platform, overlooking all the citizens of Cyan, but they were too far away to see clearly. A tap on Katrine's shoulder made her jump in surprise. She turned around to see a purple eye staring at her from only a couple centimeters away.

"Got you!" it said in a high shrill.

Two ghosts whirled from behind the ghost that spoke and surrounded Katrine's wrists before she could try to run. She attempted to pull her hands away, but it felt like razors slicing into her wrists each time she tried.

"It only hurts when you resist," one shrilled.

A purple mist began to surround her body as she tried harder to pull away from the ghosts. She couldn't help but to cry out in pain, certain her wrists had been cut so deeply they would be dripping blood

The Link – Master Rattimor

onto the black apparitions flying around them. Seeing no way to escape, she reluctantly started walking towards the fields to join the others.

As she got closer to the platform, Katrine looked up to see James kneeling on the edge, wrists bound with black rope and surrounded by a heavier purple mist than all the other citizens. He closed his eyes and shook his head when he saw Katrine approaching, and she knew she had made a huge mistake. Near the back of the platform, she could barely make out an open labyrinth door guarded by a young man who looked about eighteen years old. He was dressed in a white muscle top that hugged his body and long black shorts that fell to his shins. His head was shaved clean and he had dark skin, giving himself the appearance of a Los Angeles gang member directly out of Alyssa's time. He had to be Rehnquist, the son Zor had mentioned when he brought Alyssa for coffee at the union.

The other man, who struck fear into Katrine's heart the moment she saw him, was about forty-five to fifty years in age. He was a large, dark man with a square face and shoulder length, black hair tied into a ponytail. He wore a short, black cape with a red satin lining, black button-down shirt, black corduroy pants with a thick, black leather belt and large black boots. Though Adrian's pale, sickly looking face had little resemblance to the man pacing on the platform, their hair color was identical.

The man in black paced in front of the platform in a very business-like manner as he waited for the black apparitions to finish assembling the people. Katrine walked to the edge of the crowd and spotted Robert just a few rows behind her. The black ghosts around her wrists released her and began to fly around the entire assemblage. Katrine looked down at her wrists and saw that they weren't even red, but the purple mist around her remained, as it did around everyone.

"Why are you here?" she heard an angry voice whisper. She turned to see Robert beside her with anxiety in his face. "Rattimor would like nothing more than to get his hands on a link. Why didn't James hide you?"

Katrine started to rub her hands tightly together. "I thought you liked the classic good versus evil," she said nervously. She tried to force a smile, but felt too lightheaded.

"*Not* when it involves you. *Don't* do anything to attract attention, Katrine." Robert looked up at the platform. "You want to see evil? Rattimor is pure evil. He's a murderer with not an ounce of human decency." Katrine looked at Robert's angry face and had a feeling that Robert had encountered Rattimor before. She was about to ask him about it when a woman in the distance caught Katrine's eyes. It was her mother.

"Oh, my God," Katrine whispered.

"What?" Robert asked, turning in the direction Katrine was looking.

"My mother, the one in the green nightgown," she replied in a whisper, unable to take her eyes off the woman. Katrine ducked behind Robert to hide, but still peeked around him to see her. Dressed in a long nightgown, Mary had her hands at the sides of her neck as she looked around at the glowing crowd. Her face showed fear, as did everyone's. "If she sees me, she might give us both away."

"She's not your only problem," said Robert quietly as he pointed to the far side of the crowd. Katrine looked to see that all the guards had been assembled along with the rest of the citizens, and a few had already spotted Katrine in the crowd. Katrine tried to duck further behind Robert as she turned towards the platform.

"They don't look too happy to see me, do they?"

Katrine and Robert jumped as Rattimor began to speak. His voice sounded as if he was speaking through amplifiers turned up full blast next to their ears.

"I am Master Rattimor, father to the exalted Adrian Rattimor, who has quite mysteriously disappeared. You may choose to be victims of my fury, or you may choose to let the suffering be directed only to those who are deserving.

"Tell your founder, Zor, I have his brother. I will trade him only for my daughter. As for your fate, you will all die tomorrow at sundown if I am not in possession of a maiden by the name of Katrine Farmer."

Katrine took a deep breath and looked back at her mother's terrified face, then closed her eyes.

"If saving your pathetic lives is not enough to convince you to hand her over to me, tell Ms. Farmer I have her mother, snatched from the castle in Papau yester-morn, and I'm sure she'll be reasonable and give herself up freely."

Katrine peered around her as the citizens nearby glanced in her direction and started to whisper. Katrine shook her head.

"Robert," she said with defeat in her voice, "go over to my mother and make sure she doesn't give herself away."

"You are staying right here! Don't you dare give yourself up. Make *him* find *you*!" Robert whispered back angrily as he put his hand in front of her.

"I am *not* going to be responsible for everyone's death!"

"Master Rattimor!" yelled one of the guards.

"Guards!" James yelled. "You will keep your silence!"

The guard fell silent and Rattimor looked suspiciously at the crowd. He pointed to James and a black strap appeared across James' mouth. Rattimor took a step off the platform to the top row of the bleachers, surveying the people. "What information do you wish to share, guard?" he asked as he stared into the group of guards.

At first there was silence, then movement. Katrine looked over at the guards to see Guard Eleven walk to the front of the crowd, his body glowing as purple as everyone else's. "The Farmer girl is among us, here in this crowd, Master Rattimor," he said. "In the interest of Cyan's welfare, I feel it is my duty to share this information with you, despite the objections of our co-founder."

Robert began to fume as Katrine looked at the grass.

"Robert," she said quietly without looking up, "I hid the compass between the mattresses and the labyrinth door is still open. Get Zor after we leave. He's waiting for me in 1966, maybe even at your house." She looked back at her mother. "Go to my mother and keep her quiet. It's important he doesn't get her, too."

Robert grabbed Katrine's chin and made her face him. "I'll do this for you, but you've got to promise to stay alive! Don't die on me, Katrine!"

Katrine stared into his eyes and couldn't stop her own from tearing up. "I'll do what I can," she said with a shaky voice. He looked at her with worried eyes, gave her a quick kiss on the lips, then disappeared into the crowd behind her.

Rattimor's voice thundered. "Sweep the field, Eyes of Rattimor, and bring before me every maiden between eighteen and thirty with brown hair and blue eyes!"

Katrine started to shake as the black ghosts weaved through the crowd and dragged out every citizen that fit the description. She shuddered as a black ghost swept between her hair and her neck, then stopped in front of her eyes. Two more ghosts grabbed hold of her wrists and pulled her towards the front. She went without a struggle, not wanting to feel the razor-sharp ghosts slice into her wrists. They brought Katrine to the far end of a row where ten other women were lined up.

"Eyes of Rattimor," Rattimor commanded, "find the link."

Katrine shivered as a nearby ghost flew up to her ear and tickled the outer surface. Then it backed up and shrilled. Rattimor walked down the bleachers and stood before the lineup.

"It seems Zor has found a rather creative way to keep me from reading your minds, but it serves no higher purpose than to save a few of you from a headache. I shall simply say that if Katrine Farmer doesn't step forward, I will start randomly blasting bodies into pieces, like I did your father's remains... except these people won't be dead when I do it," he said in a matter-of-fact tone.

Katrine looked down to the grass and was about to step forward when she heard a woman in the line speak.

"I'm Katrine Farmer."

Katrine looked up to see a woman she had never seen before step forward. She had the same long, straight brown hair and was the same height as Katrine, but her face was slightly narrower. She was one of the few people dressed in the crowd, wearing light blue jeans and a white blouse. "I'll go with you freely. Just don't hurt anyone," she said without a quiver in her voice or a tremor in her body.

Rattimor stepped in front of her with a gleam in his eye and a smile on his face. "I look forward to breaking you, my dear."

Katrine watched in disbelief as the woman stood unwavering, appearing almost angry at being taunted.

"You don't scare me, Rattimor," she replied coldly. "Place me in front of a transfer vase and we'll see who breaks."

Rattimor appeared as surprised as everyone else at her speech. "Your words are careless," he finally replied. "We will see how brave you are when I dice your mother up into little pieces before your eyes."

Rattimor turned and headed up the bleachers towards the labyrinth door as two of Rattimor's black ghosts pulled at the wrists of the young woman and led her up the steps. Katrine started to fidget, unable to believe what had happened, then looked behind her. Robert was holding her mother in his arms, talking quietly in her ear. For the first time, Katrine and her mother's gaze met. Katrine couldn't help but to smile as her mother's eye flowed with tears and she mouthed the words 'I love you'. She sighed and couldn't stop jittering, wishing Rattimor would make his exit a little faster so that she could hold her mother for the first time in four years. She looked back up at the platform as Rehnquist, James, and the young woman disappeared through the labyrinth door. The ghosts began their retreat from the fields to follow behind Rattimor as he was about to step through the door, but suddenly stopped when Guard Eleven shouted, "Master Rattimor!"

"God, no," Katrine whispered to herself, losing all color in her face.

Rattimor turned toward the guard and the ghosts quickly returned to surround Cyan's citizens.

"I feel you have been deceived, and on the behalf of Cyan's citizens, I would like to correct the situation, sir," Guard Eleven announced loudly. Katrine closed her eyes and started trembling with both anger and fear.

"Guard Eleven!" yelled Robert as he charged out of the crowd to the front. "Master Rattimor has what he has come for! If you have some personal issues, then take it up with Zor once he returns!"

The Link – Master Rattimor

Rattimor walked towards the front of the platform. "What do you wish to tell me, Guard?"

"The woman you took is not Katrine Farmer. She is a prisoner who arrived just yesterday."

Katrine could hear Robert threatening Guard Eleven, but was unable to hear what he was saying over her own heartbeat in her ears.

Rattimor walked down the bleachers once more and stood between Robert and the guard. "Show me who Katrine Farmer is, then," he said with amusement in his voice.

Robert jumped on the guard and hit him as hard as he could in the face before flying through the air backwards with a wave of Rattimor's hand. Guard Eleven wiped his face, smiled, and started to walk towards the front line of blue-eyed, brown-haired women. Katrine's knees started to feel weak and she wished she felt as brave as the other woman Rattimor took, but simply didn't. The black ghosts zoomed in front and behind the front line as the guard approached. Katrine didn't lift her gaze until she heard another commotion, then looked up to see both Jacques and Robert on top of Guard Eleven, pushing him to the ground and punching him. Katrine could hear Ashleigh screaming as Jacques and Robert flew through the air and landed on their backs in front of the crowd. Rattimor stood back, enjoying the spectacle. Finally, Guard Eleven stepped in front of Katrine.

Katrine looked up at him. "I hate you," she whispered to the guard as Rattimor stepped up behind him.

"Is this Katrine Farmer?" Rattimor asked.

"Ay, Katrine Farmer she is," Guard Eleven replied with his checkered-teeth grin.

"Master Rattimor," Robert exclaimed as he ran up to him, "Guard Eleven has a personal vendetta against this woman. She is *not* Katrine Farmer."

Rattimor stepped beside the guard. "Can you offer me any proof that this woman is Miss Farmer?"

Guard Eleven and Katrine stared silently at one another as the guard considered the question. "One night, not too very long ago," he began to speak, "she nearly managed to escape through the outer log wall. Only someone with magical powers could ever hope to get clear to the outer log wall without a guard stopping her." Katrine closed her eyes, growing angrier with every word he spoke. "Zor was so furious, he burnt his name on her shoulder with a lightening bolt to remind her that she was now his property. Usually, with ordinary citizens, he would just let the guards handle them. But not this one. She was tagged instead."

Guard Eleven reached up to pull her shirt to the side, but Katrine jerked her shoulder back.

"Don't touch me," Katrine angrily warned.

Rattimor pushed the guard gently to the side and stepped in front of Katrine. Katrine's breathing quickened and she was unable to move as Rattimor slid her shirt over the edge of her shoulder, breaking the top button of her blouse. Katrine peered nervously over at Robert, who was staring at her shoulder in disbelief.

"Are you Katrine Farmer?" Rattimor asked.

"No," she quietly replied.

"Master Rattimor," Robert said calmly, "the guard has a personal feud with this woman because she made a fool out of him once. He's just using you, seeking retribution for his own humiliation."

"Whoever she is, Zor seems to have a special interest in her and she may be of some use," he said as he ran his thumb over the scar. He smiled, leaned forward to Katrine's ear and whispered, "I'll determine your value once we get out of this air." He replaced Katrine's shirt over her shoulder and two black ghosts took their place around her wrists and began to pull her towards the bleachers.

Robert stepped in front of Rattimor, about to speak, when Rattimor waved his hand and sent him flying clear to the back of the crowd.

"Simpleton," Rattimor remarked as he walked up the steps to the platform.

Katrine stumbled several times up the stairs and felt the black ghosts cut into her wrists each time she tried to regain her balance. Finally, she was at the top of the platform about to walk through Rattimor's labyrinth door. She looked down at the glowing crowd below to see her mother being tightly held in Ashleigh's arms, then walked through the labyrinth door into a tall, green hedgerow.

Chapter 30
Rattimor's Summer Hideaway

"Welcome to my summer hideaway, a luxury home so far away from any living soul that no one will hear your screams," said Rattimor as he walked past Katrine towards James. The Eyes of Rattimor released Katrine's wrists, and she held her head to try to recover from walking through Rattimor's labyrinth without holding a compass. As she did, she lost her balance and fell to a cold and wet wooden floor. She could see her breath in front of her as she exhaled into the chilly air and could hear the wind howling outside. Closing her eyes, she shook her head as if it would help her get rid of her dizziness, but it only made it worse.

"Rehnquist, seat James and let's get this over with. I was in the middle of important business when you came to me about Adrian," he said impatiently.

"How's the war going, Dad? Still on the losing side?"

"When you become less of a screw-up, Rehnquist, you'll understand that the 'means' is sometimes much more satisfying than the end, and warlocks with time labyrinths don't have to stick around until the end."

Katrine looked up for the first time to see that James, the young woman, and herself were still surrounded by the strange, purple mist, but it was harder to see in the gloom of her new surroundings. They were in a dark, single room log cabin illuminated with only candles along the walls and furnished with not much more than two wooden chairs stationed side-by-side in the center of the room. Along the far wall beside the outer door was a golden-topped redwood counter with a golden transfer vase identical to the one she had filled at Adrian's. Katrine couldn't help but to shudder at the prospect of laying her hands on one once more.

Most of Rattimor's black ghosts were hovering near the ceiling, silently dodging drops of water that were seeping through. Rehnquist had a hold of James' arm and was leading him to one of the chairs as Rattimor picked up the other young woman who had also fallen to the floor. Katrine pulled herself up into a sitting position and held her head as Rattimor sat the young woman down and bound her wrists to the arms of the chair with black rope. The woman looked down at Katrine with worry as Rattimor bound James in a similar manner, but she quickly looked away before Rattimor noticed.

"First order of business is to find out if we are short one chair or extra one person," Rattimor said. He walked over to James, leaned over, and tore the black strap of tape off his mouth. James stared expressionless up at Rattimor and remained silent. "Looks like we have a split soul. What a pleasant surprise. Now even you can handle him, Rehnquist." He stood up straight. "If you've never seen a grown man cry, now's your chance."

"I get to tell him, Dad?" Rehnquist asked eagerly. "Finally?"

"Yes, after I survey our other two guests." Rattimor's heavy boots shook the floor as he walked in front of the other young woman.

"You give off more of a witch aura than a connected link; though I have to admit, I've never been around a link that's lived as long as yourself. The two I devoured had only been linked for two days." He smiled. "Zor was quite a fool to leave you alive. I suppose he was saving you for his brother. What a mercenary."

"I know you're curious who is stronger, Rattimor. Let me out of this mist and I'll satisfy your curiosity."

Rattimor chuckled. "You are a brave one, aren't you? But because you are still in the mist already indicates that you are *not* stronger than I am. The mist will stay until I am ready for you to fill the vase."

Rattimor began to walk in front of Katrine when the young woman spoke up more urgently. "You said you have my mother. Lay a finger on her and you'll be very sorry," she said. "Where are you keeping her?"

"She's in a prisoner of war camp, getting her head shaved," he replied curtly, looking down at Katrine. "You certainly aren't interesting. Perhaps the guard *was* taking advantage of me. What is your name?"

The young woman interrupted, "Are you afraid to face me, Rattimor? Lift up the mist and..." A black strap appeared over her mouth, muffling her.

"What is your name?" he asked Katrine again.

The Link – Master Rattimor

Katrine glanced at the panicked woman in the chair beside her, knowing that if Katrine hadn't been given away by Guard Eleven, Zor's Katrine Farmer would have been able to take out Rattimor somehow all by herself. Now everything was a mess. She looked up at Rattimor and swallowed nervously.

"Katrine just called you afraid. Are you?" she asked. "Are you scared of a woman?"

Rehnquist charged up beside his father. "Show her you're not, Dad!" He looked down at Katrine. "My dad could kill a link with a wink of one eye! Lower the mist, Dad, and show them all!"

Rattimor just stared at Katrine in silent regard. "Rehnquist," he said quietly.

"What, Dad?"

"I don't blame Zor for not empowering you. You're an absolute fool and wouldn't last ten minutes as a warlock. Now disappear into a corner until I call upon you."

Rehnquist looked flustered and sulked into the darkest corner behind Rattimor until only his white shirt could be seen in the dim light of the cabin. Rattimor raised his finger and a black ghost sped from the ceiling to his side. Katrine looked down to her wet pants and took a deep breath as she remembered the screams from the head servant in Papau when a ghost had entered his head. She promised to herself that she would not scream, for a person screams when they are surprised and not expecting something; she would not be surprised and she expected it to hurt.

"Go ahead," he quietly ordered the black ghost. Without looking up, Katrine could hear it fly through the air with a buzz, then felt it enter her right ear. It felt as if someone was jabbing a stick too far down her ear canal. Then she felt enormous tension inside her head and she grasped it with both her hands so that it wouldn't explode. A high-pitched shrill began to sound inside her as all her memories flashed through her mind at an enormous rate. She struggled to breathe as the shrill grew louder and certain memories played themselves out repeatedly: the scene where she threw Adrian against the wall and shattered her bones repeated three times and the shrilling grew even louder; the scene where Zor turned Adrian into a naked mole rat surfaced, even though it was not her own memory, but Alyssa's; and finally the scene where she looked upon her mother in Cyan before disappearing through the labyrinth door. Though she thought it not possible, the shrilling grew louder and she had to groan and clench her teeth in hopes of preventing her eardrum from busting. Finally, there was an intense stabbing pain in her left ear as the ghost exited. It was now silent, though the echoes of the shrilling remained in her head. She opened her eyes and looked up in time to see the ghost zoom into Rattimor's ear.

Rattimor watched Katrine silently, his eyes growing steadily angrier as the ghost inside his head relayed the information. The howling of the wind outside intensified as Rattimor's glare became so piercing, Katrine found herself shaking and slowly inching away from him on the floor. The ghost soon whisked out of his head and Rattimor abruptly held up his hand towards Katrine, sending her in flight through the air until she hit the wall behind her so hard that when she fell on her stomach, she couldn't move, much less breathe. She watched helplessly out of the corner of her eye as Rattimor walked slowly across the puddle-filled floor towards her, then stopped a few inches from her hand. Pinning her left wrist between the sole and the thick heel of one of his heavy, black leather boots, he stomped down onto her hand with the other boot, crushing her bones. Katrine cried out in pain and tried to pull her hand away, but he still had it pinned.

Grabbing the back of her shirt, he released her broken hand and dragged her through the frigid puddles to the counter with the vase. Katrine felt a heavy metal collar appear around her neck and could see a long chain with a strong purple glow leading from the collar to the counter's bottom leg. As soon as he released her, she crouched over and clasped her broken hand under her arm, shaking with fear.

"You have forfeited your right to a chair, as well as your right to live. You shall be treated like the bitch you are, with a dog collar and a spot on the floor by the door," he sneered. He walked away quickly and began to pace. "*Nobody* attacks a Rattimor! What you did to my daughter would have killed her had she not healed herself in time!"

He kicked James' chair, almost tipping him over, but James' expressionless face changed little. He stomped back over to Katrine and knelt down beside her.

"The number thirteen has a reputation of being unlucky. It shall be your unlucky number as well." He jerked her broken hand away from her and extended her arm, causing her to cry out once more. "You're not going to crack all at once like my daughter. I'm going to let you feel it slowly, one or two bones each hour until the thirteenth hour, when I run out of patience and snap the bones in your neck. You have one hour before I break your lower arm above your broken hand. Pray Zor wakes Alyssa before I run out of patience." He threw her arm down and Katrine cowered as close as she could against the wall, no longer able to stop tears from breaking free from her eyes. "If Alyssa shows up, I suppose the game changes and I will consider sparing your life *only* if you choose to fill the transfer vase with as strong a power as your first vase."

The Link – Master Rattimor

Rattimor walked in front of James, crossed his arms, and stared at him.

"Katrine, you *do* realize that I don't need power from a link to find out the whereabouts of my daughter, don't you? I will have no trouble killing you should Alyssa remain sleeping. All the information I need is right here in front of me, in this pathetic excuse for a warlock. I may not be strong enough to read his mind without your help, but I really don't need to read his mind. It will be quite easy to break him with a split soul."

Rattimor looked up towards the ceiling at the black ghosts. "Eyes of Rattimor, you have failed me! You knew what Mary Farmer looked like and yet you failed to recognize her in Cyan! Half of you go back to Cyan and get her before Zor snatches her away from me again. Half of you go to 1998 and locate Alyssa. And you!" he yelled at a single ghost hovering in the corner. "Inform the bounty hunters that Katrine Farmer has been captured and is dead. There is no more reward to be given." Rattimor laughed to himself, "And no more space labyrinth to be given away." He shook his head. "How ridiculous. People will believe almost anything."

Most of the black ghosts silently swept through the labyrinth door and disappeared, but some stayed behind and shrieked that the door to 1693 was closed after their departure. Rattimor took a deep, angry breath. "If the door is closed, use the labyrinth named Mint. It's the new one I acquired this morning when I killed Gerard, Imperius Grumley's old gardener. It has a 1693 door, you imbeciles. Go now and don't dare fail me again." The ghosts swept out of the room as silently as the first group. "It's a royal pain when you don't have passwords, isn't it Katrine? Imperius destroyed his password notes before I could get to them, the old buffoon."

Finally, Rattimor stepped in front of the young woman. She had a solemn expression on her face, which changed very little when Rattimor approached her and tore the black strap from her mouth.

"What is your real name, Witch?"

"I'm a link, not a witch. Zor wanted me to take Katrine's place because I can defend myself after filling a vase. I don't grow weak because I've been linked for so long."

Rattimor smiled. "You've been linked for how long?"

"Five months. Ever since my other side went into a coma. She's constantly with me; you won't ever feel her leave... and it's made me powerful. So powerful, you don't need Katrine, only me. Let them go and I'll fill your vase. You'll become so powerful a warlock, you would be able to sense the whereabouts of Adrian even if she was powerless... and in a different form."

Rattimor began to pace leisurely in front of the woman with a thoughtful look, then smiled. "You're not a link. The probability of two links left alive for so long, and now in the same room, is highly improbable. Linked five months... you wouldn't last three days if you were linked. Do you think I'm a fool?"

"Yes, I do think you're a fool," she replied without breaking her gaze with Rattimor's. Katrine looked up, anticipating the worst for the young woman, but Rattimor only stared back as if trying to sort out a puzzle.

"Who is Zor's secret weapon? The game has now become very intriguing to me," he said before he reached forward and took her chin in his hand. "The mist only blocks your powers, not mine. Do you realize I could squash you like a grape, disintegrate you to ashes with a simple look?"

"Now you believe I'm the fool. Nobody's powerful enough to kill a connected link. I'm even stronger than a full-powered witch. You would have to wait until my other half left me to get your chance to kill me, which won't happen. Lower my mist and the intriguing game shall get a lot more intriguing. I promise, I won't disappoint you."

Rattimor smiled, shook his head, then let go of her chin and backed up. "I will not set you free. I enjoy the suspense too much. By what name shall I call you?"

"Anything you wish. Names don't matter."

"Then I shall call you Rebecca, after a feisty girl I dated in my youth. She was brave and foolish at the same time, as are you, and I will probably enjoy killing you as much as I did her." He looked down at a black watch around his wrist. "Rehnquist."

"Yeah, Dad?" Rehnquist asked as he stepped out from the corner.

"I have duties elsewhere and will return in an hour to break a couple of lower arm bones." An hourglass appeared in his hand. He handed it to Rehnquist and headed for the labyrinth door. "You are welcome to share our secret with James now that my daughter no longer has an interest in staying together with Zor."

A smile crept across Rehnquist's face as he looked at James. He turned to his father before he left. "Can you turn up the heat in here before you leave, Dad? I'm freezing! And a stool?"

Rattimor turned around and sighed. "It's sometimes hard for me to believe you're my son." A long, black fur coat appeared on Rehnquist and a small wooden stool appeared in front of James. "Enjoy," he said as he turned to step through the door.

"Oh, Dad!" Rehnquist yelled after his father.

Rattimor stopped again and angrily turned around to face his son. "What?"

The Link – Master Rattimor

"Don't you think the link should be bound with black rope like the others?"

"She's in the mist. Should her other side appear, she will be no threat to you."

"But her hands aren't bound. She could attack..."

"With a broken hand? Can you not handle a one-handed woman?" Rattimor asked with impatience.

Rehnquist squirmed. "Of course I can, Father."

Master Rattimor smiled at Katrine. "I enjoy seeing her chained like a dog, Rehnquist. If she gives you any problems, just yank her chain and say 'bad girl'."

With a laugh, Rattimor stepped through the labyrinth door and disappeared behind the swaying logs, but his voice could still be heard on the other side of the door. "Stay open until I give instructions otherwise."

"Yes, Master," answered the labyrinth.

Rehnquist quickly walked over to Katrine and slammed the hourglass down on the floor in front of her, then sat on the stool in front of James while slapping his hands together and rubbing them back and forth in pure joy. He waved his hand in front of James' blank stare.

"Anyone home? I don't want you to miss anything. There's so much to tell!" James made no response. "Well, let's begin," Rehnquist said as he shifted his stool even closer to James. "Seven or eight years ago, when Adrian first started dating your brother and all hell broke loose at home, Dad found out about your mom. What was her name? Oh, yes...Cyan. Died of cancer when Zor was nine and you were five, right? Well, when my dad found out, he knew it was his calling. He knew it was because of him, so he found one of his labyrinths with the right door, showed up outside your house one day when your mother was working in the garden, and screwed up her cells with a single thought. Was she in much pain, James?" Rehnquist taunted. "Even if your white-trash family *did* have the money to seek treatment, it wouldn't have done any good," he said with a chuckle. He looked at James and his smile disappeared. James' expression had changed very little. He had looked up at Rehnquist for the first time, but was far from breaking down.

"Not enough, eh? Maybe you've forgotten too much about your mommy. Well then, let's have a little discussion about your daddy." He clapped his hands together and rubbed them eagerly once again. Katrine tore her gaze from the hourglass and looked up at Rehnquist, forgetting her own troubles for the moment and wondering how Rehnquist's story could possibly get worse.

"After your mom died, Dad went to the funeral. You probably didn't recognize him as Master Rattimor, because he looked exactly like the adult version of Zor. I sneaked into Adrian's bedroom and found one of Zor's hairs, and Dad used it to change into a Zor look-alike. He walked up to your dad, and right in front of Cyan's casket shook your dad's hand and told him he planned on fighting for custody of his two children, to whom his resemblance was totally uncanny, of course. He plucked one of his hairs out of his head and said 'If you don't believe me, have a paternal test performed', even though he knew it would be an exact match to the nine year old... but it was of no concern since he knew your family couldn't afford to pay for the test. The next day on the front page of the newspaper your dad received was Zor's picture." Rehnquist raised his hands and pretended to read the headline from the air in front of him, "*Pronounced Dead at the Scene of the Accident.*" He looked back at James and gave another chuckle. "What was it like growing up with a father who didn't believe you were his own? Did he still show unconditional love?" he asked. James just stared at Rehnquist with an expressionless face, which upset Rehnquist. "Why aren't you crying?" he yelled as he stood up and kicked the stool out of his way.

"Perhaps because even with a split soul," Rebecca remarked, "he still has more of a soul than you will ever have."

Rehnquist marched over to Rebecca and slapped her hard across her face. "I didn't ask you!" He closed his coat. "I'm going outside to piss on the pond."

Rehnquist stomped over to the door and swung it open, letting bright light flood into the cabin. Katrine could hear his footsteps crunch through deep snow as he trudged farther away.

Katrine started shaking as the open door let the cold wind in, and her wet clothes seemed to turn into ice. She leaned her head against the log wall and tried to stop her teeth from chattering. The cabinet to her side blocked most of the wind, but failed to block the gusts that squeezed under the cabinet and along the wall. She crouched into a ball, trying not to smash her broken hand against her body.

"Hang in there, Katrine," she heard Rebecca say.

Katrine looked worriedly over at Rebecca, who appeared quite comfortable in the chilled air. "Are you really a link?" she asked with her voice quivering from the cold.

Rebecca hesitated. "Don't ask any questions, Katrine. It's better you remain ignorant." She looked down at James. "You're much like your brother, aren't you? It may be hard to believe, but he saved my life with a split soul. Warned *me*, a complete stranger, about my own murder. Never knew someone could be that strong inside. You have quite a remarkable brother."

A strong gust of snowflake-sprinkled wind entered the cabin, causing the door to knock against the wall and then swing shut.

"Katrine," Rebecca said with a bit of mischief in her eye. "See if you can reach across the cabinet and lock the door. You'd be doing us all a favor."

Katrine straightened up a little and peered over at the door, considering Rebecca's request. "I'm not sure I want Rattimor even angrier with me."

"I'll take responsibility if things go bad. He *expects* Rehnquist to screw up, Katrine. He won't be angry with you, he'll be angry with Rehnquist. Besides, it would probably do you some good to move around and get some body heat generated."

Katrine stood up slowly, her body shivering from the cold. She looked at the sliding bolt mechanism and decided to try it, since Rattimor was going to kill her anyway. Knocking the transfer vase to the floor, she leaned across the smooth golden counter top and stretched out her right arm as far as she could towards the bolt before her leash went taut. Barely managing to put her fingers on the bolt, she slid it towards her until it rested firmly in a hole bore into the doorframe.

"Good. I hope he freezes to death," remarked Rebecca. "Now stay standing up and bounce around a little to warm yourself up."

Katrine wrapped her arms around her body and began to shift her weight from side to side. "Why aren't you two cold?"

"The mist doesn't make us powerless, it just keeps the power contained."

"Why don't you become invisible, then? Or become so small Rattimor can't see you? Maybe he'd get rid of the mist believing you were gone."

Rebecca smiled. "He'd know I was there by the magical aura I give off. It's hard to hide."

There was silence in the cabin for several minutes, with the exception of Katrine's chain leash clanging through the cabin as she started to gently bounce on the balls of her feet. It hurt her hand to move, but freezing felt much worse. Finally, the silence was broken when Rehnquist started banging on the door, cussing.

"Hey, Link! The wind must have blown the door shut and the bolt may have slid over a bit. See if you can unlatch it!" he yelled through a crack of the door.

"Zor told me he was a dimwit," remarked Rebecca. "He wasn't exaggerating, was he?"

Katrine stopped bouncing and looked towards the door. "I can't reach it!"

"Try a little harder, bitch! My father's going to kill me!"

"Then I guess we'll go down together, asshole!" Katrine yelled back.

For the first time, James broke a smile and chuckled. Rebecca smiled in response.

"Smiling and laughing," she said to James. "Rattimor's in for a surprise if he thinks you're going to be easy to break."

Once Rehnquist stopped banging on the door, Katrine turned her attention once more towards the hourglass on the floor and nervously held her lower left arm. Adrian had broken her other arm and she knew how it felt, but it was the anticipation that made the situation so unbearable. She somberly watched the sand drop through the tiny hole, then slide down the pile of sand below it until it came to rest beside the glass. The sand that dropped seemed to be in a rush; yet the sand waiting for its turn above was ever so patient. Two different personalities, working together harmoniously. Katrine tried to come up with a profound analogy to compare the hourglass personalities, but she couldn't. Both personalities were working together to pass the hour so that Rattimor could *break her arm* when the sand finished falling. There was nothing profound about it. She rolled her eyes and began to bounce on the balls of her feet again.

The sound of Rattimor's heavy footsteps as he entered the cabin startled Katrine. He was early. Everyone was silent as they watched Rattimor survey the room suspiciously for Rehnquist. He walked across the room towards the bolted door, but stopped when the transfer vase blocked his path. He glared at Katrine as he picked it up and placed it back on the counter. Katrine considered sulking back down into a sitting position, but found herself unable to move as he looked at her. Their eyes remained locked as Rattimor slid the bolt to the side and opened the door. Rehnquist sulked in quietly without a word, his shaved head and black fur coat covered with snow. Rattimor closed the door and finally looked at his son.

"What happened?" he asked quietly.

"I went out to take a leak and the wind blew the door shut and swung the bolt over," Rehnquist replied sheepishly.

"The Eyes of Rattimor have not yet returned?"

"If they did, they didn't come get me, Dad."

At that moment, a group of black ghosts appeared from the labyrinth door and hovered at the ceiling. As they began to shrill, Rattimor held up his hand to quiet them, then he signaled one to join him. It swept down with a buzz and hovered beside Rattimor as Rattimor turned to face Katrine.

"What happened? If I think you're lying, it goes in," he said calmly. Katrine swallowed nervously, then quietly answered, "A gust of wind slammed the door shut." She paused, knowing that Rattimor wouldn't believe that the bolt had slid and locked the door on its own.

The Link – Master Rattimor

He had picked up the fallen vase and slid the bolt open himself, and the bolt was simply lodged too deep in the hole to have just slid by itself. "I locked the door on him," she added nervously.

"She wouldn't have done it if I hadn't convinced her to," Rebecca quickly cut in. Rattimor turned his head to Rebecca, then back to Katrine.

"Did she?" he asked inquisitively.

Katrine stared at Rebecca, Zor's secret weapon. "No, I acted on my own," Katrine decided to say. She looked down to the floor and added, "And if you don't believe me, go ahead and send one of your black apparitions into my head. It won't find out anything different."

Rehnquist stepped up beside his father. "Let me have a piece of her, Dad! I knew it wasn't my fault!"

Rattimor turned towards Rehnquist. "You got what you deserved, you dolt. Next time, prop the door open with your stool." He walked in front of James while Katrine let out a small sigh of relief, realizing there would be no consequences for her actions. "So did you make him cry, Rehnquist?"

"I had him bawling like a baby, Dad. You should have seen it," Rehnquist quickly said. Rattimor lifted James' chin up to face him. "Yes, his eyes are so red, he must have been begging you to stop." He dropped James' chin and turned to Rehnquist. "Is there anything you can do right, Rehnquist?"

"Well, Dad..."

"Shut up. I don't want to hear it." He looked towards the ceiling. "Well, where is Mary?"

The ghosts shrilled excitedly and Rattimor's face turned red. "How can Cyan just disappear?" He turned toward Katrine with a look of realization. "Go back to where the Main House should have been and you will find an open labyrinth door. Search every door within the labyrinth called Rose until you find Cyan and bring Mary to me!"

As the ghosts left, a second group of ghosts entered with shrills so loud, Katrine covered her right ear with her good hand. Rattimor screamed in anger, scaring Rehnquist so much that he immediately cowered in the corner. He pointed at Rehnquist. "Go to 1998 and keep watch on Alyssa Whitman's dorm room until she shows. Take a gun, the pen, and one black ghost with you. When she shows, get into position and send the black ghost to inform me. You've done this before. It's the only thing you've managed to do right in your puberty years, so don't disappoint me, Rehnquist."

Rehnquist nodded his head and quietly replied, "Right away, Dad. I won't disappoint you," then left through the labyrinth door.

231

Rattimor rushed over to James, grasped his hair and pulled his head back to face his own. "Your brother is turning into a bigger pain in the ass than I expected! As soon as I finish with Katrine, she is going to accompany you on a search for my daughter somewhere on the vast stretches of 1980's African desert! You can practice your transporting skills." He let go of James' head and glared at Rebecca. "That will allow us to have a little quality time alone with each other."

Rattimor stared coldly at Katrine as he walked over to her and tipped the hourglass over on its side with his boot. Katrine's breathing quickened as he whispered with a smile, "It's time."

"Damen, leave her alone!" yelled Rebecca.

Rattimor swung his head around with a look of revelation. "Not many dare to call me by my first name. We must have been very familiar at one time. You have now put me in a very good mood."

He turned again to Katrine, and Katrine felt her feet sweep out from underneath her. As she tried to catch herself before her head hit the floor, her broken hand slammed down to the ground and she cried out in pain.

"Damen, please don't do this," Rebecca quietly pleaded.

Katrine looked up to see two cinder blocks a foot's length apart in front of her, then closed her eyes and dropped her head toward the floor.

Chapter 31
Rude Awakenings

Alyssa opened her eyes and smiled when she saw John leaning over her, then she remembered and her smile disappeared.

"Oh, my God," she said. "I am *so* sorry. I fell asleep, didn't I? I can't believe I did that!" she said as she rolled out from under John and stood up. John sat on her bed and looked at her with a smile, but Alyssa could tell there was something on his mind. "Something wrong? Aside from the fact your girlfriend falls asleep before sex instead of after it?"

John gave a nervous laugh, then swallowed. "There is something I need to talk to you about."

Alyssa shifted her weight uneasily. "Are you breaking up with me?" she quietly asked. "I can't tell you how sorry I am that I fell asleep. I've been staying up way too late this past week..."

"Alyssa, it's not that. It's not your fault that you fell asleep. *I* put you to sleep."

Alyssa looked confused. "What do you mean? Did you drug me or something?"

"No, I didn't drug you."

Alyssa let out a sigh of relief. "John, you're *not* boring. You didn't put me to sleep." Alyssa grabbed a cola out of her refrigerator, popped it open and took a swig, then headed to the sink room where she splashed water on her face. "What time is it, anyway?"

"About ten o'clock in the morning."

"Great," she mumbled, shaking her head. "I'm late for class." She quickly dried off her face with a hand towel.

"Alyssa, you fell asleep two days ago."

Alyssa momentarily froze before peering at John in utter disbelief. "Two days ago?" She stared at John, waiting for him to correct himself, but he sat on the bed in unwavering silence. "My brain must be short circuiting or something. Weren't you able to wake me?" She threw the towel on the spare bed and picked up the phone without waiting for his answer. "I've got to call the hospital. This has got to be because of that bicycle accident I told you about. My head just hasn't been quite..." She quickly stopped herself from revealing too much about her mental state to John. "Let's just say this is *not* normal."

John stood up and walked over to Alyssa where he hung up the receiver. "Sit down. I want to talk to you first."

Confused, Alyssa sat down on the spare bed behind her. "John, I really think I should call my doctor."

"*Be quiet. I need to tell you something*," he replied impatiently. Alyssa fell silent and watched as John began to pace the small room, struggling for the right words to say.

"How should I put this?" He ran his fingers through his hair. "I've been thinking about it for quite some time and there's no easy way." John stopped at her desk, which was cluttered with papers and books, and picked up the pad on which she had written her story. Alyssa rolled her eyes, unable to believe he wanted to continue talking about the story when something was seriously wrong with her. John threw the pad on the bed beside her.

"Things have changed since the bicycle accident, haven't they?"

"No, not really," she answered without hesitation.

He pulled out a chair from under her work desk, turned it around so that it faced Alyssa and sat down. "English majors are good at analogies, aren't they? Here's one for you: Nicole is to Alyssa as Zor is to John."

Alyssa glared at John, unable to believe what he was trying to do. "That is really low, John." She shook her head. "You have no right to use me in one of your psychological experiments. It shows very bad judgment."

"I'm not a psychology major. I'm not even a student here. Check the records."

Alyssa stood up from the bed and walked to the door. "Leave, John," she said as she opened the door.

She stared at John and soon realized that no light had entered the room when she had opened the door. She turned her head and looked out to see that behind the door was a brick wall.

"What the hell?" she whispered.

"You're not in your room, Alyssa. You're not even in your own time."

Alyssa turned to John with a piercing glare, then lifted up her curtains and tore off the aluminum foil to reveal a wall behind the window. She backed away from it until she was beside John, then she

The Link – Master Rattimor

backed away from him towards the bathroom. Turning around, she charged through the bathroom to the door leading into the adjacent dorm room and swung it open. She let out a startled cry when she saw there was only another wall.

Alyssa walked slowly back into the room where John sat waiting and picked up her hairdryer by the sink for a possible weapon. "What kind of sick game are you playing, John?" she asked as she pulled the hairdryer's plug from the wall. "How do I get out?"

"Open your closet door. It's the only way out," he replied calmly.

She reached out beside the sink's cabinet to the closet door and pulled it to the side to see her clothes hanging, but then her vision began to falter. She closed and rubbed her eyes with her thumb and index finger of her free hand, then looked at her clothes again. They seemed to be swaying back and forth.

"What did you do to me? You *did* drug me, didn't you? My eyes..."

"Have never been better, Alyssa. They're much more appealing without contacts."

Alyssa turned to look in the mirror and for the first time realized she wasn't wearing her contacts, yet could see perfectly. She stared at herself, stunned. She had worn glasses and contacts since the fifth grade.

"I thought it best that you didn't have any handicaps when you face Rehnquist," John added.

"Who?" Alyssa asked, turning towards John in somewhat of a daze.

"Adrian's brother, Master Rattimor's son. He'll be coming after you. He's probably already waiting in your real dorm room for you to arrive."

With a frustrated scream, Alyssa raised the hairdryer and threw it at John as hard as she could, but the hairdryer seemed to turn in midair and miss him completely. If she hadn't been so angry, she would've been embarrassed about her throw. John rose out of his chair with a sigh and walked towards Alyssa.

"Don't you dare come near me, you lunatic!"

John began to look agitated. "I'm sorry, Alyssa, but I'm racing against the clock here and don't have any more time for small chit chat." As he approached Alyssa, she made a fist and swung it at him, but he caught it, tightly grabbed her arm, and pushed her into the closet. Alyssa struggled to get free until she noticed that she hadn't run into her clothes. She looked around to see tall, green hedges with several brown doors every few meters, a blue sky above her, and thick green grass below her. She stood speechless, staring down the row of hedges until John pulled her back into the room and guided her to her bed where she sat quietly as John sat back down in the chair in front of her.

"Are you all right?" John asked. Alyssa said nothing. She simply continued to stare at John. "I didn't want to tell you, but now I have no choice. Something's gone wrong and I need you. Adrian's father has not only my brother, but also Katrine and another young woman held hostage."

"Did it really happen?"

"Did *what* really happen?" he asked as his eyes narrowed in confusion.

"Did a psychotic witch named Adrian force my car off the road and damn near kill me last weekend?"

"Yes."

Alyssa looked away and shook her head. "Unbelievable. Why me?" she whispered.

John moved his chair closer to her bed. "Rehnquist is going to visit you, so I need to prepare you as best I can before I send you back."

"Tell me what happened last weekend, John," Alyssa interrupted, still not convinced he hadn't just read her story and was trying to play some sick mind game. "Was it exactly like I wrote it?"

John looked impatient. "All except the part that you could see me, because I showed up invisible to you... I suppose I was trying to delay the inevitable, you finding out about me... and the kiss at the end didn't happen. Satisfied?"

Alyssa clenched the bed sheets with both her fists and closed her eyes, wishing she would wake up.

"Now pay attention, Alyssa, because what I have to say will save your life." Alyssa opened her eyes and glared angrily at John as he continued. "I want you to have these," he said as he pulled from his pocket three very slim remotes that resembled garage door openers. "These are called remote disruptors. They're harmless in the twentieth century, but they're a weapon in the fifty-first. Press the button on the remote and it emits a wavelength at a special frequency. You can't detect it, but Rehnquist's auditory nerve will pick it up and send it to his brain where it will disrupt neurons in his medulla oblongata. It'll render him unconscious almost immediately. It won't work on Master Rattimor, should he decide to show, because Rattimor's altered his brain somehow and his nerve won't pick up the frequency. If, God forbid, Master Rattimor shows, keep the disruptors hidden until he's gone. Don't give him any reason for a mind probe or he'll find out about them."

John turned one of the remotes over to reveal a clip on the backside. "Clip one to the back of your pants in case he ties your hands behind your back." Alyssa took a deep, nervous breath. "Clip one to the center of your bra. Rehnquist won't look there because he's a flaming homosexual. And place one in your desk drawer as a backup. You'll be sitting at your desk most of the time."

John placed the remotes on the bed beside Alyssa. Alyssa stared at them, wondering what kind of fool John took her for, but decided to say nothing. "But don't press the button until Rehnquist sends the black ghost that will be accompanying him back to his father to inform him that Rehnquist is in position. Once the ghost is gone, press the button." John stood up and leaned against the desk. "I believe Katrine's surrounded by a mist that will contain any power she has once you connect with her. If Rattimor doesn't get word that Rehnquist is in position, he won't lower the mist for her to fill the transfer vase. So don't press the button prematurely."

"So you want her to fill the vase?" Alyssa asked skeptically.

"That's the last thing I want her to do. I want her to help me get the other young woman out of the mist. It'll take two of us combining our powers from the same side of the mist to bring it down. Once the young woman is out, she'll take care of everything else."

"Who's the woman?"

"Can't tell you that. What you know, Katrine knows, and Rattimor can read Katrine's mind when you two aren't linked."

"How are you going to get in without Rattimor surrounding *you* with a mist?"

"Can't tell you that either, for the same reason. Just be alert and smart, and you'll know everything you need when the time is right."

Alyssa rolled her eyes, uncertain what to believe. She had been struggling for so long to keep her grasp on reality, but now... she had just lost it. No longer could she distinguish between fantasy and the truth. Time to commit herself to a mental hospital.

"Here's another backup," John said, pulling a checkered red and gold pen from his pocket. "It's an ordinary pen, but it looks exactly like the one Rehnquist will give you. He will sit you down at the desk with paper and his pen before ordering you to make your connection with Katrine, then he'll have you write down everything that is happening. The pen allows him to monitor what's going on from your side of the link, to make sure there are no deceptions when she's supposed to be filling the transfer vase. You can't write down lies, and you can't hide your thoughts with his pen. You end up writing *everything* down when you are holding the pen he will give you. First chance you get, switch it quickly and quietly with this one so that you don't write down what is really happening and give me away." He threw the pen down beside the remote disruptors. "Even if you are holding the ordinary pen, be careful what you write. It's hard even with an ordinary pen to think one thing and write down another." He paused as he looked down at her on the bed. "Hopefully you'll knock Rehnquist out before he gets a chance to sit you at the desk. Just play it smart, Alyssa."

There was silence between them until Alyssa finally broke it. "So let me get this straight. Instead of just keeping me here where I'm supposedly safe, you're sending me into a situation where I might..." Alyssa raised her eyebrows and waved her hand in front of her as she looked at John, trying to finish the sentence.

"Where you might get hurt or killed. He'll have a gun with him."

"And can you remind me *why* I'm doing this?"

"Because if Rattimor doesn't believe Rehnquist is with you when you connect with Katrine, he'll never lower the mist around her..."

"And you and Katrine won't be able to get this other woman out of the mist." Alyssa stared at John angrily. "What happens if everything goes wrong and Katrine ends up filling a transfer vase for Rattimor?"

"Don't do it, Alyssa, no matter what the cost. Rehnquist will kill you, and Rattimor will become strong enough to read James' mind to find out where Adrian is, strong enough to read the young woman's mind and find out her true identity, and then he'll finish the evening by killing us all. He's already acquired transfer vases from two other links. With the power of three links, he'll probably be strong enough to kill even me."

Alyssa shook her head in disbelief. "If I break up with you, are you going to turn me into a mermaid or shoot a lightening bolt at my shoulder?"

John paused before answering, "No."

She looked him straight in the eye. "I am *so* broken up with you; you won't *believe* how broken up I am with you, John."

"Yes... I figured as much," he said quietly.

Chapter 32
Split Soul

Katrine could hear the chain that connected her wrist to James' rattle as she raised her hand to shield her eyes from the bright light of the African desert. She felt emotionally drained and her left arm and hand were in excruciating pain, especially when she moved them. She sank to the sand and took a deep breath, then her nose started to run and her eyes started to tear up. She stared down at the sand and sniffed.

"Oh, for Christ's sake," complained James, "I don't want to have to listen to you cry the entire time we're out here, so hold it in." He sat down beside Katrine. "Your soul's split. That's why you feel the way you do. Alyssa's what? About three years old in 1980? She feels exactly the same way right now, with the exception of the broken arm. Her parents are probably rushing her off to the doctor to find out what's wrong with their hyperactive toddler who suddenly quit on them." He sighed. "It sure feels good to be one hundred percent again. I certainly don't envy you right now."

Katrine struggled to look up at the empty desert and tried to remember why they were there. She thought about asking, but she didn't feel like talking.

"Rattimor doesn't seriously expect me to look for Adrian," James said. "He just wanted to get rid of us so he could have time alone with the mystery woman... to try to scare her." He paused. "Now *she* is a remarkable woman! I hope she decides to stay in Cyan after all this is over... provided you don't screw things up more by filling a vase for the 'ol coot... then *no one* will be returning home." He took hold of the chain that glowed with a purple light and started swinging it idly. "If you would have done what I told you in the first place, I'd probably be sitting in Cyan's cafeteria right about now chowing down on some nice steak and potatoes instead of sitting in the sand half a world away from

Adrian, the naked mole rat." He looked at Katrine. "You know she bit me right before I opened the 1980 door? I had absolutely had it with that woman, so I didn't exactly open the door in a place where she could roam wild and free as my brother had suggested. I found her a wonderful place to spend the rest of her years, all right," he said, nodding his head. "The witch is finally benefiting society. If she dies, it will be ample payback for what her father did to my mom. My dad, too, I suppose." He picked up some sand and threw it. "Don't you dare tell Zor what Rehnquist said, Katrine. If I decide it's something my brother needs to know, then *I'll* tell him."

Katrine closed her eyes and wished James would stop talking. She didn't feel like responding, she didn't feel like listening, she didn't feel like caring. She just wanted to be left alone so that she could wallow in self-pity. She didn't deserve to have her arm and hand broken, she didn't deserve to be chained up and freezing in the cabin like a dog, she didn't deserve to be separated from her mother for so long, she didn't deserve...

"Do you want me to fix your arm, Katrine?" James said, interrupting her thoughts. "I've never fixed a bone before, but I know I can do it. After all, you did it your first try when you were fighting Adrian." He shook his head and thoughtfully added, "That was quite an interesting clash. The witch was supposed to just put on a light show and knock you down a couple of times." He laughed with amusement. "What a cat fight! Kind of wish I would have seen the one at the Main House." Katrine tried to focus on a point in the sand to stop herself from crying. "I know you don't feel like talking, so just move a finger if you want me to fix the arm." She struggled to concentrate on his instructions, but in the end decided not to move her finger since Rattimor would probably end up breaking her arm again when they got back to the cabin. She took a deep breath and tried to raise her head higher, for the hot air lacked oxygen and was making her dizzy when she hung her head down. It still felt better than shivering uncontrollably in the freezing cabin.

"I suppose I'm annoying you by talking," James continued, "but I really don't care. I'm the one that has to go back to wherever the hell we are and once more experience the depths of despair. I found that if you focus on something and try not to think, you don't feel as low and you don't end up feeling so sorry for yourself. Unfortunately, Rattimor keeps stepping in front of the spot I'm focusing upon and interrupting my concentration with all that 'I'm going to break you' crap. The only way he's going to break me is by annoying me to death."

The Link – Master Rattimor

Katrine felt like responding 'like you're annoying me?', but that would have required moving her mouth and forming words, so she decided to remain silent.

"Hmm... I need to be more careful what I say around you. In one ear and out the other has a whole different meaning when you're around Rattimor."

He continued to swing the chain and hum until Katrine felt like yelling at him to stop, but again... that would take energy, and she didn't care enough to spend the energy.

"I'm bored," James remarked casually. "Do you want to transport somewhere? Paris, Rome, Venice... We can grab a bite to eat at a nice outdoor cafe. We wouldn't look too out of the ordinary, would we? With you and I chained together and a strange, eerie purple mist around you and the chain? I don't think anyone will notice. You're not the only one totally self absorbed in this world."

Without lifting her head too much, Katrine looked at James to see that he was no longer surrounded by the purple mist, then looked down at her glowing body and immediately started to get upset. It wasn't fair.

"He wants me to transport and find Adrian," James explained. "You, on the other hand, don't need to be de-purple-ized. If Alyssa happened to wake and connect with you and we were both out of the mist when Rattimor came to pick us up, we could overpower him, provided you cared enough. You know, tell me if Alyssa shows up. Maybe I can somehow give you some kind of supplemental motivation with my powers, then we can at least *try* to work together to get rid of your lovely purple glow." He gave a little laugh and said in a woman-like voice, "You're simply glowing." James shook his head and smiled. "At least Rattimor didn't do too bad a job when he cut your hair. It's even on both sides."

Katrine glanced to the side of her face to see that her hair now fell just above her shoulders. Rattimor had taken off a fistful of hair with his knife after he had broken her arm. Her eyes welled up once more with tears. Wasn't breaking her arm enough?

"If I didn't have a split soul, Katrine, I'd tell the ol' coot that he should become a hair dresser instead of a war criminal. That'd make him laugh, wouldn't it?" James looked across the sand dunes and stared thoughtfully, then smirked. "I wonder if Zor's going to wake Alyssa now that you've screwed everything up. That could certainly be a mistake, knowing how easy you can be manipulated in a stressful situation."

James stood up and paced as well as he could with his wrist bound to Katrine's. "Sure is strange not having you talk back or make a

241

snide remark. Even when you manage to keep your trap shut, I can tell from your eyes and face that you're simply dying to mouth off at me. It truly sucks having a split soul, doesn't it? If Zor hadn't shared with me his experiences, I would be truly embarrassed about the thoughts that ran through my head in the cabin, but you must realize a person just isn't the same when they're running on half a soul... half a personality. You become a whole different person... one with few desirable qualities, unfortunately."

Katrine did hate how she felt and couldn't stand to listen to herself think. She was whiny, self absorbed (as James had already pointed out), and simply pathetic. She wondered why it seemed only the bad half stuck around when a soul was split.

There had to be something more there than just the bad half. James managed to smile when Rehnquist got locked out of the cabin, so why couldn't *she* smile? No, the soul doesn't split into good and bad halves. It probably just gets weaker... which means it gets lazier. Alyssa would probably compare it to lounging on the couch on a hot, summer afternoon in front of mindless television. When Katrine felt lazy, she could never get away with 'lounging on a couch'. Her mother or father *made* her get up to do chores, like pick vegetables from the garden. Once she started picking the vegetables, she was thankful she was forced to do it. The laziness disappeared and she ended up feeling quite good. Katrine took a deep breath and spoke for the first time.

"Paris," she whispered.

"What?" James asked, apparently surprised that Katrine had spoke.

She raised her head as high as she could. "I'd like to have brunch in Paris. I've never been there and would like to see it," she stated a little louder, pretending that she really wanted to go, pretending that she really cared.

James broke into a huge grin. "Well, then, let's go! Close your eyes so you don't get too dizzy and we'll be there before you know it."

Katrine closed her eyes as she felt James grab her good arm. At least she would get some food in her stomach so that when Rattimor brought them back to the cabin, she would have a little more energy to shiver and a little more energy when it came time for Rattimor to break her upper arm bone, which he informed her was the next bone in line. She shuddered at the thought, but quickly stopped herself from getting upset. She would not feel sorry for herself anymore. She was going to beat this thing. Paris would be nice, she decided.

Chapter 33
Connections

"Are you all right, ma'am?" asked a man's voice.

Holding her head, Alyssa opened her eyes for the first time since John led her through the labyrinth. She remembered John offering to carry her through the passageways, which would prevent much of the dizziness, but she refused. It was hard enough to bring herself to hold his hand in her irate state of mind. She wanted to punch him, not hold his hand.

Alyssa looked over to where the man who spoke was crouched and realized she was under a staircase, sitting in an indoor planter full of bark and ivies. From the sounds of people and plastic trays being stacked, she guessed she was in the lower level of the union by the snack bar.

"I heard you moan. Are you okay?" the man asked again. Still disoriented, Alyssa tried to focus on the man. He was young and had short, neatly trimmed black hair. He wore a badge and a walkie talky – an employee of the campus' escort service.

"I'm a little dizzy," Alyssa said, again holding her head to keep it from falling off. "I wouldn't mind a little help." The man held out his hand and helped guide her from under the stairway to the edge of the planter where she sat to try to recover a bit more.

"How did you end up under the stairway?" he asked as Alyssa took a deep breath and stared at the crowd leaving the snack bar.

"I don't know," she replied, recalling that she had nearly passed out in the labyrinth. "I don't remember." She sighed and stared at the wall opposite the stairway, looking for a phone. "I wouldn't mind an escort to my dorm room after a short telephone call. Do you have a cell phone I could borrow?"

"Sure," he said as he reached to his side belt and pulled out his cell phone. "You should probably go to the student infirmary instead of your dorm room after your call."

"No, I think the emergency room at the hospital would be more appropriate," she remarked as she punched in John's phone number and held the phone to her ear. It rang four times, then like every other time before, John's answering machine picked up. Hearing his voice on the other side of the line talk so casually, as if he hadn't a care in the world, helped her snap back to reality. The whole thing was ridiculous. She had just had a second, very realistic hallucination.

She hung up without leaving a message and turned to her escort. "I'm in the Alumni dormitories." Her escort stood up, reported his actions over his radio, and then left the union at Alyssa's side.

Alyssa's heart began to flutter anxiously as they exited the glass doors and walked upstairs to the ground level where Alyssa's dormitory room door stood in clear view. She decided to err on the side of caution and have her escort search her room for invaders before she let him go.

"Alyssa!" Sami yelled. Alyssa stopped and turned to see Sami bounding up behind them, full of energy with a huge smile across her face. She lugged a heavy green backpack slung across her right shoulder. "Glad to see you up and about finally!" she said with a grin, which quickly disappeared when she saw Alyssa's face. "What's wrong?"

Alyssa turned to her escort. "You can go now. I'll be okay."

"You sure?"

"Yeah. I need to talk to her alone if you don't mind."

The escort nodded his head and began to return to the union. Alyssa watched him walk away as Sami swayed in anticipation.

"Well? What's wrong? Is it something about your food poisoning?"

"Food poisoning?"

"Yesterday morning when I called, you said you got the same food poisoning David had the night before and would be out of it for a little while."

Alyssa's face grew more disturbed. "I talked to you yesterday? What day is it?"

"Thursday," Sami replied with a look of concern.

Alyssa's heart started pounding. "I need a ride to the hospital, Sami. My mind is short-circuiting or something. I don't remember talking to you yesterday... I don't know how I ended up under a stairway in the union just now.... Twice now, I've had these crazy hallucinations – totally realistic – then I wake up in unexpected places. I'm probably going to end up walking down the center of a busy highway during my next hallucination if I don't get some help fast."

"Hallucinations?" asked Sami in disbelief.

"You know that story I've been writing?" Alyssa asked nervously. "In my hallucinations, I believe I'm actually part of it."

"What do you mean part of it?"

"I'm a character in it. I completely lose my grip on reality and become one of the characters in my book! Then I wake up God knows where..." Alyssa grabbed her hair with both her hands and her body began to shake.

"Look at yourself!" Sami cried as she put her arm around Alyssa's shoulders. "I've never seen you like this before!"

"Can you give me a ride to the hospital?"

"Yeah, sure. My car's parked way on the other side of campus, so I can pick you up in your dorm parking lot in about ten minutes. I was going to meet David in a half hour at the snack bar for lunch. Do you want me to try to find him to tell him what's going on? I know he'd want to know."

"We can tell him later," Alyssa said as she rubbed her eyes with the palms of her hands. She looked over at her dorm room door. "Would you mind checking out my room with me before you get your car. I know it's stupid, but during my last hallucination, I was told someone would be waiting for me there."

"I don't mind, Alyssa," Sami said reassuringly. "In fact," she said as she swirled her backpack around and started to unzip one of the pockets, "I'll pull out my pepper spray, just in case." She pulled out two small spray bottles, one covered in Tweety Bird and Sylvester stickers, the other with Bugs Bunny stickers. "They look like breath fresheners, don't they? If anyone ever goes through my backpack without my permission, I'm hoping they'll get a good kick in the mouth. So which is it? Bugs or Sylvester?"

"Bugs is fine," Alyssa said with a weak smile.

Sami returned the other spray bottle to her backpack pocket and zipped it up. They walked quietly across the lawn and sidewalks to Alyssa's dorm room door, and Alyssa felt inside her right pocket where she found her keys, though she didn't remember putting them there. Her hand started to shake as she tried to place the key in the keyhole.

"Here, let me do it," Sami said quietly as she gently took the key from Alyssa's hand. She unlocked the door and swung it open until it hit the bed. No one was inside. Sami walked in slowly with the pepper spray held up high and peeked behind the door and under the beds while Alyssa paused at the doorway, trying to settle her nerves. She watched as Sami slid the closet door open and looked under the hanging clothes, then walked into the bathroom where Alyssa could hear her move the shower curtain to the side and check the adjacent dorm room's door. It sounded locked. Sami came out of the bathroom with a smile.

"All clear! I'll go get my car and pick you up in about ten or fifteen, okay?"

Alyssa nodded her head. "Thanks. I'd drive myself, but I'm just a little too weirded out right now."

"Maybe you should take a quick shower to make yourself feel better. Besides, you've got bed-head," Sami teased, trying to lighten Alyssa's mood. She strolled out the door and returned the pepper spray to her bag. "The door's locked," Sami said as she reached around the door and felt the knob. "The opposite bathroom door is locked from both sides." She lifted her backpack over her shoulder. "I'll hurry."

She turned with a little wave and strutted off across the field. Alyssa swung the door shut and turned to the vacant room. A shower would feel good, she decided. She walked to her desk and reached into her pockets to empty them, then realized there were several small items in her left pocket. She pulled them out and stared in disbelief at three small remotes and a checkered red and gold pen. Her eyes quickly darted around the room as she pressed the button on one of the remotes repeatedly. There was no sound, no vibration, nothing.

Alyssa began to pace the room quickly as she jiggled the remotes and pen in her hand. She looked beside the sink to see that her contacts were still in solution. "Calm down, Alyssa. Calm down," she said before taking several deep breaths. "John gave you everything you need to protect yourself... the asshole." She walked over to the desk drawer and opened it. It was noisy to open, but she still decided to place one of the remotes inside the front tray. She closed the desk drawer, then looked at the pen. The desk drawer was too cumbersome and noisy, so she decided to put the pen in her right pocket. As she stared down at the remaining two remotes, she remembered John's instructions. One in the center of her bra, he said. Rehnquist was gay and wouldn't look there. She started to lift her shirt, but then stopped herself.

"Damn it!" she yelled. "If you think I'm staying here like a sitting duck, John, you've got another thing coming!" She threw the remotes down on the cluttered desk and headed for the door. She was about to reach down to turn the door knob when she noticed a large section of the door swaying from side to side – a labyrinth door. She backed up a little in anticipation, but nobody was stepping through. Since the door in the bathroom which led into the adjacent dorm room was locked from the other side, the main door was her only way out. She quickly reached down and grabbed the doorknob, then let out a startled cry as a man's hand appeared from through the door and grabbed her

The Link – Master Rattimor

wrist. She twisted her hand frantically to try to free herself as a leg quickly appeared stepping out from the door. Her hand finally wriggled free as a dark man with a shaved head, dressed in a white muscle shirt and shin-length black jeans, fully appeared in front of her.

Alyssa ran towards the bathroom as something black swooped down in front of her, then swirled around her midsection, cutting into her gut with razor sharp slices. She screamed as she swirled around and tried to beat off the painful apparition, then was suddenly jerked backwards against the intruder, his hand covering her mouth and muffling her cries. She squirmed and tried to pull his arm away, but he only tightened his hold on her head. Tears came to her eyes as she felt the muzzle of a gun press against the side of her head. Alyssa took several deep breaths through her nose and stopped squirming. The black ghost released her and hovered in front of her.

"That's better," the man whispered in her ear. "Settle down and you won't get hurt." He pulled her backwards and sat her down in her desk chair. "I'm going to remove my hand from your mouth. Scream or yell and I'm going to put a hole in you. Do you understand?" Alyssa closed her eyes and nodded, then the man slowly removed his hand. "Don't move a muscle. Sit as silent and still as you possibly can while I prepare."

He nestled a black nine-millimeter gun fitted with a large silencer under his arm as the black ghost swooped down so that Alyssa was eye level with its purple eye. Staring in shock at the strange black form hovering in front of her, she remained motionless and dared not break the silence.

The man grabbed her biology notebook left open from when she was studying with David and tore out several sheets of blank paper from the back of it. Alyssa nervously watched as he cleared the desk in front of her by shoving her other papers and open biology textbook to the side. To her relief, he never noticed the two remotes she had thrown on top of the desk. One was still within her reach. From his pocket, he took out a red and gold pen that looked identical to the one John had given her and threw it on top of the blank paper.

"My name is Rehn... Master Rehnquist," he said. "But you may just call me Master. This morning I will be..."

Laughing outside interrupted Rehnquist. Alyssa recognized the laughter as belonging to the girls who lived beside her. They both listened quietly as they entered the next room and slammed their door. The sounds of their voices carried easily through the wall.

"Not a sound," Rehnquist warned Alyssa before turning to the black ghost. "Scare them off," he ordered. The black ghost swept down to the floor and took the shape of a large black rat, then scurried off into the bathroom. A smile crept over Rehnquist's face. "This should be good," he said as he backed up toward the bathroom with his gun still aimed at her. "Scoot your chair under the desk so you're not tempted to do something stupid like make a break for the door."

Alyssa put her hands on each side of the chair and shifted her chair under the desk. She looked over at Rehnquist nervously as she slowly reached into her right pocket and slid out the pen with her trembling hands. The girls next door screamed and Rehnquist's smile grew even bigger. Alyssa could hear muffled yells and the sound of the girls jumping between the beds and the desks, throwing items at the black rat. Rehnquist chuckled quietly and began to step into the bathroom to better hear the commotion next door. Something hit the bathroom door.

"This door's locked, right?" he quietly asked Alyssa. Alyssa shrugged. Rehnquist waved his gun at her. "Don't make a move, got it?"

Alyssa nodded and grasped the pen at her side, ready to move. She bit her lip angrily as she remembered John's instructions not to press the button on the remote until the ghost left. As Rehnquist stepped into the bathroom to check the other door, Alyssa quickly switched the pens and grabbed the nearest remote. He stepped back into her room as Alyssa dropped the remote and pen into her lap.

"What did you just do?" he asked angrily.

Alyssa swallowed. "Nothing," her voice shook as she subtly spread her legs enough to let the pen and remote drop between them. Rehnquist marched over to her and jerked her chair back, causing the remote to fall from between her legs and bounce loudly against the tile floor.

Rehnquist looked down to the floor and spotted the remote. Alyssa lost all color in her face and wanted to pass out as Rehnquist raised the gun and pressed it against her forehead.

"What did I tell you before I went into the bathroom?"

"Not to move," she whispered.

"It appears that you moved." He reached his foot under the table and kicked out the remote. "It also appears that you've been expecting me. Am I right?"

"Yes, sir."

"Yes, *Master*, is the correct response."

"Yes, Master," she replied without hesitation. She closed her eyes and tried to control her trembling as he pressed the gun deeper into her forehead. "I'm sorry," she whispered.

The Link – Master Rattimor

"That's better." He bent over and picked up the remote. "Anything else you want to tell me before I search this room from top to bottom?"

Alyssa quickly peered across the desk at the other remote. It was partially buried under a sock, but it would still be easy to find. "I was given two remote disruptors. The other one's under that sock," she said as she peered in the direction of the second remote. Rehnquist moved her clothes to the side and the remote fell to the desk. He picked it up with a smile on his face and slipped both remotes into his pocket, then returned the gun to her forehead. "Anything else?" he asked loudly as he jabbed the gun into her.

Alyssa closed her eyes and tensed up. "No."

"Are you sure?" Rehnquist asked angrily. "If I find something during my search that I should know about, you're going to pay dearly. Do you understand?"

Alyssa took a deep breath. "There's nothing else, I swear. Go ahead and search." Alyssa felt faint, wondering how convincing her 'I didn't know' argument would be if the pen and last disruptor were found.

Rehnquist stared at her angrily, then a smile crept across his face and he took the gun away. "Good."

A scream came from next door and she could hear one of the girls yell, "It bit me!"

Rehnquist looked behind him and Alyssa thought he was going to begin his search, but instead he grabbed the other desk chair and pulled it up to her desk. "Well, at least I don't have to explain what we're doing here. It took a good twenty minutes to convince the other two links that I wasn't going to rob them. I just wanted them to daydream and write down what was happening. They never fully grasped what was going on and they thought I was a fool." He laughed and sat down, "Until the end, that is. Then they realized I wasn't the bumbling idiot they thought. I certainly showed them." Alyssa turned away from Rehnquist towards the desk. "Not that anything's going to happen to *you*!" he added, as if trying to correct a mistake.

The main door to the adjacent room slammed and they listened in silence as the girls cheered. Seconds later, the black rat squeezed under Alyssa's front door and stopped beside Alyssa, then transformed quickly back into an upside-down teardrop shape.

"Did you draw blood?" Rehnquist asked the black ghost. A high shrill pierced Alyssa's ears and she shrugged at the sound. "You idiot! You want others to hear? It's hard to believe you're from my father's brain."

Rehnquist quietly listened as the girls chattered a minute longer, ran the water in their sink, then left the room.

"Going to the infirmary," Rehnquist felt the need to explain. "Inform my father I'm in position," he told the ghost, and the ghost swept silently through the labyrinth door and disappeared. "Well, let's see what's happening on the other side. Pick up the pen and make contact with Katrine."

As Alyssa shifted her chair back up to the desk, she looked at the desk drawer. The back of Rehnquist's chair was pushed against it and she couldn't open it. She picked up the pen, closed her eyes, and thought about Katrine. In an instant, all of Katrine's experiences and thoughts flushed through her mind. In an instant, she knew of Rehnquist's incompetence, Rattimor's vindictive nature...everything. Guilt for abandoning Katrine flooded over her as she watched Rattimor replace James in his chair. Rebecca had tape over her mouth, but looked unharmed. Katrine's metal collar had already been replaced and she was sitting in a puddle beside the cabinet, cradling her arm, trying to recover from the black ghost that Rattimor had just sent through her head for a second time.

"Have you made contact yet?" asked Rehnquist. The cold, dark cabin disappeared and she looked up at Rehnquist as he hovered over the paper.

"Yes."

Rehnquist grabbed the pen and shook it. "This thing should have half a page written by now. You don't even have a single word."

Alyssa, realizing her mistake, tried to look annoyed instead of guilty. "I was about to start writing when you interrupted."

"Stupid thing's still too slow. Dad must be losing his touch." He handed it back to Alyssa. "Maybe shaking it helped."

Alyssa put the pen to the paper and started to write as fast as she could about the cold cabin, then she made contact again. Master Rattimor was now crouching in front of Katrine.

"She's back. Wonderful," Rattimor said as he grabbed hold of Katrine's chin. A black ghost swept in from the cabin's labyrinth doorway and shrilled, and a smile crept across Rattimor's face. "Glad you're in position, Rehnquist. What is the second verification?"

Alyssa wrote down the question, confused as to what he meant.

"Tell him 'Hitler'," ordered Rehnquist. "Wait! Hitler is at the end." Rehnquist looked stressed and started tapping his fingers on the desk. "Stalin! That was it. Tell him Stalin. Man, I hate history."

Katrine received the message from Alyssa and said 'Stalin'.

"Glad to see you can do something right, Rehnquist," Rattimor told Katrine. Alyssa quickly wrote his words down as fast as she could, then concentrated on warming Katrine, fixing the bones in her arm and hand, and drying her pants which were wet from sitting on the puddle-

The Link – Master Rattimor

filled floor; yet the pants remained wet despite her efforts. She hesitated at first, then quickly wrote down what she did.

Master Rattimor stood up. "Feeling a bit better, I see. I suppose it's a whole different ball game now that Alyssa's arrived. Too bad. I was looking forward to breaking more bones," he said as he tilted the hourglass on its side, then walked over to James. "Enjoy your meal in Paris? It was most definitely your last. Very creative making the chain invisible and dining out in a dark bar to hide Katrine's glow." He walked slowly around James' chair, then grabbed the back of it and pulled it to the back wall. Holding out a finger, one of his black ghosts swept down from the ceiling to his side. "Annoy him until he tells me where my daughter is."

The black ghost slammed against James' shoulder, causing him to jolt backwards; then in the whiniest voice Katrine could image, said the words, "Where is she? Huh? Huh? Tell me. Where is she? Huh? What'd you do with Adrian? Huh? Huh?" The black ghost jabbed his shoulder again. Rattimor waved his hand and a transparent wall erected, creating an interrogation room that blocked out the noise of the black ghost from the rest of the cabin. "The only sound that will pass through this wall will be James' voice, when he yells where he took my daughter."

Rattimor walked over to Rebecca. "He's got a crush on you," he informed her, seemingly amused. "Hopes you'll stay in Cyan when it's all over. He's a very optimistic young man. If you all weren't going to die, I'd be quite interested to see how it would have worked out." He sighed. "I shall take off the tape if you promise to watch your language and show me a bit more respect. You have a very offensive vocabulary, you realize."

Rebecca nodded her head and Rattimor removed the black tape from across her mouth just as the cabin started to flood with dozens of black ghosts from through the labyrinth door.

Rattimor turned red with rage. "What have you done? You've brought back the air from Cyan!"

Dozens of ghosts shrilled so loudly that Katrine quickly clasped her hands over her ears. Rattimor raised his hand and they quieted. He walked over to Katrine and crouched down.

"Rehnquist, expect an attack. I can no longer tell in this blasted air if Alyssa's connected with Katrine. What's emergency code word number one?"

Katrine waited for Alyssa to write down the question. After she did, Alyssa looked over at Rehnquist and stretched her aching hand as she waited for his response.

"Tell him I am aware of the deception and have already taken care of it. Emergency code word number one is 'Mussolini'," Rehnquist replied.

Alyssa placed the pen back to the paper and wrote down the response, then reconnected.

"He found out about the deception and already took care of it. Mussolini," Katrine quietly replied.

"What happened?" Rattimor asked Katrine.

Katrine fidgeted, knowing everything about Alyssa's situation from the second she had made contact. "Zor gave her two remote disruptors to knock him out, but he found them both."

"Where were they?"

"Alyssa was supposed to clip them to her clothes, but she just threw them on the desk."

Rattimor's eyes narrowed in confusion. "Why would she do that?"

Katrine quietly explained, "Partly because she didn't believe they worked, partly because she was about to leave – angry that Zor knew Rehnquist might go after her, yet he still chose not to hide her."

Rattimor nodded his head in satisfaction, then stood up. "The Eyes of Rattimor have found Cyan. It's only a matter of seconds before your mother arrives. Does she take pain as well as you do, or do you plan on sparing her pain by filling the vase?"

Katrine clenched her fists and looked away, wondering why Zor hadn't arrived to save them. Her heart began to pound when she heard her mother's voice yelling through the doorway from a distant labyrinth passageway. She leaned her head against the back wall and concentrated as hard as she could on the mist around Rebecca, but it remained. She stared and concentrated on the mist surrounding her own body, but it also failed to disappear. All Alyssa could do for her was keep her warm and keep her bones from breaking.

As her mother's yelling grew louder and a second wave of ghosts began to fly through the labyrinth door, Rebecca looked nervously over at Katrine and whispered, "Fill it and we're all dead."

Tears came to Katrine's eyes as her mother was dragged through the door by two of Rattimor's black ghosts. Mary was in a grass-stained, long, lavender dress Katrine recognized from four years ago when on the farm; and her long, grayish-brown hair was fastened in the back by a barrette. As soon as the two ghosts released her arms, she struggled to lift herself up, but immediately fell back down, dizzy from the trip.

Rattimor approached her and stood above her. "I'm so glad you could finally make it, Mrs. Farmer. I apologize for overlooking your presence this morning. Seems I had other things on my mind at the time."

As Mary struggled to lift herself a second time, Katrine's eyes caught sight of her locket dangling from around her mother's neck, the one Zor said he would keep until all the 'Rattimor' business was over. With wide eyes, she watched as her mother lifted her gaze to Katrine. It was not a look her mother would have given her under such circumstances, but it *was* a look Zor would have. Katrine gave a quick nod to show she understood, then her mother returned her gaze to the floorboards. Katrine's breathing became more rapid as she realized that the purple mist had not surrounded her mother's body. After all, Zor was just a normal woman.

Alyssa started to scribble, not knowing what to write in place of Katrine recognizing the locket and realizing her mother was Zor in disguise. Rehnquist grabbed the pen and shook it, then handed it back.

"There, see if that's better," Rehnquist said, not suspecting a thing.

Chapter 34
Discoveries

"Leave her alone!" Katrine stood up and shouted as Rattimor shoved Zor against the wall with his foot.

"Shall we complete our business before she gets hurt, or after, Katrine?" Rattimor asked smugly as he towered above her mother's body.

"Don't give him anything, Katrine," said Zor defiantly. "He's not worth the spit I put on his boot."

Rattimor kicked Zor against the wall. "Quiet, woman!" A large dagger appeared in his hand and he pushed it gently into the woman's neck. "Well, Katrine?"

Katrine tried to look as stressed and confused as she possibly could, trying to mask how eager she wanted to agree to fill the vase.

"You've got to promise to let everyone go unharmed after you have Adrian back," Katrine said, appearing hopeful.

"Katrine! He doesn't keep his promises!" Rebecca yelled in frustration.

Rattimor gave a curious look at Rebecca, then walked over to Katrine. "I will let your mother go. That is all. She's the only one here I have no personal grudge against," he said before he glanced over at Rebecca. "If I had no grudge with you before, Mystery Woman, I do now."

"Can't take a little constructive criticism?" Rebecca replied curtly.

He looked back at Katrine, seemingly annoyed, and said, "The offer to release your mother is rescinded in one minute. Then I start sawing off her arms. You know I would do it."

"Don't do anything for this monster, Katrine," Zor said quietly as Rattimor picked up the hourglass from the floor and placed it on the

The Link – Master Rattimor

counter in front of Katrine. Much of the sand disappeared, leaving only a minute's worth behind. Katrine bit her lip as she nervously looked between Rattimor, Rebecca, and the hourglass. After about half a minute, Rebecca hung her head, realizing that Katrine was close to giving in. Katrine waited nervously for a little more sand to drop.

"I'll do it, but you've got to keep your promise," Katrine said, her voice shaking ever so slightly for just the right touch.

Rattimor smiled and threw the dagger behind him on the floor. "Place your hands on the vase and I'll lift the mist. No tricks. Rehnquist, what's the transfer vase pre-verification word?"

The word's 'Napoleon'.

"Napoleon," Katrine said as she placed her sweaty hands on the vase.

"Good. First the water, then the power," Rattimor said with a greedy smile. He stepped on the opposite side of the vase, ready to watch the light show. "Begin," he instructed as the purple glow around Katrine's body disappeared. Katrine immediately began to concentrate on the mist around Rebecca. She peeked to the side without turning her head to see the purple color around Rebecca steadily grow fainter.

No! Not now!

Alyssa broke her connection with Katrine. Katrine looked over at Zor with a panicked look, then quickly returned her attention to Master Rattimor. "Alyssa's gone."

"What happened?" Rattimor asked angrily.

"I don't know," Katrine replied as she took her hands off the vase.

"Contact her!"

Katrine closed her eyes for a moment, then looked back up at Rattimor.

"Alyssa's friend is knocking at her door. Rehnquist won't let Alyssa continue until she gets rid of her."

Katrine leaned against the wall, feeling weak. Rehnquist was going to find the pen when Alyssa stood up to answer the door. She glanced behind Rattimor at Zor, who appeared both angry and worried.

"Sounds like my son is using half his brain today. I suppose I should be proud," Rattimor grumbled. "We shall wait," he said as he raised his hand and the mist returned around Katrine's body.

* * *

"Come on, Alyssa!" yelled Sami from outside the door. "I can hear you in there! This is not funny!" Sami banged on the door again.

"Answer the door and get rid of her!" whispered Rehnquist.

"She'll go away!" whispered Alyssa in return. She turned back to the paper. "Katrine needs to fill the vase before her mother gets hurt."

She tried to reconnect with Katrine, who was also trying to reestablish the connection, but Rehnquist grabbed her shoulder and pulled it back so that Alyssa faced him. Their connection lasted only long enough for Katrine to find out what was going on.

"It can wait! We're not going to do a rush job here. Get rid of the distraction!" he said as he waved his gun in her face.

"Who's in there with you?" yelled Sami from outside. "I'm going to call the police if you don't open this door in five seconds!"

Alyssa jerked her shoulder away from Rehnquist and returned her pen to the paper ready to write, but Rehnquist pressed the gun against her cheek. Alyssa closed her eyes, unable to breathe.

"I'm pleased that you are so willing to fill the vase, but I choose to get rid of your friend before she calls the police. Tell her I'm your cousin, here for a visit," Rehnquist instructed. Alyssa groaned, uncertain how to hide the pen once she stood up. "Now!" Rehnquist ordered impatiently as he jabbed her cheek with the gun, then withdrew it to a more comfortable distance.

Alyssa placed both her hands on the chair to lift herself up. As she stood up, she quickly reached under with her right hand and scooped up the pen, then hid it in her palm and held it against her shorts as she turned to get out of her chair. As she turned to pass by Rehnquist sitting in his chair, he grabbed her arm and stopped her, then slid his hand down until it touched the pen. He took it from her and eyed it angrily.

"We will discuss this after you get rid of your friend. Remember, I'll be pointing the gun at her, so don't try anything stupid. Appear casual and relaxed. Smile even." He reached behind him and grabbed a sweater from the spare desk to cover his gun.

Disheartened, Alyssa opened the door. "Hi, Sami. Haven't seen you for a couple of days."

"You had me seriously worried," Sami said angrily. Alyssa opened the door further before Sami could mention the hospital, wondering if she could see Rehnquist and even hoping Rehnquist was just a third hallucination. "Oh, hello," she said to Rehnquist. Rehnquist smiled and nodded; Alyssa felt faint.

"This is my cousin," Alyssa said. "He just dropped by for a visit, so I can't get together right now."

"Oh, I didn't know you had any cousins," Sami said enthusiastically. "You look Italian. Are you from Italy?"

"Sicily," replied Rehnquist with a smile.

Alyssa wanted to roll her eyes, but stopped herself. "Hey listen, Sami," she decided to say, "I was going to meet David in about twenty minutes at the union." Sami's face became confused. "We were going to study psychology together for the quiz tomorrow on Chapter Five."

The Link – Master Rattimor

She hoped she had remembered the right chapter: the 'hostage situation' chapter. "Tell him I can't make it because I'm visiting with my cousin. Okay?"

Sami immediately looked nervous, but then quickly smiled. "Sure! Can do!" she said with a little bounce. She leaned over and waved at Rehnquist. "Nice meeting you. Maybe we can have lunch together sometime."

Rehnquist gave a wave back with his free hand and Alyssa began to close the door. Just before the door closed entirely, she could see Sami back up from the door with extreme trepidation. Alyssa returned the look and the door shut. Immediately, she felt as though she had made a huge mistake.

"Sit," ordered Rehnquist. Alyssa quickly sat down without a word as he slammed Rattimor's pen down in front of her and picked up the ordinary pen. "I swear a bullet is going to fly if I find out about any more tricks. For the last time, is there anything else I should know before we continue?"

Alyssa swallowed. "No, there's nothing," she answered with a small tremor in her voice.

He placed the muzzle of the gun against her shin and Alyssa took a deep breath. "You and I both realize I have orders not to kill you until my father gives the word, but you are making this so difficult. I hope you realize I have full permission to shoot you, as long as I don't kill you. Two disruptors and a fake pen. There had better not be anything else," he warned.

Alyssa closed her eyes, struggling not to tell him about the third remote resting in the top drawer only a couple inches from where he was sitting. "That's all John gave me."

"John?"

"Zor," Alyssa quickly corrected herself.

Rehnquist cocked the gun and Alyssa tensed in anticipation, but still said nothing.

"Start writing," Rehnquist ordered. "I want to find out what's really going on. You will be telling my father about the pen as soon as you are able."

Alyssa's hand shook as she picked up Rattimor's pen and placed it to the paper. Unlike with the ordinary pen, she became unaware that she was writing once she connected. Her dorm room completely disappeared and the sensation of being in the cold, dark cabin became more intense than when she held John's ordinary pen.

* * *

Master Rattimor turned away from Katrine as she stood in a stupor, waiting for Alyssa's return. He began to pace past Rebecca, but he immediately stopped when something caught his eye.

"The mist is weaker!" he announced. He stomped over to Katrine, shoved her abruptly against the wall, slid his hand under her collar, and squeezed her neck with his large hand. "I told you no tricks! Now your mother is going to pay for your mistake." He released her neck, picked up the dagger, and marched over to her mother.

"I'm sorry!" Katrine yelled after Rattimor, desperate to divert his attention away from Zor. "Please! I'm sorry!"

Rattimor grabbed Katrine's mother by the front of her dress, shoved her against the wall, and held the knife to her arm. The glimmer of candlelight reflected off the locket, attracting Rattimor's attention for just a moment, but it was long enough. Shock swept over Rattimor's face just before an intense explosion of light, both purple and green, radiated outwards from between Zor and Rattimor. Katrine shielded her eyes until they adjusted to the light, then looked up to see the black ghosts zoom from the ceiling into Rattimor's ears, leaving several ghosts behind who rapidly circled the pair, blocking most of the light that escaped into the rest of the cabin. Only two silhouettes could be seen in the explosion of rays.

"No," whispered Katrine as she realized the purple light was slowly becoming more dominant over the green. She looked down at the vase in front of her, picked it up and threw it as hard as she could at Rattimor, but it merely bounced off the black ghosts that were circling them.

The light was nearly solid purple and the black ghosts started to shrill louder and louder. Over the racket, Katrine could hear Rebecca say, "Come on... Don't let him win."

Finally the light began to dim and Zor, still in Mary Farmer's form, sank to the ground surrounded by a purple mist. The ghosts still present swept silently and swiftly back up to the ceiling as Rattimor towered over Zor.

Katrine started to shake and sank to a sitting position as she realized how terribly wrong everything was turning out. No one was left to save them.

Alyssa reconnected.

Katrine.

Immediately, Katrine knew that Alyssa's pen had been discovered, and Alyssa was scared.

You have to tell Rattimor I'm back or Rehnquist is going to put a bullet in my leg.

The Link – Master Rattimor

"Alyssa's back," Katrine whispered, breaking the silence in the cabin.

Suddenly everyone jumped as James yelled, "She's in Montreal! Now leave me alone!"

A smile crept across Rattimor's face. "I love it when things begin to go my way." He looked up at the ceiling to his black ghosts. "Go to Montreal and search every zoo, every testing and research lab, every pet store, every animal collection..." He looked down at Zor with a disgusted look. "Bring back every naked mole rat you find in Montreal."

From Rattimor's ears, hundreds of black ghosts squeezed out to join the rest as they swept out the door to begin the search for Adrian.

You have to tell him about the pen, Katrine, and Rehnquist wants to apologize to his father for his mistake.

Katrine sighed and put her head down on her arms as they rested across her knees.

Please hurry, Katrine. He seems particularly trigger-happy.

"Alyssa switched pens when Rehnquist wasn't looking and was writing with an ordinary pen. He found the right pen and sends his apologies," she said without looking up. She couldn't face Zor.

"Anything else my son should know about?" Rattimor angrily asked.

"No," she answered truthfully. Rehnquist *shouldn't* know about anything else, she reasoned. If he wanted a different answer, he should have worded his question more carefully.

Katrine heard a ghost whirl down from the ceiling. She looked up to see it at Rattimor's side and knew what was coming.

"You know," she said angrily, feeling she had nothing more to lose, "when Zor probes memories, it doesn't hurt!"

"Everyone develops his or her own style," he said with a smile. "Go ahead," he instructed the ghost. The ghost raced down to the entrance of Katrine's ear and she cringed in anticipation, but it seemed unable to enter. It returned to the ceiling with a shrill.

"Rehnquist, disconnect Alyssa for a minute or two."

* * *

Rehnquist pulled Alyssa's chair away from her desk as Alyssa stared over at the paper in amazement. Not only did she not remember writing the two pages that sat on the desk before her, but her hand didn't hurt and the writing on the paper wasn't her handwriting. Rehnquist grabbed her chin and turned her away from the paper.

"What color is the sky?"

"What?"

"Answer the question. What color is the sky?"

"Blue," Alyssa answered with confusion in her face.

"What color is the grass?" Alyssa paused and Rehnquist slapped her. "You are answering too slow."

"Green. What's the point of this?"

"To keep you from connecting with Katrine. Daddy wants her alone so he can read her mind. How many fingers on each hand?"

"Five," Alyssa answered as she glanced over to the paper on her desk, worried that Rattimor would find out about the third remote.

* * *

After Alyssa disappeared, Rattimor signaled for the ghost to try again. Once more, it shrilled just outside her ear and returned to the ceiling.

"Blasted air," remarked Rattimor. He grabbed Katrine's chain and yanked her up, causing shooting pains in Katrine's neck and shoulders. He quickly threw open the heavy log door and pulled her outside where the sunlight had just broken through the clouds. Katrine squinted in the intense brightness, then closed her eyes completely and cringed as the shrilling of a black ghost sounded a third time right outside her ear. When it finally grew silent, Rattimor grunted angrily, then jerked Katrine's leash as he pulled her back through the doorway and secured the chain to the bottom of the cabinet once more. Katrine sank to the floor, slipped her hands under the collar, and massaged her aching neck as Rattimor stomped across the floor toward Zor.

"How'd you do it?" Rattimor yelled at Zor. "Not even I can manipulate the air the way you have. Whose help did you acquire?"

Zor looked up at Rattimor and said quietly, "I suppose I have a friend even more powerful than you."

"Impossible. I'm the most powerful warlock alive," he said, turning away in disgust.

A gust of wind entered the cabin from the open door and Katrine quickly let go of her neck and wrapped her arms around her shivering legs. Alyssa returned, then quickly warmed Katrine.

Zor sighed as he watched his dress flap in the wind. "If I change back into my own body, would you change my attire? I would rather face you with my own face than that of a woman."

Rattimor turned to him. "You may change and I will dress you appropriately. I can't stand transvestites."

The lavender dress burst at the seams as Mary's body changed shape and grew into Zor's. As Zor grasped the locket around his neck, Rattimor waved his hand and a black tuxedo with a white shirt and black bow tie took the place of the shredded dress that Katrine's mother used to wear.

The Link – Master Rattimor

"Now you don't have to dress for your funeral," Rattimor remarked. He walked in front of Rebecca. "There are certainly benefits to your arrival, Zor. I can finally find out the identity of your mystery woman. Would you like to tell me outright, or shall we play a game?"

"Since I don't intend on telling you outright, I suppose we shall have to suffer through one of your games," replied Zor dismally before tucking Katrine's locket under his shirt.

"I was hoping you would say that," Rattimor said as he walked over to Katrine. "Rehnquist, play your little question-answer game with Alyssa until I come for a visit."

* * *

Once again, Rehnquist pushed Alyssa's chair away from the desk so that her chair faced him. Before Rehnquist could ask a question, Alyssa anxiously interrupted.

"What's he going to do to them?"

"Now get this straight: *I'm* the one asking the questions. How many tires on a tricycle?"

Alyssa peered nervously at her desk. "Three."

"Answer faster. How many seasons are there?"

"Four."

* * *

Rattimor grabbed Katrine's chain and it released from the cabinet once more. "Get up. I haven't shown you the pond. It is particularly beautiful this time of year, especially nice for a swim."

Katrine shuddered as she experienced a flashback of when Paul had pulled her from the water after nearly drowning. She glared at Rattimor. "I never said I wanted to play in your game."

"You aren't a player, you *are* the game."

"But I had nothing to do with Zor's mystery woman," Katrine angrily retaliated.

"Leave her alone, Damen," Rebecca warned. "You've already put her through enough."

Rattimor smiled and knelt in front of Katrine. "Does the peasant Mädchen need *reason* to be chosen for my game? I have plenty. First, I'm gambling that Zor cares more about you than he's willing to admit. It's either you or James; and since James won't cry out for help or beg for mercy, I shall use you... because I love a good show." He stood up. "Second, it's much easier to kill you than James, should it come to that. Even with a split soul, warlocks will find the willpower to fight death." Rattimor glanced at Rebecca. "And third: you need to be taught a lesson for trying to dissipate Rebecca's mist instead of doing what you were told." He pulled on the chain and the edge of the metal collar again dug into the base of her sore neck, prompting Katrine to quickly stand up. He turned to Zor, who was already on his feet.

"Follow us to the pond, Zor, and we shall play," Rattimor said as he pulled Katrine around the cabinet to the open doorway.

Katrine stepped back onto the porch and shielded her eyes as she clenched her other arm close to her body. Without a ghost screaming in her ear, she managed to keep her eyes open long enough so that they could adjust to the brightness. They were in a large canyon meadow speckled with pine trees that were weighted down with large clumps of snow that periodically fell to the snow-blanketed ground. Rehnquist's footsteps forged a path leading from the cabin to a large frozen pond about fifty meters straight ahead in the center of a meadow. She could hear Zor's footsteps on the wooden floor as he approached the door behind them.

"Zor," Katrine could hear Rebecca say. "He's not going to kill her. He wants the vase filled."

Rattimor shook his head. "How little she knows. Come on," he said as he jerked Katrine's leash in the direction of the pond.

Katrine stepped off the porch into the snow and hugged herself even tighter as the chilled breeze once blocked by the cabin hit her wet shirt. Zor stepped out from the cabin and paused a moment before stepping into the snow behind Katrine. She looked back at him and tried to interpret his expressionless face.

"She's wrong, you know," Rattimor said loudly as he glanced back at Zor. "I am perfectly willing to let this one die." He started to lead them through the fluffy, dry snow. "You realize," he continued, "I am the only warlock throughout all of history that has succeeded in actually *creating* the links I have used. I've done it twice already, I can do it a third time."

"How many healthy minds will you retard with your next one?" Zor responded coldly. "One hundred fifty? Two hundred? Your average is not very good. Seems you have no idea what you are doing when it comes to manipulating brain connections."

"I know plenty about the mind. The Eyes of Rattimor, for example. They are cells taken from a useless part of the brain, but I have successfully turned them into valuable servants."

"I was unaware that any part of the brain was useless," Zor responded. "Perhaps this explains why you are so incapable of functioning in society."

"Don't be a hypocrite, Zor. Unlike you, I don't feel the need to create an entire separate society to live happily. I am quite pleased with my chosen lot in life."

"Murdering and harming the innocent..."

The Link – Master Rattimor

"No, the *inferior*. Am I really so unlike you? You and I both reject those who fail to meet our standards."

"I save people. I don't kill them."

"All hail to the kidnapper-of-the-ages!" Rattimor replied sarcastically. "Before we near the pond, I shall explain the game we're about to play, if you haven't already figured it out. It's simple. Katrine goes into the water below the ice, heavy boots, chain and all. You may choose to save her, since you believe yourself to be such a mercenary, but I won't let you onto the ice until you tell me the identity of the woman, *and* I believe you are telling the truth. It is truly a shame that truth rope doesn't work on warlocks. It would save us a little time should you decide to reveal her name. You lose the game, of course, if you choose to save your precious little link, because I will know the identity of your secret weapon and I will still have Katrine." Rattimor laughed. "You win if you let her drown, because I will *not* know the identity of the woman and I will have lost my link. Consequently, your stay with me will be lengthened while I try to create my third link, and a possible two hundred more victims lose their sanity."

"Still haven't figured it out, even after creating two links," Zor said with contempt.

"*Altering* billions of connections in a single mind is harder than merely *shrinking* them during your animal morphology experiments. You would do no better," he angrily replied as he continued walking towards the pond.

Katrine took a deep breath and stared down at the snow in front of her as she walked, wishing she had chosen to steal the tennis shoes instead of the hiking boots. With each step, she started to shake more violently, partly out of fear, partly from the cold. Rattimor stopped suddenly and Katrine looked up, unaware that they were already at the banks of the frozen pond. When she saw the smooth ice in front of her, her heart began to pound in her chest.

"I will give you a moment to make your pleas to Zor, Katrine," Rattimor said before letting go of her chain and backing away from her.

Katrine nervously looked at Zor. What was she supposed to say? Please, oh please, don't let him kill me? Did Rattimor seriously believe she was going to beg in front of him? She paused before finally deciding on what to say.

Katrine's voice shivered as she spoke. "You're the only person I know who looks good in both a tuxedo *and* a dress." A small smile crept across her face. "My mother's green dress would have complemented your eyes better."

A smile slowly spread over Zor's face, then he quickly took her locket from around his neck and put it over Katrine's head and through the metal collar. "I believe this belongs to you. Your mother is no longer in Cyan. Rattimor will never find her."

"Thank you," she said as she looked down at her locket.

"That's enough!" yelled Rattimor in disgust. He stepped forward, and with a wave of his hand sent Katrine sliding on her stomach across the wet ice to the middle of the pond. Before she could lift herself, she heard the ice below her crack and looked down to see a section below her shoulders quickly break into little pieces. She cried out in shock and frantically searched for something to grab onto as she felt her legs and body drop through the chunky ice that had taken the place of the smooth surface.

"Hold onto the chain," Rattimor called out to her from the shore. "It will lengthen the game's running time a bit."

Katrine quickly slid her arms across the smooth ice in front of her and clenched onto her chain to stop sliding. She struggled to pull herself out of the water, but was barely able to hold on as she began to lose feeling in her fingers from the cold. Her boots became heavier as they soaked up the water, and kicking to stay afloat seemed to only cause her to slide farther down. She stopped kicking and concentrated on breathing and maintaining her grip on the chain as she peered over to the shore where she saw a glass wall surrounding Rattimor and Zor. Zor stood silent.

The chain started to slide so that it slowly lowered Katrine into the water. She felt the ice stir around her as she sank deeper into the pond. With a grunt, she released the hand closest to her and tried to grip the chain farther up, but her hand slid back down to its original position. She closed her eyes, waiting to hear Zor say the name of the woman, but there was still only the sound of the breeze blowing through the pine needles and knocking snow to the ground. She could barely feel her legs and the rest of her body was quickly becoming numb. Her upper chest, which had just entered the water, seemed to burn from the ice that bumped against her. As her neck began to hit the water, she tried kicking one more time to try to lift herself up. She could hardly believe that there was still no sound from the shore.

She took a deep breath and closed her eyes before her face sank below the surface. The ice shards delivered a stinging bite as they hit her face, but she quickly dropped past them into the dark waters below. Where was he? Why hadn't he pulled her from the water?

As Katrine sank quickly towards the bottom of the pond, she curled up and tried to untie her boots, but her fingers couldn't bend to start untying the knots. It became harder and harder to hold her breath, harder and harder to move and try to swim to the surface. She was numb... it was quiet... she released her breath, inhaled deeply, and jolted

The Link – Master Rattimor

as her lungs reacted to the water. She closed her eyes and thought about the last time she saw her mother. Ashleigh was holding her, comforting her. She placed her hand flat against her locket and wished she could grasp it with her numb fingers. Her daughter would not be returning... ever.

There was a light. She had seen it before.

The light grew brighter and Katrine had an uncontrollable desire to cough. As she did, her lungs burned and convulsed. Her body curled up and she choked and hacked to push out the water from inside her. Sharp pains stabbed her lungs and throat. Again she coughed, unable to inhale a clean breath of air afterwards. When she opened her eyes, she was on top of the ice being held by Zor, the water from his hair dripping down on her face. She closed her eyes again and inhaled, but the air still struggled to enter.

"Try to contact Alyssa," Zor said quietly. "Get her here for just a moment so she can warm you and get the water out of your lungs."

As she continued to struggle for a clean breath, Katrine called out to Alyssa over and over in her mind until she responded. Alyssa warmed her and cleared her airways, then immediately left.

* * *

Rehnquist slapped Alyssa hard across the face and nearly sent her flying off her chair. She held her red, sore cheek and looked back at Rehnquist with wide-open eyes.

"You answered too slowly! What did you just do?" Rehnquist yelled.

"Nothing! I was just thinking of a response."

"It does *not* take that long to answer *what color is your shirt?!*"

"I'm sorry. I just wasn't concentrating."

"Name a mountain range in the United States."

"Rocky Mountains," Alyssa answered. She straightened up in her chair again and faced him, ready for the next question.

* * *

Katrine opened and closed her fists, amazed at how fast the numbness had disappeared. Her clothes were still wet and she was quickly getting cold again as the wind rushed past Zor's body and hit her own; but along with a little warmth, Alyssa had thrown in a little more energy, a little more comfort, and had returned her breathing to normal. She looked up at Zor, who was still holding her.

"It seems you lost the game," Katrine whispered. Zor stared down at her with a look of trepidation, then glanced briefly at the shoreline towards Rattimor. Katrine also looked over and saw Rattimor nervously pacing through the snow. "You told him then?"

"Yes," he said disappointedly. "I didn't call his bluff."

265

"It didn't feel like a bluff to me," Katrine said, irritated that Zor sounded as though he regretted saving her. "It would have been nice if you would have spilled the beans a bit sooner, in fact. That wasn't exactly a pleasant experience."

Zor looked her straight in the eyes. "Are you complaining that I didn't save you fast enough? Perhaps I should throw you back in the water."

Katrine quickly pushed herself out of his arms and clumsily sat up beside him. "Why is it with you I never know whether to thank you or..."

"I find you equally frustrating," Zor interrupted.

Katrine wiped the water from her face and clenched her arms around her body as she once again started to shiver. "Well, do you mind telling *me* who she is?"

"Rebecca Grumley," Zor replied staring back at Rattimor. "Once I warned her about Damen's plan, she waited until Damen came to kill her, then had her father transport her away at just the right moment. Imperius conjured up an illusion of a screaming Rebecca, wriggling in pain as Damen tried to make all her cells spontaneously combust. After the show, Imperius left spare ashes he found in a crematorium behind on the floor."

Katrine smirked. "He named her after Rebecca Grumley without knowing. Said she reminded him of her."

"She's the only one who can take back the power she gave to him, and we nearly had her out of that blasted mist," Zor said, shaking his head. "She's not going to be too happy with me right now." He sighed and looked up and down Katrine. "We need to get you out of this wind and back to the cabin before you freeze again. I'll carry you unless you want to walk, but I don't think you have the strength."

Katrine stared across the snow at the cabin, desperately not wanting to return to the darkness where she would be chained again to the cabinet and faced with Rattimor's next ultimatum. She wanted it to be over. "I have the strength," she quietly replied, shaking her head. "But I believe I'm going to need to save it for other things."

Chapter 35
Visitations

"What color are my pants?" asked Rehnquist.

"Please! How long is this going to go on?" Alyssa questioned impatiently. She had been answering questions for well over twenty minutes.

"The game is over," boomed a deep voice from behind her.

Alyssa jumped up from her chair and spun around. In front of the door towered Master Rattimor, dressed entirely in black. Alyssa immediately turned pale as he stared at her with suspicious, judgmental eyes. Rehnquist also rose from his seat.

"Everything is going well, Dad!" Rehnquist announced proudly. "I searched the room from top to bottom and didn't find any more remotes, any more pens, nothing."

"Hold your hand over her mouth so no one can hear her scream," Rattimor instructed as a black ghost squeezed out of his ear. Alyssa panicked and quickly charged past Rehnquist to the bathroom door, determined to break it down if she had to. Rehnquist grabbed and pulled the back of her shirt, causing her to topple backwards. She spotted a small steak knife on top of her refrigerator and grabbed for it as she lost her balance, but was quickly jerked away and held tightly from behind by Rehnquist. She squirmed as he dropped his gun on the spare bed and clamped his hand over her mouth. Alyssa looked up to see the black ghost hovering at Rattimor's side, waiting patiently to enter her head.

Rehnquist spoke, sounding slightly nervous. "Dad? There's really no need to send your Rattimor Eye in. I'm certain she's not hiding anything more."

"Foolish boy. The only way you will know for certain that she's not hiding anything is to do a thorough mind probe." He surveyed Alyssa and his eyes narrowed. "You share a remarkable resemblance to a witch who gave me a tremendous amount of trouble in my younger days." He glanced at the black ghost. "Make it more painful than usual."

Alyssa's eyes filled with panic as the ghost zoomed towards her. In a final attempt to free herself, she squirmed enough to free up an arm, then she gave Rehnquist a sharp blow with her elbow to his ribs, causing him to become more aggressive in his struggle to hold her. She felt a vibration outside her left ear, then became paralyzed as it jabbed into her ear and a loud shrilling resounded inside her head. She wanted to hold her head to keep it from exploding, but Rehnquist had managed to secure her arms. She clenched her eyes and screamed through Rehnquist's hand as the shrilling became unbearable. She was only vaguely aware of the scenes replaying in her mind, such as when John told her he was Zor and handed her the remotes and pen, or her conversation with Sami and her message to David. She stopped screaming and took a deep breath through her nose as the shrilling exited her right ear, leaving a throbbing, splitting headache behind. Rehnquist let her go and she fell to her knees. Holding her head, she looked up to see that the black ghost was nowhere to be seen. Rattimor, however, appeared as though he was receiving information.

Rattimor looked over at the desk drawer before glaring at his son. "You conducted no search, you lazy, worthless excuse for a son. I'm embarrassed we share the same blood. And you will *not* go around insisting you be called Master, for that is a title reserved for only one individual... the most powerful warlock alive. And you certainly have not earned that title."

"Yes, Father. Sorry," Rehnquist sheepishly replied as he cowered a few steps backward.

Rattimor looked over at Alyssa. "Sit in your chair. We will wait for your company to arrive."

Alyssa's heart began to race. "I can get rid of him without him suspecting a thing."

"Sit. I do not want you to get rid of him."

Alyssa stared in shock at Rattimor, unable to believe the danger in which she had placed David. Rattimor sat in Rehnquist's chair and motioned for Alyssa to sit in front of him.

"Don't make me repeat myself again," he said calmly.

Alyssa stood up and weakly walked over to her chair where she sat and stared at Rattimor as he drummed his fingers directly above the desk drawer where the third remote was placed. The silence in the room, although lasting only a few minutes, seemed to last an eternity. Alyssa closed her eyes and hung her head as she heard David's footsteps outside approach her door. He knocked.

The Link – Master Rattimor

"Alyssa," David called from outside. "I just wanted to drop off the study guide to the quiz."

Alyssa whispered, "Please let me get rid of him."

Rattimor looked over at Rehnquist. "Invite him in," he said as the gun flew off the bed into Rattimor's hand. With a smile, he raised the gun and pointed it at Alyssa's forehead.

Rehnquist walked over to the door and opened it far enough so that David could see Alyssa and his father.

"We've been expecting you," Rehnquist said in sheer delight. "Come and join us."

David appeared stunned as he spotted Alyssa with the gun to her head. "Don't hurt her," he said quietly as he slowly stepped inside with his hands slightly raised. Rehnquist quickly closed the door and searched David from top to bottom, exposing one of Sami's pepper spray bottles from his pocket and a knife tucked into the back waistband of his jeans. Rehnquist put them on the desk beside his father and they disappeared. David watched wide-eyed as a pair of metal handcuffs appeared in its place.

"Sit down at the foot end of the bed, David," Master Rattimor instructed as he held out the metal handcuffs to Rehnquist. David sat down facing Rattimor, and Rehnquist quickly secured David's left hand to the metal frame of the bed before Rattimor handed the gun over to Rehnquist.

"Rehnquist, now is your chance to make me proud. You swore to Alyssa that a bullet would fly should you find out she's deceived you again."

With terror in her eyes, Alyssa placed her hand over the drawer to keep Rattimor from opening it. "I wasn't going to use it!"

"Stupid girl," he commented as he easily slid the drawer open, despite Alyssa's best efforts to keep it closed. He picked up the remote and held it so that Rehnquist could see. Surprised and angry, Rehnquist pointed the gun at David's foot.

"No!" yelled Alyssa as Rehnquist fired the gun, sending a dart-like noise through the room. David cried out in pain as blood sprayed from his left foot, then trickled onto the floor. He leaned over, grasped his foot with his right hand, and held his breath to stop from crying out again. Alyssa sprang out of her chair, grabbed a shirt under the bed, and tried to wrap his foot.

"Oh my God, oh my God, oh my God," she uttered hysterically as she pressed the shirt on top of his shoe, causing David to cry out in pain. She quickly withdrew her hands and shook them back and forth in the air, uncertain what to do. "Sorry, David!"

Rattimor grabbed the back of her shirt and sent her flying back into her chair. He stood up and leaned over so that they were eye to eye.

"You will fill the transfer vase or David is going to get it in the head! If you continue to screw up and try to escape, or try to get Rebecca Grumley out of the mist, then we'll start with your friend Samantha after David. I suspect she'll be dropping by in a short while as well." He smirked. "The daughters of policemen are sometimes the worst about calling the police." He looked over at Rehnquist. "I shall keep the labyrinth door open for you. If her dear friend, Sami, does call the police, bring the hostages through the labyrinth door and close it. We don't have to do this here."

"Yes, sir," Rehnquist quickly responded.

"Sami has pepper spray. You *do* know what pepper spray is, don't you?"

"Of course, Dad," Rehnquist said with a wave of his gun. "I know a lot about weaponry."

"You don't know everything. The pepper spray will look identical to the spray bottle you pulled from David's pocket. Don't let her spray it in your face," Rattimor instructed.

"I know, Dad. I know what pepper spray is," he said, annoyed.

"You can handle her friend, Sami, alone, can't you?"

"Yes, easily, Dad. She's a girl."

"Good. There's one last errand I have to get done before I return to the cabin. Connect Alyssa with Katrine in about twenty minutes. I should be back in the cabin by then. Understand?"

"Yes, sir."

Rattimor stood up, gave a final look around the room, and then walked through the labyrinth door without a word.

"Shit. How'd he do that?" David whispered as he stared at the swaying dormitory door.

"Explain it to him, Alyssa," ordered Rehnquist. "I don't want him interrupting when you start to write."

Alyssa sighed and searched for her tablet with the story. She found it partially buried under a pullover on the extra desk. She reached over slowly so that Rehnquist wouldn't get nervous, grabbed the tablet, then threw it on the bed beside David.

"The extra brain activity after the bicycle accident? It allows me to make contact with Katrine, my past soul. I'm Nicole in my story. It's not fiction or fantasy, or whatever you may call it. It's more like a journal of what I see through Katrine's eyes."

David looked at her confused. "That's impossible."

Alyssa turned and put her head down on the desk. "So is making things disappear and appear, and walking through doors, David."

The Link – Master Rattimor

"And who are you?" David asked Rehnquist before he took a deep breath and closed his eyes in pain.

"Adrian's brother. I'm here to get her back."

"Alyssa obviously doesn't have her," David angrily replied.

"But she is the means to an end. Once my father has one more transfer vase full of power, he'll be able to find out from James where she is. He can almost do it already," Rehnquist bragged. "Then I get to watch him kill a full-powered warlock. That'll be cool." He picked up the tablet and started to turn the pages.

Alyssa raised her head. "May I please try to help David?"

Rehnquist looked thoughtful, then waved his gun towards David before returning to the tablet. "What do I care? Go ahead."

Alyssa slipped out of her chair and carefully untied David's running shoe. The bullet was lodged between the bottom of his foot and the rubber sole of his shoe. David held his breath as Alyssa slowly slipped his shoe off, removed the bullet, and snugly wrapped her shirt around his bloody foot.

"What the hell is a naked mole rat?" Rehnquist angrily yelled, startling Alyssa and David. Alyssa looked up to see that he was reading the second to last chapter. Before she could figure out how to respond, she was distracted with the sound of footsteps approaching from outside.

Chapter 36
Imperius

"I see you received my father's gift for warning me about Damen," remarked Rebecca to Zor as she sat facing him, still bound to the chair with black rope. She had changed into her own body and was now taller and more slender with long, wavy red hair and brown eyes. "The only one who could ever cloud up the air like this was my father," she said proudly.

Zor stood leaning against the wall facing Rebecca, shackled to the logs behind him with black rope and surrounded by the purple mist. His tuxedo and hair were still wet from retrieving Katrine from the pond. Katrine sat curled up in a ball beside the cabinet with the vase, rocking back and forth to try to keep warm in her soaked clothing; and James continued to get harassed by one of the black ghosts along the back wall behind the glass bar rier, just in case he had lied about Montreal. Other than the single black ghost behind the barrier, they were left alone.

"I was never sure he intended for me to have the sword until a couple of days ago. I covered up the inscription 'My Deepest Gratitude for Saving Rebecca Grumley' on the blade long ago so Adrian wouldn't see it. I thought for sure it was meant for someone else." He thoughtfully nodded his head. "It's a nice sword."

"Which snake told you how to cloud up the air like this?"

"The middle snake, the same one that told me how to summon Imperius Grumley's *'Book of Unmemorizable Spells'*. It's the only one that will talk to me."

"The middle snake is female. She must like you. The others are male. They'll warm up to you once they begin to trust you. How long ago did you get the sword?"

The Link – Master Rattimor

"Seven years ago, at the exact time and place I built Cyan. The snakes didn't say anything to me, but it was strange. They somehow called me there... and then kept me there. Can't explain it."

Rebecca glanced down at Katrine, then looked back at Zor. "The snakes know the labyrinth passwords. Once we get the labyrinths back from Damen, I suspect my father would want you to keep them."

Zor appeared worried. "Perhaps we shouldn't talk so openly about a few things until we have some sort of plan to get out of here."

"Well, there is *some* good news. My father hasn't showed up yet. He said he'd come save me if I didn't check in before... you know..." Rebecca paused, looking very uncomfortable, "before the younger Damen and Zachariah came after him. He'd find us, I'm sure. After all, he is a genius," she said with a tone of worry. "The fool."

"Fool?"

"He's going to let those two sadistic cretins be the end of him." Rebecca took a deep breath, growing steadily angrier. "My father says he's tired of being known as a mutation and wouldn't mind coming back in another life, a little more normal... a little more average. Plus it would give him the chance to prove that a person can manipulate his own reincarnation. Before I left for Cyan, he was planning his 'life after death', figuring out how he was going to do it, who to be, when and where to be born, what life he wanted to lead..." She shook her head in worry. "He says he'll be a redhead like me so that every time he looks in the mirror, he'll remember the daughter he left behind. I don't know why he thinks he'll remember me," she said disappointedly. "Nobody's capable of keeping their memories."

Rebecca looked down to the ground and watched herself anxiously tap her feet. "I've got to get out of here to talk some sense into my father before it's too late. If mother were alive, she would have had a fit if she found out he was just going to lay down and die without a fight. After all, it was always my father who loved the 'good versus evil' battle, and now?" Rebecca became choked up and stopped her sentence to avoid breaking down any further.

"I'm certain your father will make the right decision. Don't underestimate his genius, Rebecca," Zor said quietly.

"He may be a genius," Rebecca said angrily, "but he approaches everything he does with such a lighthearted, flippant attitude. He's going to overlook something important and end up reincarnated as some sort of street bum, eating bugs on the sidewalk... not that he ever objected to a bug in his food every once in a while," she said with a faint smile.

Katrine took a deep breath. Too many things Rebecca said reminded Katrine of Robert. She recalled her first day in Cyan when

Robert had told her the story about the fate of the Grumleys – which was *not* a story told by Woester, as Robert had told her; and the anger on Robert's face when he saw Master Rattimor in Cyan. She stopped rocking and looked up at Zor. He had once called Robert a *special case*. A quick nervous glance from Zor told her that her suspicions were not too far off the mark.

"Sounds like someone *I* know," Katrine said without looking away.

Again Zor looked at Katrine, this time with a look of warning. Katrine shook her head and sighed, then leaned her head backwards against the log wall and closed her eyes.

"You should tell her, Zor."

"Tell her what?" Zor asked with a hint of irritation in his voice.

Katrine opened her eyes and looked between Rebecca and Zor. "I'll be the first to admit that it's my fault we're here. I should have left Cyan when James told me, and Master Rattimor would have thought Rebecca was the link. But it is ultimately *your* fault, Zor, for your inability to peacefully break up with a psychotic witch... especially one with such a powerful, demented, deranged family. You owe it to Rebecca to give her a *little* peace of mind if we don't make it out of this alive... if I'm correct in what I suspect, that is," Katrine said quietly before she closed her eyes again.

"What are you talking about, Katrine?" asked Rebecca, shaking her head in confusion. "What do you suspect?"

There was silence in the cabin, for Katrine didn't consider it her duty to respond.

"What is she talking about Zor?" Rebecca asked louder.

Zor sighed and paused a moment before finally saying, "I ran across your father's soul during a collection several years ago. He had a dozen or so memories carried over into his new life, and some were of you. The memories were dormant until I read his mind."

The cabin was quiet. Even the wind outside seemed to quiet down.

"My father's a prisoner?" Rebecca asked angrily.

"Cyan is not a prison, it's utopia," Zor politely retaliated.

Katrine jumped back in the conversation. "Cyan *is* a prison, Zor! Until you get rid of the guards and let Cyan's citizens leave if they want, it's a prison!" She turned to Rebecca. "And Robert is not your father, he just has his soul," she hastily explained, bothered to think of Robert as a grown woman's father.

A shrilling sounded through the labyrinth door.

"They're returning from Montreal," Rebecca said gloomily. "I wonder if they have Adrian."

The Link – Master Rattimor

"Not a chance," Zor responded. "My brother lied about Montreal."

The shrilling grew louder and the ghosts swept through the doorway, but they instantly silenced themselves when they realized that Master Rattimor was not present. No one spoke as they watched the ghosts hover above them. The minutes passed slowly and Katrine closed her eyes and rested her head on her knees. Only the sounds of a chain through the labyrinth door made her raise her head.

"No," Katrine whispered as Master Rattimor pulled Robert into the cabin. She felt as though she had just been stabbed in the heart with a jagged knife. Robert's wrists were bound in front of him with metal handcuffs that were attached to a chain held by Rattimor. Robert appeared drunk with dizziness as he tried to recover from the labyrinth. Rattimor had a gleam in his eye as he watched Katrine's reaction.

"Found this one loose in Canada," Rattimor announced to Zor proudly. "Thought you might like your prisoner back. His mother is in an air-proof, metal box waiting to suffocate as her youngest son and a Mr. Coal are pounding on the outside, desperately trying to save her."

Katrine clenched both her fists, wanting to scream, but immediately became paralyzed as Robert noticed her for the first time.

"Damen!" yelled Rebecca. "You've got to stop this! It's insane!"

Rattimor pulled Robert so that he stood in front of Rebecca. Robert broke his gaze at Katrine and looked at Rebecca, then a look of recognition spread across his face.

Rattimor smiled and spoke. "Rebecca, there's something you should..."

"Don't tell her," interrupted Robert without breaking his gaze at Rebecca.

Rebecca's mouth dropped slightly open in disbelief.

"Appears I don't have to." Rattimor sneered at Rebecca, "I can't begin to explain the sheer pleasure I felt when I saw your image tucked comfortably away in the mind of Katrine's heartthrob. It's like getting two for the price of one, *and* if your father comes to try to save you, he'll now have a split soul."

Rattimor pulled Robert over to the cabinet and connected his chain to the opposite side as Katrine. Katrine slowly stood up and stared at Robert, not knowing what to do or say.

"Robert attracted my attention ever since your first mind probe, Katrine," Rattimor casually commented. "That vase is going to have to glow like the sun if you want me to let *this* one live."

Rebecca screamed in frustration, then yelled, "Kill him, Damen, and I swear I'll kill you! You are *not* going to be the end of Imperius twice!"

"Yes, I understand your concern," Rattimor smirked. "Seems he now has little control over where he might end up in his next life."

A single ghost on the ceiling shrilled and Rattimor sighed. "No matter. I will know the whereabouts of my daughter soon enough."

Katrine backed against the wall and took a deep breath, dreading Alyssa's return.

Chapter 37
Ignorance

"Not a word," Rehnquist warned as they listened to the footsteps outside stop in front of the doorway. There was a light tapping on the door.

"Alyssa?" Sami called from outside with a slight tremor in her voice.

Rehnquist dropped the tablet on the bed and pointed the gun at Alyssa, who was still kneeling in front of David. "Answer it."

Alyssa stared up at the barrel of Rehnquist's gun and took a deep breath before yelling, "Sami! Get out of here!"

Rehnquist immediately kicked Alyssa backwards, sending her across the tile floor and into the spare bed, then quickly turned and opened the door.

"Come in, and put the pepper spray on the desk," he ordered as he pointed the gun at Sami.

Sami's face turned white as she stared down at Rehnquist's gun, then she slowly walked in and reached over to the desk where she slowly placed the Bugs Bunny spray bottle on the desk.

"Sit down at the foot of the bed behind David." He closed the door and waved the gun at Alyssa sitting on the floor. "*You* are really getting on my nerves. Tie your friend's hands up to the bar under the bed's bookshelf."

"Oh, my God, David!" yelled Sami as she noticed his bleeding foot.

Rehnquist impatiently shoved Sami between the beds, causing her to nearly trip over Alyssa on the floor.

"You're not moving!" he yelled at Alyssa. "Do you want me to shoot another foot?"

"No," Alyssa replied in a defeated voice. "What do you want me to tie her up with?"

"Hell if I know! Do you have a bathrobe belt or something?"

Alyssa nodded her head and lifted herself up with the help of the spare bed behind her. After yanking a green cloth belt from her robe hanging in the closet, she knelt in front of Sami.

"Sorry, Sami," Alyssa whispered.

"It's not your fault," Sami said as she held out her hands. Alyssa started to tie them together as Sami looked up at Rehnquist. "You know, I called the police just a couple of minutes ago. You're going to have a hell of a time getting out of here."

"I doubt I will," replied Rehnquist with a smile. The room was silent as Alyssa finished tying the other end of the rope to the bar under the bookshelf. "Now sit in your chair. We'll reconnect in about ten more minutes. I suspect there'll be no further delays, unless the police decide to show, that is."

Rehnquist picked up the pepper spray bottle from the desk. Alyssa sat in her chair and laid her head sideways on the desk, watching Rehnquist slowly pace in front of the beds as he examined the bottle carefully. He tried to peel the stickers off, but they tore apart, turning the bottle's surface into a sticky, white mess. Alyssa began to have her suspicions.

"Is that the peppermint flavor, Sami?" she asked quietly, without lifting her head.

"Yes."

"The cherry spray is much better. It's new on the market. Flavor lasts longer than the pepper spray, and it still delivers a nasty sting when you spray it in the eyes."

Sami paused before answering. "My boyfriend likes the peppermint flavor best."

Alyssa fought back her smile as she watched Rehnquist place his finger on the tip of the bottle. He turned the spray bottle different directions, eyeing it with curiosity, then lifted it to his mouth and sprayed it inside. Alyssa sprang out of her chair as Rehnquist dropped his gun and clenched his throat with both hands. He gagged, struggling to breathe as his eyes bulged and watered. Alyssa knocked him down on the spare bed, coughing and eyes tearing up from contacting the small amount of spray still left in the air, then frantically searched for the remotes in Rehnquist's pocket.

Chapter 38
Warlock's End

"There's no reason to wait any longer. Contact Alyssa. We're ready," Rattimor ordered Katrine.

"Not until I know your full intentions," Katrine replied somberly.

"My intentions?"

"Who's getting out of this cabin alive?"

Zor spoke. "No one is, Katrine. Don't let him deceive you."

"The way *you* deceived me?" Katrine asked. "How do I know this isn't just another one of your elaborate deceptions? Who's really going to get this vase? You and Rattimor are probably best friends, aren't you? James is probably back there faking everything. Rebecca Grumley is probably just Adrian in disguise. Shall I just fill three or four so we can get this all over with?"

Rattimor smiled, then laughed out loud for several long minutes. "Yes, by all means," he finally managed to say, "fill three or four and get this all over with. She's onto us, Zor."

Zor shook his head and looked disappointedly at Katrine.

"Contact Alyssa and fill the vase," Rattimor repeated. "Robert and his mother will be set free. Alyssa's friends will be set free. You and Alyssa will be kept alive to serve me for the remainder of your lives, and two hundred or so people will have you to thank for their sanity. That's the best you'll ever get from me."

Katrine looked over at Robert, hoping for advice. Robert looked pale and shook his head. "It's your decision," he said. "All I know is that my mother is probably suffocating and I desperately don't want to be here right now."

Katrine looked at the vase on the cabinet between them just as Alyssa reconnected. Katrine paused, then put her hand on her forehead and backed up against the wall, shaking.

"What has happened?" asked Rattimor.

"David's dead."

"How?"

"He was shot in the head by Rehnquist after Alyssa tried to attack him and get the remote from his pocket."

"My son finally did something right," he said, nodding. "There may be hope for him yet. Does he have Samantha?"

"Yes, she's tied to the bed."

"I would have let David go, Alyssa," Rattimor said as he stared at Katrine. "Now your foolishness cost him his life. Don't let it cost Samantha her life as well. Fill the vase."

Katrine closed her eyes and bit her lip, then looked at James, Rebecca, and Zor. "I'm sorry. If I can at least save Robert, his mother, and Sami..."

"Katrine, don't do this," Zor said quietly. "He'll be unstoppable."

"Shut up, Zor. I don't *want* to do this; I'm being *forced* to do this."

The purple mist around Katrine disappeared. She placed her hands on the vase and filled it with water... as pure as water could be. Then came the power. A yellow light radiated from the top of the vase. She concentrated on making the light brighter until it filled the cabin, and she had to close her eyes so that she wouldn't become blinded. She took her hands off the vase and leaned against the log wall, weak. She watched as Rattimor approached the cabinet with a gleam in his eyes, the same gleam Zor had when she had filled a vase for him.

"Rehnquist," Rattimor said. "What is the transfer vase verification word?"

Katrine swallowed and stared at the floor. "Hitler," she whispered.

Rattimor picked up the vase. "Of course, Alyssa already knew that, didn't she? My idiot son let it slip. We shall test the contents before I drink it." He walked in front of Rebecca. "Drink some."

"Let me drink it," Zor quickly said. "If something's wrong with it, I'm the one who should drink it."

Rattimor held the vase up to Rebecca's lips. "Drink it." He lifted up the bottom of the vase so that it poured into her mouth. She took three gulps, then put her head down. Her body glowed yellow, then slowly faded until the purple mist could be seen again. Rattimor lifted Rebecca's chin and inspected her eyes without a word. After several minutes of silence, Rattimor nodded his head in satisfaction.

The Link – Master Rattimor

"It's good," Rattimor said before letting go of Rebecca's chin. "Rehnquist," Rattimor said turning to Katrine. "Dispose of Samantha."

Katrine closed her eyes, sank to the floor, and clenched her hair with both hands as Rattimor lifted the vase to his mouth and quickly drank the entire contents. He wiped his mouth with the back of his hand and a smile spread across his face.

Katrine raised her head, grabbed hold of the cabinet and pulled herself up as Rattimor's body glowed yellow. The first time Katrine had filled a vase, she had become weak because Alyssa had just watched. This time Alyssa gave her back her strength. She watched as Rattimor closed his eyes and took a deep breath as if soaking in the sun's rays on a warm summer day. Then his smile disappeared and he quickly looked over at Katrine.

"What have you done?" he asked her. "Rehnquist, what is happening?" Rattimor grabbed his head and groaned in pain.

"Rehnquist was hauled away by the police about ten minutes ago," Katrine responded coldly. "Shortly thereafter, Sami and David left for the hospital to get David's foot treated. Alyssa's in your labyrinth with Rehnquist's compass... writing the last chapter of Master Rattimor, the warlock. She couldn't stay in the room because of the pepper spray your son sprayed in his mouth."

Rattimor fell to his knees, still holding his head, and the black ghosts from the ceiling swooped down and entered his ears. "My head!" he yelled as his body started to violently shake.

"Your brain is being liquefied by a virus I put at the bottom of the vase," explained Katrine. "It traveled through the roof of your mouth and has lysed several hundreds of your neurons by now. Alyssa's biology book was still open on her desk, giving her the virus idea. When she realized it would be non-living and difficult to detect by a warlock, such as yourself, she decided it would be the best way to attack that incredibly powerful and screwed-up brain of yours. She came up with the details on how it would work, and David came up with the idea of making it denser in case you made someone drink from the vase first. He nailed *that* one on the head, now didn't he?"

Zor smiled. "I knew you had done something to it."

Katrine looked over at Zor, still uncertain whose side he was on. "How would you know?"

"I knew you were lying about David getting killed. In my youth, I used to always read David Lopez's comic books... about a warlock named Zor, the Collector," he explained, looking away.

Katrine's attention returned to Rattimor when she heard him groan and saw three small red clouds squeeze out of Rattimor's ears. Two of them swept out the labyrinth door before Katrine could stop them; the third seemed much slower and became trapped in a glass box Katrine quickly conjured up. The red cloud banged repeatedly against the glass in an attempt to escape while Katrine dropped the glass box to the ground in front of the doorway, then slid it towards her.

"What is it?" she asked Rattimor.

Rattimor laughed a strange, peculiar laugh despite the apparent pain he was in. "It is the entire copy of my mind... my entire being... my thoughts and memories, my genius," Rattimor cried in such a voice it sent shivers up her spine. "The two that got away will fuse with the minds of two of my loyal comrades, who will then come to save me... and end you." Rattimor wrapped his arms around his head and screamed an ear-curdling cry before collapsing on the floor unconscious.

The cabin was silent as everyone stared at Rattimor sprawled across the floor in front of them. It was the sound of the red cloud banging against its glass container that seemed to break their trance.

"Bravo, Katrine," whispered Rebecca.

"We have no time to lose," Zor said. "You're not the first one to knock Rattimor down, Katrine, and it could only be a matter of minutes before he repairs himself. You need to get us out of the mist *now*, which means you've got to superimpose your body with mine."

Katrine looked at Zor, baffled at what he was telling her to do, but then realized if she was capable of creating a virus without knowing the specifics of the genetic material inside, she would be capable of walking into matter. It would be the same as walking through walls, which she had seen Zor do the night he had burned his name into her shoulder.

"Why you? Why not Rebecca?" asked Katrine, uncomfortable at the thought of being merged with Zor.

"If you superimposed with Rebecca, your combined powers may still not be enough to lower the mist, then you'd be stuck inside. I don't think she would appreciate that."

Katrine looked back down at the red cloud and took a deep breath. "Not until I know for sure whose side everyone is on."

The cabin fell silent until Rebecca spoke. "Are you sure you want to do that? I'm not sure even I would be able to handle his secrets. He's changed so much since when I knew him... when I *thought* I knew him, I mean."

"It's not going to be pleasant," Robert interrupted, "but would you please hurry? My mother may be dying."

Katrine dissipated the glass box around the red cloud and ordered it to enter her head with a wish. She cringed, expecting it to be painful and loud, but she felt nothing. As Rattimor's experiences poured forth, she witnessed a young Rattimor who was an exact copy of Rehnquist -

same stupidity, same abusive father. She witnessed his joy when he bragged to his father that he had killed Rebecca, and his arrogance and pride when he had helped kill Imperius and steal the labyrinths. She witnessed the loveless lust for two women from which he acquired his children, and the hatred and anger when Adrian betrayed him for the love of Zor. Then there was the murder of Cyan, a gorgeous woman with long, flowing blond hair and dark green eyes; the devastating lie to the boys' father at her funeral; the destruction of hundreds of lives in his attempt to create a link; and his activities in war-time concentration camps. The last disturbing thought relayed from Rattimor's cloud was that the last red cloud was *meant* for Katrine, not for a third comrade of Rattimor's, for reasons not revealed.

Katrine found herself shaking on the floor when his memories and thoughts had finished pouring into her own. She was thankful that the cloud did not contain memories of his *entire* life, as Rattimor had said, for she was certain she would have lost her sanity if it had. She at least knew now that Zor, James, and Rebecca were not Rattimor's accomplices, but his victims.

Katrine felt someone grab hold of her hands. She opened her eyes to see Robert kneeling down in front of her, barely able to reach her because of his handcuffs. Katrine released Robert's handcuffs with a wish, then was held by him as she tried to regain her composure.

"Rattimor moved, Katrine," Zor said. "We've got to hurry."

Panic struck at the thought of Rattimor regaining his senses and Katrine quickly stood up and tried to bust her glowing chain that held her to the cabinet, but couldn't. Rollers appeared on the bottom of the cabinet so that Katrine could pull it across the wooden floor to where Zor was bound.

"Just walk right in?" she asked uncomfortably as she approached him.

"Yes," he replied, glancing between Katrine and Rattimor. "Both of us occupying the same space. Concentrate on lowering the mist around me, then Rebecca. Quickly."

Katrine glanced backwards to see Rattimor's hand move towards his head, then she quickly stepped forward into Zor's mist. He was warm and she could hear him already concentrating on the mist surrounding him. She joined in and the mist soon grew faint. Once it completely disappeared, they quickly concentrated on Rebecca's mist until it faded, then completely disappeared.

Staring down at Rattimor as he began to lift himself up, Rebecca spoke in an unforgiving voice:

C.R. Kwiat

*"The gift I gave you, you no longer deserve -
so I take the gift back, you it no longer will serve."*

"No!" Rattimor yelled as a bluish-green light began to stream from his mouth.

The transfer vase that had been dropped to the floor by Rattimor righted itself before the light began to stream inside, filling it. Katrine stepped out of Zor and watched as the last of the bluish-green light left through Rattimor's mouth. A stream of yellow, red, and bright orange light immediately followed. Unlike the first light, the second stream split into their separate colors before spreading thinner and thinner above their heads. Katrine watched the red and orange lights as they faded away, knowing the painful story behind each. Four linked individuals, each killed after seeing their loved ones die. Katrine stared at the dark ceiling, numb and unable to move.

"You will all pay for this!" yelled Rattimor.

Katrine looked down from the ceiling and watched as Rattimor's body flew backwards across the floor and slammed into the wall beside the labyrinth door. So many ropes appeared around his body that he looked like a mummy, and a black tape that covered his mouth looked the same as the one Rattimor had used on James and Rebecca.

"Have a taste of your own medicine, Damen," Rebecca sneered. "Are you all right, Katrine?"

Katrine stared vehemently at Rattimor. "I've been better."

"The vase is yours if you want it, Katrine," Rebecca said. Katrine peered down at the glowing vase. All she could picture as she watched it glow was the light coming out of Rattimor's mouth. She wanted nothing more from him; she already had too much.

"I don't want it."

Rebecca nodded her head understandingly. "Robert?"

There was only a slight pause before Robert answered, "As I understand it, I gave up my last life because I didn't want to be a warlock. I'll pass."

Rebecca smiled before turning to the vase. "No one gets it," she said with some satisfaction before the bluish-green light rose to the ceiling and thinned until it completely disappeared.

Robert glanced nervously from Zor to Katrine to Rebecca. "My mother..." he said quietly.

Katrine immediately visualized the terror of Robert, his little brother, and even Mr. Coal as Rattimor placed Brandi Tebeau in a large metal box. She shuddered, barely able to stand herself now that she had Rattimor's memories.

The Link – Master Rattimor

"Robert," Katrine reassured him, "your mother still has about twenty minutes of oxygen. We'll get her out in time."

"Katrine, give us the passwords to the black rope," Zor said.

She stared at Rattimor and recalled the passwords. "Rebecca's is gas chamber, James' is guillotine, and yours is electrocution, Zor."

As Zor and Rebecca released themselves, Rattimor's eyes narrowed hatefully at Katrine. Katrine slowly shook her head; her voice was cold as she spoke. "If the people in this cabin choose to kill you for what you did to their families, I certainly won't shed any tears."

Everyone in the cabin fell silent.

"Katrine," asked Zor, "What did Rattimor do to my family?"

Katrine shot a wild glimpse over to James, realizing her mistake, but he had not heard because of the soundproof wall. She paused uncomfortably, trying to figure out how to justify her statement without mentioning Zor's parents.

"I..." She closed her eyes, unable to come up with any reason.

"Zor," Rebecca said, "she's a little disoriented. You would be, too, after absorbing Damen Rattimor's memories. Now help me get her collar off."

Katrine felt the collar release around her neck and heard it fall to the floor. As she placed her hands on her neck and rubbed it, she looked at Zor staring back at her suspiciously.

The transparent wall at the back of the cabin disappeared and Zor walked over to his brother where he laid his hands on the black rope and said the password. He helped James up as Rebecca retrieved the labyrinth's compass from Damen Rattimor's pocket.

"I'll get Robert's mother out if you can handle matters here," said Rebecca while giving the compass a small toss in the air.

Robert quickly stepped forward. "I want to go with you."

Zor lifted James' arm over his shoulder to help him walk. "Robert, you may go, but carry Rebecca so neither one of you get dizzy. Katrine, do you know of a labyrinth door close by in the 1500's?"

Katrine searched Rattimor's memories. "There's a door not too far: 1574."

"Good. Come back and get us in 1574, Rebecca. Don't drag Robert back with you. It'll be hard enough getting all of us back to Cyan without someone passing out," explained Zor. "I'll get him later through my labyrinth."

"Katrine," Robert said softly as he placed his hand on Katrine's shoulder. "Catch up with you later?"

A warm feeling flushed over Katrine, and she nodded. "Tell your mother thank you, for letting me stay with her."

"My ride?" Rebecca asked Robert with raised eyebrows. Robert lifted Rebecca in his arms, and they disappeared through the swaying wall.

Zor approached the door holding James in his arm. "Wait for us in the labyrinth, James. I want to talk privately with Katrine for a moment."

Katrine clenched her fists and groaned as Zor and James left the cabin through the labyrinth door. Rattimor's bound body slid through the door by itself as Zor reentered the cabin.

"I would *really* like to get out of here, Zor. Can't we talk somewhere else? Two of Rattimor's friends will be arriving shortly."

"This will only take a second. Who's coming for him?"

"Fireball, the bald man you knocked out in Gardenstadt..."

"Imperius Grumley's nephew, Zachariah."

"...and Rattimor's apprentice, Razor. Rattimor shared his second link with both of them."

"Did Rattimor know where to find them?"

"He had a vague idea."

"Do they have compasses?"

"They know where to get one."

"Just one?"

"Yes, just one. There are only three compasses to this labyrinth."

"Then chances are only one of his friends will be lucky enough to make it this far, and my guess is we have a second or two to discuss what you're hiding from me?"

Katrine swallowed. "Hiding?"

"Why might I have reason to kill Adrian's father? What did he do to my family?"

James shouted through the labyrinth door. "Katrine! What did you tell him? You weren't supposed to say a word!"

Zor looked toward the labyrinth door suspiciously, then erected a transparent wall between themselves and the door. "It appears both of you know something I should know. Do I need to probe your mind or Rattimor's to get my answer?"

Katrine looked at the floor and shook her head. "James wants to be the one to tell you. It's not my..." Before she could finish, she heard an ear-curdling cry from James; but it was not from the sound-barred labyrinth door, it was through Alyssa's mind right before she broke off her connection with Katrine. "James!" Katrine yelled, staring at the labyrinth door with fear-stricken eyes.

Zor quickly dissipated the transparent wall just as James stumbled back into the cabin, screaming with his clothes ablaze. Zor quickly put out the flames and healed James' burnt skin, then looked up to see that the labyrinth door had been closed. Katrine stared at the wall in shock.

"I'm sorry," whispered James, trying to catch his breath. "I didn't hear him coming. I couldn't put the flames out. He was too strong."

"Be thankful you're not in a hundred pieces," Zor said, shaking his head. He stared at the wall along with Katrine as James sank to the floor, expressionless. "I guess we're stuck here until someone comes for us. Let's hope it's Rebecca."

"I told you we should have talked somewhere else!" Katrine yelled at Zor. "Now they'll be going after Alyssa!"

Zor turned to Katrine with worry. "Tell her to find a labyrinth door where both Fireball and Rattimor have split souls. It's her best chance until we can get to her."

Katrine let out a frustrated cry and sat on the ground. She buried her head in her arms and reluctantly sifted through Rattimor's memories to find the right year in which Alyssa should escape. Any year when Rattimor was a boy, for Fireball was a childhood friend. She closed her eyes and attempted to reconnect with Alyssa.

Chapter 39
The Hunt

Alyssa could hear Rattimor and Fireball's voices in a distant labyrinth passageway, steadily approaching. She dropped the writing tablet to the grass and stood up. Looking down at the compass in her trembling hand, she whispered, "The door closest to me around the year 5135, please."

The compass needle pointed directly at her, so she turned and hurried down the pathway behind her. She made a left, then two rights, then several more turns before she faced a very long hedgerow in which several other passages met.

"I said the door *closest* to me!" she whispered to the compass. She looked down at the compass and the arrow still pointed straight ahead.

Alyssa took a deep breath and walked slowly forward. She stopped, believing she had heard footsteps, but all was quiet. She nervously peered down at the compass, hoping it would turn towards one of the shorter passages, but it remained pointing straight ahead. Her heart was pounding by the time she came to the end of the long hedgerow and the arrow shifted to the right down a shorter passageway.

The sound of a gas torch igniting sent Alyssa spinning around. At the far side of the row she had just walked stood a bald man in a tuxedo with a ball of fire in his hand; behind him stood Master Rattimor, holding his head. Alyssa dodged into the adjacent row of hedges as the fireball flew and smashed into the bushes behind where she had just stood. Leaves and twigs flew through the air ablaze, leaving a large hole through the labyrinth hedge. She stopped at the first door on her left and laid her hand on it, noticing that the labyrinth doors were not marked with years.

The Link – Master Rattimor

"Open."

"Where?" the door asked in a man's impatient voice.

Alyssa could hear Fireball running down the hedgerow towards her. Frustrated, she yelled at the door, "Anywhere with a lot of hiding spots!"

The door opened to a solitary desert canyon riverbed surrounded by scrub as well as oak, birch, and sycamore trees. A cool breeze rustled past the trees, sending leaves of red, yellow, and brown to the rocky, dry riverbed in front of the labyrinth door.

"No!" Alyssa yelled. "Like a shopping mall where there are lots of people!"

"If I close now, I can't open until tomorrow unless you have the password, and I seriously doubt you do. You've got an hour. Take it or leave it," the door rudely replied.

The sound of a torch igniting only a few meters from the corner sent her running through the door into the colorful, smooth rocks and leaf litter resting on the canyon riverbed. Without looking back, Alyssa knew Fireball was directly behind her by the sound of the fireball resting in his hand. She cringed in anticipation as she ran clumsily across the rocks, expecting to end up like James or the young warlock in Gardenstadt, but nothing happened. She looked back to see Fireball just outside the door, slumping to the ground with his head hanging to his chest. The ball of fire in his hand dwindled to a tiny flame, then extinguished completely. She slowed and turned towards him, wondering what had happened, then ducked behind a couple of large fallen logs entangled with green and brown vines at the edge of the riverbed only thirty meters from Fireball.

Master Rattimor soon appeared through the door, almost losing his balance and tripping over Fireball. After he seemed to regain his senses from the labyrinth, he stared down at Fireball, then scanned the densely covered canyon slopes for Alyssa. Alyssa watched through a crack between the logs and tried desperately to quiet her heavy panting as Rattimor hoisted Fireball up by one arm and dragged him back through the labyrinth door. Only seconds later, Rattimor reappeared with a crossbow on which a sight equipped with a red laser was mounted on top. Numerous small arrows were stashed behind him in a red holder decorated with yellow flames.

"Which direction do you think she went?" Master Rattimor asked.

Fireball's voice from beyond the labyrinth door sounded agitated. "I don't know. I collapsed the second I entered the canyon."

"Don't worry about it, Fireball. This will be more satisfying anyway. I haven't been on a hunt for several years." As he loaded his first arrow, Alyssa started to breathe heavier and feel lightheaded. She was glad there was a breeze rustling the leaves or else she would have been heard. "You take care of Rebecca and her friends should they come, though I really don't expect them. Rebecca won't be able to reopen the door into the cabin until tomorrow. Stay close by."

Alyssa watched nervously as Rattimor carefully surveyed the ground, apparently looking for clues as to her whereabouts. He brushed some leaf litter to the side with his boot.

"Rocks don't leave very good footprints," Rattimor said before he looked up and pointed his crossbow up the arroyo beside Alyssa. "I'll just start up the riverbed and see if I can spot some footprints in the sand. See you in about fifteen minutes. This shouldn't be too hard."

"Have fun," was the reply from beyond the door.

Alyssa searched below her for a stick to use for a possible weapon while she listened to Rattimor's heavy boots slide sideways off the rocks with each step. She grabbed for a branch and began to pull it up, but it was still rooted to the ground. Leaves and dirt shifted and tumbled down to the bottom of the riverbed.

"Alyssa?" Rattimor asked with a smile, peering in her direction. Alyssa held her breath and searched for another stick, but there was none. "I hope you don't make this *too* easy. After destroying my family and causing me to lose my power... my future... I'd sure be upset if you chose to rob me of a satisfying kill as well."

Alyssa shook her head and picked up a couple of hand-sized riverbed rocks to throw. She peered through the space between the logs and gasped as she saw Rattimor only fifteen meters away, heading straight for her. She clenched the rock in her right hand, wishing she hadn't given up softball in high school, then stood up and threw the rock as hard as she could at Rattimor. The rock hit the edge of his right pant leg before colliding with the rocks behind him. She quickly threw her second rock and ducked just before she heard his arrow release and strike the log directly above her. She immediately scurried up the steep, sandy slope of the riverbed to the brush-filled canyon floor, hoping that Rattimor was slow at reloading his crossbow.

Once the slope leveled out, Alyssa glanced back and gave a startled cry as she saw Rattimor standing by the fallen logs below, the red laser above the crossbow aimed straight into her eyes. She quickly dodged sideways behind a large oak tree and watched as an arrow ricocheted off several trees to her side. She took a deep breath, then bolted as fast as she could up the painted slope towards the next dense stand of trees.

Chapter 40
Waiting

I'm going to die out here, alone in the middle of nowhere, if I don't get some help soon!

Katrine rubbed her eyes with worry. *We're stuck here, Alyssa. We can't get to you until Rebecca comes to get us.*

HOW LONG IS THAT GOING TO BE? The only thing I've got going for me is the old man is out of shape and is having trouble keeping up with me! That's not a lot, Katrine.

Don't get too far away from the door.

You **know** *I have absolutely no idea where the door is! I'm completely lost!*

Head to the opposite slope and go to your left.

Aaargghh! You are no help at all!

Alyssa cut her connection with Katrine. Katrine stood up from a couch, interlocked her fingers on top of her head, and began to pace. Katrine's clothes were now dry, and the cabin was warm and well lit. Zor had added two couches, carpeting, a central fireplace with a large fire, several windows on all sides of the cabin, and a table with fruit, bread, and hot cocoa.

"Were you talking with Alyssa just now?" asked Zor as he rested on the opposite couch. Katrine nodded and continued to pace. "How's she doing?"

Anger swelled from deep inside and Katrine had a hard time not exploding. "She's being hunted like a wild animal by Rattimor and there's no possibility of escaping back into the labyrinth because Fireball is on the other side of the door."

"He stayed in the labyrinth?"

"Split soul problem, I believe." She stared out the window at the pond and would have thought it scenic had she not become so intimate with the water below the ice.

"Things will work out," Zor said. "Rebecca's smart. She'll get us out of here soon."

Katrine became enraged. "She thinks we're in 1574! When she finally figures out where we are, she's going to have to get the passwords, which are either with her father or in your sword in Cyan! Does she even *know* where you moved your little utopian society?"

"No, but Rose knows."

"The labyrinth?"

"Yes. Robert knows Rose's location. Rebecca will ask him."

"Rattimor took Rose to his residence after he grabbed Robert," Katrine remarked with scorn. "He found cells on my hair he cut, used it for its DNA, changed into me, and moved the labyrinth to his residence." She shook her head. It almost hurt knowing so much about Master Rattimor's actions.

"That's not too different from how he stole Rebecca's labyrinth before giving it to Adrian. Rose thought Rebecca had gone through one of the doors and let it close behind her, releasing her ownership." Zor sat in silence and watched Katrine pace and rub her hands together. "All Rebecca needs to do is go to Rattimor's residence at the entrance of his labyrinth..."

"Then of course, she'll run into Razor there, looking for the compass Fireball has already taken."

Zor paused with a thoughtful look on his face. "She's probably evenly matched with Razor. He may have received power from a link, but she received her powers straight from Imperius... plus she had a couple sips from your vase."

Katrine plopped back down on the couch and folded her arms. "Alyssa's running out of time. If she dies, it's your fault."

Zor looked away from Katrine, nodding his head. Katrine closed her eyes and made contact once more. Alyssa was nearly finished crossing an exposed portion of the riverbed to get to the opposite side of the canyon. She jumped up on a small boulder, then plunged to the sandy banks leading up and away from the riverbed as an arrow hit the rocks below her feet. Katrine could hear Rattimor laughing from high up the distant slope.

Alyssa panted. ***Got past the riverbed. I should be okay for a little while.***

Katrine leaned forward on the couch and sank her head into her hands. "I can't believe this is all because of a freak bicycle accident."

"It will all work out fine, and when it does, you and your mother are welcome to stay in Cyan. Your mother would make a fine addition to the Gardener House."

Katrine looked up, angry. "Perhaps, if you get rid of the guards."

Zor shook his head. "I like the guards too much. They serve a real purpose. Without them, my newcomers would try to leave before they became truly acquainted with Cyan, just as you tried. Just be in by curfew. It's not that hard."

Katrine clenched her teeth and took a deep breath to regain control of her emotions. "And remind me why those already *acquainted* with Cyan still don't have the opportunity to leave? Oh, wait! I remember! They haven't realized the service you have done for them and they need to stay longer!"

Zor stood up, walked over to the table, and poured a cup of hot cocoa. "If I let my citizens leave, word would get out about Cyan and I'd have to constantly deal with mediocre people banging at the door, trying to get in. Besides, Cyan citizens don't actually *need* to go home. There are countless millions that leave their homes every day, never to return. *Maybe* they'll call home on Christmas and on birthdays." He sipped the cocoa. "The only problem with bringing people to Cyan is that – for obvious reasons – the families cannot be informed where they are being taken, and so everyone is worried. The family worries about their missing family member; my citizens worry about their families. It's unfortunate, but no harm comes from it."

Katrine shook her head and said under her breath, "Yes, very unfortunate." She stood up and walked over to the table. "What would it take for you to allow them to go home? Those who know what Cyan is all about and still want to go home, that is."

"Nothing. They stay."

"What about a transfer vase in exchange for their freedom."

"I can't use it. Don't you realize all the past links would still be alive if the same individual could reuse them? I would drink the vase and nothing would happen."

Katrine looked over at James, sitting on the couch. "What about James?"

Zor sipped his hot chocolate with a thoughtful look on his face. "Maybe for visitation rights, not a full release."

Katrine nodded her head, feeling as though she was making *some* progress. "And no guard games."

For the first time since apologizing for letting Fireball sneak up on him, James raised his head and spoke. "Don't get rid of the guard games, Zor."

Zor smiled. "Guard games stay, James. Don't worry." He put his cup down on the table and walked over to the fire. With a poker, he rearranged the wood. Sparks flew to the ceiling and disappeared into the woodwork. "There would have to be some restrictions and conditions regarding any visitations. I can't spend all my time escorting over four hundred citizens back home, then spend the time to retrieve them. I'd be spending all my days in the labyrinth instead of Cyan." He put the poker down, and turned to Katrine. "You're going to be the one who escorts them through the labyrinth. If they don't return to the labyrinth door after their little get together... *alone*... they'll be horribly mutated. Those are the terms. If someone feels they can't trust themselves to return, then they shouldn't go on the visit."

Katrine stared down at the table, not wanting to be responsible if someone was *horribly mutated*. "Let me think about it," she said uncertainly.

"Finally!" cried a woman's voice. Everyone in the cabin turned to the wall to see Rebecca step through. "You have no idea what I had to go through to get this blasted door open again!"

"We have an idea," replied Zor as he rushed over to help James up. "Katrine, stay here while we get Alyssa. You'll be no help if you follow us; you'll just end up splitting Alyssa's soul when we least need it."

Katrine gave a frustrated scream, then yelled, "But I can't stand to stay in this God-forsaken cabin any longer!"

"Fine," Zor said as he helped James through the door. "We'll pick you up in the Caribbean when we're finished." He reached forward and touched her.

Katrine was about to object when she found herself standing on a crowded beach in front of miles of beach and ocean wearing a large straw hat and a blue swimsuit covered with a short, white dress made of lace. She looked behind her to see a large towel with an open cooler of beer, a bottle opener, and a lawn chair. She plopped down, angrily grabbed a beer, and popped it open.

Chapter 41

James

I'm glad to see someone's *enjoying herself*, thought Alyssa as she ducked behind a tree. An arrow whizzed by and landed in a bush behind her.

I am not *enjoying myself*. It was your boyfriend who put me here, not mine.

Ex-boyfriend.

I just wanted to tell you that help is finally on the way.

Good. Ever since I got on the opposite slope, this psycho's got more shots in at me. I'm farther away, but easier to see.

Get closer to the riverbed where the vegetation is thicker.

Then I won't be able to see him! *The only true advantage of being on this side is that he's running out of arrows.*

Alyssa peeked around the tree and watched as Rattimor started to descend the opposite slope towards her. When he disappeared behind a stand of trees, she dodged behind the next clump of tall bushes and peeked out. He was nowhere in sight, but she could hear his footsteps echo through the canyon. She took a deep breath and ran behind several large boulders. The sound of an arrow ricocheting off the rock above her sent her to her knees, crouching and holding her arms above her head. Rattimor's footsteps continued down the opposite slope.

"Alyssa!" a man's voice called out from the riverbed not too far down the canyon. Rattimor stopped walking and the canyon fell silent.

Alyssa looked up, wide-eyed, unsure whether to yell back in response. She quietly crept to the other side of the rocks to try to get a view of who was calling her name, but the vegetation below her became so dense, she was unable to see the rocks of the riverbed. She listened for Rattimor, but he remained quiet.

"Alyssa!" the man called out again.

The voice was familiar, perhaps James, but she still wasn't entirely certain it wasn't Rattimor's apprentice, Razor, trying to flush her out.

"Katrine," she whispered. "Is that James?"

I'm not sure. It's harder to hear through your mind than with my own ears.

"Why would he call out my name? If he was a warlock, couldn't he just pop up here?"

Maybe he's powerless? I don't know. But since Razor has the power from a link, he'd be able to find you, no problem. It's got to be James calling you.

Alyssa was getting irritated. *Why wouldn't John come? Or Rebecca? They send a powerless warlock to save me? Is this some kind of practical joke?*

They may just be busy with Fireball... or something.

Alyssa held her breath and decided to risk going back down slope towards Rattimor to see who was calling her. If it *was* James, and if he was powerless, she figured their best chance to get out of there was to get back through the labyrinth door. James knew where it was; she didn't.

She peeked around the corner rock and counted to three, then sprinted down slope and slid to a lying position beside a large fallen tree trunk resting in leaf litter and small rocks. Safe.

"Alyssa! It's James!" the man called out again, not too much farther away.

Alyssa crawled to the edge of the log, then crept to the next group of thin trees below her, trying her best to avoid stepping on the dried leaves and brittle sticks. She listened over her own breathing for Rattimor in an attempt to determine his whereabouts, but could only hear the rocks shift in the riverbed as James continued to walk towards her.

Alyssa inched her way past the trees and looked down the slope. She was almost to the riverbed, but the slope immediately before her was steep and rocky. She stepped onto a small, rocky outcrop below her, then stepped onto the dirt below it with her other foot. She started to slide helplessly until she managed to grab hold of a vine jutting from the canyon floor. In a sitting position, she scooted down until the forest floor seemed to level out. She could hear James' footsteps pause a little ways up the riverbed before continuing on at a faster pace towards her. Rattimor still made no sound.

Alyssa stood up quietly, now worried that James was walking directly into Rattimor's line of fire. She weaved her way silently through the trees in front of her until she came to a rocky cliff a little over three meters high that bordered the riverbed. She quickly scanned up and down the rocky bed. James had spotted her from downstream and was heading around a curve to where she stood; across and up the riverbed, she could see no sign of Rattimor and his red laser.

"Alyssa!" James exclaimed as he approached. Alyssa quickly put her finger to her lips to quiet him.

"He's somewhere close by," she whispered as loud as she could.

James glanced around nervously. "I need to get you back to the labyrinth door. Can you climb down from there?" he whispered loudly in return.

Alyssa looked down, then to each side of her. She was at the shallowest part of the cliff. She sighed.

"So my guess is, you don't have any powers to get me down?" she asked, trying to conceal her anger.

James shook his head and approached closer. "Bad year for me. I tried to return to the labyrinth the second I realized I was quite useless, but an inferno exploded through the door and didn't allow me to return. The best I can do is get you close to the door so that when Zor and Rebecca are finished with Fireball and Razor..."

"Razor showed up?"

"I think he's pretty close to passing out... but so is Rebecca, unfortunately."

Alyssa scanned the trees and several tall boulders across the riverbed, looking once more for a red laser beam, then looked down to the rocks of the riverbed below her. "I can climb down, but I'd appreciate it if you could spot me, should I fall."

James walked over until he was below her, then she reluctantly turned and searched for a spot on the steep slope to rest the tip of her shoe. As soon as she found one, she swung her other leg down and searched for another step. As she began to take her next step down, the rock on which her foot rested broke free from the wall. She cried out as she slipped and tried to grab hold of some vegetation on the embankment, but soon found herself falling on top of James and knocking him down. She flew sideways off his body and the back of her pelvic bone slammed into a large boulder. She winced in pain and grabbed her back.

"Are you okay?" James asked as he pulled himself up.

"That *seriously* hurt," she answered before holding her breath. She struggled to untangle her legs, then sat on the bumpy riverbed bottom, rubbing her hip. From the corner of her eye, she caught sight of a red light flying swiftly along the cliff beside her until it stopped comfortably on top of her heart. Her face flushed white as she looked across to the other slope to see Rattimor standing on top of a tall boulder with his crossbow aimed at her. She sat, unable to move, expecting each breath she took to be her last.

"Don't do it," James warned as he turned away from Alyssa towards Rattimor. "You'll regret it."

Rattimor smiled. "You don't scare me, you powerless and pathetic excuse for a warlock. I have nothing left to lose and would die a happy man if my last arrow pierced the heart of the woman who caused my downfall."

James stepped in front of Alyssa, blocking her from Rattimor. "She did what she did out of self defense. You gave her no choice."

Rattimor waved his crossbow to the side. "Stand aside or I shall shoot you, then kill her with my bare hands."

"Shoot me and you will never find out what happened to Adrian, and I so dearly want to tell you."

Rattimor's eyes narrowed in hatred. "What did you do to her?"

"First, Alyssa walks away," James demanded.

Alyssa closed her eyes, hardly believing what she was hearing.

Rattimor appeared thoughtful, then laughed. "The motives behind your apparent bravery couldn't be more obvious. Tell me, what good will come from saving Alyssa's life if you are dead? Even if you *were* alive to receive a vase from Katrine, would you trust her to make it clean and pure? You are a fool if you do."

"You have no idea what my motives are, Rattimor, and I resent the fact that you believe I'm as shallow a person as you."

Rattimor nodded his head. "We shall see. Alyssa stays here to see how valiantly you accept the arrow meant for her. My promise to you, brave and foolish soldier, is that I shall not kill her should you reveal the whereabouts of my daughter."

"Your promises are a waste of your breath and a waste of my time. Alyssa leaves now, not later."

They stood in silence until Rattimor shook his head. "If your tactic is to stall long enough for your brother to save you, you are doing well. Alyssa shall disappear into the forest to my side, then we shall have our little chat."

James turned to Alyssa and instructed, "Get up, but stay behind me the entire way."

Alyssa pushed herself up with her hands and stood directly behind James. He turned and took hold of her arm, then escorted her across and down the riverbed from Rattimor until they were about five meters from the forest trees. Rattimor had meanwhile climbed down from the rocks, never lowering the crossbow aimed at James.

"Stop there, James. You've gone far enough."

The Link – Master Rattimor

James paused and looked at Alyssa. "Are you okay enough to run?" Alyssa glanced nervously between James and Rattimor, then nodded to James. "Then run like hell until you're behind that tree," he said, eyeing the tree closest to them.

Alyssa swallowed and peered warily at Rattimor as he aimed his crossbow at them. James let go of her arm and she backed slowly away without taking her eyes off Rattimor, then quickly turned and sprinted until she was behind the first tree.

"Get back to the door," instructed James, still watching her. "It's downstream about a hundred meters in the center of the riverbed."

Alyssa reluctantly moved behind several more trees, but couldn't make herself run away.

"Appears she's not listening to you, James. She and Katrine definitely have the same spirit," Rattimor said with amusement. "I held up my end of the deal. Now... my daughter's whereabouts."

James peered angrily through the trees at Alyssa, shook his head, then turned to Rattimor. "I brought Adrian to a cancer research laboratory somewhere in New England and placed her in a wire cage not too much bigger than she was, fitted with a nice litter pan under the wires. As her father, you should be truly proud. I believe she was considerably more valuable to the researchers than the furry hamsters beside her cage because they can retrieve additional data on skin rashes after they inject her with their experimental drugs. I haven't had time to check in on Adrian since I dropped her off, so I don't know if she's well. Maybe if we're all lucky, she'll get cancer and die, just like my mother. Of course," he said, nodding his head, "she did have a *nasty* temper. They'll probably just put her to sleep because she'll be too difficult to work with."

There was silence before Alyssa heard the arrow release and strike James. James let out a quiet groan and collapsed backwards onto the rocks.

"God, no," Alyssa said before she dodged back through the trees towards James. She clumsily ran across the rocks and leaned over him, her hand shaking as she placed it on his bloody, gray shirt beside the arrow in his chest. "Don't die, James," she begged. "I think he missed your heart. Just hang in there until your brother comes."

James stared blankly at the sky and held his breath as Alyssa gathered the bottom of his shirt and wrapped it around the entrance point of the arrow. She gently pressed down to try to stop the bleeding and looked up to see Rattimor throw the crossbow to the rocks and walk towards them.

"Bastard!" she yelled at him before turning back to James.

"Get out of here, Alyssa," James whispered before taking another deep breath and holding it.

"Don't hold your breath. Keep breathing," she told him as she grabbed his hands and placed them around the arrow. "Try to press down to slow the bleeding."

Alyssa looked up to see Rattimor only ten meters away, pulling his belt from his pants and snapping it taut in front of him with a gleam in his eyes. She reached down and picked up a large rock, stood up, and threw it at him as hard as she could, but it seemed to just bounce off the tall figure of a man like paper.

"Back away!" she warned as she took several steps backwards, wobbling on the rocks for several seconds after she stopped her retreat. Once she regained her balance, she knelt down and grabbed two more large rocks.

Rattimor kept approaching until he towered over James, then looked down. Smiling, he lifted his foot and gave the arrow a nudge, causing James to cry out and convulse in pain.

"Leave him alone!" yelled Alyssa as she threw a second rock at his head.

Rattimor turned away so that the rock ricocheted off the back of his neck. He shook his head and narrowed his eyes angrily, then charged after her with a monster-like growl. Heart racing, Alyssa quickly threw the last rock in her hand, then turned to run towards the trees. She could hear his red and black satin cape descend on top of her like a bat pouncing an insect and cried out as her legs were kicked out from underneath her. As her knees slammed into the rocks, Rattimor flung the belt over her head to her neck and yanked her backwards against his knee. She grasped frantically at the belt with both her hands, trying to loosen it to breathe, but he squeezed even tighter, causing tears to flood Alyssa's eyes. Closing her eyes, she pulled at the belt digging into her neck in vain. She could feel her face tighten and turn red from lack of oxygen; her grip on the belt grew weaker. After a short while, she could no longer hear the breeze through the trees and she opened her eyes to get her last glimpse of the world before she left it. The riverbed and trees in front of her were blurry as white specks darted across her eyes. Heart aching, she dropped her hands and thought of her mother and father.

"No!" Rattimor yelled.

A green light whisked across Alyssa's face, and she felt the belt release. She fell forward, grasped her neck, and began to gasp for air as she watched the belt fall to the rocks and dirt below her. As she tried to recover, she turned and looked back to see Rattimor swirling silently in a green, funnel-shaped cloud, arms and legs flailing in every direction,

The Link – Master Rattimor

growing smaller with each turn. Below him stood Zor, staring at his victim with a heated, unforgiving look upon his face. Alyssa turned and sat on the rocky ground to watch as Rattimor seemed to completely disappear. The green tornado disappeared and a small jar appeared in its place, hovering in mid-air. Zor approached the jar and took hold of it.

"I shall let my brother decide your fate, dirty little insect." He walked over to James and knelt down.

"You had me worried there for a little while," James whispered. "I stalled as long as I could and tried to keep Alyssa safe for you."

Zor glanced up at Alyssa, then back down at his brother. "You saved her life, James. You did more than I ever would have expected." He grabbed hold of the arrow planted in his chest. "This won't hurt." He pulled the arrow out effortlessly, then placed his hand over the wound. James' breathing returned to normal and his tense body relaxed on the rocks where he lay.

"Thank you," James said. "How's Rebecca?"

"Both Razor and Rebecca are passed out in the labyrinth. I just left them there because I figured you might need me more here."

"And Fireball?"

"He's now a very powerful mountain kingsnake. I thought he would appreciate his new red, yellow, and black stripes, but he has a split soul and isn't motivated enough to thank me, much less slither away to hide under the leaf litter. I'll cloud the air so no one can find him, should someone try to rescue him." Zor held out his hand and helped James stand up. "We need to get back to Rebecca. I don't feel comfortable leaving her alone with Razor in the labyrinth." He looked over at Alyssa. "Are you okay?"

Alyssa took a deep breath, then calmly stated in a rasping voice, for it hurt to talk, "I want to go home, and I want you to help David... and then I want you to disappear from my life forever."

Zor looked down the riverbed and sighed, then looked back at Alyssa. "I can help you out with the first two requests, but the third might not be possible." He walked over to Alyssa and offered her a hand. "At least you have a good ending to your book."

Alyssa looked up at him, then struggled to her feet without his help.

Chapter 42
Home

The dim lighting on the periphery of the thespian's living room was warm and friendly, illuminating dozens of laughing thespians sitting on the soft couches surrounding the center of the room. In the center of the floor were two men in a spotlight, acting out Abbot and Costello's "Who's on First" skit. Katrine snuggled closer against Robert's chest with a smile on her face as he wrapped his arms around her and held her tightly from behind. She closed her eyes peacefully, hardly able to believe that such a horrible day could end so wonderfully. Weak and tired, she was looking forward to falling asleep in Robert's arms. She listened to the audience laughter and the comedians' bant er, but became curious enough to open her eyes when the door was heard opening and the room fell silent. Zor had entered. Several guards dawdled outside in the cool night air, peering inside to catch a glimpse of Katrine.

"It's time for you to retire to your separate rooms," Zor announced to the thespians. He looked at Katrine and Robert. "You two will stay."

The thespians filed quickly and quietly down the hallway and shut their bedroom doors behind them, leaving Katrine, Zor, and Robert in silence. Robert started to remove his arms from around Katrine and shift to a more upright position, but Katrine quickly grabbed his arms and replaced them around her.

"It's past curfew. Why aren't you in your room, Katrine?"

Katrine looked Zor straight in the eyes and replied, "I'm staying here tonight."

"I don't recall assigning you to the Thespian House." Katrine took a deep breath and looked away without a response. "Let me get a few things straight. If you are going to stay in Cyan, you will still live under my rules, under my command. You will *not* use your powers here, *not* interfere with the decisions I make or any discipline I choose to implement, and you will still reside at the Main House in your old room. It's safest for you there."

"No one is coming after me," Katrine quietly replied. "Rattimor sent out word that I was dead."

"But Razor disappeared from the labyrinth. It's only a matter of time." Zor took a few steps, examining the room, then returned his gaze at Katrine. "You won't be alone at the Main House. Rebecca is moving into the room beside James'. She wants to keep an eye on you, Robert. Make sure you're being treated right, I suppose."

Katrine struggled to keep her eyelids open. "May I please stay just tonight? After the day I had... it's only one night..."

Zor looked between Robert and Katrine several times with a hint of jealousy in his eyes before he reluctantly nodded his head. "Okay, but tomorrow you're back in your room. James sends his thanks for the transfer vase. It lights up the entire Main House. He's a little weary about drinking it though."

"Tell him not to worry. He saved Alyssa's life, after all."

"That's what I told him." Zor sighed. "I suppose you now expect me to work out visitation rights?"

"I would appreciate it."

Zor shook his head and headed for the door. "Visitation rights. I want you to know that you are becoming a royal pain in the ass. I'll be especially peeved at you if that vase makes James' stronger than me... in Cyan, anyway."

"I don't think he will be," Katrine weakly replied.

He paused at the door. "I almost forgot. Tomorrow morning in the courtyard, I'll have a terrarium set up so that you may view a spider devouring a fly. Both of you are invited to attend. It will be a ceremony to honor the memory of my mother."

Katrine knew who the fly was, but was wondering about the spider. Robert beat her to the question.

"Is the spider anyone we know?"

"Guard Eleven. Be careful from now on when you sit on the courtyard bench," replied Zor before he left the room and shut the door.

Katrine closed her eyes and rested her head sideways against Robert's chest.

"Visitation rights..." Robert said with amusement. "Impressive."

"It's a start. My next project is year-round mail service."

Robert laughed. "You're going to drive that man absolutely crazy." He rested his chin on Katrine's shoulder. "Does he know about your 'Zor' scar, yet?"

"No."

"What do you think he'll do when he finds out?"

"To tell you the truth, I have no idea. If he puts it back on, though, I'm taking it right back off. Both Alyssa and I agree that he's not going to win *that* battle."

Robert brushed a piece of her hair that had fallen across her face to the side. "How's your mother adjusting?"

Katrine smiled. "She's never been better. The gardeners are making her feel very welcome. She's got a nice room to herself, too."

"Hmm. Speaking of mothers, mine seems very taken with someone who claims to be your Irish uncle. Know anything about that?"

Katrine groaned, "I *completely* forgot about Mr. Coal."

"I don't think he minds. He told me he's died and gone to heaven. Besides, he's just what the farm needs. My little brother even likes him."

Katrine sighed, "I love happy endings." She sank further into Robert's chest, no longer able to stay awake.

Robert raised his head from her shoulder and kissed her neck. "I love them, too."

Chapter 43
New Beginnings

Alyssa sat on a grassy hill outside the university's union, writing the times of her final exams in a small pocket calendar. It was May, a little over three months since the day Rehnquist and his father had attacked her. She looked down the sidewalk to see Sami and David approaching, so she quickly packed her books and papers away in her backpack and stood up.

"Ready?" she asked as they approached.

"We can't decide on pizza or hamburgers," Sami remarked.

"Personally," said Alyssa as she swung her backpack over her shoulder, "I don't feel like either."

"That's because you've been in a constant state of depression ever since February and you never have an appetite," remarked David.

"Let's drop off our bags in my room before we go," Alyssa said, trying to ignore David's comment.

They walked up the sidewalk until they passed the east end of the union, then started to cut across an outdoor stage area toward Alyssa's room.

"Alyssa," Sami said quietly. "In front of your room."

Alyssa looked over to see John, pacing in the grass not far from her door. When he noticed Alyssa, he stopped, stood straight up, and stared at her. Alyssa looked down at the grass and continued walking.

"Ignore him," said Alyssa. "He's here on business. Rehnquist is being psychologically evaluated again today and they requested that his lawyer be present."

Sami ran in front of Alyssa and stopped her from walking. "Alyssa," she said impatiently. "They don't do that on campus. He's here to see *you*, just like the other dozen times he's been here and you ignored him."

305

"Look, Alyssa," David said with a sigh. "Maybe it's none of my business, but I believe you've been blaming him for things he's not entirely responsible for. After all, he *saved* your life. He gave you protection against Rehnquist, and he stopped Master Rattimor before he did you in. And have you ever stopped to consider what might have happened to you if he had never become involved with Katrine? Some other warlock might have come along and ended her within days. Instead, he's protecting her." He shook his head. "I'm just not sure you should consider him the enemy. If you or Katrine encounter one of Rattimor's friends in the future, I would sure want him on my side."

"Besides," added Sami, "you've been absolutely miserable since you two broke up."

Alyssa dropped her backpack down to the grass and put her hand on her hip, irritated. "So, what are you saying? I should start going out with him again?"

"We're not saying that," David explained. "We're just asking you to at least talk to him and make amends. I want the old Alyssa back."

She looked at David thoughtfully. "Aren't you going to get jealous?"

"Well," David smiled nervously, "I've been meaning to tell you. I've dumped you for another woman."

Alyssa slowly broke into a smile, then gave a little laugh. "Who?"

"Me!" Sami cried out with a huge grin.

Alyssa chuckled and shook her head. "Fine. I'll talk to him. Go eat your pizza, or hamburger, or whatever."

David and Sami smiled and nodded.

"Good luck," Sami said. "Call me tonight."

David and Sami turned and headed back towards the union, leaving Alyssa peering across the grass and sidewalks at John. She picked up her bag with a small groan, slung it over her shoulder, and slowly made her way over to him.

"So, is Rehnquist still insane?" she asked as she approached him.

"Yes. Keeps spouting off things about time travel and warlocks. I don't even have to influence him to say anything. They believe him to be completely crazy without my help."

Alyssa stared at the parking lot on the south side of the union. "Why are you here, John?" she asked without making eye contact. "If that's your real name..."

"It is," he replied hesitantly. "I just wanted to talk to you... see if you're doing okay."

The Link – Master Rattimor

"Finals are coming up. Nothing too difficult, so I'll do well. Soccer season ended last week. I miss it a little." Alyssa broke her gaze at the parking lot and looked back at John. Before she could stop herself, her eyes started to tear. "Well, I've got to go," she said, turning away to head for her dormitory.

"Someone once told me true love was messy," John quickly said. Alyssa stopped, but didn't turn around. "Look, Alyssa. I've given nearly every citizen the opportunity to visit their home, I've allowed five to return home permanently, I've let two bring their children back, and I've put restrictions on the guards' activities and allowances. And as for Katrine..." He shook his head. "I've done all I can to help alleviate the headaches and nightmares caused by Rattimor's red cloud. I'm sorry I can't do more, but I don't want to risk damaging her brain." After a slight pause, he sighed. "I've tried to change for you, Alyssa, but I find myself still at a loss. What do I have to do to get you back?"

Alyssa held her breath and looked up at the sky, then turned towards him. A tear broke free from her eye, and she quickly wiped her cheek dry with the back of her hand.

"I suppose I wouldn't mind kicking the ball sometime," she said quietly. "Do you want to meet me at three today by the intramural fields?"

A smile crept across his face. "Not going to make this easy on me, are you?"

"No," Alyssa replied. "I'm curious to see how someone with such high standards copes with his own imperfections."

"Or maybe you just want to embarrass me."

"Boy, you *are* good at reading minds."

"How do you know I'm not better than you?"

"Maybe you are. Is it a date or not?"

John sighed and appeared a bit nervous. "See you at three."

Alyssa nodded her head with satisfaction, then turned back around. She walked up to her front door and grabbed her keys from her pocket.

"And perhaps dinner, afterwards?" John asked hopefully.

Alyssa smiled, leaned her head against the door and closed her eyes. Unable to mask her smile when she turned around, she replied, "We'll see. Perhaps dinner, afterwards."

Look for
Book Two, *Razor's Box*, and Book Three, *Saber's Edge*,
available in paperback in the future.

Printed in the United States
37279LVS00003B/1-18